Fletcher and the Mutineers

Also by John Drake

Fletcher
and the Mutineers

JOHN DRAKE

LUME BOOKS

LUME BOOKS

This edition published in 2021 by Lume Books
30 Great Guildford Street,
Borough, SE1 0HS

ISBN 978-1-83901-371-3

Typeset using Atomik ePublisher from Easypress Technologies

www.lumebooks.co.uk

In fond memory of
David Burkhill Howarth

----------- DBH -----------

1946 – 2009

PATRIFAMILIAS AMATISSIMO
MAGISTRO DOCTISSIMO
INGENIOSISSIMO TECHNITAE
OPTIMO AMICO

INTRODUCTION

Readers of *Fletcher's Fortune* and *Fletcher's Glorious 1st of June* will know that the Fletcher series is based on the memoirs of Jacob Fletcher, in twenty-five bound volumes, as transcribed by his unfortunate secretary, Samuel (later the Reverend Doctor) Pettit, who later added footnotes to the journal, in revenge. The memoirs are amplified by chapters of my own writing in which I've done my best to tell what happened when Fletcher wasn't there, based on data in my archive of Fletcher papers.

This third book gives Fletcher's explanation of the catastrophic loss of HMS *Calipheme* in Boston Harbour on October 4th 1795, a mystery which has excited interest ever since. Thus *Morning Chronicle* of Monday May 13th 1799 thought a sea-serpent was involved, while *True UFO Reports* of January 1959 claimed that the ship was blasted by an alien death ray. But truth beats fiction ever time.

The telling of Fletcher's further adventures in Boston prompts me to say how much he liked America. He was proud of his American citizenship (acquired in 1794) and regarded the sundering of the English-speaking peoples after the American Revolution, as the greatest tragedy in the entire history of the world, blaming it upon:

"The malign, crass, wrongful, perverse, arse-upwards, unforgivable piss-head stupidity of a raving mad King and a blockhead parliament."

His own words, and you can imagine him bellowing as he thumps the table in emphasis.

Also, as Fletcher makes several references to actual sums, a rough measure of 18th money should help readers. Thus, the Pound Sterling had such huge value in the 1790s that a good salary for well-paid professionals like Admiralty Clerks (senior managers) might be just £30 per year. But that was then and this is now, after two hundred years of inflation. So if you want to equal the value of George III's mighty, golden pound you must put down at least *one thousand* of our miserable plastic equivalents.

Finally, one for the pedants: Sarah Coignwood, wife of Sir Henry Coignwood (who was a Baronet), is referred to as Lady *Sarah*, throughout this and previous Fletcher books because she was universally known as that in her lifetime, despite the fact she should have been called Lady *Coignwood*, since only women of higher rank (such as the daughters of Dukes) might use their Christian names after the title *Lady*. Others were supposed to use their husband's surname, and the full details of this complex matter can be researched by anyone who likes a headache, because it certainly gave me one.

John Drake, Cheshire, 2015

PROLOGUE

New York Harbour,
Night
September 6th 1776

George Washington's army was trapped because Admiral Lord Howe's British fleet lay anchored in the narrows, blockading Manhattan Island. The fleet was safe because the rebel colonists had no warships and no means of attack: or so the officers said, despite hideous rumours on the lower deck that the rebels were floating gunpowder barrels out on the tide with fuses burning. But any man who said that got flogged, so the men kept quiet and kept a good lookout.

They were right to do so, because three miles to the north, in the dark of the night, the oarsmen of two American whale-boats sat gazing at the lights of the fleet, while others attended to the fantastical contrivance they'd towed behind them. It floated just clear of the water like a huge brass hat with a dome-shaped crown and a flat brim: a hat three feet across, with glass ports, two vertical pipes crooked at the upper ends like walking sticks, and a foot-long, steel screw, while a cord ran from the screw to something under water because most of the beast lay below: an egg-shaped, oaken barrel, ballasted upright with lead, and just six feet deep and three feet wide.

"Ah!" said a voice, "She's open!"

"Hand me the bolts," said another voice.

"Ezra!" said the first voice, "She's ready." Hands pulled the hat up on hinges, revealing a dark hole just big enough for a man to pass through into the mysteries within.

"Ezra!" said the first voice, "Make shift!" and a dark figure moved, but then stopped, shuddered, and sank back.

"What is it lad?"

"Nothing," said Sergeant Ezra Lee, but he couldn't move.

"It's the typhoid!" said another voice, "He said he'd shaken it off, but look at him!"

There followed a furious argument. One faction admired Lee for turning out when sick, while the other damned him for putting everything at risk. An extreme splinter of this latter conviction was all for cooling Lee's fever by heaving him over the side.

"Shut your mouths!" said the first voice, "The only thing now is, who's to go in his place?" and everyone looked at Mr Francis Stanley, apprentice to David Bushnell who'd designed the craft, because Stanley was now the only man present who could master it. To his credit he instantly volunteered, and was lowered into the tar-stinking machine.

"Due south," said the first voice, "Chose any man-o-war!" Stanley nodded, and eased himself on to the transverse plank that was the operator's seat.

"Due south," he repeated and reached up to close the brass hatch.

"God speed!" said someone as the hatch came down. Stanley secured it, stood up, got his head into the dome and peered out through its little windows, and from his viewpoint just above the waves he saw the whalers pulling for New York, leaving him alone. A horrible fright stabbed, but Stanley crushed it, checked the bearing of the British lights, and settled down to work towards them. Sat down, he couldn't see through the ports and had to steer by compass, which he could do in the pitch dark because the compass card, and the depth gauge beside it, were marked out with fox fire fungus that glowed in the dark.

Stanley's feet worked cranks below, while his right hand heaved an iron lever. These motions, via rods running out through the hull, moved paddles by which the *Turtle* swam: *Turtle* being Bushnell's name for the craft.

It was heavy work, and Stanley soon had to stop to turn a handle working a fan, to draw fresh air through the crooked pipes above. During these breaks Stanley looked at the British, to check his course. In the open sea *Turtle* would have got nowhere. But in still waters, making a few knots, she was closing on her prey and fulfilling the hopes of the desperate Americans, because on her back, made fast by a bolt and connected to the line that ran to the steel screw, was a formidable weapon: a waterproof charge of one hundred and fifty pounds of gunpowder with a clockwork time fuse and flint lock detonator.

Stanley pressed on, even though he hadn't got the strength nor experience for the work. Ezra Lee, who'd been chosen for the job, was muscle from neck to ankle and had tested the machine for months, while Stanley had made just a few trials. He knew how *Turtle* worked. He knew what to do. But could he do it? He was already tired and the real work was yet to come.

Finally, a sick and dizzy Stanley stood up, and was amazed to see that the British ships were all round him. He'd done it! So he cranked his fan to freshen the air and wiped the sweat from his eyes. He was mortal tired and now he had to dive into the airless depths. But he hated the British and he'd come this far, so he picked the nearest ship and went after it, which by pure chance was HMS *Eagle*, no less than the British flagship herself.

Whirring the air-fan one last time, Stanley checked his compass and pressed his foot on a brass valve at his feet. Water gurgled into a tank and *Turtle* sank. Fear jumped and Stanley's hands shot to the handles of the pumps that would empty the tank and bring her up. But the strong hull never even creaked, so he took her down to twenty feet by the depth gauge, and there, in the waters of the Narrows, in a space like a coffin, with his muscles aching and the air getting stale, Francis Stanley carried out the first attack by a submarine boat in the entire history of the world.

Placing himself under the target was guesswork but Stanley did it, getting right under *Eagle*. Then he worked the pumps to bring him up against the enemy's hull, rising until a bump sounded. Stanley stopped pumping, and felt for the crank that turned the dome's steel screw, which should now be digging into the hull of the ship above. All he had to do was fix that screw, unbolt it from inside the hull, and unbolt the explosive charge. The two were joined by a line and unbolting the charge set its fuse going. He could then withdraw and leave the powder to blow the son-of-a-bitch, damned British to hell!

He turned the handle but the screw didn't bite. He pulled down and jabbed up, trying to force the screw in. But he failed and failed again. He was so tired that he hadn't the strength, and in his awkwardness, he trod hard on the valve that opened the diving tank, and the valve stuck and *Turtle* sank hideously, and Stanley hauled on the valve, and still it stuck, and he hauled again, already below the lowest depth on his gauge, and the

11

hull began to groan, and he pulled again, and appalling crackling sounds came from the timbers, then *pop* the valve came free, and Stanley worked pumps furiously, emptied the diving tank, and *Turtle* shot up, up, up!

Boom! *Turtle* hammered into *Eagle's* hull, knocking Stanley senseless off his perch, such that by the time he'd gathered his brains, *Turtle* was under attack with things bounding off her hull, because the British tars, mindful of hideous rumours when they heard the great bump, looked over side, saw *Turtle* wallowing alongside and pelted her with cold shot, musket fire, and anything else to hand.

Stanley worked crank and pedals mightily to get away, with water splashing, and cannon balls raining down, and moving at a slugging walking pace, that was just enough, because *Turtle* was so low and small in the dark, that she was soon out of sight and Eagle's crew had nothing to aim at.

When the battering stopped, Stanley cranked the air fan, filled his lungs with salt breeze, knew he didn't dare attack again, and began the long haul, north to safety. But first, he stopped and stared back at the great warship now blazing with lights. He cursed the British and didn't even notice that the explosive charge ... with clock ticking ... was gone: shorn off in the collision. So he turned for home in misery.

It was near dawn, and Stanley was aching, shaking and drenched in sweat before he met the waiting whale-boats. Just after they'd got him aboard, there came a flash of light followed by a heavy explosion from the British anchorage. The Americans cheered and thumped Stanley on the back. He tried to explain his failure but they wouldn't listen and it didn't matter anyway. It didn't matter because, for the moment, King George's fleet was no longer a threat to the Americans, because King George no longer ruled the British fleet. Not him or his Sea Service officers.

All discipline was gone from the fleet because the same British tars who'd fight any foe that ever floated on the waters, were un-manned by a thing that came unseen at night, all horribly from down below, to take the bottom out of a ship, and drown them every one, and never even the chance to fight back. And seafaring men were profoundly superstitious anyway, and all too ready to identify the deep dark of the underseas with the deep, dark of the occult. So panic ruled the fleet and not the King.

This was especially so aboard *Eagle* when a huge explosion thundered close by, and all hands bawled their terror and tried to slip cable, make sail and hoist out boats all at the same time, and all the ships around her did the same, blundering into one another, carrying away spars and bowsprits in a cacophony of splintering timbers and snapping lines, such that by noon next day, the entire fleet was working out to sea, and Lord Howe didn't regain command until the day after that, by which time the shock to British naval confidence, had rattled their army ashore, enabling Washington to retreat with his army, cross the Hudson and Delaware, and found a mighty nation.

Meanwhile, David Bushnell despaired of what he saw as *Turtle's* failure, and abandoned submarine navigation entirely. He forgot all about it, but Francis Stanley did not, and neither did Admiral Howe. The one was inspired and the other disgusted to the very core of his being.

CHAPTER 1

The thing to remember about Jamaica in those days was that in a population of three hundred thousand people, nine out of ten was a slave and there'd been many slave risings in the past, all of them ferocious, with unspeakable acts of cruelty performed by all sides. And when I first got there, there wasn't more than three thousand British regulars and militia, most of them sick or exhausted by the heat, to keep control over one hundred thousand virile black men every one of them fully accustomed to the climate.

At least that's how it was on Monday September 29th 1794 when I first saw the island from the mizzen top of *Lady Jane* out of Shadwell Basin, Wapping, after a voyage of eighty-six days.

Landfall is odd in Jamaica because the winds are odd. During the day they blow steadily onshore, and at night they blow steadily offshore, which is just as well or no ship under sail would ever have found land, since you wouldn't go blundering into the Jamaican coastline at night, not if you wanted to live.

Lady Jane came westward past Pedro Point up in the north east of the island, heading for Rio Blanco Bay. There were little islands (keys they call them) all along the coast: just coral rocks breaking clear of the waves, with weed and seabirds on them, and enough to wreck a ship. But the ship's master, Captain Cloud knew the coast and he knew his ship, a three hundred and fifty ton, three-masted vessel. He brought her to safe the mouth of Rio Blanco Bay and lay to.

Then he and I (as first mate) went up into the maintop to examine the shore with our spyglasses. The sky was deep, pure blue, the sea beneath us was so crystal clear you could see the fishes and turtles swimming over the sea bed below. The heat was intense and all the clothes we could bear was a cotton shirt, calico drawers and a straw hat for the sun. The hands went barefoot as a matter of course, but Cloud kept his shoes to show his rank, and so did I.

"The trick of it, Mister Fletcher," says he examining the channel, "is to go in with a steady wind, with full water under her, to swim her over the rocks. *That* and a pilot, naturally!"

Since the ship lay in plain sight no more than a mile out from the bay, we didn't have long to wait and we saw a large boat run down to the waves by dozens of hands, from a snowy-white beach with big mangroves hanging over it, with brilliant green leaves. The boat launched and forged out among the big black rocks covered with pelicans.

Behind the boat and the white shoreline, there was a cluster of wooden houses with verandas and broad roofs, some black folk looking out at the ship, and little more. Cloud pointed out a white man among them, and behind them, the green feathery mass of the Island rose up to the purple mountains and wisps of steam rose here and there as the sun pulled water up from the hot, moist jungles.

The boat plunged over the waves with six oarsmen pulling like bulls and a man in the stern sheets at the tiller. Every one of them was black. I snapped my glass shut and turned to Cloud.

"Captain," says I, "Shall we do our business here, or shall we have to go inland?" He grinned and tapped his finger along the side of his nose. He was older than me by a long shot, agreeable enough, and a Welshman and conscious of it. He thought himself a mysterious fellow: a dark Celt.

"Now then, mister," says he, "As agreed previously, you do *your* business, which you'll do better than I could do it myself, and you leave *my* part to me. The less you know, my boy, the better it'll be for you."

"Aye-aye Captain," says I, letting him get away with this, to keep him happy. After living together in a ship a hundred feet long by twenty-five feet wide, and with only six of us quarter-deck folk to talk to, there wasn't much of each other's little secrets that we didn't all know, "Well and good! " says I, "But I'll remind you I've put gold on the table and I'm in this venture alongside of you! You know my circumstances."

In fact Captain Cloud knew just as much about me as I wanted. He knew that I was Jacob Fletcher, 20-year-old heir to the late Sir Henry Coignwood, the Potteries millionaire and my natural father. He knew too that I'd been driven out of England by my stepmother, Lady Sarah

15

Coignwood, who'd brought evidence before the Court of Admiralty such that I was wanted on a charge of murder. He knew that before I ever came on board of his ship, and the exorbitant price of my safe passage out of England had taken account of the fact.

He also knew that my companions aboard ship were Sammy Bone, a white-haired, veteran Royal Navy seaman now wanted for aiding and abetting my escape from Naval custody, and Miss Kate Booth (known aboard ship as *Mrs Fletcher* to preserve the proprieties). Katy Booth was the only one of the three of us not wanted by anyone for anything, except in the sense that every man aboard wanted her, which was no more than natural where a girl of her beauty was concerned.

What Cloud didn't know was that I was guilty as charged, because in February 1793 just after the war began, I was pressed aboard the impress tender, *Bullfrog* where the Bosun (one Dixon) was such a sadistic, vicious bastard[1] that I had to batter and drown him, which is easily said, but the act was murder, right enough, and it had penetrated what passes for my conscience to the degree that I dared not face a Court Martial.

So that's what Mr Cloud knew and didn't know. For my part I knew, in the first place that he was a rogue or he'd never have taken me into his ship. I also knew that the good Captain had two cargoes battened under *Lady Jane's* hatches. The first was a normal assortment of supplies for the plantations: tools, nails, clothing for the slaves, salt fish etc. This would be discharged further east at Montego Bay and was perfectly legitimate.

The other cargo was fifty long cases each containing a dozen Tower muskets with GR stamped on the lock-plates, plus further boxes and kegs containing powder, shot and 25,000 made-up, service cartridges. These items were to be unloaded at Rio Blanco Bay and sold to a Mr Vernon Hughes, of *The African Society*. These beauties were a chip off the block of the abolitionist movement, who'd got fed up trying to push bills through a House of Commons dominated by Jamaica Sugar millionaires, finally realising that nobody in government was going to abolish slavery when the slaves were making all that money for Britannia. So Mr Hughes and his chums had decided on other means, and their people in England had

---

1   No entreaties of mine could dissuade Fletcher from the uttering of obscenity nor even profanity, and it was only under direct threat of violence that I was compelled to set down the words that he spoke. Thus all should remember, who read these volumes, that I transcribed under extreme duress. S.P.

approached Captain Cloud in deepest secrecy and offered gold for every musket he could deliver.

Now you don't need to be Sir Isaac bloody Newton to work out that should the Jamaican Authorities find out what was going on, then there was a hanging in it for all concerned. On the other hand, the African Society was offering *twenty times* the legal price for guns, powder and shot. So I bought a share of Mr Cloud's arsenal (having come away from England with a considerable sum of money) and persuaded him to let me conduct any negotiations of price: a skill which is my pride and my joy and which I value above all other. Certainly I value it above mere brute strength or the clumsy trade of the sea. Rum-soaked, pot-bellied morons can take a ship to sea, I've seen them do it, so what's so clever in that, I'd like to know? [2]

"Pilot boat," said Cloud, stating the obvious. The steersman was standing and waving his hat with a merry grin as the boat came alongside and made fast to a line thrown down by one of Cloud's men. "Time to go below," said Cloud and led the way down the shrouds to the main deck. His men had run out the guns and rigged boarding nettings while we were aloft: a wise precaution in the business we were at. Sammy Bone was among them. He was a paid-for passenger like me and Kate, but constitutionally incapable of not working. He'd been forty years at sea and was a magician with the great guns. By mutual consent, Cloud had rated him Master Gunner, and was grateful to have him.

"Cleared and ready, Cap'n!" says Sammy as we clambered down on to the deck. Sammy winked at me, he knew what was going on and was content with it. He trusted me to run our business affairs just as I trusted him to defend the ship. Miss Booth on the other hand, had gone sour the moment she got a whiff of my piece of enterprise. She frowned at me from the quarter-deck rail then looked away when I tried to smile at her. Women! What can you do with them? I'd saved her life in England and rescued her from a career in the rogering trade. And now she was looking down her nose at me just 'cos I was selling a few firelocks on the

---

2   It is necessary here to state that Fletcher stood six feet six inches tall, weighed 18 stones and was immensely strong. Furthermore he was an excellent sea officer, trained to King's Navy standards, being particularly adept at navigation and gunnery. His affected contempt for these attributes stems from the fact that his possession of them frustrated his lifetime's ambition to make a career in commerce S.P.

sly. Lovely little thing she was too, with a big hat with a ribbon and a dress that showed off her figure a treat.

But I had no time to think about her moods. What we were about to do in this quiet, lonely bay, could be dangerous. We could hardly seek the protection of the law, after all. Fortunately, *Lady Jane* had a heavy broadside for a merchantman: eight six-pounders, as well as half a dozen one-pounder swivels.

The guns were loaded with canister, and the swivels with a score of musket balls each. We had thirty hands to man them and nothing short of a man-o-war or a massed attack by thousands could give us cause for worry so long as we stayed in the ship.

Cloud led the way to the quarter-deck, and nodded approvingly at his Second Mate, Mr Harvey, who was armed with cutlass and pistols and holding out an armful of the same for him.

"You can clap some 'o that tackle aboard of Mr Fletcher," says he, "While I go below and prettify m'self. I'll take my share later." He jabbed his thumb at the Pilot boat, "Bring him aboard, Mr Harvey: just the one, mind! Take care there ain't half-a-hundred of 'em hid under the thwarts."

Harvey smiled but he took a good look over the side none the less, and Sammy had men at the swivels ready to blast the boat's crew to minced meat, if need be. It was all very purposeful and I'd seen the like on the slave coast in west Africa. The aim was to put wicked temptation out of the minds of innocent natives who vastly outnumber a ship's crew and who otherwise might take liberties with them.

The merry, laughing Pilot, with his gold earrings and a red-silk hand-kerchief bound round his head under his hat, noted this as we brought him aboard, unlashing a portion of the nettings to let him through. I saw him take a good look all round even before he drained the mug of rum that Harvey offered him for goodwill. Then he chattered away in the sing-song accent of Jamaica (the first time I'd ever heard it) pointing out the safe channel into the bay, and where the dangers were.

"Him there, him big-man-rock, Sah! An' him there, sah! An' him there, him big-man-san-bank! But *dis* way, him all o-kee, sah! All o-kee! "

Harvey set reefed topsails and took her in nice and easy, with the Pilot beside the helmsman, pointing and jabbering all the while, and the Pilot boat dashing ahead of us, back to the shore. Meanwhile I buckled on a cutlass and stuck a brace of pistols into my belt and had another go at sweetening Kate. But she wouldn't have it. She just ignored my friendly words and stared fixedly ahead of the ship. Finally, she condescended to look up at me and pointed at the beach.

"Why," says she, all sarcastic, "It must be market day. "See how the good folk come to buy!" I bit my lip. The *good folk* were mostly men: hundreds of 'em and all of them armed. Each man carried some sort of long gun and a long, broad-edged blade at his side.

"Musket and cutlass!" says Sammy, who'd come up from the waist and his guns. "They give a volley then go at it with the cutlass, which ain't like our Navy cutlass: it's shorter and broader, but they're buggers with it!" He'd been everywhere in his long seafaring life, and that included Jamaica. He peered at the men gathering on the beach. We were only a few hundred yards out now and they were in plain view. He pointed out the tall, upright figures "Them there ain't no common natives, lad," says he, "Them's *Maroons*!". He shook his head emphatically, "Finer set of men you'll never see."

By George he was right, too. Most of 'em were naked from the waist up, for they scorned to wear hats even in this blazing heat, and their costume was a pair of loose breeches with a belt to support a sheathed cutlass, and a bag slung over the shoulder for powder and ball. They were a browny copper colour rather than black and they had sleek bulging muscles like athletes. They had precisely that look of perfect readiness that a prize fighter brings to the ring after months of training.

At that moment there came a roar and a rumble from the bow as an anchor was let go and the cable ran out the dozen fathoms to the sea bed. The instant it had settled, *Lady Jane's* people doubled like madmen to get a spring (that's to say a hawser) on the cable and led it through one of the gun ports to the capstan so we could swivel our broadside around to any point by a few turns on the capstan. Harvey never said a word because the men were going at it as hard as they knew how, having seen the committee of reception on the sea shore.

Soon after that, Captain Cloud came on deck togged out in his finest. He had a long blue broadcloth coat, with rows of shiny buttons, his best shirt, silk stockings and silver buckled shoes, a small-sword with a glittering cut steel hilt and a big three-cornered hat with silver lace. His men stirred with pride at the sight of him, even though the sweat was already streaming down his brow from the weight of cloth on his back.

On sight of him, Sammy shot off, nimble as a goat, down the companionway to the waist and took station by one of the six-pounders which, of a purpose, was loaded with powder and no shot. The gun-crew stood by with a rammer and linstock and a ship's boy waited with a fresh cartridge in his box.

"Twenty-one guns for the Cap'n, Mr Bone" bawled Harvey, and three cheers from all hands … Hip-Hip-Hip…"

"*Hurrah!*"

'Hip-Hip-hip…"

"*Hurrah!*"

Boom! Went the six-pounder, and ponderous echoes shattered the silence of the bay and shook the birds out of the trees. The crew reloaded as smart as man-o-war's men.

"Hip-Hip-Hip…"

"*Hurrah!*"

And, boom! Went the gun again. Sammy laughed aloud as he gave the Royal Salute, all twenty-one guns, and filled the air with dense clouds of rolling smoke.

It was all very impressive. The crew cheered again and again, the Pilot stuck his fingers in his ears, and the men on the beach leapt and jumped and waved their guns and fired them off in the excitement of it, their little pops and cracks feeble against the deep voice of the six-pounder.

In the middle of it all, Captain Cloud threw out his chest and waved majestically, like King George reviewing the fleet. He caught my eye and yelled at me over the noise.

"That's the way, damn my bloody eyes! Show the buggers what's what, Fletcher me lad, 'cos I'll not creep in like a bloody mouse!"

Now don't ask me if he was doing right. On the one hand he punctured the anxiety that was building on both sides. Our men, and the maroons were grinning and laughing now, instead of fingering their weapons and scowling. On the other hand he set off something wild among the maroons. Drums were pounding from among the houses ashore and drink was produced. There was dancing under way and singing, and women flitting about between groups of carousing men bearing food and other attentions to keep their menfolk happy. All very well, my jolly boys, but I'll point out that I was about to go ashore among that jamboree.

Had I been in command, I'd have dropped anchor out at sea, took the customer aboard to talk business, and then let him ship his goods ashore piecemeal in the Pilot boat or whatever else he'd got to carry them. That way there would be no risk to the ship at all. But Cloud wouldn't have that. He'd traded here before and claimed he was known and trusted. In short he had hopes of further business. In any case, whatever were the arguments, Cloud was determined to go ashore and do his dealings direct with Mr Hughes, and so we did.

With the smoke of his guns drifting slowly across the bay, Captain Cloud told the Pilot to whistle up his boat again, so that he and I and Mr Pilot could go ashore. When the actual moment came to climb over the rail, I didn't pretend that I was pleased. It was serious faces all round, among the crew and Sammy Bone shook my hand as I went and said he'd not let Kate fall into the hands of *them heathen* come what may. I knew how much he liked me so I assume he meant to cheer me up with this comforting reference to saving the women from rape.

We went over the side Navy fashion: juniors first. The Pilot went down like a panther, easy and graceful, I heaved my weight down by main strength, and Captain Cloud puffed and grunted like a walrus and muttered to himself in some ungodly tongue (Welsh probably).

The oarsmen gave way and whisked us the half cable's length to the shore, where hundreds of their companions were waiting for us.

At close range the maroons were even more impressive than they'd been at a distance. I've never seen men with such an air of athletic grace. They'd have made the most capital set of tumblers. They were smaller men than me (as most are) but lithe and active. They were free men too, and acted like it. They were different as could be from the plantation slaves I met later. Mind you, most of them were drunk by then, or on their way to it, for the rum was going round merrily. Their women were something splendid too. The same brown colour but dressed up in more clothes and in bright colours. They had fine legs and bouncing breasts and they laughed loudly and joked with the men, with shining teeth and red lips. By Jove, I forgot Katy's airs and graces on the instant and I could just have done nicely with a maroon girl or two.

But there wasn't the opportunity. Among the fun and games under way on the beach and round about the half-dozen houses, we could see a small group of men standing waiting. One of these was a white man in dark clothes and a round, civilian hat. Cloud tugged his coat into place, wiped the sweat from his eyes and turned to me.

21

"Keep under my lee now, Mr Fletcher," says he, and the pair of us trudged forward under the blazing sun, across the soft, clinging sand that sank you ankle deep and filled up your shoes. It was heavy going and the maroons laughed at the clumsiness of us. They skipped across the sand like a sprung dance-floor.

As we went, two or three brown girls kept me company, giggling and chattering and offering rum and fruits of all kinds, which was very jolly. But we also had a file of men on either hand, neat as a light infantry company. These gentlemen, about a dozen of them, were stone cold sober and carried their muskets ready for use. Partly this was to keep off those of their own men who tried to act saucy but they gave me and Cloud the hard eye none the less.

And then at last, we were face to face with Mr Vernon Hughes and his chums, standing out in the sun in front of the steps leading to the veranda of the biggest house on the beach. It was a rickety timber shed, but probably passed for the town hall in these parts.

Cloud drew himself up to his full height, splendid in his formal clothes (heat or no heat). I drew myself up, rather less splendid in shirt and breeches. He swept off his hat, I swept off mine. He bowed, I bowed. The guard of honour fell back, out of respect for their betters, hundreds of maroons closed in behind them to watch, and all eyes turned to our hosts.

"Have I the honour of addressing Mr Vernon Hughes of the African Society?" says Cloud.

"I am he," says the white man, a very tall elderly fellow with thick grey eyebrows and a soft voice. He looked like a scholar and, he too was dressed up under a sweltering burden of wool and linen. He was suffering from it too and mopped his face continuously with a handkerchief.

"May I present Captain Whitefield and Captain Mocho," says he indicating his companions, who were done up in maroon full ceremonials: the usual breeches plus a grubby shirt and a fancy silk sash. "These gentlemen represent Captain Montague of Trelawney Town," says Hughes, as if he were presenting the ambassador of the Emperor of all the Russians. (*Captain*, incidentally, was the standard politeness among the maroons towards superior men, and used where an Englishman might say *Mister* and touch his hat.)

We shook hands all round and I saw Hughes cast a longing glance up at the veranda with its shade and a table and chairs with a big jug and an odd assortment of cups, mugs and glasses (mostly chipped and dented). I was beginning to feel sorry for the poor old fellow, suffering under the climate as he was, when he spoke again.

"And now, friends," says he, quite gently at first, "Let us begin this great work which shall strike the chains of oppression from the wrists of countless thousands. Let us cleanse the European oppression from these islands with purifying fire, and the sharp sword, till not one shall live of that vile race to carry home – to a corrupt and viciously intransigent legislature – the tale of that, which their abominable mistreatment of their fellow man has wrought!"

He had full steam up now. There was white all round the pupils of his eyes and the spittle sprayed from his mouth as he ranted with head thrown back and fist raised to heaven. Out of the corner of my eye I saw Cloud struck rigid with horror, "Death to the planters!" screamed Hughes, "Death to the English! Death to every white face in Jamaica!"

CHAPTER 2

"...thus I shall see you damned before one penny shall I pay, and I shall defy you in the courts to the end of days, denying any shred of negligence on my behalf, and insisting only that had not your son hid coin in the disgusting cavities of his body, for purposes of bribery, and had I not been betrayed by false servants, then he would this day remain safe confined in my house."

(Extract of a letter, 24th July 1795, from Dr Ephraim Crick, *Crick's Insane Asylum*, Staffordshire.)

The barouche stood gleaming in Dulwich square. The glossy body swayed on its high springs over the bright-yellow wheels, two exquisite greys were in harness, two footmen in livery of red and gold stood on neat steps at the back, armed with long white staves against the common herd, while the driver sat on the box in front, and all waited patiently for their mistress to emerge from number ten: the finest house in the square.

When the lady was quite ready, the doors were thrown open by her butler and she and her companion emerged: two of the most beautiful ladies in London. The more striking of the two was voluptuously lovely with a waterfall of heavy, black curls descending from a snap-brimmed hat topped with an ostrich plume and bound with a broad pink ribbon. Her voluminous gown was pink-striped silk drawn tight beneath the bust and with a ruff of lawn at the neck. Since the day was cold there was a swansdown tippet across her shoulders. She was Lady Sarah Coignwood, who set the style that London followed and was embarking on a carefully-planned day of perfect pleasures.

It was one day of many such days, devoted to abolishing painful memories of the detested Jacob Fletcher, illegitimate son of her late husband Sir Henry, and true air to the Coignwood fortunes: fortunes so great that even she could not spend the money faster than it came in from her late husband's investments, estates and enormous pottery manufactories in Staffordshire. To protect this wealth, she'd had Fletcher pressed into the Navy, where her beloved son Alexander (a sea-service lieutenant) should have killed him, but Alexander was himself killed by Fletcher. Sundry murders had failed to solve the problem, although she was acquitted of all blame at the Old Bailey having corrupted witnesses, and been obliged to sacrifice her second son, Victor, as bearer of all guilt. She shrugged at the thought: at least he hadn't danced the Newgate jig. They put him in the mad-house instead, still spitting hatred against herself.

Meanwhile, her companion (in sprig muslin and swansdown) was Clarissa, née Morton, who as a sixteen-year-old actress had enjoyed such decent good sense as to persuade the entire world, including the Duke of Bannockshire (a fine man apart from pock-marks, belly and squint) that she'd fallen in love with him, and His Grace had been so captivated with her blue-eyed, golden haired loveliness that he married her, and she decently presented him with a son (almost certainly his) whereupon the seventy-one-year-old Duke, exhausted by the intimacies of marriage, promptly did the decent thing and died of a stroke, leaving the Duchess in command of his money.

Chattering happily, the two great ladies were ushered into the carriage, cushions and rugs snugged around them, and the hood strapped back because it was a strategic aim that the two beauties should be on display.

With all preparations complete, the footmen gripped their hand-holds, the driver took up the reins, and a fourth servant in exotic oriental coat and silk turban, took his place beside the driver. He was a tall, slender young man in his late teens: a gold-coast African: strikingly handsome with the most lovely eyes and milk-white, perfect teeth. He was named Rasselas, after the Ethiopian Prince in the play by Johnson the Lexicographer, which Lady Sarah had once seen and found deathly dull. But she remembered the name.

"Where did you get him, my dear?" said Lady Clarissa as the vehicle moved off.

"From an advertisement in *The Morning Post*," said Lady Sarah, "I bought him from a West Africa merchant who'd raised him up for service."

"You *bought* him?" said Lady Clarissa, puzzled, "Is not the owning of slaves unlawful on English soil?" Lady Sarah shrugged. She hadn't the slightest interest in such matters.

"I bought him and he is now mine," she said, acknowledging a lady and gentleman in a passing carriage. She and Lady Clarissa smiled at each other in satisfaction at the mortified expression on the other lady, caught out wearing last season's fur when Sarah Coignwood and the Duchess were in swansdown.

"He is very beautiful," said Lady Clarissa, looking at Rasselas.

"He is indeed," said Lady Sarah.

"And does he … *give satisfaction?*"

"I cannot yet say, my dear. I bought him only yesterday."

"But you will tell me, will you not? Once you are better informed?"

"I will tell you everything, dear Clarissa," said Lady Sarah, "Do I not always?" And they laughed as their magnificent vehicle swept out of Dulwich Square and turned right into Grosvenor Street, heading for New Bond Street.

(A beggar in a long, dirty coat, watched them go with a fixed look. His hands were mutilated: the tip of the middle finger was gone from his left hand and the entire middle finger missing from the right. He shuffled off in the same direction as the carriage, rattling his bowl as he went.)

The first act of the perfect day was that which gives more pleasure to ladies than true love's kiss: shopping. First they visited David Rigge & Sons of Bond Street to purchase fragrances. Next, Spiratils of Pall Mall, for Leghorn straw hats. Next Peacock's of Titchfield Street for kid-leather shoes, and next to Laroudils of Queen Street (Stay makers to Her Majesty). There they bought absolutely nothing but thoroughly enjoyed themselves.

In all of these places they were attended with the utmost solicitude of which the proprietor was capable, and in none of them was the vulgar matter of money even mentioned, because Lady Sarah's credit was indisputable and her steward would settle accounts in due course.

Thus they pursued their zig-zag course within the fabulous lozenge delineated by Hanover Square to the north, St James's Square to the south, Berkley Square to the west and Golden Square to the east. The short distances could easily have been covered on foot, but the carriage displayed its occupants to fashionable London, which waved and smiled on either hand and in great numbers.

(But nobody noticed the beggar with the mutilated fingers who, from time to time, appeared outside one or another of their destinations, as if he were anticipating their movements.)

Happy hours later, Lady Sarah and Lady Clarissa enjoyed act two, in St James's Park, where they reviewed the Tenth Light Dragoons, magnificent in Tarleton helmets, silver-frogged coats, and white breeches of inconceivable tightness. Armed with broadsword and carbine, each man was mounted upon a chestnut warhorse fit for a king and knew himself to be the smartest soldier in England.

In strict point of military etiquette, it was His Royal Highness, the fat, handsome, George, Prince of Wales who reviewed the Tenth: in his uniform, on his horse, on a dais with mounted cronies around him. He was a past lover of Lady Sarah's who couldn't stop sighing at her, though he did it sidelong in the vain hope that nobody would notice.

But in reality it was the ladies who took the salute, in carriages lined up along the route to the Prince, though not *every* lady, because a lady's beauty was measured by the number of young officers who gallantly saluted with their flashing swords as they rode past, their men giving eyes-right behind them. Not every lady could stand such assessment, because what if nobody saluted? So most carriages hung back just a little to avoid the test.

Naturally, Lady Sarah's barouche stood out front and centre, confidant that no man in the British Army could resist Lady Sarah or Lady Clarissa individually, let alone the two together. HRH couldn't resist them either, and he drew sword and saluted as he led his regiment off the field at the end of their manoeuvres. He was graciously acknowledged by the small wave of two slim hands.

(The beggar made his way to St James's park just as the Tenth moved off to their barracks. He was tired and thirsty, having been to several wrong places. He was just in time to see the tail end of Lady Sarah's barouche as it pulled away, heading for Dulwich square. He cursed viciously and spittle ran down his unshaven chin.)

Later in the perfect day, Lady Sarah and Lady Clarissa entered Lady Sarah's box at the Theatre Royal, Drury Lane. Three entertainments were offered: the play *Virtue Triumphant*, then a new ballet, *Terpsichore's Progress*, and finally a pantomime: *The Apprentice's Wife, or the Cuckold's Curse Confounded* (*with entirely new scenery, machinery, music, dresses and decorations*). The house was sold out and four thousand people were crammed into the pit and the five successive tiers of galleries. Hundreds of candles blazed in dozens of chandeliers and the murmur of the waiting multitude was like the snoring of a monster dragon.

The two beauties chose their moment. The interval between play and ballet was the acknowledged time for an entrance, and Lady Sarah's box was designed for entrances. Immediately to the right of the stage, in the second tier, the box faced the audience giving a poor view of the proceedings. But that didn't matter. What mattered was that the audience had an excellent view of the box. Thus as Lady Sarah entered with gemstones gleaming in her shining hair and upon her perfect bosom, there came a great gasp as the audience sat up, nudged its neighbour and pointed out La Belle Coignwood and her lovely companion. A pattering of applause grew to a roar and the common herd in the cheap seats near the ceiling, drummed their heels on the floor and bawled out their noisy approval, while the two ladies smiled, waved and sat down, smoothed their gowns and affected thereafter to ignore the commotion. Rasselas stood behind them with his arms folded and his nose in the air.

Then there was a tap at the door of the box. Rasselas opened it and in came a most tremendously handsome man. He was very young but had the manner and confidence of maturity and he wore clothes that were a triumph of the tailor's art.

"Ah!" said Lady Clarissa, "My dear Lady Sarah, I present Mr George Brummel, recently gazetted Cornet in the Tenth."

"Your Grace, My lady," said Brummel, "When I saw you in the park today, I could not deny myself the pleasure of your closer acquaintance, and so I sent my man with a letter…"

"To which I replied, and so here you are!" said Lady Clarissa.

"Here, with Venus herself, except that she is two!" said Brummel, looking from one lady to the other, and smiling with perfect self-assurance. Lady Sarah was much amused at such confidence in a boy. But he was such a pretty boy.

"You are late, Sir!" she said. Brummel waved a hand at his complex neck-cloth,

"Two dozen failed attempts to get it right," he said, "But one perseveres."

"Mr Brummel has made a science of elegance," said Lady Clarissa to Lady Sarah, "As you will have noticed." Surprisingly, Brummel frowned at this compliment.

"The test of true elegance," he said with perfect seriousness, "Is that it should *not* be noticed." Lady Sarah laughed, a delightful peal of amusement.

"Bless you, dear boy!" she cried, "Would you choose not to be noticed? God save you from yourself!" She laughed again, and noticing this the pit and three or four tiers of galleries laughed with her. Brummel blushed and bit his lip. He was very young after all. So Lady Sarah smiled upon him and placed her hand upon his. She looked into Mr Brummell's eyes and sent a certain signal. His long lashes swept up and down and he stared straight back. He placed a hand on hers.

But then she fell into doubt concerning the final act of a perfect day. She looked Rasselas and she looked at Mr Brummel. Both were very much to her taste. But she reflected on what she'd heard concerning men of Rasselas's race, and made her decision. It was a decision that would make Mr George (Beau) Brummel, extremely thankful.

(Outside the theatre, the beggar stood among the dirt, and the traffic, and the Drury Lane whores. Soon he grew bored and set off towards Dulwich Square. He muttered spitefully as he walked, and fingered the surgical knife in his pocket.)

CHAPTER 3

Mr Vernon Hughes was a foaming lunatic and one of the most dangerous men I have ever known. There's only one way with the likes of him: calm him down with a belaying pin, clap a straight-waistcoat on him and cart him off to a padded cell. But such enlightened measures are only possible in civilised parts of the world.

When Cloud and I heard Hughes calling down fire and damnation upon everything white, we thought we were dead men. Our ship was beyond reach, we were surrounded by hundreds of warriors and one false step would have seen us hacked into offal. You could see it in the eyes of the mob behind us. They were yelling along with Hughes and calling out his name and just itching to set about somebody.

I still had my cutlass and pistols, and Cloud had his little court sword but we might as well have turned out empty handed for all the good they would do. The only safe thing in such a case is keep your hands by your sides, and ask God very nicely indeed if He wouldn't mind letting you off, just this once, thank you kindly, Lord if it ain't too much trouble, and this time, by George, I really do promise to give up tarts and strong drink and farting in church, amen.

What saved us was not the Almighty but Captain Whitefield and Captain Mocho. All other opinions on that beach were for starting the crusade then and there, but these two gentlemen (sharp-eyed fellows that they were) had noticed the absence of fifty cases of muskets about the persons of Cloud and myself, not to mention the powder and ball.

So they hung on to Hughes's arms (very respectful mind and with much bowing and scraping) and they talked reason into him like a pair of nurses with little Lord Pissbritches in a tantrum. Also the chaps that had marched up the beach with us, took their lead from the two Captains and closed in and about-faced to keep back the rest with their musket butts. They were steady as guardsmen and if they'd had such a thing as a drill sergeant (which they didn't) then he'd have been proud of them.

Finally Whitefield and Mocho got Mr Hughes to belay his spouting, they found his hat where it lay in the sand, brushed it off, stuck it back on his head and led him up the stairs into the shade and sat him down, gasping and slobbering, and poured him a drop of drink for his thirst.

Whitfield, who seemed to be the senior of the two, beckoned me and Cloud to follow, and had a private word with us in the corner, while a bunch of brown girls bustled out from the house and fussed over Hughes like a Turk in his harem, mopping him down, throwing off his neck-cloth and fanning him.

"Cap'n Hughes, he very great man," says Whitfield, whispering, and looking at the proceedings around Hughes. "Him great, man. Him tell me how me goin' fight for de freedom." He gave a little sneer, "Me!" he says, "Me, which is free from me father an' *he* father before him!" he nodded at Hughes, "Him there, he say me goin' fight for the freedom of *everyone*: even the poor-damn-shit-arse slave on the plantation." I caught his drift. Not all were brothers who weren't white, and the good Captain was not entirely of the Vernon Hughes persuasion. I looked at Cloud and he winked at me, cool as you please. He'd read the signal too.

"Now," says Whitfield, "Cap'n Hughes, he goin' buy guns for de maroons," he pointed to the mob that was all sullen now, with the chance of a blood bath gone away. "An' all these men, they love Cap'n Hughes, "he said, "and they do just like he say. So Cap'n Hughes him de master, and him got de money," he frowned and turned nasty, "So, if him got de money and you got de guns, then nobody get cut! So where de guns, Cap'ns?"

The next few minutes were worst of all. If you're too eager to please in such a case then you might as well give up your goods for nothing, 'cos your customer knows he can do with you as he wishes. But should you act up too bold, then you could find your customers crisping the crackling on your tits and arse alternately as they rotate you, live on a spit, over the red hot coals (which thought may make you laugh, but not too loud, please, as I once saw it done to a man and believe me it ain't funny).

Fortunately Cloud was a tough old trader who'd done the like a dozen times before, and as for me, it comes natural. We quickly came to an agreement that I would stay on the veranda accepting Whitfield's hospitality (that's to say I was hostage) while Cloud went back to the ship for a crate of muskets to show the quality of what was on offer. But the bulk of the cargo would stay aboard until our deal was struck and monies paid.

After that things looked up. Cloud went off in the Pilot boat, Whitfield smiled, Mocho smiled, we all sat down and food was brought and more rum. Hughes recovered and chatted civil as a poor clergyman visiting a rich widow, except for the girls still fanning him and combing his long white hair to sooth him. And of course, every soul present treated him like a king, so when he talked, they shut up and listened.

By rights, he should have been the most thundering bore 'cos he hammered on about the abolition of slavery to the exclusion of all else. And he seemed to have memorised every last word ever spoken on the subject in the House of Commons and quoted them at length. But he had the most amazing gift of speechifying, which I guess was what earned him his respect among the maroons. He was like those actors that can make any line interesting. His voice went up and down, and the maroons edged closer and closer to hear: hundreds of brown faces, hundreds of figures squatting in the sand, and they repeated his words and chanted and mumbled among themselves, their deep voices rumbling and echoing and dying away.

I must confess I enjoyed listening to him. He was mad as a hatter, but a rational madman if you see what I mean. You could almost believe the nonsense he was blathering, what with brotherhood and freedom and all, though he spoiled it a bit when he got on to his plans for the Jamaica planters and their families.

Cloud was over an hour getting back 'cos he took the opportunity to reinforce our position. He had the long-boat swung out and manned, with a brass four-pounder in the bow. And he brought a dozen men, all armed. Of course, this was just for show: it meant they'd now take ten seconds to massacre the lot of us instead of five. But it cheers a man up to have a few friendly faces around at such a time, and I certainly felt my spirits lift as Cloud laboured up the beach with half the boat's crew behind him, carrying the crate of muskets and some powder and shot to go with them.

Whitfield and Mocho jumped up and had the crate broken open, while Hughes smiled benignly and looked on. Out came the brand new muskets and dozens of men pushed forward to have a look. Their own guns were old and worn, with thin barrels that looked ready to burst and take the fingers off your left hand. And they were every size and shape from fowling pieces six feet long, to antique Spanish carbines with external mainsprings, and most of 'em would have cut their mother's throats for a regulation Tower musket.

One of these was duly handed up for Hughes to look at, and he clumsily strained to cock it and snap it off to test the lock. But later when we set about striking a price for the whole cargo, he revealed another of his talents. He was damn near as good as me, even without the advantage of enough men to butcher me should the business not go his way. On top of that, for a man who looked like a preacher, he had the most amazing knowledge of the goods on offer.

"There must be a serious reduction on your price, Mr Fletcher," says he, peering at the opened crate, "Because I see that your muskets come with bayonets, for which my followers have no use. And as for the made-up cartridges: these are useless without cartouche pouches – the which you have not provided - to keep them from the rains!" Beyond that he wanted to know how many spare ramrods we were providing free, and how many packets of flints, and bar lead, and bullet moulds and mainspring vices, and turn-screws etc, etc, etc.

I could see that Cloud was out of his depth. If I'd not been there Hughes would have had the drawers off him and tarred his bollocks. But I shrugged my shoulders and told Hughes, man to man and eye to eye, that we'd another customer among the Froggy blacks in Santo Domingo, and if he didn't want our merchandise then I knew who did! Whitfield and Mocho didn't like that one bit and there was some angry mumbling that spread through the maroons like wind over a field of corn (another dangerous moment, but you have to keep your nerve or give in). Of course it was all bluff, and Hughes damn near guessed it too, but I stared him out and in the end he wasn't sure, and backed off.

Eventually, by evening (which comes down like a curtain in Jamaica with no twilight) we had a deal that left both parties content and I'd more than trebled my little investment in Cloud's special cargo. We parted like friends and we mariners went back aboard for the night having agreed to unload the goods on the morrow.

The next morning we duly exchanged our merchandise for the agreed sum which Hughes himself counted out in new-minted French gold and this I record as the beginning of my success as a dealer in hardware on the fair Island of Jamaica. [3]

Then when all the goods were ashore, we took an anchor out on a boat, dropped it in the seaway, bent the anchor cable to the capstan and heaved round the capstan bars to haul *Lady Jane* bodily out into deep water to make sail. The last I saw of Hughes was him standing just out of the surf, waving solemnly and raising his hat with his brown girls hovering in attendance. I thought I was well rid of him, but I was wrong.

Two days later I was established ashore and finding my feet as a man of business. Cloud landed his main cargo at the port of Montego Bay which was about the size of a large Cornish fishing village, and was the third biggest town on the Island. It was set in the most lovely bay and had wharves and warehouses, a couple of churches, a Town Hall, a Court Room, a Gaol and a Common Workhouse. It was neat and pretty place, mainly consisting of the usual whitewashed wooden houses with their big verandas for shade: *piazzas* they called 'em.

This was ideal to me. It was big enough to give me leeway for my activities and far enough from the main port of Kingston where the Navy was, or the capital, Spanish Town where the Governor and the Parliament were, to keep me from attention of the authorities, and I soon found that I was safe so long as I didn't actually grab folk by the collar and say:

"Good day to you, sir, I'm Jacob Fletcher the celebrated mutineer and murderer,"

Thus it was a rough and ready place, was Jamaica in the '90s. It was dominated by the planters as a class, who mainly lived on their estates, and whose idea of culture was monster banquets, heavy drinking, making money, and covering every slave girl they could grab hold of.

When we left Captain Cloud and *Lady Jane*, Sammy, Kate and I took up lodgings with a Mrs Godfrey, a musteefino widow-woman who had her own house and a string of children by her late, so-called husband who in fact had been her owner. But he'd left her the house and her freedom, and the freedom of the nippers too because under Jamaican Law the white/musteefino offspring were free in their own right, and could never be bought or sold.

---

3   Note the depravity implicit in these words! The gold coin obviously came from England's implacable enemy - the French Government - whose slithering agents were using Hughes as a catspaw to strike a blow against Fletcher's own native land. S.P.

And that gives clue to the way in which a few thousand white men held sway over a vast slave population. It went like this: the child of a white and a black was a mulatto, the child of a white and a mulatto was a sambo, and the child of a white and a sambo was a musteefino. There were also quadroons and octaroons and others from various combinations of these mixtures, and it all seems ludicrous but was taken deadly seriously, and each one of these had his place in the hierarchy, and of course there were the maroons who were no part of this at all because they lived free in the mountains and thought themselves better than anyone.

Consequently, just so long as everyone was busy scrambling for place, there was no combining against the whites.

By the end of October, after a few weeks in Montego Bay I was beginning to become very comfortable. I'd re-invested my profits when Cloud sold his cargo, which he did before sailing for more business in Kingston. I bought a stock of his wares, carefully choosing only items that Jamaica could not produce for itself: bars of copper, lead and tin, tools, nails and bolts. These I was selling on at a handsome profit to the planters or their agents when they came into Montego Bay to buy.

On the other hand I was alone. Kate Booth demanded a sum in gold, so she could seek her fortune in Kingston. I was sorry to see her go for she was a lovely creature and I knew she had wounds inside her that needed healing, from hurts that she'd taken years ago. So I gave her the money and off she went and I never saw her for years.

Sammy on the other hand, took to Jamaica wonderfully. He even put on weight and pronounced himself ready to give up the sea and settle down. The reason for this was Mrs Godfrey's sister Chloe, a pretty little musteefino woman half Sammy's age, who did the washing for the house and had taken a fancy to Sammy's jokes and his laughing. So Mr Samuel Bone, mariner, moved in with her and lived better than ever he'd lived in his entire life, with good food, a lively young woman, Jamaica sunshine all day, and rum at night: a sailor's paradise.

He was close enough that I saw him every day or so, which was good because it meant I had someone to talk to without having to guard my tongue all the time. So I kept the cash flowing his way as I prospered. I could hardly do less considering all he'd done for me: if Sammy hadn't got me out of the Navy's clutches I'd have long since been hauled up the yardarm for some *hearty-choke and caper sauce* as they say on the lower deck.

I took the name of Boswell, for trade, and since commerce is the natural inclination of my life, I prospered well. I specialised in hardware and metal goods, and bought a fresh stock from each incoming ship. As I'd thought, tools, nails, and bar metal proved excellently profitable and by the beginning of November I had my own warehouse by the harbour, complete with a counting house and my name (Boswell) painted over the door. As for staff, there was an endless supply of slaves hired out for the day, to do the heavy work and some of the younger ones were smart and willing and served customers too. The problem was keeping accounts. At first, I did it myself but I soon had to give this up as demands on my time grew and grew.

Finding a clerk was the devil of a job. Not one slave in a thousand could read and write, let alone serve as a book-keeper. And there was a dreadful scarcity of white men capable of working to the standards I demanded. Such men as I could get, proved to be idle rogues who bodged the figures so they could dip their hands in the cash box. As you may appreciate, they might as well have tried to fly to the Moon as play that game on me, and each one was duly found out, chastised and heaved out through the back door by the collar and the seat of his breeches (not the front door: that would be bad for trade). Finally I solved the problem and considerably advanced my interests all in one jump.

From the very beginning I'd sought to build up a string of loyal customers who knew me and trusted me (a most advantageous and excellent thing to do in business and which I most particularly draw your attention to). One of my best customers was a fellow by the name of James Lee, a coppersmith and plumber who'd established himself in the highly specialised art of building and repairing the pumps and pipe works to be found in the distilleries of the big plantations. He'd done very well at this since there was a shortage of skilled mechanics of all kinds in Jamaica, and the likes of coopers, carpenters, masons, and blacksmiths could make their fortunes if only they applied themselves (the fact that not all did, is a monstrous indictment of some of the dull heads and fat arses that were to be found upon the island).

Mr Lee however, was a diligent fellow, known throughout Jamaica and whose services were much in demand. But he was over sixty and feeling the strain of the constant travelling that his work involved. And so, he put me a proposition. He came to see me at Mrs Godfrey's the first Sunday in November. He was done up in his best, English clothes (taken out the chest after thirty years probably for they were a generation out of fashion and even included a round, 'scratch' wig).

"Mr Boswell," says he, as we sat on the piazza with a jug of rum punch, "You a straight man, an' me want to put a straight thing to you," like many whites who'd spent their lives in Jamaica, he'd picked up the local accent and tricks of speech. It was an odd thing to hear at first, but you soon got used to it.

"Me lookin' for a partner for me business," says he, "For to keep me people straight, and for to keep me people jumpin'." He took a pull at his drink, and licked his lips, "But him got to be man me can trust. An' him got to be man of substance!"

He said it *sub-stance* in the musical up-and-down accent of the Jamaica people. What he meant of course was that his offer didn't come cheap an' he was inviting me to bid. So we talked about the details and what the thing amounted to was this.

Lee had a workshop and warehouse plus a dozen experienced slaves, trained up to the work, with a white journeyman to supervise them. He also had a couple of mulatto freed-men who'd had a proper education and kept his books. All the skills were there to run the business. There was only one problem. "Me journeyman, Higgins," says he, "Him good man, him very good workman, but him too fond of the drink and sittin' in the sun, and it take the right kind of master to keep him to the mark."

He looked at me and grinned and I had the nasty suspicion it was my size and muscles he was thinking of rather than my abilities as a man of business: the one damned thing that's dogged my footsteps all my life and which is sure to set my blood boiling when it's mentioned. For it is my desire to advance myself by brains, and not by strength like a stupid bloody cart-horse. [4] But I knew a good thing when I saw it and we soon got down to money.

Old Mr Lee was a good craftsman who'd worked hard and made his way by his own hands, but he was no dealer – certainly not a man to rate

---

[4]   Affectation and posturing! Fletcher was proud of his strength and in later years would entertain the ladies after dinner by taking up the iron poker from the fireside, and twisting it into a knot. On wilder occasions, with wilder, so-called ladies present, he would clasp one on each shoulder and run up and down stairs with them while they squealed with incontinent excitement. S.P.

alongside of Mr Vernon Hughes – and I could've taken advantage of him if I'd wanted. But it is the profoundest principle with me never to do such a thing, for it leads to no good in the long run.

So after a very little talk we came to an agreement that on the morrow I would inspect his books to check he really was making the money he claimed. All being fine, I would pay him a substantial sum in cash, we would merge our businesses (Lee and Boswell of Montego Bay: it's still there as a matter of fact) and I would run both for a 40% share of total profits, with an option to buy a greater share in one year's time.

And that's what we did. It was an excellent piece of business for both of us. Lee had a near monopoly of the pumps and pipes trade and was making enough money to return to England and buy an estate if he'd wished (which he didn't). So I embarked upon the road to real wealth, I got my book-keeping done, and I learned the new business.

Lee's people were well-chosen and good at their work, including the book-keepers who were a cut above their white brethren and had the sense to try no tricks. The journeyman, Higgins was a skinny little Irishman with long hair tied up at the back. He was a most gifted craftsman and worked well as long as I was there to keep an eye on him. As Lee had said, that meant I had to travel with Higgins and his men whenever work was to be done at a plantation, but that was no disadvantage as it gave me the opportunity to meet the planters on their own ground and to sniff out new business of all kinds.

And so, for about the next eight months I spent some of the happiest days of my entire life. Those golden times comprised one of longest and best chances I ever got to follow my true vocation and if I'd been left alone for a few years then I'd have become a sugar millionaire and never a doubt of it. But I didn't get the chance.

CHAPTER 4

"… thus I am sickened, and thus shall I leave Dulwich Square. I do not care that I lose my station without reference and – if you will have me – I would chose honest work beside you at the cobbler's last rather than spend another instant in her service. Indeed I would wish rather be a plantation slave groaning under the lash."

(From an undated letter from Mr Edmond Morris, unaddressed, to his brother Harold Morris, Shoe-Maker of Macclesfield, Cheshire.)

Late in the evening, inside 10 Dulwich Square, Lady Sarah Coignwood climbed the grand, richly-polished staircase that lead to the first floor of her magnificent house. Two maids followed, stooping to retrieve the garments she cast off on her way, while Morris her Steward proceeded her, backing elegantly up the stairs in grovelling unction, while performing the intellectual duty of arranging everything to her pleasure.

(Outside, the beggar shuffled past. He peered through the railings, looked down into the area and saw what the servants were doing in the bright-lit kitchen. Hot water was being poured into large cans and placed by the fire to keep warm.)

"Bath for My Lady in her dressing room," thought Morris, "Bath for the blackamoor in the back bedroom. Then the usual wines and refreshments in My Lady's bedchamber. Then the bedding turned back …" As he went through the list, he held aloft a massive, five-branch candelabrum to light the way, hoping that My Lady's good spirits meant nobody would get the edge of her filthy tongue this night. "Just so long as that piece of black fancy measures up to requirements," thought Morris, and swivelled left rearwards as his questing heel told him he'd reached the landing.

Without looking he reached back with his free arm, bowing like a dancer, and accurately located the handle of My Lady's dressing room, and threw open the door to reveal her bath laid out with all linen, towels, fragrancies, oils and iced Champagne in a silver bucket, and another maid standing by.

"Ah!" said My Lady, with the smile of a goddess, "You are my treasure, Morris!"

"My Lady!" said Morris, sighing inwardly. It'd been a safe bet that she'd want the bath but you never knew with her.

"You may go, all of you" she said, disrobing completely as if Morris were not capable of a man's feelings. He ground his teeth, pulled the door shut behind her and cursed her to Hell.

Inside the dressing room the solitary maid bowed awkwardly at her naked mistress. The bow was awkward because she was a very large woman, thick about the middle, with muscular arms, and broad, red hands. She had a better moustache than many a French Grenadier and she'd hauled up the heavy cans of hot water, steaming from the kitchen, as if they'd been feather pillows. She was Mrs Maggie Collins, who'd pulled Lady Sarah bleeding and unconscious from the roaring inferno of number 208 Maze Hill Greenwich in July last, when My Lady's bastard stepson Jacob Fletcher had come to rescue Miss Kate Booth.

(Out In the street, the beggar looked again and carefully noted how many servants were still in the kitchen.)

Sarah Coignwood stared at Mrs Collins and frowned. Gratitude was now overcome by the distaste of employing such a creature as a body servant. When in her bath, Lady Sarah liked to be soothed and stroked by slender girls with soft round arms and white skin. Mrs Collins noted the look and flinched. She was deeper in My Lady's power even than ordinary servants because My Lady knew that her former profession had been the removal of embarrassments left inside ladies by selfish gentlemen.

"Out!" said Lady Sarah, waving Mrs Collins away having decided that she'd be sacked on the morrow. "I cannot be served by apes and trolls," she thought.

An hour later, bathed, perfumed and wrapped in a robe of Chinese silk, Lady Sarah admired herself before the enormous mirror in her bedchamber and decided that the moment was come. She tugged the silken bell-pull that would set Morris into action like touch on a hair-trigger. Within seconds there came a tap at her door and Lady Sarah breathed deep in anticipation of the first encounter with a new lover.

"Yes?" she said and Rasselas entered wearing a long robe that she had bought for this purpose. He was gorgeously handsome and the colours set off his skin to perfection.

"My Lady calls," said Rasselas with a smile, "And it is my pleasure to serve." He set his right hand over his heart and inclined his head towards his mistress. Lady Sarah sighed in contentment. His voice was cultured and smooth with just a flavour of the exotic. Standing tall and splendid in the candlelight, Rasselas was the most perfect incarnation of the un-tamed panther.

"Come here!" she said urgently and snapped her fingers, pointing at the thick carpet by the bedside. Rasselas grinned confidently, revealing gleaming white teeth. He walked the few steps and stood before her, looking down into her eyes, his hands on his hips.

"Perhaps M'Lady would tell me what is her pleasure?" He said.

"Oh yes," she smiled "But first I must know the truth of what I have heard."

Rasselas laughed, "That is what my last Mistress wanted to know, first of everything," and drew open his robe.

"Ahhh!" gasped Sarah Coignwood. He was slender and finely muscled, with narrow waist, wide shoulders and every glossy contour sharply defined like the work of a sculptor in black marble, while stirring into life beneath his flat, hard belly was everything she'd ever dreamed of. Instantly she sank to her knees, threw her arms around his tight muscular buttocks and buried her face in his loins.

Despite his experience of such matters, and despite his full awareness of the supreme importance of delivering a professional performance, Rasselas was close to being swept away. But he clenched his teeth and screwed up his eyes in the intensity of his control, because truly there were times when a servant's life was hard.

He stood the torment as long as he could then raise her up. He kissed her deeply while sliding the silk robe off her shoulders to slither, whispering down the length of her naked body. After that it was easy.

"At least there's no stays to unlace," he thought. Though having got My Lady stripped for action, and having seen the stunning loveliness of her body, that was as far as Rasselas could go with rational thought and

41

she was swept up in his arms and spread over the bed's gorgeous silken coverlet for a thorough and comprehensive servicing.

(In the street, the beggar cocked his head he heard, faintly, from an upper floor of the great house, the piercing cries of a woman in ecstasy. He jibbered and jabbered to himself. He spat out curses and peered again down into the area. The cook was alone, sitting by herself in the kitchen.)

Some minutes later, Lady Sarah stretched her tingling limbs and enfolded Rasselas in her arms. She stroked his head In satisfaction, she kissed him long and luxuriously, she stroked his soft skin slowly and gently, and allowed herself to drift easily, comfortably, deeper and deeper into warm and sensual slumber.

The beggar saw his chance. He threw open the iron gate. He scampered down the area steps. He knocked at the kitchen door. He chewed his fist as the cook drew the bolts. She opened the door. She saw him. Her mouth gasped. He grunted with effort and hit her in the face with a heavy cobblestone. He leapt the body. He was in! He ran across the flagged floor. He ran to the door to the stairs. He slammed it back. He shot down the lower corridor. He flew past the open door of the servants parlour. Those within leapt up, too late. He took the stairs three at a time: ground floor, first floor, second floor, bedrooms … *her bedroom*!

Lady Sarah woke sharp and ugly. Rasselas bellowed in pain and limbs thrashed beside her in the very bed. The stink of a foul body filled her nostrils and some rough and filthy fabric scraped over her skin like a file. A shoe kicked her leg as blindly she pulled herself out of bed and fell to the floor.

"Ahhhhh!" screamed Rasselas.

"Ahhhhh!" screamed someone else.

"Morris!" screamed Lady Sarah, "Morris! And all of you, damn you! Here! To me! Now! Now! Now!"

Rasselas and someone in disgusting rags were locked in fight in her bed. Blood was spraying from slashes all over the beautiful black body. And – oh Jesus Christ! Oh Sweet God In Heaven! She saw the other's face! Oh Christ, oh Christ, oh Christ!

Exerting all his strength, Rasselas suddenly leapt back and clear, hurling himself out of the bed. He was young and strong and rolled nimbly to his feet, his streaming bleeding arms raised protectively from the threat of the terrible knife. He snatched up a chair as a weapon, but his assailant had turned away and was scrambling like a spider across the great bed, after the woman.

Rasselas sprang forward and swung the chair over his head, but it slipped in his blood and he caught the wriggling legs rather than smashing his enemy's spine as he'd intended. The wild, filthy, mad creature got himself out from chair, bedclothes and encumbering rags and threw himself upon the naked form of Lady Sarah Coignwood, who was frozen with horror and unable to move so much as an eyelid.

The monster enfolded her in his arms He spun her round to get her between himself and Rasselas and the terrified servants massing at the bedroom door. The mangled right hand put the blade of a surgeon's knife under My Lady's jaw and pressed it to her throat. To the disgust of all present, he drew her head round by main force and kissed her full on the lips.

"Mother," he sighed, "I have come home."

CHAPTER 5

On Wednesday February 26th 1795, some three months after I'd taken over the running of Lee and Boswell, I went with my men to the Powys Sugar Plantation In Cornwall: Jamaica being quaintly divided up into the three Counties of Cornwall, Middlesex and Surrey, each of which had five parishes. It was a thirty-mile journey from Montego Bay and took seven hours including stops for refreshment and resting the horses. We travelled in style, in a pair of big waggons laden with our tackles and kit, and two teams of powerful, well-fed draft horses that were in themselves an advertisement of the success of Mr Lee's business. Myself and Higgins the Journeyman took the lead, with five of our slaves in the second waggon, in line astern of us. Our slaves loved such an outing and lorded over those we passed trudging in the dust.

Even winter makes no difference to the climate in Jamaica and it was hot, with a big sun blazing out of a blue sky. As we neared the plantation, the road wound up through mountainous country and I ordered all hands over the side to walk, and ease the task of the horses. The slaves knew me by now and tumbled out without a murmur, but Higgins whined about his *poor suffering feet*, and I had to help him down with a boot up his beam ends, and so we proceeded, as happy a band of comrades as ever was.

The scenery was something to wonder at. Big mountain peaks with jungle growth dense on every side: bamboos, log wood, trumpet trees and broadleaf of all kinds, and everything green, green, green. It was a wonder when you came across a stone or a boulder that wasn't smothered in growth of some kind or another.

The Powys Plantation was one of the finest on the island and we had a good view of it as we came down the mountainside to the level grounds below. Your average Jamaica sugar Plantation of those days was a thousand acres. One third laid down to cane, one third provision grounds for the slaves to raise crops on, and one third virgin forest for the timber. To run it, you'd want two hundred and fifty slaves. Then you'd need a watermill or windmill to crush the canes, a boiling house, a curing house, a distilling house, a hospital for sick slaves, huts for them to live in, stables for your beasts, sheds for your mechanics, and a fine dwelling house for yourself and family. You should think of a combination of village and manufactory rather than any sort of farm that we know in England.

At the end of a good year, a big plantation like the Powys might clear £3,000: a huge sum indeed for those days. If you took it into your head to buy one (as I had done) the asking price was some £30,000, a colossal sum. You could build a squadron of frigates for that. I knew all this already as we hauled on the brakes of our waggons on the way down to Powys, and my mouth was fairly watering at the thought of it.

Later as we drove past the rows of cane, the neat lines of the slave houses, and the busy slaves toiling at their work I thought what a fine thing it would be to be a planter. I'd seen other plantations but none quite so prosperous and orderly. Even the slave houses had neat thatch roofs, whitewashed walls and gardens with flowers, and they had furniture and beds inside.

"Oh, yes sir, Mr Boswell," says Higgins when I commented on this, "Them Powys slaves live better than many a white man, sir. If I had the choice of being a slave here or a poor freeman in England, I know the which it must be, sir!"

"What?" says I, irritated by the stupidity of this remark, "Don't try to gammon me, Higgins or it'll be the worse for you!" I thought he was trying to get his own back in some way for my making him walk in the hot sun. But I was wrong.

"Oh, no sir, beggin' your pardon, sir," says he, looking me straight in the eye, "See it like this, Mr Boswell: if times be bad in England, why, it's starvation or the workhouse and there's many as prefers starvation of those two," I nodded. That was true enough. "While take these here, sir," says he pointing at the slaves bending to their tasks in their neat shirts and breeches, "Why them, sir, they've a roof over their heads, they've their crops and their pigs, and a good dinner each night and rum on Saturdays. And they got the sunshine, sir! Every day, mostly."

He made a good case. It occurred to me that there was many a mill-hand grinding out his fourteen-hours work, for sixpence a day, under the cold wet skies of Lancashire, that was worse off by far than these slaves. That's what I thought at that moment, anyway.

So I mulled that over as Higgins drove past the big house where the family lived. This was a giant version of the veranda-ed, piazza-ed Jamaican house I'd seen all over the island. It was wood-built, white painted and stood in its own grounds with a high, white picket fence all around. Higgins, who knew the plantation, took us to the overseer's house where we were expected. This was a more ordinary building, but passably clean and staffed with a couple of slaves to keep it in order.

The plantation staff of hired servants was the overseer at the top, with a few mechanics (carpenters, coopers and the like), plus a number of book-keepers who were a disgrace to that name and no more than slave drivers. Needless to say, all of these beauties were white men.

The overseer was out in the fields as we arrived, but slaves were sent running and eventually three or four white men turned up. They swaggered comfortably under broad-brimmed hats, and were much what you'd expect of a team of men hired to keep slaves up to the mark. They were a greasy, self-satisfied crew, led by the overseer, whose name was Alderton. He greeted Higgins as a friend, and introduced the rest to me.

There were two book-keepers of no special account and a third fellow that I took against on sight, which partly explains what happened later.

"An' this here's Mr Slade, *The Jolly Jumper*," says Alderton. "He's come on speculation to see what's doing in his line!" Everyone laughed at that, including Higgins. I had no idea what this meant but I had no inclination to admit ignorance in this company.

Slade was a big man with a thick neck and a permanent sneer on his face. He had a cutlass hanging at his waist and a knife in his belt besides. He carried a thick cow-hide whip coiled in his right hand and he stared me in the face with an insulting familiarity that I didn't like one bit. If he'd been aboard a ship of mine, he'd have got what he was asking for, that instant minute. But I was here in pursuit of business and personal pleasures must be subordinated.

"What'll you take to whet your whistle, gentlemen?" says Alderton beckoning one of his house slaves, and I saw Higgins grin happily.

"Most courteous of you, Mr Alderton, says I, but it is a principle with me that work comes first." It was a risk refusing his hospitality, but I saw from the look on Higgins's face that if I let him near drink, there'd be no work done that day. Alderton was a bit surly at this, but he led us to the distillery, a stone-built structure about sixty feet long, with a high chimney to take away the furnace smoke, and four enormous copper stills, each one of a thousand gallons at least, and there were huge cisterns for water and fathoms of copper piping, with pumps to impel the various liquids about.

Having served afloat and seen the indispensable importance of rum to the running of a ship of war, it was interesting to see one of the places where rum was actually made. The distillery stank of rum, and steam and molasses and Higgins beamed with pleasure and inhaled deeply. But he set to work quick enough when Alderton pointed out where his services were needed. Higgins sent one of our slaves for the tools and materials for the work, and put on a long leather apron to protect his clothes. Alderton soon excused himself and wandered off, while I got myself a stool and sat watching Higgins to see what I might learn of the trade.

But I'd not been sitting long when we were interrupted. In came a busy little fellow with a penetrating expression on his face: a man in his forties with a sharp look about him, wearing gentleman's clothes which spoke money in loud, plain words.

"Bid you good day, sir!" says he, all in a breath, "My name's Green. I'm Planting Attorney for Mr Powys who these six weeks past is gone to England. I stand in full authority for my owner." The words *my owner* meant that he owned the owner if you understand me, for a Planting Attorney was one who supervised a plantation for an absent owner, and took a nice 6% of turnover for doing so: it was a position I had my eye on.

Green pumped my hand vigorously, and poked his long nose into Higgins's work, while Higgins and my slaves stood back out of his way. Higgins treated him odd and not one bit to my liking: not quite rude but not quite polite, and with a half-smile on his face. The slaves followed his lead and grinned to one another. I ground my teeth at this behaviour towards a client and marked Higgins down for a boot up the breech later on. But Green seemed not to notice and asked a number of pertinent questions about time to finish the job, and cost of materials and labour. When he'd done, he turned to me.

"Sir," says he, "I hear your name's Boswell and I hear good of you, as a straight dealing man. A man of business, in fact." Well … he couldn't say fairer than that, now, could he? Mind you, my first thought was to beware of him attempting some deceit, having blown a hole in my defences with flattery. But that wasn't what he was at. He meant only what he said and proposed that we took a turn about the plantation while my men were at work.

"'Taint many days a-month I get the opportunity for conversation with an educated man, sir!" says he, "The nature of my work forcing me into the company of plantation overseers and such." Now this was a puzzle because I wanted to keep an eye on Higgins. But here was a man of importance in the world of local business, who was seeking out my company. And he was a customer besides.

"Mr Higgins," says I, fixing the shifty swab with my eye, "You may expect my return within the hour, to see what progress has been achieved." I did my utmost to signal by my expression and manner, that he'd get a walloping if he'd been slacking.

"Yessir!" says he, knuckling his forelock.

"Yezzah!" says the slaves.

"Hmmm…" says I, giving them a final glare before going off with Green, out into the boiling sun.

Green was a serious fellow, honest and interested in his work, and I'd guess he gave *his* owners full satisfaction. And he truly seemed to have no other motive than a desire for conversation. Mind you he did have a damned good try at talking down the price he was prepared to pay for our work.

I soon put him right on that, and I think we were both enjoying the cut-and-thrust of it when a commotion broke out among a group of a half-a-dozen slaves off to our right, a couple of hundred yards off. We were in the provision grounds where the slaves grew their food, and a crowd of women were out hoeing and watering. Two male slaves were holding on to a woman who was far gone in pregnancy, with a great belly bulging under her dress (all the slave women on the Powys being respectably covered in cheap cottons bought from England). The Overseer, Alderton was there with one of the book-keepers and Slade, the Jumper, who was shouting at the woman. Without any conscious thought in the matter, I started walking towards them.

"Mr Boswell!" says Green, nervously, "This is overseer's business going forward here. No place for you nor I," and he laid his hand on my arm, but I shrugged it off and kept walking. A hot thick feeling was filling my head and my heart was beginning to pound. "Pay no attention, sir!" says Green, "I do advise you," I looked at him, and his eyes widened in supplication, "You are newly come out to Jamaica, Sir, and ignorant of our ways." But I was paying him no heed, because Slade was yelling at the woman.

"Dig, you idle slut!" says he, and shoved a hoe into her hands. She pleaded with him in floods of tears but he cuffed her back-handed and pointed at the ground, "Dig!" says he, "'till I say to stop!"

She took the hoe and scraped out a hole in the ground. Green and I stopped a dozen yards from them and Alderton and the book-keeper nodded at Green as we came up, though not with any great show of respect. Slade ignored the pair of us, and when he thought she'd dug enough he snatched the hoe from the woman's hands and flung it down.

"Now then!" says he to the two male slaves, "Off with 'em!" and the two promptly stripped the women of her few clothes and left her stood up exposed to all the world. I'd had my share of rough living by then, and seen plenty, but I could have blushed for the swollen, pendulous nakedness of her, and the clumsiness and awkwardness of it. This wasn't a young girl revealed in her beauty, but a mature woman with the marks of her years upon her and the right to be decently covered, whether she were snow white or night black.

But Slade was shouting again and pointing to the hole. The wretched creature left off crying and sank clumsily to her knees, then lowered herself, half falling in the process, so her belly fitted into the hole she'd been made to dig. At once, the two slave men, kicked her legs and arms apart and got out of the way, leaving her spread-eagled in the dirt. Meanwhile, Slade carefully measured out three or four paces, and uncoiled his whip.

"What's this, Green?" says I, turning to my companion.

"'Tis Mr Slade, at his work," says Green, "Mr Slade, the Jumper."

"The what?" says I.

"The Jumper," says he, "The itinerant flogger of recalcitrant slaves. He is paid by the stroke to chastise persistent offenders: the slack and the idle and the insolent. How else should we go on?" He was trying to be matter of fact but he was going a sickly colour and wanted to be off. "Come, sir!" says he, "This is no place for us. Such business is beneath my dignity."

"What's that bloody hole for," says I, "Why's she made to lie in that hole?"

"Ah, ahem," says Green, "Why, sir," says he, licking his lips and clutching

49

at my sleeve, to be away, "The child sir. Valuable property of my client. Should she lie upon it, some harm may follow and so … Ah!" He broke off and his fingers bit into my arm, for Slade had swung the lash and brought it whistling down across the victim's back with a snap like a pistol shot.

I'd seen plenty of floggings, both in the King's service and the American. But that was men being flogged, and some of 'em stupid crass lumps that could be shown no other way to good behaviour. And while a Navy cat came down hard enough to make a barrel jump, the seven lines spread the blow so it hurt like the devil and scarified the skin, but it didn't go deep. A ten-foot cowhide whip on the other hand, delivers all its force into the narrow plaited cord at the tip, and applied the way Slade was using it, the filthy thing cut like a knife. His first stroke pulled skin and blood out of the long wound it created.

The victim shrieked like a pig in a slaughterhouse. The other field women threw up their hands and moaned in horror. Slade and the book keeper goggled, open-mouthed and Green turned his back and mopped his face with a handkerchief, while Slade shifted his feet slightly for another stroke.

"Belay that!" says I, in a great roar. Slade froze and all eyes turned to me.

"Mr Boswell," says Green, anxiously, "This is a legal and proper punishment, recognised by the competent authorities. Do you not appreciate the fact?" I bit my lip. He'd hit me in a most sensitive spot. I did indeed appreciate the fact. Slaves were whipped every day in Jamaica and I knew it. But this was the first time I'd seen how they went about it. You must understand that I hadn't the slightest wish to rock the boat. I felt myself on the way to success in Jamaica and making trouble with a man like Green was the very last thing I wanted to do. He saw the doubt in my eyes and smiled a feeble smile.

"Come away now, my dear sir," says he, "And let these good fellows get about their work."

I looked around me. I saw the fat, naked figure face-down in the dirt with blood running out of the cut in her back. I saw Slade and Alderton sneering at me and at Green. I saw the field-women holding their breath, and I saw Green himself whom my instincts told me was the key to a new and superior class of business upon the island. The clever side of my mind was all for keeping out of this. How many floggings had I witnessed aboard ship? Ten? Twenty? A hundred? So what was one more? And if I made a fuss and stopped this one, then what of the hundreds I'd never even know about? And above all there was the powerful, overwhelming desire not to make a bloody fool of myself over matters I did not understand. For all I knew the damned woman was an idle slut that no work could be got out of by reasonable means.

"Ah!" said Green, seeing the change in my expression, "Then we'll be off, shall we?" He looked at Alderton, "I'm sure Mr Alderton can delay matters until we have gone?" He looked unsure about it but Alderton grinned.

"Surely can!" says he, tipping his hat with one finger in a lazy salute. He looked at Slade, " Obliged if you'd stand easy for a while there, Mr Slade," says he, and the two of them leered at one another and at us, and Green dropped his eyes. He might have been a sharp 'un for business but he'd got no proper control over his hired hands and I think he was actually frightened of Slade and Alderton. Green started off at once and tugged at my arm. I followed, stamping down on the emotions boiling up within me. I fixed my eyes on the big, white Planter's House and fixed my mind on trade and profits. I wasn't no abolitionist and I wasn't no reforming radical and I wasn't going to upset things just when they were looking bright.

I'd gone a dozen paces when the smack of the whip and the shrill cry rang out, loud and piercing. Slade couldn't contain his impatience or more likely he wasn't even trying. And that, unfortunately, was that. In spite of every consideration of trade and business, I couldn't let *any* man treat *any* woman like that.

And it weren't no half-hearted feeling neither. The blazing bloody anger that swept over me was like the explosion of a powder mill. I'm a heavy man for a runner but I hit Slade before he knew what was happening, and did my level best to tear him limb from limb. I knocked him clean off his feet and we rolled over and over, kicking and biting and gouging. The fact that I made a dog's breakfast of the thing is what saved his life, for I'd have killed him then and there if I could have.

His mates tried to help him and piled in milling and booting. They bellowed and cursed and hauled us to our feet, which cleared my head from the dizzy rolling in the mud. Slade had got the worst of it and was staggering like a drunken man, clumsily trying to haul out the cutlass that had worked round to the back of his belt and couldn't be got at.

"You bastard!" says Alderton and struck a blow at my head, with the butt end of a horse-whip, but I blocked it and gave him my fist in the middle of his face and put him down, with closed eyes and a nose like a smashed tomato. The book keeper had the sense to back off with his hat in his hands, claiming it weren't no part of his affair,

"Not no-how, not at all, Mr Boswell, sir."

Then Green was screaming out a warning as Slade finally got his cutlass out and swung it glittering at me in a side-swiping slash: the Jamaican cane cutter's blade, sharp as a lancet, near three inches wide and half an inch thick at the spine. He damn near got me too. He actually took hair off the top of my head and shaved me bald over a patch the size of a shilling. It was only by luck that I dodged him and I jumped back, looking around for something to fight with. He came on again and missed again. His head was still sick from our tumble on the ground or he'd have split my skull to the Adam's apple.

Then I snatched up the hoe that the slave woman had used and held Slade off with the long shaft, jabbing the iron repeatedly into his face while I watched for advantage. We danced like that for a while, till I manoeuvred him into Alderton's prone body, and so he tripped and I stamped on the fist that held the cutlass.

There's little more to tell after that. I hauled him up, took my time, and gave it to him properly with both fists, until he dropped to his knees, spitting teeth and begging for mercy, and finally falling semi-conscious on his face. I didn't even take my coat off and stood over him, gasping with the effort of it and wiping the sweat from my eyes, with Green at my elbow chattering with excitement. He seemed greatly pleased with himself and with me. But I wasn't listening, "You there!" says I to one of the two male slaves who'd manhandled the woman, "Get her out of there." I pointed at the wretched, naked figure still snivelling into the dirt. "Get her some clothes and take her … take her …" my knowledge of plantation life was limited, "Take her home," says I, "Take her to her family."

"Take her to the hospital," says Green, joining in.

"Aye!" says I, "And no more flogging. No bringing her out for the rest of it when the surgeon says she's fit!" For that's how it was done in the Navy under some Captains, and I didn't want the like done here. If I'd made a fool of myself, so be it, but I didn't want it to be for nothing.

"Of course," says Green, quickly, "She shall not feel the lash again."

And so the slaves fussed around the woman and got her up and dressed her, and she muttered something at me in a tearful voice, and grabbed my hand and kissed it, and without thinking I put my arms around her, and gave the Jolly Jumper a few more good, hefty kicks, (him being conveniently near) and I threatened bloody murder to all comers if anyone even so much as thought of another flogging. I think I must have yelled at them for some while because, by God Almighty, I was never in such a passion in all my years, and you don't know some of the things I've seen and done.

Then I let her go, and they took her off and Green led me towards the big house, grinning about I-knew-not-what and talking all the way. I was still full of what had happened and paid him no proper heed. But as we went up the steps to the piazza, I saw something that I did take note of. There came out of the house to receive us, two cracking fine women, in dresses like English ladies of quality. They were in their thirties, fair-skinned with big almond eyes, long-legged and tall with saucy lips.

Enough to catch a man's eye, you might think. But what I haven't said was that they were identical twins and not even their mother could have told the one from the other. But their mother should have told them not to look at a man the way they looked at me that day.

"By George," thinks I, "We shall have some fun here!" And I did too, but only at the cost of drawing myself to the attentions of an enemy that made Mr Slade and his cutlass seem like a baby lamb.

CHAPTER 6

*"Did I arst wot yu done wiv my boat? Did I arst what yu was
adoing of? But I spied yu and I noes. So now I says be damned the
gelt what I owes yu and no more shal yu have of me for the hard
herted cow whot yu are to yore own flesh and blood."*

(From a barely-legible letter of 25th August 1794 to Mrs M. Collins at
Dulwich Square, London, from Mr H. Collins, Waterman of Wapping
Stairs.)

"Tell them all to be gone, my darling," said the beggar drawing Lady
Sarah close to him, while sliding the flat of his knife over her breasts and
belly. Suddenly his eyes bulged and his mouth foamed, "Get them all out
now!" he screamed and the knife shook in his hand, "Get 'em out or I'll
slit you before their eyes."

He stank fearfully, his hands were filthy, with ragged nails, and his face
was wild. But, except for Rasselas, he was known intimately to all present,
and the horror of the moment was intensified by the ghastly change from
the elegant exquisite they'd known, to the howling madman pricking his
mother's flesh with a blade. Because this was Mr Victor Coignwood, Lady
Sarah's last surviving son and heir to her millions.

He was also the son whom she'd betrayed to escape a murder charge,
who'd suffered wounds and mutilation as a consequence, and whose weak
mind had snapped when she deliberately tortured him with the details of
what she had done. But only she and he knew that.

"Out!" said Lady Sarah, fighting to be calm, "And you, Morris! See to
this good man's wounds." She pointed to Rasselas, now swooning from loss
of blood, "See that he receives every conceivable attention." She spoke in

a soft and lovely voice. She was playing a part. She became the Madonna, the saint, the gentle *parfit* lady. She did it to calm Victor and to persuade those watching (who all might have tales to tell), that her own position was one of snowy-white innocence. "My poor Rasselas," she breathed, softly, "Let him be attended by…" But she touched the wrong key.

"No surgeon!" cried Victor, and the knife-point trembled, quivering, snicking skin and drawing blood. "No surgeon or any other comes to this house, or I'll cut this bitch in slices!" He stamped and raved and dragging his mother with him, past Rasselas where he crouched on the bloody carpet. "Take him with you," he cried, "And out! Out! Out! All of you."

The servants vanished, taking Rasselas with them and the door slammed.

Then Victor turned on his mother, "I've come for you, my love," said he, "I've come to pay you back at last, and it shan't be done quick. I've a lifetime to pay you back for." This was no more than the truth. She knew it and she had to get his mind on to some other course. She was close to howling in despair. Close to giving up. But she held on by a whisker.

"How did you escape?" she said, "How did you get out of Dr Crick's Asylum?" Victor smirked.

"By God's own hand," he said, "Or rather by the hand of his representative."

"Oh?" she said, managing to sound as if enjoying the conversation.

"Oh?" he repeated, "Oh? My darling I shall tell you. Now guess who was the Chaplain to Dr Crick? Guess who came to pray for the poor lunatics?"

"I cannot guess," she said.

"Ilkley," he said, "The Reverend Mr Ilkley."

"I do not recall the Reverend Gentleman," she said.

"No, you never knew him. He and I were never close, for his penchant is the dear little bottoms of dear little boys while mine is the richer pleasures of full grown men."

"I see." she said, "And he proved loyal to you?"

"Not really," said Victor, "Even when I threatened to expose him to the world, he said he would deny my words as the ravings of a madman. And yet he brought money to help my silence," he paused and frowned, "I was searched every day. Did you know?" His lips twisted in viciousness, "Yes of course you know for you paid the good Dr Crick to keep me nice and tight, didn't you mother dear?"

"So what did you do?" she said, desperate to keep the lid on the bubbling pot of his anger.

"Do?" said he, "I hid the damned money," he laughed, "I put it where the sun don't shine. Nasty business mother. Dirty business."

"And then, and then what did you do?"

"I saved the money, and found a greedy gaoler, and walked out through opened doors."

"And then?" she said.

"And then I walked to London. And here I am."

"My dear, clever boy," she said, stroking his matted hair. Victor trembled. At the bottom of his cess-pool mind he hungered for his mother's approval.

"Do you think so?" he said.

"Oh indeed," she said.

"Truly?"

"Yes."

"Truly? Mother … am I truly clever?"

"My darling, you were always the one for special cunning. Do you not remember? All others were simple brutes," she whispered in his ear as a lover might, "Only you had that special cleverness upon which I came to rely."

"And do you … do you … love me?" He choked over the words, driven into utterance *only* by the victory of hope over bitter experience.

"Of course darling, always and forever," she said, and flawlessly named past events which (when duly edited) demonstrated her love for him. Thus Sarah Coignwood was walking barefoot through broken glass. She was doing it with extreme skill and playing on her knowledge of Victor's crooked mind, and as she spoke Victor began to relax. She scratched his filthy scalp and kissed his cheek. She forced herself to ignore the sickening stench and the vermin that hopped in his hair.

"And shall I come home to you mother? To live with you again?"

"Of course, my love."

"And shall I be well again?"

"Of course."

It was going well. Her confidence was surging back and her quick mind was already wondering what to do with Victor afterwards? Thus her concentration slipped and she missed his next few words. He shook her. She blinked.

"Mother!" he was saying, sharply, "*Am* I? You must tell me!"

"Are you what?" she asked.

"Mad," he said, "I must know if I am mad."

Coming from a wild-eyed monster holding a knife to her throat, the question drew from her a hysterical gasp, half way between shock and laughter, and the result was catastrophic.

"*You fucking bitch!*" he screamed, and gibbered and chattered and spat out the mutilations he would perform upon her body: vile fruits of the dreams he had lingered over during his empty days at Dr Crick's. He pulled himself up, sat squarely across her body, and fumbled in his rags producing scissors, pincers, a green-glass stoppered bottle, a brass funnel, and a bodkin with a coil of waxed thread ready drawn through its eye and secured with a knot.

Sarah Coignwood struggled with total, desperate strength to fight free, she clawed his face and arms with her sharp nails, but in vain. He held her down and seized the four-inch needle and its trail of thread.

"Now, mother," he said and took hold of her upper lip …

Tap-tap-tap! Victor spun round to look at the door.

Tap-tap-tap! The door was thrown open by a maid who instantly vanished to make way for a large woman dressed as a domestic, bearing a tray with a silver tea-service, the household's best china and a dish of macaroons. The woman advanced calmly into the room, as if a madman were not squatting on My Lady's naked body preparing to sew up her mouth.

"Tea, Madam," said Mrs Collins in the purest tones of Billingsgate, "'as hordered by yerself. His it your Ladyship's pleasure that I put it dahn?"

"Mmmm!" said Lady Sarah. It was the best she could manage. Even she had her limits.

"Get out!" cried Victor, throwing down his needle and seizing his knife, "Get out or I'll cut her blasted eyes out!"

"Certainly Mr Victor, sir," said the big woman, completely unperturbed, "Han will you be takin' Tea wiv 'er Ladyship? I 'av fresh lemon 'ere, hacordin' to your taste." Moving slowly as if with the clumsiness of age, she found a table, put the tray in place and smiled respectfully at Victor. She carefully noted the distance between them.

"Get out!" said Victor, but with less anger. He was actually thirsty. He'd not eaten or drunk all day. And he'd always preferred tea with lemon (as Mrs Collins knew, having taken advice in the matter).

"So 'ere we hare then, Mr Victor, sir," said Mrs Collins, pouring tea. She added a slice of lemon and advanced slowly towards Victor, with a dainty cup and saucer on a silver tray. She was the picture of demure deference, the very icon of the aged serving woman. Lady Sarah held her breath. Mrs Collins held her breath. The servants on the landing held their breath.

"Stop!" said Victor, and pointed with his knife, "Put it there!" he snapped, indicating a spot within reach of his hand and about one pace in front of Mrs Collins. Mrs Collins curtseyed and sank to her knees as smoothly as her bulk would allow. She put down the tray and clambered awkwardly to her feet. Victor took the cup quickly keeping out of her reach and keeping his mother under threat with the knife in his left hand.

"Will that be hall, sir?" she said.

"Yes!" said Victor, "Now get out!"

"Macaroons, Mr Victor, sir?" said Mrs Collins, again offering what she had been assured was a favourite of his.

"Macaroons?" he said, "Chocolated?"

"Hof course, Mr Victor sir," she said and brought the tray. She put it down beside the saucer seeming to concentrate her attentions on the pile of macaroons but studying Victor Coignwood as a hawk does a mouse. She caught My Lady's eye, made a business of preparing to get up as Victor leaned forward, looking at the plate of his favourite dainties.

As he moved, Sarah Coignwood suddenly heaved herself upward, propelling him further forward, within reach of Mrs Collins who leapt like a tiger and dropped her weight flat on top of him. She had the knife out of his hand in seconds and got her beefy forearm under his chin and squeezed his neck inside the crook of her elbow.

Victor kicked and wriggled furiously, but Mrs Collins had a grip like a wrestler and fourteen stones of bulk. Victor's eyes began to bulge and his face darkened. Mrs Collins secured her grip by getting a fat thigh across Victor's legs and her slitted eyes glared out of her big red face, relishing Victor's death struggles.

"No!" said Lady Sarah, "Collins! No!" she slapped the big woman across the face to get her attention. Lady Sarah looked at the servants. Eyes to see and tongues to wag. Mrs Collins looked and understood. She relaxed her grip and let Victor breathe. But with admirable foresight, she clapped a big hand over his mouth to stop him speaking.

Lady Sarah nodded, then got to her feet, found a robe to put on and ran her hands through her long, tousled hair, pulling it back from her face. She looked around her polluted bedroom. Everything would have to go. She could not support any reminder of this. But for the moment.

"Shut the door!" she cried, "Any one of you! Shut it! Now!" The door closed, hiding the frightened faces. At once she knelt beside Mrs Collins and Victor, still locked together beside the great bed with its jumble of bedclothes. The two faces looked into hers.

"You," she said to Mrs Collins, "will be rewarded beyond your dreams for this. For what you have done ... *and for what you must do next.*" Victor struggled violently at this, but he was a dwarf in the arms of a giant. Mrs Collins blinked and nodded.

"Collins," said Lady Sarah, "I want him dealt with tonight, but I want it done quiet. I want..." But at that, Victor's struggles grew so violent that the conversation had to be delayed. Resourceful woman that she was, Mrs Collins had come prepared. She had a long coil of rope under her skirts and a length of linen folded and knotted to make a gag. Between the two of them, they got Victor trussed like caterpillar in its cocoon, in which state he could be left on the floor while his mother pronounced his fate.

"The thing must be done by stages," said Lady Sarah, "I shall shortly summon my staff into the withdrawing room. Once this is done, you will then take this," she gestured contemptuously at her son, "You will take this down to the cellar and put an end to him by whatever means you chose.

"Umm! Umm! Umm!" said Victor, writhing on the floor with eyes rolling white around the pupils. He could hear every word, but was swaddled so tight that he could utter no sounds other than these wretched pleadings.

"Yes, M'Lady," said Collins, "And has to the disposin' hof the remains?"

"Ummm! Ummm!"

"What do you suggest?"

"The river, M'Lady."

"Ummmm! Ummmm!"

"How?"

"I've a brother what's a waterman M'Lady, what works out o' Wapping stairs. 'e howes me money and 'e'll loan me a boat han no questions hasked."

"Who'd man the oars?" said Lady Sarah, "I want no witnesses !"

"Bless you, M'Lady," said Mrs Collins, "I'm a better waterman than any man! Do it meself, M'Lady, nice and dark, out in the middle o' Hold Father Thames where tis deep and ... *Plop!*" she said, miming the heaving of a body over the side. "But I'd need the Cook's Gig, M'Lady han a steady nag 'arnessed. I can't trudge the streets with 'im over me shoulder."

"You shall have it," said Lady Sarah.

A quarter of an hour later Lady Sarah addressed her servants in the first-floor withdrawing room. Morris the Steward, stood to the right of the company, as head of the household. Then came the butler, the head footman, the coachman, three footmen, two ladies' maids, three house-maids, two kitchen maids, one maid of all work, and one boy page, and the outside servants stood to one side as their lower situation required: head gardener, two gardeners, and one stable boy.

There were just two absences: the Cook and Rasselas, both of whom were laid out in their beds, bandaged as well the household could contrive. Neither would receive the attentions of a surgeon, who would ask questions and demand answers. The Cook would undoubtedly live, though with a pugilist's nose. Rasselas was another matter, still bleeding from his un-stitched wounds, and whether he lived or died was a matter of chance.

Normally Lady Sarah gloried in the number of her servants, but not now because the task of shutting their many mouths was all but impossible. None the less she would try. As she began to speak, there came the faint sounds of somebody going down stairs outside the room, with a heavy object bumping behind. She raised her voice to cover this and warned her audience to pay attention solely to herself.

"You all know me," she said, "You know how dangerous it is to act contrary to my wishes," she ran her eyes from one to another of them stood silently in a room, lit only by a few candles.

"Bump!" A sound from the staircase, "Bump-bump!" The servants looked at one another. Lady Sarah continued.

"I wish to make clear that this house received no visitors this evening and spent a quiet night. Do you all understand?"

"Yes, My Lady."

"Good," she said, "But should any other story emerge, then all of you without exception will be dismissed my service in disgrace, such that none shall ever gain any other employment thereafter."

"Yes, My Lady," said the room.

"So," she said, "The future prosperity of you all, is in one another's hands. I shall be savage in my punishment of any person who so much as mentions this night's activities, even among yourselves." Since her household had always been controlled by the systematic encouraging of one servant to inform upon another. Lady Sarah knew that all possible precautions had been taken. She now offered her most profound prayers that Rasselas should not die and put all to the risk of a coroner's enquiry. She shrugged. Another day, another way. She would contrive in any case.

Mrs Collins decided not to make use of the cellars. The stables would be better, having two sets of doors: an inner set in the garden and an outer set leading into Dulwich Mews behind the house, where My Lady had ordered the gig to be harnessed and waiting. Yes, the stables would be the best place. She let herself quietly out through the ground floor dining room, heaved Victor over her shoulder and walked as quickly as possible across the dark gardens. He'd stopped struggling since she'd winded him with a few heavy blows under the ribs. He was easier to carry that way. He was blindfolded too, so he wouldn't see what was coming to him.

She got him into the stables, dumped him on the cobbles and all the horses snorted and clattered in their stalls. She found a couple of buckets. She filled one from the pump outside the stables. She went back inside, to the smell of horses and hay and leather, and put down the bucket that was brim full of water. She up-ended the other beside it to make a seat for herself. Then she fetched Victor, sat herself on the up-turned bucket and hauled him across her lap, face downward. His arms and legs were tight-wrapped in turns of rope and he was entirely helpless. She shuffled about to get things conveniently nice, with Victor's blind, gagged, head and shoulders sticking out over her thighs with his nose poised an inch over the water. Then she pushed down hard on the back of his head. It was nice and quiet that way. Just a bit of bubbling.

CHAPTER 7

"My dear Ladies," says Green, "May I present Mr Boswell of Montego Bay, newly arrived from England and already become a man of property in the Island." A fine introduction, but the way the two of 'em looked me up and down had more to do with my own broad shoulders and curly hair.

"Mr Boswell," says he, "Mrs Alice Powys, the wife of my principal, and Mrs Patience Jordan, her sister, the wife of Major Oswald Jordan of the militia, and owner of the Jordan Plantation in Middlesex. Two of the foremost ladies in the island's society and known to us as *The Stewart Sisters*, that being their maiden name."

I made my bow and smiled and the two sisters smiled boldly back and an understanding flashed between us as clear as a hoist of signals. It was not so much a matter of what was going to happen between us as when and where. Also I supposed there was the running order to settle, seeing as there was two of them and only one of me. All in all, things bucked up wonderfully in those few seconds.

"A pleasure to make your acquaintance, Mr Boswell," says Mrs Jordan.

"Indeed," says Mrs Powys (at least I think it was her, for I couldn't tell 'em apart).

"Anything is a relief from the infernal boredom of life in this wilderness," says number one.

"Indeed," says number two. Then they frowned slightly and looked puzzled.

"Do we know you, Mr Boswell?" says number one.

"Indeed?" says number two.

"I think not, Ma'am … and Ma'am," says I, "For the possibility does not exist that any man could meet you and not remember the happy occasion." (Damned good, what?)

"Sir!" says number one prettily affecting modesty, "You are a flatterer!"

"Indeed!" says number two.

You'll have recognised their manner of speech by now, so I'll save myself the bother of writing down the addendum henceforward. I think that whichever of 'em spoke first, expressed the thought they were sharing at that moment, with the other bringing up the rear. Of course it's possible that one of the pair was dominant as is the case with some twins, and so always spoke first. But how could you know? For they played all manner of games for devilment: switching costumes, and jewellery, and places at dinner, to make a jumble of all the ways you might've used to tell which was which.

Meanwhile Green was singing my praises as we went up the steps on to the Piazza and out of the hot sun.

"You should have seen Mr Boswell remonstrate with Slade and Alderton!" says he, "Slade was just about to put a few stripes across the back of that lazy Jemima, when Mr Boswell says…" That was about the tone of it and gives you the key to Jamaican society. Nice matters to raise before the ladies, don't you think? But he told a good tale and all in my favour and all three laughed over Slade getting his comeuppance as we sat down in a sort of open drawing room, with great slatted windows that looked out over the Piazza, across the plantation.

It was cool and shady in there with some good furniture and paintings, clearly brought from England, and a beautiful deep polish on the floor which was made out of local hardwoods. They make no use of carpets in Jamaica, for it's too hot to need them and they give cover to the cockroaches.

"Slade is an impudent fellow," says the twins, "And a good thrashing once a week will make a better man of him!" They looked at me with big eyes, "Perhaps you might stay to deliver it, Mr Boswell?"

"I'll be here for a day or two, Ma'am," says I to the one who'd spoke first. "My man Higgins tells me he'll have to rebuild the brickwork beneath one of your stills. It's a considerable piece of work." This was odd too, and unlike life at home. These were what passed for ladies of quality on Jamaica, and yet they were passing the time of day with a glorified plumber like myself. But I suppose that out here in the colonies, they were all in trade one way or another.

"Then you'll stay in the house, Mr Boswell," says number one, "I'll order a room made up."

"Thank'ee Ma'am," says I, "Does that mean I shall have the pleasure of making the acquaintance of Mr Powys, later on?"

"No," says one of 'em, speaking alone for a rare exception, "Mr Powys is gone to London on business," by implication this must have been Mrs Powys. She pouted and sighed with mortal boredom, "Leaving me here to rot, "Do you know, Mr Boswell there is but one theatre upon the island worthy of that name and that a wretched little place in Kingston."

"Indeed Ma'am?" says I, "But you have the solace of your good sister's company, do you not?"

"And I have hers!" pipes up the other, and they laughed and leaned across from their chairs to fan one another merrily. Number two turned to me, "You see how my sister is abandoned, Mr Boswell? And my own husband little better than Mr Powys."

"Indeed?" says I, scenting already that neither of 'em was in tow of her lord and master. There are few things better to stiffen man's pecker than a ripe married woman left lonely by her husband, and crying out for a rogering.

"Alas," says number two, fluttering her eyelashes, "My husband is so enwrapped with the affairs of our estates that he comes but seldom here to visit. And I, for my part, could never abandon my poor sister" She flashed me a wicked smile and giggled at number one. Number one giggled back and they looked me over like thirsty matelot sighing at the grog tub.

I flicked a glance sideways at Mr Green, embarrassed for the poor devil. He might as well not have been there for all the attention they paid him, the pair of trollops. Surely the little grub would pick up messages that were crackling across the room? But either he didn't or he knew to keep his nose out. He just nodded politely and smiled a careful smile.

So we chatted a while, refreshments were brought, I told a few tales from my travels, and a pleasant hour passed. Then the twins declared they must order dinner. and bathe and change and whatever else went on between ladies and their servants. So Green and I took a stroll back to see how the plumbing works were progressing. In fact he was itching to get me on my own as he had an offer to make me.

"I like the manner of you, Mr Boswell," says he as we made our way to the distillery, in the late afternoon sun. It was past the full heat of the day and more comfortable. "The plantation business is a robust one. Sometimes rough. And a tight rein needs to be kept." I could see what was coming and mixed feelings of pleasure and distaste filled me up. I guessed the offer before he made it and I resented a good half of it. "My work as a Planting Attorney is most arduous", says he, "Calling as it does for a good head for figures, a sound base in commerce, and good practical sense ... but also..."

And there it came. The old story. He wanted a pair of heavy fists to keep his toughs in line. The likes of Slade and Alderton were to be found on every plantation – it wasn't the kind of business to attract poets and scholars – and they didn't take kindly to taking their orders from a pipsqueak like Green. He had the law to back him, of course, for Jamaica had its writs and magistrates and the rest. So Green couldn't be denied in his lawful powers. But that didn't save him from the embarrassment of endless sneers and insolence.

"So you'd like me to act in your behalf?" says I.

"Yes," says he, "To act between myself and the staff of each plantation under my hand." He shook his head solemnly, "I act for five absent owners, Mr Boswell: a heavy responsibility!"

"Aye," says I. "And what's my percentage?"

"Oh?" says he, eyebrows shooting up,

"Percentage?" he shook his head and smiled patiently, "No, Sir! My offer is one hundred pounds per year, plus expenses." I actually laughed aloud. And so we had a very jolly little game of pounds, shillings and pence. At the end of it, Mr Green was properly educated of the full range of my skills and knew that a talent for knocking down bruisers is by no means incompatible with the ability to bargain nose-to-nose with a sharp customer like him.

In the end we shook hands on a most sweet partnership. I got 25% of his 6% of the business of each plantation. He kissed farewell to the jibes of rum-sodden bullies and could devote himself to living like a gentleman of leisure in Kingston. Of course it also meant that I'd have to find myself someone to look over Higgins's shoulder, for my responsibilities as Acting Attorney would mean extensive travel throughout the island.

More important, the new opportunity was so great I couldn't let it go. I was now deep in the swim of the Jamaica sugar trade. Aside from the money I'd make directly out of the work, there would be endless opportunities from close connections with Green's five plantations and the constant opportunity to meet members of the planter class as I went about the island. All this, plus the income from the pipes and plumbing business, if only I could keep old Mr Lee happy with the new arrangements.

Do you see what this meant to me? It was the realisation of my dream. I was making my fortune in trade. I was on my way. I was going to be a Nabob, a Sugar Millionaire, never doubt it. Look how far I'd come already, in less than three months! I landed in Jamaica in September 29th 1794, remember, and here I was in only in mid-December. Do you wonder that the pride of my life is trade and commerce?

The only problem that faced me on that happy evening was which of the twins should be first in line after sundown. But for the moment, my new partner and I popped into the distillery for a look at Higgins and the slaves. He'd taken my earlier warnings seriously and done a good job, but there was much yet to do. Just for Higgins's own good (and to show Green what a good bargain he'd made) I put the fear of God into the good Journeyman for what he'd get on the morrow if he didn't do better than that, and I blew the ears of the slaves too, for sniggering behind Higgins's back while I did it. But I never laid a hand on any of them for I was still galled at the thought of Green perceiving me as a tamed ape, hired to frighten his bullies.

Alderton turned up in the middle of this performance, to invite Higgins to sup with him and to find a place for our slaves to sleep. He was speaking out of thick lips and had a fine big nose, puffed up twice its normal size. He blinked at me as he came in and looked properly nervous. But I nodded curtly at him, to let him know he was forgiven. After all, I could always punch his head again if need be. So I let the fellow settle accommodation for my people and then Green and I strolled back to the big house for our dinner and a comfortable bed. Mine more so than his, most likely.

"Well, Boswell," says he, "You'll be pleased to know I'm not one to sit up late o'nights."

"Oh?" says I, my mind occupied with thoughts of finding someone to keep Higgins up to snuff."

"So I'll not be a skeleton at y'r feast," says he.

"You'll not?" says I peering at him in surprise.

"Not I, man!" says he, straight-faced, "D'ye think I'm quite stupid, Boswell?" Strange little chap, he was. Most fellows in those days would've slapped me on the back and begged me to *give her one on my account whilst you're at it*. But not Green. "You'll not be the first," says he, "Nor the last."

"Oh," says I, a little deflated.

"Bah!" says he, "why d'ye think Powys is in London? He'd the choice of suffering ridicule, or fighting duels for the supposed honour of his lady, or packing himself off. And he ain't the crack shot that Major Jordan is, so he chose the third option."

"Major Jordan?" says I, feeling a sea-change in the weather.

"Aye," says he, "Mrs Patience's husband: the other sister. He don't live with her no more, but he puts pistol balls through those she takes to bed." And then he smiled at last, "Of course the problem is, my boy, as a sharp 'un like you will've seen by now, the problem is, how the devil does a man tell which one has the husband in London, and which one has the husband with the barkin' irons?"

Now that put a damper on the evening, and no mistake. Duels are damned nasty things. I'd not the slightest inclination to stand up at twelve paces and let some red-neck Jamaican take pot shots at me. And you couldn't refuse the invitation neither. Chaps took it deadly serious in those days, especially in a place like Jamaica, full of merchants aping gentlemen, and planter militia officers who felt they had to shite fire harder than the regulars, to prove they weren't the vulgar boobies they actually were.

So I was quiet and thoughtful all the way back to the house. Quiet while the slaves showed me to my room, quiet while they brought in bowls and water for me to wash, and quiet all through dinner. Well, nearly so anyway, because I do love a good dinner and a glass or two of wine.[5] Especially I do in female company, and the Stewart twins were a pair of corkers. They had the most gorgeous brown eyes, with sloping eyebrows, and long lashes, and full lower lips with a gleam of white teeth showing, even when they weren't laughing (which wasn't often).

They kept a fine table, laden with the fruits, flesh, fish and fowl of the island. They had Sheffield silver, Irish Linen, French wine, furniture by Hepplewhite with chairs upholstered in brocade, and a splendid service of tableware in the new *Athenian* range by none other than Coignwood's of Staffordshire!

The slaves were done up like servants at home, complete with powder in their hair, and they came and went so soft, you hardly knew they'd been, as course followed course.

---

5 For 'glass' read 'bottle'. S.P.

With two fine women flashing their eyes at me, and no restraining influence whatsoever (Green was soon dozing over his plate) I took a little more wine than was wise and all thoughts of Major Jordan slipped away. About half way through dinner I noticed Green was gone, and when the covers were lifted and the Ladies withdrew I had to sit by myself to observe a token five minutes with the port, before proceeding into the withdrawing room on somewhat unsteady pins.

My memory is imprecise on the exact turn of events after that. They had a long sofa in the withdrawing room and came and sat on either side of me, prim and proper for the benefit of the servants, but brushing their arms against me and laying their hands on mine, as if casually, to empha- sise some point or other in the tales they were telling me. It's grand being centre of attention like that and I drank it all in merrily.

And then the servants were dismissed and the big mahogany doors, were closing behind the last maid and I was alone with the Stewart twins. One of them instantly leapt up, skipped across the room and turned a key in the lock. Then she was back with me and her sister (the two now inextricably confused in my mind). And that was the signal to *Engage the enemy more closely* as Nelson would have put it.

I don't think I ever met even one woman quite so desperate hungry for it as those two were. They positive leapt on top of me upon me on that sofa and fought for possession!

"Avast there!" says I (ain't it amazing what you say when taken aback?) "Which one o' you's which now?" I'd had a good drop to drink, but a bit of my brains was wondering which trollop had the dangerous husband and which had the one in London. But then they were all over me, sighing and moaning and making every hair of my body shiver with delight. "Shove off!" says I weakly, "You can't both have me!"

By George but they did though, and my brain dragged its anchor and thought no more of husbands, and I joined in the struggle and we had a match to see who could get the clothes off one another the quickest. The ladies were more expert than me and had the nimbler fingers for buttons and hooks and lacings. So the three of us heaved and rolled together, with enough noise to wake the dead and a final crashing descent, stark naked and entangled, from the sofa to the polished floor-boards and a damn good thing this was Jamaica, for we'd've taken our deaths of cold doing that in England.

But now here's the queer part. To the best of my recollection I had one or another of them, separately or together, on the floor, on the stairs, numerous times and in various bedrooms until we all fell asleep together with them purring in my arms like a pair of kittens. They were jolly enough in the morning too, but that was the end of it and I never enjoyed their company again, because once Higgins had finished his work (which he did that day), I got no further invitations to dinner and though the Stewart twins were cordial, I was kept politely at a distance.

To tell the truth. I was grateful because I didn't like Green's comments on Major Jordan and his duels. I ain't no coward and I've stood fire a thousand times in my career, mostly unwillingly it's true, but if I must then I will, and it's no more than thousands of poor devils are obliged to do, who wear red coats or blue jackets.

But I don't like duels, because with the date fixed, you've got days to get through in the certain knowledge of facing a bullet. What's more, being so big a chap is entirely to my disadvantage, since I'm all the easier for the other man to hit. And above all, a duel is risking death over somebody's idea of injured honour that ain't worth two pence, and I pronounce duels to be a damn fine thing for Frenchmen, monkeys and bloody fools, but not me.

So, as the two Lee & Boswell waggons pulled away from the Powys Plantation, I congratulated myself on having time in the best of all entertainments, and on having fixed an appointment with Green to have papers drawn up by a lawyer in Montego Bay (he jibbed at this and wanted me to come to Kingston, but I wouldn't have that, what with Navy ships in the harbour). As far as the Stewarts were concerned I assumed that the fire had burned hot and burned out quick. And of course I congratulated myself that there wouldn't be no duel with Major Jordan – not so long as Green held his tongue.

He did too. I had no problem with the Major. I met him, not long after and he proved to be a decent enough fellow, much in the planter mould, though you could see the temper in him in the way he cursed his staff and slaves alike.

And so the busy months passed in one of the golden and happy periods of my life. Between December 1794 when I met the Stewarts, and June '95 I gave myself over entirely to business. I toured the island as Acting Planting Attorney for Green, and developed numerous subsidiary trading activities.

I was making money hand over fist and the only thing that worried me was the degree to which I was becoming known about the island. There was always the possibility of my being recognised as Jacob Fletcher the fugitive from justice. But I wasn't going to sink into obscurity when, day by day, my business activities were going from strength to strength. It just ain't part of me to do such a thing.

In fact, in all the time I was in Jamaica, nobody ever did 'peach on me to the Authorities, though I suspect some guessed. After all, the colonists took the newspapers from England, my doings had been widely reported, and I'm a damned easy man to describe and to spot. Thus the two threats that I recognised, both passed me by while another threat that I'd forgotten came winging across the sea to find me. If I'd been given the choice I truly think I'd have preferred to take my chances against Major Jordan or a Court of Admiralty trial in England.

CHAPTER 8

*"From the moment of our seeing him we recognised a likeness
but could not place him in memory, because we met Sir Henry
Coignwood but the once, when he was deeply unwell. Moreover,
there was a vast disparity of context. It was only on the following
day that we recollected."*

(From a letter of Thursday February 27th 1795, from Mrs Alice Powys
and Mrs Patience Jordan, of Powys Plantation, Cornwall, Jamaica, to
Lady Sarah Coignwood, 10 Dulwich Sq, London.)

As soon as the very tremendously energetic Mr Boswell left the plantation
and the tiresome Mr Green had been packed off to go about his business,
the Stewart twins went to their writing desk in the withdrawing room,
now hot and darkly shaded from the boiling sun outside, and one of them
(who could say which?) took up her pen while the other fanned them
both to get a breath of air to breath in the stillness of the room. They were
excited with the discovery of a great secret and the telling of it to someone
whom they regarded with the uttermost admiration.

"They are so alike!" said one, "Fletcher and he."

"Indeed," said the other.

"We are agreed then. We may not see Fletcher again. *She* would be angry."

"After all that we have read in the London newspapers."

"What will she say?"

"What will she do?"

"Indeed!"

When the letter was written, it was rushed to the post office in Kingston
as fast as a trusted slave and a good horse could bear it. It went aboard ship

for England the next day, post-marked for February 28th. The ship, *Amelia Jane Smith* under Captain Ignatius Bottomley, and bound for Gravesend, weighed and worked her way out of Kingston harbour three days later on Tuesday 3rd March. Afterwards *Amelia Jane Smith* made a slow passage of seventy-two days, and anchored at Gravesend on Thursday May 14th 1795. There she unloaded her cargo plus a mail bag of letters including one for Lady Sarah Coignwood. The letter took two days to get from Gravesend to Dulwich Square, where it arrived on Saturday May 16th 1795.

But much had happened at number 10 Dulwich Square while the letter was rolling across the Atlantic.

The shock of Victor Coignwood's visit took months to smooth over. The Cook recovered, and her injuries were soothed with gold. Rasselas too, finally gave up bleeding and became a substantial pensioner of Lady Sarah's who could no longer bear to have him in the house, but sealed his lips with a large quarterly allowance which she warned would cease the instant that the cause of his scars became public knowledge. So he opened a Coffee House in Covent Garden and prospered considerably, but not as greatly Mrs Maggie Collins did.

When Mrs Collins drove back alone, in the cook's gig in the early morning of Sunday August 24th, she found the Coachman waiting at the Dulwich Mews entrance, and orders to go directly to My Lady in the library: *Sir Henry's Library* the servants called it, because it had always been his favourite room.

Mrs Collins knocked at the door and was summoned from within. She was shocked at My Lady's appearance: the fright was still upon her and she sat in a huge wing-backed leather armchair, still in a night robe with her hair undressed. There was a decanter of brandy at her elbow and a glass.

"Collins!" she said, glaring steadily at the other woman, "Is it done?"

"Done M'Lady," said Mrs Collins. She wore a man's greatcoat over her clothes and it was stained with dirt and wet.

"Into the river?" said Lady Sarah.

"Yes," said Mrs Collins, "As you ordered M'Lady."

"You followed *all* my orders?"

"Yes, M'Lady. Stripped 'im hof every stitch and tipped 'im in naked as the day he was…" She stopped, remembering.

"As the day he was born!" continued Sarah Coignwood, and shrugged her shoulders like Pilate washing his hands of Christ, "Have you children, Collins?" she asked.

"*Had*, M'Lady."

"Hmm," said M'Lady, not in the least interested any private sorrows her servant might bear, "No matter," said she, "You burnt the clothes?"

"Yes M'Lady, and tipped his things into the river after him: the knife and suchlike."

"Yes," said Lady Sarah with a shudder, "No doubt you did." She looked around the room with its tiers of books, uniformly bound in red, green and gold, to her husband's own style. She looked at the neat patent furniture: the chairs that folded into steps to reach upper shelves, the expanding desk for folio volumes. He'd loved such things, the old monster.

"Do you know why I sit in this room, Collins?" she said.

"No, M'Lady."

"Because my house is spoiled. It is made filthy. Everything must go, at whatever cost. I can take no pleasure in any of it. But this room which was never mine, does not disturb me."

"Yes, M'Lady."

"Oh, sit down, Collins," said Lady Sarah, irritated and wanting somebody to talk to. Anybody. Even this creature. She pointed to a second armchair, facing her own.

"Yes M'Lady," said the big woman and eased herself into the chair. She was tired after a night of heavy work and disturbed by the intense concentration of her mistress. She shifted in her chair, nervous of the ruthless intellect that she was facing.

"You have done very well indeed, Collins,"

"Thank you M'Lady."

"I propose to keep you in my service for so long as I shall live. I furthermore propose to pay you wages that you will find extremely generous."

"God bless you, M'Lady!"

"I doubt he will!"

"Whatever you say, M'Lady."

"Do you understand me, Collins?"

"M'lady?"

"Do you understand the full meaning of my offer?"

"Er ... no M'Lady."

"I shall explain. You are now privy to secrets that you may suppose to give you power over me."

"Never M'Lady!"

"You think not? You are a remarkably stupid woman if so. But listen to me. You killed my son. You dropped him into the Thames. I assure you that if this came to light then you will hang and *I* will go free."

"But…"

"Ah! You say *but*?"

"No, M'Lady!"

"Good! Then you must understand that the law is a thing that I bend to my will."

"Yes, M'Lady."

"So never suppose, Collins, that you are beyond my control, or I will dispense with you in every sense of that word."

"Yes, M'Lady."

"But should you serve me faithfully, then there could be considerable advantage to you. I am impressed with you, Collins! You showed resource and courage last night that no other in my service was capable of. There might again come a time when I have need of your talents."

"You may rely upon me utterly, M'Lady" said Mrs Collins who could recognise a very big stick and a very rich carrot as well as anybody.

"Good," said Lady Sarah, "Then begin by summoning my butler and informing him that I will have my bags packed for a month. He is to find me rooms at the best hotel in town. He is further to arrange for me to receive plans and designs for an entire re-furnishing of this house. I shall leave today and I shall not return until the works are completed. Tell him that money is not to be spared."

"Yes, M'Lady."

But Lady Sarah's estimate of one month to complete the gutting and re-furnishing of her house, fell victim to the eternal struggle between mankind and the interior decorator. Thus it was not until February of the following year that the transformed house was acceptable to her. By that time, she'd almost managed to forget Victor's visit and her life had resumed its steady pursuit of pleasure. By March she was her old self again, and all her friends were congratulating her on the elegance of her house and begging to know who'd done the work, that they might follow her example.

As a consequence, the letter that her butler brought on a sliver tray, to her private sitting room, on Saturday morning, May 16th, came like a blow. But the blow didn't fall at once. First she recognised the writing and the Jamaica postmark, and smiled with pleasure. Sarah Coignwood was as nearly genuinely fond of the two Stewart girls, as it lay within her capabilities to do so.

Three years ago they'd been in London with their husbands, whom her own husband, Sir Henry, had known. The husbands were pure trash: specimens of the colonial planter at its worst. But the girls were beautiful and had so openly modelled themselves upon Lady Sarah, and had so completely applied to her for advice that Sarah Coignwood could not help but like them. And certainly, their opinion of herself had been close to worship, since she was living the very life that they could only dream of, in their stinking, festering swamp of an island, surrounded by dirty slaves, poisonous reptiles, and hideous fevers.

So Lady Sarah smiled, almost as a mother would have smiled upon receiving a letter from her daughters. But she'd not read far before the colour drained out of her face and she sprang to her feet.

"*Collins!*" she screamed, and throwing open the door she rushed out and leaned crazily, dangerously far out over the stairs towards the servants hall, below, "*Collins! Come here this instant!*" The big woman lifted up her skirts and thudded up the stairs as hard as she could go, her flat face anxiously looking up at her mistress.

"In here!" snapped Lady Sarah, leading the way into her sitting room and slamming the door in the butler's face with a boom that shook the house.

"Damn that bitch to buggery!" said the butler, to himself, "And God save us all!" Much the same thoughts were in the minds of the rest of Lady Sarah's staff, so none of them knew that this particular rant was entirely out of the ordinary.

"It's him!" said Lady Sarah, "Jacob Fletcher, he's in Jamaica!"

"Fletcher?" said Mrs Collins, "'im what left us to burn when 200 Maze 'ill burnt dahn?"

"Him!" said Lady Sarah, and the two were united in hatred. "We shall go together. Collins, you and I. We shall see to Mr Fletcher ourselves. I could hang him through due course of law but I chose not to do that." She spat out the words in manic fury. She had scars of the mind from what had happened to her in the past months. Scars deeper and more lasting than she knew. A predisposition to insanity was in her blood and the extremes of her moods were dangerous, and frightening.

She even frightened Maggie Collins, who alone in the middle of the dark Thames had chuckled and as she'd plucked Victor Coignwood of his feathers and who'd never turned a hair as she cradled the white limp figure with its wide-open eyes before dropping him over the side. She'd even kissed him goodbye and taken a number of other liberties with the body. None the less, she was unnerved by Lady Sarah Coignwood whose lovely features were, in that instant, composed into absolute ugliness.

"Pay attention Collins," she said, "for this is what we shall do…"

CHAPTER 9

From March to July of 1795 my business in Jamaica forged ahead like an express locomotive with the devil shovelling the coals. I was making money at a furious rate and more than that I was becoming a man of consequence among the planters and tradesmen of Jamaica. I was even offered a commission in the militia (Captain, too, none of your Ensigns or Lieutenants!) and useful though this would have been for business, I had to refuse the honour since I feared being brought into the company of officers of the regulars.

The company of regular army officers I avoided like a clap of the pox, and for a damn good reason too, but one you'll hardly credit and you'll have to take on trust from your Uncle Jacob. The fact is, my jolly boys, that despite being block-head Fauntleroys with commissions got by purchase, and not one hundredth the professional skills of a Sea Service officer; despite all this, some of these army buggers *could actually read and write!* And they read the newspapers out from England. As consequence, I was afraid being recognised by someone who might arrest me and haul me back home for a hanging.

I did get to a few militia dinners though and staggered home in the small hours, arm in arm with some of my new friends, bawling out songs and waking the dead, since this was excellent for business, what with the gallant officers of the militia being drawn almost exclusively from the ranks of my customers or future customers, and by now I'd got comfortable with the idea that none of them was likely to poke his nose into my business.

My home port at this time was the counting house at Lee and Boswell's, and to keep the business running while I travelled the island, I took on a solid, middle-aged fellow named Wright as my deputy. Wright had been twenty-three years a Royal Marine and had reached the rank of Sergeant.

He was far from ideal, having no brains at all, but choice was severely limited and he offered two vital qualities: ingrained obedience to his superiors (me) and the knack of putting the fear of God into his juniors (principally Mr Higgins, my journeyman).

Apart from that, my mulatto clerks were intelligent fellows and easily able to run Lee and Boswell's as well as keeping the books for my other enterprises. Mind you, I checked the books every month, always without warning and on different days. This I did for their own good, as it would have been wicked to put temptation in their way by not watching how they handled my money.

So I grew richer and richer and if things had gone differently, then never a doubt that I'd have become a millionaire In a few years, and moved to America. And then who knows? Maybe I'd have become President. But things did go differently and that's that.

In the first place things grew hot in Jamaica towards the end of July of '95 and I'm not talking about the weather. There was a rumour that the Trelawney Maroons had kitted themselves out with muskets and all of Montego Bay was scared silly. I must admit I felt uncomfortable on this matter and always changed the subject when I could. But one of my customers or militia friends would never leave the thing alone, especially friend of mine by the name of Major John James.

He was a gentleman who'd risen high In Jamaican Government circles as regards the administration of Maroon affairs. He had the grand title of Major General of Maroons, and strangely enough had a really genuine affection for the rogues, having lived among them for many years. He was a big, red-faced old cove in his sixties, with a liking for flash clothes and bright colours. He had a great fancy for old-fashioned, silver-laced coats and wide-brim hats with feathers.

He'd been a powerful man in his youth and still had much of his strength left but he'd grown a vast belly and had the gout, so he had to stump about with a stick. He had a furious temper and little patience with fools but he took a liking to me, saying that I reminded him of himself when young. He used to challenge me to wrestle arms across the table, which I did to humour him, making sure that I let him win enough times to keep him happy.

"Give your best, now, Boswell!" he'd roar into my face, snarling and sweating with the effort, "Give your best or be damned!" and I'd heave and strain and let him force my arm over. Then he'd call for strong ale and a rum chaser (seeing as his chosen place of business was always a tavern) and he'd slap my back and invite me to feel the muscles of his arm. He wore his heart on his sleeve and there wasn't an ounce of guile in him. He was like a child in many ways.

He was a good customer too. He had a couple of large farms, run by freedmen (he wouldn't own slaves) but he couldn't get out to manage them anymore, and so he employed me to do it. His wasn't a large account compared with some I had at the time, but it was sweet business for he always paid up prompt and paid in cash. None the less I can't help wish that he'd taken his business elsewhere.

I've mentioned that my affairs were charging onward like an express train, have I not? Well, it was Major John James and his precious love for his precious maroons that derailed my train and pitched me into disaster.

I was away on my travels from mid-July until the 20th, but when I got back into Montego Bay, I found it under military law with the militia going up and down the streets trying to keep in step, and the civil population in a state of terror. One and all were convinced that an insurrection of Maroons was imminent, so earthworks and palisades were being thrown up around the court house and town hall, as a fort for the townspeople in case of need. But there were furious arguments as to where the lines of earthworks should run, and how to get enough drinking water inside, and food as well. It gave me a nasty fright, as I hadn't taken the rumours of Maroon trouble seriously.

When I got to my lodgings I found a messages waiting from Major John James begging me to go to his house at once. I thought he'd know what was going on so I went to him first and he dragged me off to a council of war that Mr Tharp the Custos had convened just shortly before (the Custos being chief magistrate and the representative of the Governor). So: crammed into the judge's robing room at the court house was a crowd of militia officers, the Mayor, assorted prominent civilians, Major John James and Mr Tharp the Custos.

There was a furious debate: Tharp was for summoning the 83rd Foot, a regular regiment stationed at Kingston, to protect the town. Others wanted to evacuate everyone by ship, others were for getting inside the new fort, and others were for an immediate attack on Trelawney Town (the main Maroon settlement) by the militia. But all these plans were hopeless: the 83rd was far off at Kingston, there were too few ships in harbour, the fort wasn't complete, and the Maroons would fight like demons to defend their homes. Unfortunately nobody had any better ideas. Nobody except John James.

"Let me try 'em!" says he, loudly and repeatedly, "I'll go alone. They'll listen to me and no other life need be risked!" But the meeting ignored him, because he'd made himself poisonously unpopular, a few days earlier, by taking the part of a Maroon, my old friend Captain Mocho, who'd been caught pig-stealing in Montego bay and later flogged (serve him right too in my opinion). But James persevered until eventually they paid him heed. In fact I was instrumental in getting him a hearing.

"Gentlemen!" says I in my best mast-head bellow, "Give Major James a hearing. What have we to lose?" Heads turned and they all looked at me. By then I was known and respected by every man present.

"Well, Major James," says Tharp, "Here's Mr Boswell pleading your case. What have you to say?"

"Give me leave to go up into Trelawney Town and settle this matter. I can talk sense Into the Trelawneys for they trust me and they need…"

"Need, sir?" says a voice, "What those villains need is the edge of the sword!" It was a fellow named Craskell whom the Maroons had turned out of Trelawney Town with a boot up his bum. He'd been *superintendent* there, a Jamaica government post supposedly putting him in charge of the Maroons. There was a superintendent at each Maroon settlement and the Maroons didn't give a monkey's piss for any of them. But there was a growl of support for Craskell but I and some others shouted this down and called for silence.

So Major James carried the day. He talked them round to letting him go to Trelawney Town, in the name of Mr Tharp the Custos, to see if there weren't some grievances to be found that could be settled and so prevent a descent into general bloodshed. Tharp insisted that if the 83rd did come, then Major James's expedition wouldn't be needed, that he might make ready in the meanwhile. At this everyone perked up something wonderful and told one another what a fine fellow John James was and how much the Maroons loved him, and I thought I'd done a useful piece of work in supporting James, but in fact I'd opened my mouth too wide.

"I've one more thing to ask of this meeting," says James and he turned to look at me, "Or rather of my friend Mr Boswell," he smiled and put a hand on my shoulder. "Will you come with me, lad?" says he, "I know my Maroons and they'll pay heed to a man of your size, and I'll may need to a man of your cunning!"

"Aye!" says the whole room.

"Capital suggestion," says the Custos. "We all know young Mr Boswell's reputation for straight dealing."

"And hard bargaining!" says another voice, and they all laughed.

And that, children, was your Uncle Jacob pitched in headlong. There was no refusing the offer; not with all my best customers looking on. Anyway, they'd caught me square on my vanity. Just for once in my life I was being invited into danger mainly on the basis of my brains. But it was a few days before Major James and I set forth. This was consequent on Lord Balcarras the Governor's dithering over the matter of sending the 83rd Foot to Montego Bay, because he thought the Montego Bay Militia was well capable of dealing with '*a few wild blacks in the hills*'. Finally on the 25th July Tharp realised he must solve his own problem and that Balcarras wasn't going to send the 83rd to Montego Bay until the Maroons had proved the danger was real, by burning the town. He therefore produced a compromise plan. James and I were to go to Trelawney Town for Major John James to act in the name of the Custos, while he, Tharp would follow a day later with sufficient force to take Trelawney Town if James failed to make peace.

And so it was. That same day found Major James and I on the road to Trelawney Town, on horseback. What with his weight and mine, the stables of Montego Bay had been scoured for two of the biggest saddlehorses in Jamaica. Mine was a great, ugly brute named Black Tom, that'd killed two stable-hands but was spared because they were only slaves while he was worth stud fees, which they were not.

I could barely control him for I'm no rider and horses are mysterious beasts and my understanding of them has always been limited. As you know, a horse has a limb at each quarter (fore as well as aft) and is steered by tiller lines which perversely run for'ard instead of aft as they do in a boat. Hauling on the starboard line sends him to starboard. Hauling on the larboard line brings him about on the opposite tack. Hauling both together, throws him all aback and causes him to heave to. Sammy Bone told me that, and it's all I know or care to know of horsemanship. But Major James insisted on horses despite the fact that he was even more awkward aboard a nag than me.

"'Tis the manner of our entrance that counts with the Maroons, lad!" says he, "The power of the animals, the strength and the stamp of the beasts! You've to strike a man's attitude before the Maroons." He was right too, and our entrance into Trelawney Town was more of a royal progress than a diplomatic mission. I was nervous all the way of the long ride from Montego Bay, but the first contact with Maroon sentries set the tone of the whole day.

They were out like picquets of Sir John Moore's light infantry and spotted us well before we saw them. But we got no hostile challenge. Rather, a group of half a dozen finely-built men suddenly rose up out of the rocks and undergrowth of the highland trail that passed as a road in these parts, and came leaping and bounding down towards us, crying a glad welcome.

They all but ignored me and fell upon James, laughing and weeping with joy and seizing his hands, and his boots and his stirrups or any other trappings they could catch hold of. The joy was mutual too. Old James was like a father greeting his children and calling them by name. And so we went forward, with the best runner sent ahead to warn the town and other sentries joining us on the way in.

When we arrived at the *New Town* which was the first half of Trelawney Town, we found thousands of men, women and children awaiting us where the road wound in from the surrounding hills into a collection of several hundred thatch-and-timber shacks. The noise and the cheering and the calling out of Major James's name, was deafening and we rode forward surrounded by some of the most splendid men and women I've ever seen in my life. The overall standard of fitness, uprightness and sharp-chiselling of the muscularity in the men was something to see. They were like the Zulu or the Cheyenne. The fact of their being near naked had much to do with this, but even the Grenadiers of our Guards regiments ain't so damned athletic in their bearing. They don't do so much leaping about in their trade, after all.

As before, the Maroons pressed forward with raised hands to touch their old hero and the women held up their children for his blessing, while the old Major leaned down to grip their hands and stroke their heads in the most amazingly affectionate manner.

The official chieftain here was an old Maroon named Captain Montague, and we were taken to his house where he had his principal people gathered together and I recognised my old friends Mocho and Whitfield. All these Maroon leaders were done up in sashes and feathers and all of them were armed, as was every other man present. My guess would be that they could muster over a thousand fighting men.

Also, and to my horror, there was that wicked old bastard Vernon Hughes, unmistakable among Montague's elite. This was a dreadful development. One word from Hughes to Major James about my selling muskets and I'd be a ruined man. Oh God and Jesus and all the little angels! The traps I've dropped into in my life. And my own fault too. But fortunately Hughes never got the chance for John James made a speech calling for peace between black, white and brown, which was received with rapturous cheers. And then when Vernon Hughes tried to speak against him he was howled down by the community in united voice.

After that, the common people were pushed back and a circle of chairs and stools was set out, in front of Montague's house and James and I sat down with Montague and his councillors, which Included Vernon Hughes, who obviously had his own faction among the Maroons. Hughes was still foaming and ranting for a slaughter of the whites in a way that made your blood run cold. But for me this was good news, for Hughes was so bound up with this. and with quarrelling with Montague that he had took no interest in me. Montague, I thought was a thoroughly decent old cove who clearly detested Hughes and did his best to argue against him.

Nonetheless, there was a swell of opinion among the younger Captains like Mocho and Whitfield for some immediate blood-letting, and the Maroons did have a series of grievances against the Island Government. In particular they wanted more land and more rights to run their own affairs.

But Major John James warned them that troops were on their way and he promised to bring the Custos himself tomorrow, to listen to their demands, and since it was John James who was saying this, and since the Maroons trusted him, John James did what he had set out to do which was to prevent any immediate outbreak of fighting.

Late in the afternoon, James and I rode back towards Montego Bay, to meet Tharp and his troops at an agreed rendezvous point, about ten miles from Trelawney Town. There we found a battalion of militia stepping up the road towards us with drums beating and colours flying. Their continuous drilling had taken effect, so they looked reasonably like soldiers and came on at a steady pace. On the other hand there was only about five hundred of them, not counting the officers riding at the front of the column with Custos Tharp and Colonel Jervis Gallimore. My guess would be that the Maroons could muster something like twice this number and that it was plain foolhardy to bring so few men. To my surprise, John James disagreed.

"They'd never stand fire," says he, "Maroons are artful cunning at ambush and irregular warfare, but they'll not form line and fight it out with regulars, nor even militia. If the town be attacked they'll take to the hills."

That night we slept in camp with the militia battalion, and reported what had taken place. Tharp nodded solemnly and agreed to give serious consideration to what the Maroons had to say. He'd brought a couple of assemblymen with him too to represent the island's Parliament in Kingston and these seemed inclined towards compromise also. Colonel Gallimore on the other hand, was not. He was a friend of Captain Craskell's and wanted to make an example of Trelawney Town.

"I tell you frankly. gentlemen," says he as we sat around a camp fire with the night insects twittering around us, "I await only the excuse to purge this nest of wasps once and for all."

"You will follow orders, Colonel," says Tharp, with a frown, "I stand for the King here, not you!"

"I'm well aware of it, Sir" says Gallimore with a sneer, "Only too aware of it."

On the morrow a small delegation, led by Custos Tharp and Major John James. rode into Trelawney Town. Colonel Gallimore was with them, and the two assemblymen, and of course myself. If I could have got out of it I would have, for I was still afraid of Vernon Hughes blabbing. But any hint of my holding back would have been seen as cowardice, as Tharp had decided to leave the troops formed up a mile from the town, with bayonets fixed and ball cartridge loaded. That way the Maroons wouldn't feel too threatened but swift retribution would follow any harm to the delegation. Mind you, we members of the delegation wouldn't be there to see it, would we now, because we'd be dead.

This time there was no glad crowd out to see Major James. This time the women and children were away, hidden in the hills and armed men were placed in small groups where they could best defend the town from attack. A larger group was held in reserve in the Old Town, through a narrow pass in the hills, and others were posted up in the high ground overlooking the New Town. Gallimore made a great play of pointing out all these preparations to the rest of us, and laughing at them in a forced and affected manner. But Wellington himself couldn't have placed the Maroon warriors to better advantage.

The circle of chairs was still there, though, and a table in the middle with food and drink as a gesture of hospitality. Montague was there too, waiting with his followers. But as we dismounted and walked towards them, one of the assemblymen stopped dead in his tracks and pointed dramatically at Vernon Hughes, standing close to Montague.

"Mr Tharp! Colonel!" says he, spitting out his words like poison, "That man is Vernon Hughes the abolitionist. I have a warrant for his arrest on a charge of stealing slaves out of my estates! He is furthermore a…"

"How can there be stealing of a living man?" cried Hughes, "Rather it is liberation."

"By God!" says the assemblymen and pulled a pistol from his belt. He cocked and levelled at Hughes's head, "You filthy traitor to your own blood!" Well, there was a man who knew Mr Hughes and no mistake. I couldn't have agreed with him more, but it wasn't the time.

"Put it up, you fool!" says I, "Can't you see how we're situated? Look about you." Several score of muskets were aimed at us from close by and there was a deadly tension In the air. One shot would start the war. With bad grace, he put the pistol away and we all sat down.

There were few formalities and little respect given in that long, tense negotiation, and great distrust on either side. Or at least that was the case at the beginning. Without Major James's constant diplomacy nothing would have been achieved at all. But once again he proved a master of the spoken word and at the end of several hours we'd reached agreement on a list of Maroon grievances to be set before the Assembly at its meeting on August 3rd.

When it came down to it, all they wanted was a token compensation of ten pounds for Mocho's flogging, and a few square miles for themselves of a big island that was still under-populated. It wasn't as if they were asking for a weekly supply of white virgins. Tharp was smiling, the two assemblymen were smiling and old Montague was smiling. Vernon Hughes and Colonel Gallimore were not, but that was no surprise.

And so agreement was within reach when something blew up like a squall at sea. The only point outstanding between us was payment to Mocho, who insisted on cash in hand. Tharp said this was impossible and only a promissory note, redeemable in Montego Bay could be issued. Not surprisingly Mocho had no wish to go near Montego Bay and things began to look ugly. Crazy as it may seem, this small matter looked set to upset everything and men were inching their hands back towards their guns.

"Gentlemen," says I, "Can't we find this sum among ourselves?" I took off my hat and put gold and silver into it, out of my own pocket.

"Here's three guineas," says I, and went from man to man. All contributed with more or less good grace, and Mocho grinned … and then Gallimore ruined the whole thing. As I came to him, he stood up and made a great act of tearing open some pistol cartridges and extracting the bullets.

"Here!" says he, in a loud voice, "Here's the only coin I'll give in such a cause!" He tossed the lead balls into my hat and snapped his fingers at Mocho. The insult was gross and it was fathomlessly stupid. There came a roar of anger from the Maroons and Mocho leapt up with wild. staring eyes and whipped out his cutlass, and click-click went the musket locks all around us as the Moroon sharpshooters took aim.

"No!" cried Mocho glaring at his companions, "Me own man!" and he sprang at Gallimore, who drew his own sword and caught Mocho's first swing by a whisker. Clash-scrape! The blades met and sparks flew off the edges. Gallimore staggered back, round eyed and sweating and defending by instinct alone as Mocho laid on. Gallimore was clumsy and slow and Mocho leapt like dancing master. Gallimore couldn't win but I couldn't let him take his medicine. Not when Tharp and the two assembly men had drawn firearms (one of them even pulled a bloody carbine out from under his coat as well as a pair of barkers) and fingers were tightening on triggers. One shot would have drawn return fire from a hundred muskets and blown us to rags.

But for all my profound irritation at being taken for a bully boy, there's been times when I've blessed my size and my prodigious strength, and this was one of them. So I skipped round the two men with their deadly blades and seized the table laden with food. It was thick oak and few men could have moved it, but I heaved it up, spilling fruit, flesh and fish to all points of the compass, I spun it round and shoved one end between the swordsmen. *Clunk*! *Thud*! The timber took a couple of swipes and I saw Mocho's mad eyes staring at me, as I hurled the bloody thing on top of him.

Down he went with the table uppermost and his arms and legs sticking out on either side. He was stunned but he was alive. I straightened up, gasping, and looked at the faces all around me: the white as well as the black and there was a moment of hideous silence when the thing could have gone either way. For nobody had put down his guns just yet. And then John James threw his arms around me and let out a great booming laugh, "That's the boy!" says he, "That's how I used to settle a fight when I was a young 'un!" He laughed again and turned me to face towards the nearest group of Maroons. And would you believe it, he presented me to them like a stage manager getting the pit to cry bravo for a Prima Donna at the opera. By George he had bottom, did that one and didn't the Maroons love him for it! There came a great roar of laughter and the day was saved.

And that should have been the end of the Maroon War. Mocho was hauled out from under and given his money (I saw to that). Montague shook hands with Tharp for all to see. The assembly men were sick and trembling with relief and thanked God for another sunrise. Gallimore scowled, Vernon Hughes scowled and our delegation saddled up and rode out of Trelawney Town with peace secured and a list of Maroon grievances for the next assembly meeting, and all over the island men and women sighed with relief, happy in the supposition that there would be no war with the Maroons, for folk will believe what they want to believe.

I would also place It on record that in due course, when Colonel Jarvis Gallimore got round a table with his friends and got a bottle of claret inside himself, he concluded that he'd have slain Mocho unaided and that my interference was a stain on his honour. He was just barely persuaded that he need not call me out and he pointedly snubbed me when next we met. Stupid bastard.

But I didn't care about him, for in Montego Bay I received visitors who offered me the prospect of a holiday of the most intriguing and exciting kind.

CHAPTER 10

"Mrs Curtis was outraged, as was myself, when our cabin was given over to La Belle Coignwood. Then I saw the creature and was utterly undone. For no lovelier a female did God ever make, and such gracious condescension as would melt the heart of a hangman."

(From a letter of Wednesday August 5th 1795, postmarked Kingston, Jamaica from Mr Oswald Curtis, Merchant in Fine Spirits, to his partner Mr James Cutler of Chatham Street, London.)

There followed two weeks of intense activity driven savagely forward by Lady Sarah's will. First, and to her intense annoyance, she found that as one of the greatest owners of property in the Kingdom, she could not leave its shores at a day's notice. Her lands and properties were managed through layers of agents, lawyers, bankers, head clerks and others who could demand her signature and approval from time to time. And this was even more true of the great profit-turning engine of the Coignwood Pottery Manufactories.

In all these things Lady Sarah Coignwood had not a shred of interest. But she was too sharp to neglect the source of her wealth, and when it was explained to her by nervous underlings that she was likely to be away at least a year, and that things could not be left, and that powers of attorney must be drawn up etc, etc, etc ... once she'd heard this from enough quarters to believe it, she applied herself to a ferocious chastisement of lawyers used to functioning at a speed barely distinguishable from dead stop, causing the whole, great and temporary shift of power to be completed in the incredibly short time of twelve days.

Thus at dawn on Thursday 28th May 1795, her preparations were complete and she was being helped up the folding stairs into her posting chariot. Like every vehicle in her stable it was the finest work of the coach-builder's art. The glossy black body and roof were flat and box-shaped, the underside curled elegantly forward into a sharp flat chin. Big glazed windows at the front and sides gave an excellent view and carriage lamps stood out for night-driving.

To the front, a large luggage boot was slung between the springs, while further trunks were built beneath the body, and to guard My Lady on the journey, two footman, in multi-caped coats and cocked hats, were sat high up on a double seat behind the coach body, each armed with a brace of pistols and a twelve-bore double carbine.

The doors were slammed, sealing Lady Sarah and Mrs Collins into the snug interior with its dimpled leather seats and long brass foot-warmer filled with piping hot water, because the day was chilly for May. In their long coats, fur hats and muffs, they at least, would travel warm and dry, whatever the outside weather.

Then the post boy in his enormous boots, mounted the left-hand front horse, the entire staff of servants paraded on the steps of number 10, bowed and curtseyed, and the chariot pulled away at a smart pace in a rattle of hooves and creaking of springs.

Stowed in the luggage boots was a small fortune in ready gold and Bank of England notes, plus letters of credit to various banks, and jewellery and gowns to dazzle the world. More important still, there was a letter of introduction to Lord Balcarras, the Governor of Jamaica, signed by His Royal Highness the Prince of Wales (wheedled out of him by offers he could not resist but which were never quite realised). Finally there was a letter from Mr William Pitt the Prime Minister.

Thus did Lady Sarah Coignwood, have at her fingertips every privilege that limitless wealth and rank could provide to speed her on her way. None the less, the journey before her was of such discomfort and inconvenience as later ages could not dream of.

By travelling non-stop, day and night, with heavy payments to ensure an immediate change of horses every ten miles or so, and with hired postilions who knew the roads, Lady Sarah completed a mind-numbing thirty-five hours on the road, arriving at Falmouth in Devon in the evening of Friday May 29th. There she planned to embark aboard a fast ship of the Falmouth Post Office Packet Service.

But even Lady Sarah Coignwood could not buy fair weather and had to endure a three-day wait in an indifferent inn with intolerable company drawn from the commercial classes, before the wind would shift to allow any ship to set sail. Then more money (much more) had to pass hands since the Jamaica Packet *Cumberland* had already filled its six passenger cabins, and an impudent colonial merchant at first refused to take himself and his wretched wife, out of his cabin and into the hold among his barrels and stores, so that Lady Sarah might be properly accommodated.

At last, on Monday June 1st, *Cumberland* went out on the ebb tide and spread her wings for Jamaica and Lady Sarah suffered the creaking, groaning hell of eight stinking, sickening weeks at sea.

The only consolation of that vile experience was that the weather steadily improved as the ship ploughed southwards. The grey northern waters and skies became blue and lovely. The very smell of the sea changed, and in the absence of any supportable society, Lady Sarah devoted herself to considering exactly what she was going to do to Mr Jacob Fletcher. In this, she never knew how closely she was duplicating the adventures of her son Victor: he trapped in a madhouse, she in a ship and both nurturing their souls with lurid dreams of revenge, an addictive poison that must be taken in ever-larger and ever-stronger doses.

Cumberland anchored in Kingston harbour on Thursday July 30th 1795 and Lady Sarah immediately sent her card ashore, for the attention of the Harbour Master, with a copy of her letter of introduction to the Governor, that she might be received with the dignity befitting her rank. In due course, even she was gratified by the reaction she received.

CHAPTER 11

It was Monday 27th of July that I met Francis Stanley the submarine navigator. It was a couple of days after my visit to Trelawney Town and I was feeling exhausted with months of work and my adventures of the previous week. I was relaxing by going through the books (always a pleasant occupation for me), sitting on a tall stool in the counting house behind the shop when two gentlemen came into the shop followed by a seaman pushing a barrow load of copperware. I heard a Yankee twang and poked my head round the door to see what was doing.

You see, since April of the previous year we'd supposedly been at war with the Americans though in reality the thing was a sham on the part of the Yankees who'd declared war on us to try to impress the bloody Frogs into buying American wheat. The war hadn't amounted to much more than a few naval battles, the worst of which I'd taken part in myself: the fight between HMS frigate *Phiandra* and the US Republican frigate *Declaration of Independence*. However, by the end of '94 It was common knowledge that Yankee and British envoys were in Lisbon, wrangling over a peace treaty, and the war had run out of steam with neither side wishing to carry it forward. But for all that, here was a gen-you-wine Yankee, supposedly an enemy, on my own premises.

Mind you, as soon as I got a look at him and his companions, I knew who they were, for they were the talk of the island. He was Mr Francis Stanley of Connecticut, who practised the wonderful art of underwater salvage.

Stanley was a middle-aged, tired-looking man, bald on top with a halo of hair and the veins broken all round his nose and cheeks giving him a red complexion. He had stooping shoulders and was much given to introspection; daydreaming really. When I got to know him, I found that he was totally obsessed with submarine navigation and would always bring the conversation round to it if you let him.

His companion, Captain Marlow of the brig *Amiability* out of Boston, was a more straightforward man. He had *Sea Captain* writ large upon him, from his tanned-leather face with its hard eyes, to his old-fashioned tarred pigtail. He had an air toughness, and was obviously one of the tarpaulin school who'd fought his way aft from the lower deck.

When I first saw them, Marlow was chewing tobacco and looking for somewhere to spit, while Stanley seemed to be feeling the heat, and he was sat in a chair, fanning himself with his hat.

I'd heard them discussed endlessly, as a subject of mighty fascination for it was an open secret that they were engaged in the incredible business of raising gold coin from thirty fathoms of water, off Montego bay point, where a ship had gone down in May of last year carrying £30,000 in gold coin fresh from the Royal Mint and on their way to the Kingston, Jamaica branch of the bankers Dean Barlow and Glynn. Stanley would reputedly keep 25% of anything recovered, since no other man in the world could salve at that depth.

Seeing the pair of 'em there in the flesh, I was smitten with fascination of the thing they were doing, and a whole new side of my character stirred into being. It was a side of me that I never knew existed before, and which in time became as much a source of pleasure to me as my life-long dedication to commerce. This new love was a fascination for mechanism. I suddenly conceived a great curiosity to know what sort of undersea craft might be needed to fish for gold in thirty fathoms? What might it look like, and how precisely might the cogs and gears of it turn upon one another?

Of course, the bridge to this new fascination was the familiar one of gold, and I could see that a most excellent business opportunity had just hove in sight, for when I looked at the wheelbarrow in charge of a lower-deck hand from Marlow's ship, I saw that packed carefully in sawdust was a load of pumps and copperware of large and ingenious size. Here was some of the very tackle and kit that was employed in their wonderful art, and it was the Royal Mint to a bent farthing that the said tackles were in my shop to be mended, for the looks on the faces of Stanley and Marlow showed frustration and desperation … and so … and so … be still my beating heart! They were balked in their plans and needed Lee and Boswell's to haul them out of the bog-house pit. Now, I'd be a garlic-breathing Frog-eater if I didn't admit that I saw the chance to get my hands on some of the guineas. But separate and aside from that was this strange new interest in the thing itself.

I found that I badly wanted to go out to Captain Marlow's ship to see what there was to see. It was a powerful feeling too. Like falling in love. And the feeling wouldn't be denied. All these thoughts tumbled over one another in a trice as I was going forward into the shop.

"Gentlemen!" says I, "I am Boswell, the proprietor," I dismissed the man who'd been serving them and shoved out my paw, "How may I be of service?"

"Good day, sir," says the smaller man, "My name is Stanley and this is Captain Henry Marlow of the *Amiability*. I presume you already know us, for this damned island of Jamaica is full of gossips and my client appears to have babbled my business to every damned fool one of them!"

That was bitter and no mistake, and unfortunately for him it was dead accurate too. But I forced a smile and nodded politely. I shook his hand, and Marlow's too: he proved to be one of the bone-mangler brigade but I gave him back as good as I got once I got the measure of him.

"What seems to be the problem, gentlemen?" says I peering down into the wheelbarrow at the brass and copper tubes with their compound levers and their valves and filters.

"They tell me you have the monopoly on the fixing pumps in this island" says Stanley. He was no hand at bargaining and I could see he was resigned to being fleeced. Marlow was shifting from one foot to another, grinding his teeth and glaring alternately at Stanley for saying such a damn fool thing, and at me whom he saw as a rogue about to skin him alive. He was bursting to deliver some oath and kept his temper with much effort.

They were in my power. I knew it and they knew it. Without my repairing the contents of that wheelbarrow, their operations off Montego Bay Point were at an end, so I wondered why they'd not brought their own craftsmen for such work, with his tools and materials. It was an obvious thing to do, on such an expedition as theirs, and they were very fortunate that it is a fundamental principle with me to deal fairly.

"Gentlemen," says I, "The whole island knows who you are and what your business is," Stanley's face sank and Marlow clenched his fists and looked ready to punch my head, "And I suppose you'd not have come ashore and sought me out, unless you were in dire need." I looked at

Stanley, "Might I guess your works are suspended, awaiting these repairs?" Stanley looked sickly and fanned himself the faster, while Marlow said,

"Dammit!" and stumped off boiling with rage to stare out of a window into the street. "Dammit, dammit, dammit!" says he.

"I see!" says I, "Then I've an offer for you," I pointed at the pumps, "This work will be done free of charge, plus any similar work that may arise, in exchange for five percent of whatever gold you recover." Marlow spun on his heel to stare at me. Stanley dropped his hat and picked it up. They couldn't believe their luck. I could have asked for far more than that. A greedy man might have got twenty or thirty percent.

"But I want something else besides," says I, and their expressions changed again, as they feared the worst, "I want to come out to your ship and see how the thing is done. How do you descend to the bottom of the sea? How can you enter the hold of a lost ship? What light is there to see by? What tools are used…" I chattered away like a small boy whose Papa has promised a trip to the toy shop. I wanted to know everything, all at once. And so I made a pair of friends.

Stanley and Marlow grinned with relief and told me some of their secrets. I invited them into a little sitting room I had in the back, and offered rum punch and lemonade. But first I summoned Higgins from the workshop so Stanley could tell him exactly what was wrong with the pumps.

Higgins had a good look, blessed his soul. marvelled, begged the saints to preserve him, and said It would take two days and a half, for he'd to make new pistons, and grind them into the bore where the old were broken and worn, and he'd to cut new screw threads on sections of pipe to replace a part corroded beyond use, and a big valve would have to be re-built from scratch, all of which was highly-skilled handicraft in those days before standard sizes and machine-tool manufacture. But I told Higgins he was an idle rogue and that he'd work all night if necessary and have all complete by Wednesday. He'd got the measure of me by then so be blinked a few times, swallowed nervously and asked if he might set to work at once.

And so we left him to it and retired to my little room, which was a cool shady place, away from the shouts of the street traders and rumble of waggons outside, and open to our stockyard at the back, by a window taking up most of one wall, and shaded with a venetian blind of broad slats. It was an untidy little den, with a few old chairs and a table and a bed where I slept on occasions. But I wasn't in the habit of entertaining high company and it suited an old tar like Marlow and a mechanic like Stanley. Suited me too, come to that.

"Mr Boswell," says Stanley, when we'd got most of the punch inside of us, "I tell you true, It was in despair that we came in to Montego Bay."

"Why's that, sir?" says I, though I knew already.

"I'll tell you," says he, "We'd planned for all eventualities before ever we set sail, with two skilled men to put right all that might break or wear out in my apparatus. But one died of the yellow jack and the other we lost in the capsize of a boat, with all his tools and the best part of my stock of spare fittings. So when we came into your shop, why, we was expecting a skinning for you had us in your power!"

"Capsize eh?" says I, shaking my head in sympathy, "Sir, these things will happen at sea and there's no preventing 'em."

"Ah!" says Marlow, "Knew you was a seaman, sir, the moment I clapped eyes on you. A man-o'-war's man I'd guess, and you ain't no common seaman, neither."

Damn the fellow! How the hell did he know that? A cold fright shot up my spine. Perhaps I was discovered. Perhaps there was gossip about *me* just as there was about them. But he smiled back at me and winked, and raised his glass as one old tar to another and I realised he'd spotted me just as I'd spotted him. That's the trouble in being a blasted sailor; there's just no hiding it. And there was me thinking what a clever fellow I was in burying my past. But there was no use denying it and all I could do was turn the subject away from myself as fast as could be.

"Aye, Cap'n!" says I, "I can hand, reef and steer if need be."

"Hah!" says he, slapping his thigh, "I knew it. What ships were you in, sir?"

"First tell my about yours, sir!" says I, seizing the one subject no sea Captain could ever refuse, "I hear she's a brig. How does she serve for your present purposes?"

"Well enough, sir," says he, "She's Boston built, five years old and copper-bottomed. She'll steer her course within seven points of the wind…"

And so on, and so on, and so on. I let him prattle. It kept him happy and kept him off my own personal history. Stanley's eyes soon glazed over as Marlow and I discussed every aspect of the brig *Amiability* from the masthead trucks to the keelson bolts.

After an hour or two, we parted company like old friends and it was agreed that I'd go out to the ship on Wednesday when they came back for their pumps, and moreover that I would stay aboard for a week or two which would be a sort of vacation for me, and one which I felt I needed. In fact they'd have taken me that very day, but I was invited to dinner with Sammy Bone and his wife.

Later on when I told Sammy all about Stanley and his submarine boats, he turned nasty for one of the very few times I ever knew him do such a thing.

"Bloody buggers!" says he, smashing his fist down on the table so the pots jumped, "Damned Yankee sods with undersea mines and torpedoes! The bastards!"

His musteefino girl was staring horrified eyed at this, and I felt embarrassed for her. I could see that like myself, she'd never seen this side of Sammy Bone, who would never normally swear before a woman.

But he wasn't done. He jabbed a finger like a steel rod into my ribs and his sharp eyes stabbed at me under snow-white brows, "I seen the buggers in the American war," says he, "Filthy, filthy things! D'you know what they was trying to do, lad? Eh? Do you?" I shook my head. I had no idea where he was driving, "I was a gunner aboard the old *Eagle*," says he, "Black Dick Howe's ship. An' some swab in a devil's craft shaped like a barrel with oars, was laying alongside of us, under the water, at night to explode a mine beneath us and sink us and drown every soul aboard!" He was shaking with anger and most bitter in his detestation of the thing he was describing. "You know me, lad!" says he, "Fair quarter for the enemy as steers boldly forward with his colours flying. But as for him as creeps up, like a blasted coward, under the water, to take the bottom out of a ship where never a man can see him come?" he sneered in profoundest contempt, "Why, shoot him like a dog, says I!"

And that, in a nutshell was Sammy's opinion on underwater craft. It was useless my pointing out that Stanley was purely engaged in salvage operations for such was Sammy's loathing of under-sea warfare that he could not even discuss the matter. I was very fond of Sammy and soon let the matter slip, because it was upsetting him, and if I'd had any sense I'd have let slip any idea of closer acquaintance with Stanley, because Sammy's attitude was an accurate sounding of the general opinions that Englishmen held on the matter. Especially Englishmen who followed the sea.

But I'd found a new love and I couldn't let go and so I kept my thoughts to myself. Later on when I went home, Sammy was more himself again, and as I went out into the hot tropical night under the blazing stars, with the song of the insects all around, he had one more heave at steering me off the rocks.

"I know you, you daft bugger," says he, "You'll go your own way come what may, but just remember this," and he fixed me with his eyes, "The man that sinks a ship from below will be despised by all England, and he could never face his friends again. You remember that when the time comes!"

Damn the man! He was a precious sharp 'un, was Sammy, but surely even he couldn't spy into the future, because he was warning me off of things I'd not yet even dreamed of. It was uncanny. Or maybe my memory of that moment is at fault. Maybe he never said, '*when the time comes*'. But, by George, he did!

None the less, I couldn't keep away from Stanley and his underwater engineering, and on Wednesday morning I was sat in the stern sheets of *Amiability's* long-boat, with Stanley's mended pumps under a tarpaulin. Higgins was beside me already complaining of the sea-sickness while we were still in harbour. I'd decided the sea air would do him good, and he might be useful in fitting the pumps into whatever it was they were part of.

The long-boat, with four hands aboard besides Higgins and myself, was under the command of Marlow's First Mate, an Englishman by the name of Laurence who came from Bristol. It was common in those days to have a sprinkling of our tars aboard Yankee ships and Yankees aboard ours, but it gave me a fright when I met him, because though I'd grown reasonably comfortable in the company of Jamaicans I never got rid of the fear that some newcomer, fresh to the island, would recognise me as Fletcher the runaway, for I'm too big to fade into the background and folk tend to notice me.

But, with the weather blowing up a bit, Laurence was kept busy with his command. The boat was rigged single-masted with a gaff mainsail and a long bowsprit with a pair of headsails. To my irritation, Laurence kept fiddling with his for'ard sails, bawling at his people to set first one and then the other, and then both, except that I doubt he quite knew what he wanted and he'd have done better leaving things alone. I've got no great love for the sea[6] but I was itching to take over and do the thing myself.

---

6   Vanity and affectation yet again. Fletcher loved the sea, loved ships, and was deeply proud of his skills as a seaman yet would never admit to it in plain words. S.P.

But eventually he got it more or less right and we plunged merrily along with the salt spray coming over the bows and Higgins hung over the side, pleading for all the saints to receive him into their bosom. So, as old seamen will, Laurence and I had a bit of harmless fun with him, suggesting he might chew a sheep's eye-ball or take a draft of luke-warm fat, to add more power to his heavings. By the time we made fast to *Amiability's* quarter, we'd pumped his bilges so clean that he'd nothing more to bring up than empty air.

Amiability was anchored about seven miles off Montego Bay point, among a cluster of five little islands called the Montego Keys. The spot was known as Morgan's Bay ever since that bloody-handed old savage Sir Henry Morgan, once Governor of Jamaica, had used it in the 1670's. It was a fine, safe anchorage, once a ship got herself in to it, but it was deadly perilous to enter in rough weather, as coral reefs ringed it round with few ways in that were deep enough for a ship to pass over. That's why on May 21st 1794, His Majesty's sloop *Brigand* had ripped herself open trying to enter Morgan's Bay to shelter from a freak storm and had gone down with all hands and a cargo of gold under hatches. And now, here was Mr Francis Stanley with his submarine devices to perform the magic feat of raising the gold.

Amiability was a perfectly ordinary brig, bobbing at anchor with sails furled and topmasts sent down. Her crew lined the rail as we came along-side and Stanley and Marlow waved to me from the quarterdeck. I looked her over as we approached and everything seemed taut and seamanlike, which is what I'd expected having seen Captain Marlow. But two things took my attention at once.

First, *Amiability* had four anchors down: two ahead and two astern, which was twice as many as any ship needs under ordinary circumstances. And second, she had hoisting gear rigged, as if she were about to lower a boat. Any seaman would say this was perfectly ordinary, but it wasn't for what was waiting to be hoist over side, was not a boat at all but a black, tarred shape with a copper dome twinkling on its humped back and another on its blunt round nose. I was consumed with wonder at the sight of this object: for this could only be Stanley's diving machine.

CHAPTER 12

As I went up the side of the Yankee brig that morning, I had no idea of the trouble I was getting into, nor how I would be held to account for it in due course. Instead, a excitement was upon me as if I were about to embark upon some great enterprise of business.

Stanley and Marlow greeted me warmly, I noted that the ship was smart enough with lines coiled down and brasses polished (though she weren't half so sharp as I'd have had her), and I noted she was short-handed. I also noted the ever-present burning sun and the blue skies and the blue seas and the long palm trees sloping their green heads over the white sands of the little islands around us. I noted all this with a little part of my attention, for above all else I noted the submarine craft secured in the waist, lashed over the spare spars, where a ship's boats normally were stowed.

Like most men of those days I knew such craft had been made. I knew the Yankees had invented infernal engines of all kinds to attack our shipping in their Revolution. Sammy had made that abundantly clear, after all. But knowing was one thing, and seeing was another.

Stanley's machine was about thirty feet long and eight feet high. It was round and fat and sausage-shaped and made of heavy timbers running fore and aft like the planking of a ship's hull, but bound around with iron hoops and tarred heavily overall. At one end, which I took to be its bow, a copper dome stuck out front and centre fitted with round glass scuttles screwed shut with thumb-screws.

Another dome sat on top of the machine and was provided with hinges whereby it could swing open to form a hatch allowing men to descend into the craft. At the stern was a rudder connected by short iron rods that lead into the machine through the hull, and below the stern was a thing of mystery which now we know as a screw propeller, but in those days even Stanley called it an *oar*. There was a second propeller rising out of the top of the hull for forcing the vessel up and down, alongside other pipes of all kinds, including ventilators to admit fresh air when running on the surface and a pair of big eye-bolts to take the lifting tackles.

Underneath, there was a heavy keel of solid lead running along the craft. Finally, jutting out from beneath the blunt round bow, just where the curve of the planks straightened out to run down the underside, was a pair of spars about ten feet long each hinged and jointed where they met the hull so as to enable them to be pulled this way and that by stout ropes wound upon brass spools secured to the hull. One spar had a big iron hook at its free end and the other a pincer like that of a giant crab. One jaw of this pincer was rigid, while the other was hinged and could be caused to open or to bite upon its partner by ropes like those which moved the spars themselves.

"D'ye appreciate the principle of the thing, Mr Boswell?" says Stanley proudly displaying his creation, "The brass spools here," he pointed them out, "Are wound by hand-cranks within the vessel which turn rods passing through water-tight seals. The spools wind In the ropes which, in turn, haul upon the spars and move them fro," he paused and drew my attention to the dome with its glass scuttles, set in the bow, "I take my place here," says he, "With head inside here, and my eyes pressed to these windows, and there I give orders to those operating the cranks. and so I cause objects to be seized or moved or pulled this way and that." He grinned at me, "Would you like to enter my *Plunger*, Mr Boswell?"

Plunger was what he called the thing and I didn't need asking a second time. There was a short ladder against the sticky, black side and I was up it in a trice, collecting tar on my knees and elbows, and lowering myself carefully into the hot interior. Stanley followed me and we sat on our haunches grinning at one another like a pair of schoolboys crept out of bed to share a stolen cake.

If you've been aboard of a modern ironclad: one of the new giants like HMS *Warrior* or perhaps the steam Monitors the Yankees built for their civil war, then you'll have an idea of what *Plunger* was like inside. Similarly, the fireman and driver of a railway locomotive would have been on familiar ground. But not me. Not me nor any other seaman in that year of 1795.

You must understand that in those days, if you left out the chronometer (and by no means every Captain had one of these) then the most complicated mechanism aboard a ship was the chain pump. Aside from that then the whole vessel, including her guns, was worked by men hauling directly upon lines or simple levers, with their bare hands. The rigging was tied together by lashings, splicings and knots and the hull was secured by simple wooden treenails and copper bolts. A ship was mainly made of oak, hemp and canvas and the whole thing was nothing that Francis Drake wouldn't instantly have understood, nor the Greeks and Romans neither, with a bit of effort.

But here, my jolly boys. inside of the *Plunger* in a narrow space, too low for him to stand up properly, your Uncle Jacob found a new world of wonder. There were brass cranks and valves on every side and you couldn't move without ducking your head and squeezing past. There were instruments and glass tubes. There were metal pipes of mysterious purpose. There were copper globes that Stanley said were pumped full of air under great force for the crew to breathe. There were iron levers and steel clamps. There were tools neatly secured in racks: spanners, wrenches, files and little hard saws to cut steel.

"Here's the key to it all," says Stanley pointing at the place where the shaft of a hand-crank met the inside of the hull, "Ain't no point going below if you can't do work when you get there. You got to move the *outside* from the *inside*." He tapped his finger against a copper ring that seemed to encircle the shaft, "First I bore a hole through the hull, which is two foot thick of seasoned New England live oak, and I drive a copper tube real tight into the hole. Then I cut the tube off flush and file down the shaft so it *just* goes through with a little oil to seal it."

He pointed at the copper dome in the bow, "Get your head in there, boy, and watch," says he. I got past him and found that by sinking on my knees and placing my elbows on the rim of the dome, I could lean forward and see outside through the glass ports. They were cleverly placed to give a line of sight in every direction.

He wound busily on one of the hand cranks.

"The larboard claw, boy!" says he, "Watch the claw!" I gasped as one of the spars raised itself up. Stanley switched from crank to crank, turning and chuckling and glancing my way from time to time. Faintly from outside the hull I could hear the spools and ropes creaking as the spar with the pincer moved up and down and side to side. "Marlow!" bawled Stanley towards the open hatch. "Feed her a round shot!"

I saw Marlow laugh and collect a six pounder ball from a shot rack. He offered it to the jaws of the big pincer.

"Haul away" roared Marlow and Stanley spun another of his cranks. The pincer closed on the iron ball and Marlow let go. "Aye-aye!" called Marlow and Stanley made the claw prance up and down with its prize.

"Below!" cried Stanley.

"Aye-aye!" cried Marlow, stepping back, and Stanley opened the claw and dropped the shot to fall with a boom on to the deck where a seaman ran to retrieve it.

"Well, Mr Boswell?" says Stanley. "How d'ye like that? It works in thirty fathoms too, for I've proved it." For once I was speechless. I'd never seen the like before and I was stunned with the fascination of it. Stanley laughed and slapped my back, "How d'ye like her, eh!" says he.

"Wonderful!" says I and waved my hand at the gleaming metal all around me, "All this. It's the work of genius. There's never been the like of this before."

Stanley was mightily pleased, and he laughed again and leaned back, sat against the hull with his legs stretched out and his hands in his pockets, "Well," says he, "You're wrong there, my lad, but never worry," then he put his head on one side and looked at me odd, "How'd you like to go down with me?" he said suddenly. "There ain't many men as would have the taste for it," says he, "And there's still fewer I'd make the offer to, but I like you Mr Boswell, and that's a fact. What do you say?"

"Yes!" says I, the reply bursting forth as gunpowder responds to a spark. I was as completely seduced by fascination for this amazing craft as any green boy is seduced by a woman.

"Good man!" says Stanley, and it was settled.

But first there was the matter of fitting a pump into the *Plunger*. Stanley explained that the purpose of this particular kind of pump, an extremely powerful one, was to drive out water from the inside of the vessel when she was down below.

"See here," says Stanley, pointing at the narrow, cluttered grating beneath our feet. This passed for a deck and ran over a narrow bilge running the length of the vessel, "With the bilge dry, and the lead keel in place, she's ballasted to keep her stiff upright, and give her a little buoyancy. So when I want to go down, I open this valve here," he showed me a brass wheel that turned a shaft running down into the bilge to control a valve set in the very bottom of the hull. Then he looked me in the eye with a mischievous look and added, "And the sea pours in and I sink her!"

"Sink her?" says I.

"Aye!" save he, enjoying himself, "I sink her, Mr Boswell, and down we go among the sharks!"

"And how d'you bring her up again?" says I.

"Four ways, Mr Boswell," says he, "I can signal the ship to haul her up, by lines made fast to her the hull," he rapped knuckles against *Plunger's* heavy timbers, "I do that by releasing a red, danger float. Or I can pump out the bilge to lighten her. Or I can row her up and down with the oar," (by which he meant the vertical screw propeller), "And if all else fails, I can cast off the lead keel and send her up like a cork. But mostly I pump the bilge with those pumps your man has been working on. A gallon or two of water, give or take, and she'll float or sink to a nicety, especially if I row her up and down with the oar," he pointed to yet another crank which operated the vertical screw. "So let's get the pumps in place and I'll really show you what my *Plunger* can do!"

He led the way out, via a small ladder and we left the thick closeness of the vessel and climbed out into the bright sunlight. Marlow and his men grinned at me, as if proud of their incredible toy and Stanley set his men to work, with Higgins assisting at my suggestion, though it took a couple of hours for the pump to be installed and Higgins had the time of his life. If anything he was even more smitten with sub-marine navigation that I'd been, though he loudly declared that he'd not go down himself, not if all the saints in the calendar were to line up and beg him to.

Meanwhile I chatted with Stanley and Marlow under an awning rigged on the quarterdeck, to keep the sun off. I was surprised to hear that they'd been at their salvage for some months and had already brought up quantities of gold.

Finally, at about three o'clock in the afternoon, all hands were turned up to hoist *Plunger* over the side and Stanley and I got inside of her, together with a seaman named Brunswick who was trained in the arts of whizzing the cranks and levers to Stanley's command. They swung us up and out and once we were bobbing in the water they cast off the lifting tackles and lashed lines to the ring-bolts in the upper hull. These lines would be paid out as we descended, and as Stanley had said, would be used to haul us up in an hour's time.

As soon as that was done, Potter closed the hatch and screwed it tight shut.

"Any last thoughts, Mr Boswell?" says Stanley and the three of us looked at one another inside the cramped, awkward space. I just shook my head, like a child on the way to the Christmas Pantomime.

"Open the valve!" says Stanley.

"Aye-aye, sir" says Potter and a few turns of the big brass wheel brought forth the ungodly, sound of water rushing into the bilge under our feet.

"Well!" says Stanley, like a gun-captain in charge of his crew. He had his head and shoulders into the copper dome at the bow and was watching the little waves, lapping just below his nose. At once, Brunswick shut the valve and the sound of rushing water was replaced by a gentle slopping sound. With nothing to do myself, I climbed one rung up the little ladder under the hatch, so I could peer out through the scuttles in the upper dome. Already I could feel *Plunger* settling beneath me as the sea was rose up and up until the upper hull was awash.

Next the water was rising up the sides of the dome to the level of the glass scuttles. I gasped. A sudden fright came over me, and without thinking I raised my head in a futile attempt to keep above water level. Donk! I rapped my skull on the inside of the dome and the waters closed over my head.

And then I saw such sights as few men have shared. I saw the underside of the brig, her copper shining dull, for all the fierce strength of the sun was gone to pale greens and blues within a few fathoms depth. I saw fish swim past and I saw the surface of the sea from below! I was overwhelmed with wonder, as down and down we went until I could see the bottom of the sea all around us. It teemed with fish of every colour and shape and size that imagination could conceive. I actually laughed with the joy of it.

Crack-crack-crack! Went something sharp and sudden.

"What's that?" says I, taking another fright Stanley looked back at me from his station in the bow.

"Nothing," says he, "'tis but the timbers shifting as weight of the sea pressing in upon the hull. The deeper we go, the greater the weight," he grinned at me wickedly, "Should we go too deep then the sea would crack us like a louse."

"My God!" says I, "Then how deep can we go, in Heaven's name?" I spoke because no man understood such things in those days. At least I certainly didn't. I'd assumed that if the hull would hold at one fathom then it'd hold at twenty five.

"Calm yourself, Mr Boswell," says he, turning back to place his head and shoulders into the copper dome. "Before ever a man went down in this vessel, I lowered her to the bottom at thirty fathoms and left her an hour."

"And she came up safe and sound?" says I.

"Safe and sound," says he, "Barring a little water she'd taken in."

"What water?" says I.

"A little water forces its way in through the crank-shaft tubes," says he.

"Does it?" says I and looked about me. Sure enough where each of the many cranks and other fittings pierced the hull, there was a trickle of water. In some cases it was a steady stream that ran down the curved insides of the hull and passed through deck grating into the bilge. I suppose that's why there wasn't a proper deck. But Stanley paid it no heed and neither did Brunswick who was sat in the stern steadily turning a heavy crank shaped exactly like the handles of a chain pump. It was secured to a transom for'ard, and connected to gearing astern, so one turn of the crank caused several turns on the propeller.

Brunswick was a squat muscular man, and seemed well fitted for the work. Meanwhile Stanley steered her by levers fixed by his dome in the bow, which worked the rudder by long, iron rods running back to the stern. There was a second set of steering levers at the upper dome so she could be conned from there if need be.

"Yes," says Stanley, "We take water aboard constantly, but we do not permit more than a certain quantity to remain. Should we sink too much then we pump out, and restore our trim."

"But what if .." says I but Stanley interrupted.

"Ah-ha!" says he, "Come for'ard, Mr Boswell, and you shall see what you shall see!" I ducked my head under the cluster of brass cranks and levers, got on my hands and knees and joined Stanley. There wasn't room for both of us to look out of the scuttles in the dome, so he moved aside and wriggled myself into his place.

It was sort of short tunnel, cut through the thickness of the hull and lined with a collar of heavy cast brass, bolted firmly into the timbers. The dome with its scuttles was clamped tight against the brass collar, by a dozen heavy screw-bolts. By pulling with my hands against the curved brass, I could just about squeeze my shoulders into the tunnel and get my head into the copper dome, which had five discs of glass some six inches across and an inch thick, set in its sides at regular intervals to let the pilot look to either side and up and down. Also there was a sixth disc about eight inches across, set plumb in the centre.

"Look ahead and downwards," says Stanley, but I'd already seen the thing he wished to point out, and once again I was speechless with wonder. It was the remains of the sloop *Brigand* in her grave on the bottom of the sea. She was less than fifty feet away and every detail was clear in sight.

She was dim and grey with the weeds sprouting from her, laid broken-backed on her side, with her masts at crazy angles and the rags of her sails waving from her yards, and her shrouds and her standing rigging half intact and half sundered. Her decks were burst open and the silt and sand piled smooth over her fo'c'sle. I shuddered, for it was a sight to freeze the blood of any mariner. It was like seeing a dead soul in hell. But Stanley had seen it all before and was itching to go about his business.

"Now then, Mr Boswell," says he, "I've used gunpowder to blow the ship open and I'll show you later how we scoop up the bullion-boxes with my spar claw, but what I'm going to do now is pull her open a little more with the help of our friends above. And he did too, and it was as neat a piece of teamwork as could be, between *Plunger* and *Amiability's* longboat up above. The boat, laden with ballast to make her heavy, had dropped a grapnel on a stout line and with careful manoeuvring, Stanley took up the grapnel with his pincer and hooked it into the jagged hole in the side of the wreck. This done, *Plunger* released a float as a signal to the surface and the long-boat pulled hard away till the line tightened and the grapnel tore out a chunk of timber.

It was damned clever but the trick had limitations. Even when it worked it took out only small or broken timbers and sometimes the grapnel slipped or the timbers simply refused to budge. That's why the job was taking so long and that's why I had two splendid weeks enjoying the sea air and dives in Stanley's magical machine as he chewed his way into the sunken ship. So I went down again and again in *Plunger* and saw bullion boxes fished out of the silt, and dropped into baskets lowered from above, and hauled up. But eventually we needed to break open the remains of the strong-room where the remainder of the gold was still lying, and sterner measures were needed.

Stanley solemnly informed me that he would blow open the rest of the strong room with a 50 pound charge of gunpowder in a watertight sub-marine mine that was provided with a clockwork fuse and trigger. A thrill of fear and wonder ran through me at the thought of this, and I tried to question him on the how and the why. But he just clammed up tight and wouldn't say how the thing worked other than what he'd already said. He let me have a look at it though, not that there was much to see. It was an unusually heavy cask, with some bolts and fittings about it and a socket for the long screw that held it to *Plunger's* hull. The real works were inside and Stanley wouldn't let me or Higgins see them.

And so on the 10th of August I went down in *Plunger* once more. I was having such a grand time and was so impressed with Stanley's machines that I thought nothing of the use of gunpowder, other than the expectation of a new treat. By George what a fool I was! And you youngsters take note: just because the sun's shining and you're happy and rosy, it don't mean that you ain't about to be dropped down the hole of the privy. And down, indeed we went, and Stanley got us within sight of the wreck, with *Plunger* ballasted to float just above the sea bed.

"Now then," says he, and he reached for a big wing-nut set on a shaft that led out through the hull, just below the copper dome in the bow. "I shall turn this nut," says he, busily spinning the nut and its shaft, "And this will unscrew the outside end from the interior of the device ." He worked for a while until the nut went loose in his hands, "Ah!" he said, "Tis done," he smiled at me confidently, "All is in order. The mine is dropped to the sea bed in front of us. I will now take up the mine with my spar pincer and place it accurately upon the wreck to secure greatest benefit from the detonation. Then we shall rise to the surface and move to a place of safety. Brunswick!" says he, jamming his head and shoulders into the dome. "Lift ship a fathom and row her astern so I can see the mine to take it up with the pincer."

"Aye-aye, sir!" says Brunswick and reached for the pump lever.

As he did so, one of the crank shafts that was leaking more than most, suddenly shot inward with the force of a bullet and a jet of water, hard as an iron bar, drove in from the inch-wide hole in the hull and threw Brunswick down as if he'd been struck by a round shot. At once *Plunger* began to settle on the sea bed.

CHAPTER 13

*"... my dearest girls it is with utmost anticipation that I await the
opportunity to renew our acquaintance and apologise once more,
that I am arrived all unannounced. Apropos of this young man
who resembles my late husband, it might be amusing to meet him.
Might this be arranged? Or rather, put yourselves to no trouble,
merely send me his address."*

(From a letter of Tuesday August 4th 1795 from Lady Sarah Coignwood
at the King's House, Spanish Town, Jamaica, to Mrs Alice Powys and Mrs
Patience Jordan, Powys Plantation, Cornwall, Jamaica.)

From the moment she set foot ashore in Jamaica, Lady Sarah received
every honour of which the colonists were capable. The news of her arrival
ran through Kingston like lightning, carried on the wings of excitement
and the pounding feet of pages, slaves, maids and servant speeding from
door to door with hastily-written notes.

The instant they heard the incredible news, those arch-rivals for social
leadership, Mrs Lucy Fitzgibbon (wife of the Mayor of Kingston) and Mrs
Sandra Portland (wife of Mr Saul Portland, the richest man in the West
Indies) each, separately in her own house, leapt to her feet and screamed
for her carriage, knowing all too well that her enemy would be doing the
same. On the road to the docks, the carriages literally raced for position,
coachmen flaying the wretched steeds and heavy vehicles swaying dangerously behind them as the iron tyres lost grip on the bends and skidded
sideways in a shower of sparks.

The Mayoress won. Her carriage scattering stevedores, slaves, porters,
clerks, redcoats, idlers, whores, coopers, chandlers and the myriad other

forms of humanity that infest the cobbles of a busy dockside, not to mention grinding beneath its wheels numerous chickens, hats, pies, fruits, dogs and such other small objects as got themselves in the path of its irresistible onrush.

But the Mayoress's carriage, with its triumphant coachman leering over his shoulder at his beaten rival, and its lathered, sweat-soaked animals, effectively placed the Mayoress opposite the gangplank of the Mail Packet *Cumberland* and denied access to Mrs Portland. At least it did if the Mayoress looked sharp, and she screeched for the carriage steps to be let down, hopped out with skirts lifted and her black page in her wake, and hysterically urging her footman to announce her this instant to those on board. But seeing the steps slamming down and the door springing open on the rival carriage astern, she scuttled up the gangplank without further ado with her servants following.

Seconds later, heart fluttering with triumph and exultation, she was received in the Captain's cabin by La Belle Coignwood herself. But first, there was a sudden pang of disappointment. For the Mayoress was met on deck by Lady Sarah's maid, who proved to be a huge, ugly woman with a hideous moustache. She was incongruously dressed in fine clothes, almost like a lady of quality herself, but none the less was such a creature as no woman of discernment could keep on her staff, and Mrs Fitzgibbon briefly wondered if, perhaps, this Lady Sarah Coignwood was not all that the London newspapers and magazines claimed.

For Mrs Fitzgibbon, at twenty-nine years, was at the peak of her beauty with four pretty children, an adoring husband and the (almost) unchallenged leadership of Kingston society. She was furthermore dressed in a high-waisted, voluminous morning gown of blue silk with tight, wrist-length sleeves. The shimmering fabric was printed with tiny yellow flowers and worn with a huge, loose mob-cap with ribbons to match the gown and enfold her tumbling curls. This splendid ensemble had been made up, by Mrs Fitzgibbon's maids, in accordance with the coloured fashion plates in *The Lady's Magazine*, sent out to Mrs Fitzgibbon by her mother in London.

Briefly, Lucy Fitzgibbon preened herself, and then the gross maidservant was opening the door into the Captain's cabin and she was face to face with Sarah Coignwood.

"Mrs Lucy Fitzgibbon, M'Lady," said the maid, "Wife hof 'is worship the Mayor of Kingston."

And so the bladder of pride was pricked. The gorgeous woman sat at her ease in the cabin was dressed in a sleeveless cotton shift, knotted at the shoulders to expose the wearer's sleek white arms in their naked loveliness from wrist to shoulder. The simple gown was bound around the waist with a broad silk sash matched by a few turns of thin ribbon that miraculously held up a mass of heavy chestnut curls.

Lucy Fitzgibbon could not know that the inspiration of Lady Sarah's style, was the new and outrageous portrait of the courtesan Therese Tallien by the French artist David, prints of which portrait were freshly smuggled into England but would not reach Jamaica for many months yet. But Lucy Fitzgibbon knew in the deep soul of her that she was looking at the new fashion and was herself wearing the old.

Worse still, she felt clumsy and she felt that her complexion was spoiled despite all her care with broad hats and parasols, and she felt that her nose was too big, her hips too wide, her eyes too small, her lips too thin, her clothes ill-made and her arms as rough and hairy as those of the creature she had just despised. In short, she was making the inevitable and foredoomed comparison of herself with Lady Sarah Coignwood. So Lucy Fitzgibbon bit her lip and sighed.

An observer more penetrating than the Lady Mayoress would have noted the tiny smirk of satisfaction crossing the face of La Belle Coignwood, A fleeting expression which grew, blossomed and faded in an instant, to be replaced by a smile as soft as love.

"My dear Mrs Fitzgibbon," said Lady Sarah, "I am so pleased to meet you. Every man and woman on this ship has spoken of no other person than yourself, these weeks past, and I look to you to show me how everything is done in Jamaica," she hesitated with just a shadow of anxiety in her eyes, "I do so hope that I may name you as a friend?"

Until thirty seconds ago, Lady Sarah had never even heard of Mrs Fitzgibbon but Lady Sarah was so very lovely, and she was so irresistibly accomplished in the art of being charming that the unfortunate Lucy Fitzgibbon went down like a snowdrop under a hammer.

And so, Lady Sarah was whisked out of the ship (graciously bidding farewell to her fawning, adoring Captain and crew) and into Mrs Fitzgibbon's carriage. A great crowd had crammed on to the dockside, growing by the minute as newcomers arrived at the run from all directions, buzzing with the name of La Belle Coignwood. A cheer went up as the fair one appeared and Mrs Fitzgibbon's coachman had to lay on with his whip to force a way through the press. As they passed Mrs Portland, fuming in her splendid vehicle with its satin upholstery and beautiful painted blinds to keep out the sun, Mrs Fitzgibbon drew Lady Sarah's attention her friend, and she and Lady Sarah waved politely to her as they moved off.

That was Thursday July 30th. By the following Sunday, Lady Sarah had contrived to vault socially over the backs of Mr and Mrs Fitzgibbon and she and her servant and all her luggage were removed, at request of the Governor, the Earl of Balcarras, to his own residence, the King's House in the Capital, Spanish Town.

She was thereby at the summit, such as it was, of Jamaican society with no higher place left to climb. The only hard part was to avoid sneering at the rickety, shabby, dirty town with its narrow streets, and wooden houses interspersed with pathetic brick built remains of Castilian grandeur. Even Government House where the Assembly met, in the same square as the Governor's residence, was crumbling and clumsy with the stucco falling off its walls, and there was a ridiculous statue of Admiral Rodney as a Roman General, a thing with neither grace nor sense.

In fact there was just one small peak still for Sarah Coignwood to surmount: the noble Earl the Governor himself. He took little urging and was delivered sufficient favours to keep him sweet but he was not to her taste any more than anything else in this ridiculous, sweltering, bourgeois, hell-on-earth. Fortunately Lord Balcarras was too busy to be troublesome, with a rebellion to deal with among some of the island's natives. Lady Sarah had not the slightest interest in the doings of black savages, and since the troubles were far away in some God-forsaken place by the name of Montego Bay, she crushed the topic whenever it was mentioned. None the less, the matter had been so much in the minds of others that she made enquiries of her servant.

"What are these Maroons, Collins?" asked Lady Sarah as she took her bath on the evening of her arrival at King's House, "These maroons who make such trouble?"

"Precious fine 'uns, M'Lady," said Collins with a look of wonderful fascination on her face. She'd been talking to his Lordship's cook who was an expert upon the subject. "Big black-men wiv big muscles M'Lady, what lives wild in the woods and kills pigs bare-handed by wringin' hof their necks, and eatin' the flesh raw. They runs around stark naked except for a musket and a cutlass and takes what girls they pleases among the slaves, and the owners glad to 'ave the women covered by 'em and the girls pleased of the sport. The smallest of 'em's six feet high and..." she risked a sidelong, leering look at her mistress (whose interest she had somewhat caught) "...and," she said, "The manhood of 'em's *this* long!" She held her palms about two feet apart.

"Enough!" said her mistress and thought of the beautiful Rasselass whom she'd not even begun to enjoy before he was ruined. She snarled viciously as unfortunate memories crowded in. "Enough of this!" she snapped, "We are here for a purpose and I'll not suffer interference from any one or any thing. His Lordship has troops to deal with these Maroons. I shall Speak to him later and I shall insist that the proper steps are taken."

CHAPTER 14

It's commonplace that disasters occur only when several things fail at once. Take the case of the *Plunger*: there were at least four ways to bring her up off the bottom. As a consequence of this, although Stanley was as shocked as I when the crank-shaft failed, he at first acted as a man should who knows his drill and is ready to deal with a predictable accident.

"Get him up!" cries Stanley, shouting over the terrifying hiss and spatter of the fierce waterspout that ran horizontal across the craft, tearing into the bilge-pump's lever which bent – actually bent under the force of it. "Get his head above water while I plug the leak!"

Brunswick was laid out senseless on the planking of the cramped, narrow deck, and already there was water sloshing about seeking to fill his mouth and lungs. I reached across and hauled Brunswick up by the scruff of his neck. His face was cut open in a deep gash from temple to jaw from a collision with some fitting or other and he was limp as a corpse. Stanley pushed past me, ducked under the deadly stream of seawater and made his way to a rack of tools.

"Here," says he, throwing me a coil of stout line. "Lash him upright so he's clear of the water." I got the rope under Brunswick's arms and got him into a sitting position with his legs sticking out across the deck and his back against the hull. Then I lashed him to a copper ventilating pipe to keep him there. He sagged forward with his white face on his breast and he looked like a corpse but he was bleeding strong and fresh, so he was alive right enough, and in the absence of anything better, I cut a sleeve out of my shirt with my pocketknife and bound the linen round Brunswick's head.

Meanwhile Stanley was dealing with the fearfully ticklish job of sealing the leak. In his left hand he held a tapered iron spike about a foot long, pointed at one end and a couple of inches wide at the other. This implement was tight-wrapped with a thin sleeve of sheet lead to act as a gasket. In his right hand was a heavy iron hammer with a four-pound head and he was working his way round the glittering shaft of water like a snake charmer with an angry cobra. The game was to get the sharp tip of the spike just into the stream, so as to line it up on the hole and yet not so far into the stream that the pressure of incoming water would throw it out. And then, if Stanley looked sharp and timed his blow right, one heavy blow of the hammer should jam the spike into the empty copper tube that had spat out the crankshaft, and thereby plug the leak.

Easily said, but desperate hard to do in an awkward space with rods and levers all around, sticking into your elbows and the small of your back, and the upper hull curving in over your head so you can't stand up properly, and the force of the water throwing the spike out of your hands every few seconds. Once or twice Stanley picked the thing up for himself, carefully avoiding the water that shot just over his head. Once or twice I got the thing for him and handed it over. He tried again and again, and I could see him tiring and his hands beginning to shake.

"D'you want me to try?" says I.

"No," says he, "You don't know the way of it," and he bent once again to the task. No one could fault him for courage and steadiness in a dreadful plight. But then, without that he'd never have taken to sub-marine navigation in the first place, would he, the little swab? And then I'd not have been down there with him. But eventually, with a foot of water swilling above the deck, he got the spike in place and caught it a terrific blow with the hammer. Boom! And, boom-boom-boom! As he drove it home.

Silence. My ears still rang with the fierce gushing of the leak, but the sound was gone. Stanley slumped exhausted to the deck and sat panting with water up to his waist. He dropped the hammer and we looked at one another.

"Well, Mr Boswell," says he, "If you'd be so good as to man the pump, we'll lift ship and resume where we left off." He blinked at me, solemn as you please. You had to admire the bugger. I'll make no bones about it and admit that I was scared silly at that moment and quite totally out of my depth (if you'll admit such a figure of speech in that circumstance). I hadn't a bellow or a spark of temper in me. I was sodden dripping wet for one thing and the sea's damn cold at 25 fathoms, even in Jamaica. So I might not have said Aye-Aye, Sir, but I got up on my knees and worked the pump lever like a good 'un. Pumping the bilge you will recall was the first method to raise the *Plunger*.

But the lever was crooked and wouldn't act properly, and worse still, there was a strong resistance to my efforts. No matter how hard I leaned on the lever, it seemed I couldn't properly drive the water out of the vessel. In fact I was bending the lever rather than working the pump.

Stanley watched me for a bit then got his head into the dome and looked out. There was mud and all sorts swilling round out there from where we'd settled on the bottom and he took a while to make anything out. I watched him out of the corner of my eye as I pressed on with my futile efforts.

"Avast pumping, Mr Boswell," says he, "The pump outlets must be fouled. We're settled firm in the bottom and I would suppose that the outlets are crushed on rock, or coral or suchlike." He looked at me and I looked at him. He smiled weakly and shrugged his shoulders as if to say that he was sorry. A thick, hot fear surged up my breast and filled my head. Oh God Almighty, was I going to die in this horrid little machine? Was I going to drown or suffocate or be smashed as the hull was pressed in by the water?

I must have said something of the kind to Stanley for when the wave of fright subsided a little, he was chattering away, to reassure me.

"I will release a danger float, and the ship will haul us up by the lines made fast to the deck," says he. That sounded good, and up went the red float, and soon we felt *Plunger* twitch as those above hauled on the lifting lines. They hauled and hauled, but it was no good. She was stuck fast. But Stanley persevered.

"The vertical oar, Boswell!" says he and pointed to the crank that turned it, "That'll bring us free!" I was on my feet in an instant and spinning it round. But that was no good either. The vertical screw was for fine adjustments when the boat was nicely ballasted. We'd taken in too much water and the damn thing did no good at all.

"Well," says I, "It that the best you can do? The mine's sitting right under our bow, with the clockwork ticking. Are we to sit here till we're blow to atoms?" I looked about me for some way of escape. "Can we not open the hatch and swim to the surface?" says I and I stood up and reached for the hatch in the upper hull.

"No!" says he, in a sudden fright, "I cannot swim!"

"Well I damn well can," says I, "How'd you open this hatch?"

"No" says he, jumping up and grabbing at my arm, "Tis too deep, and the weight of water would crush us, and we could never open the hatch, and … and…"

"Shove off!" says I and pushed him clear. I mounted the short ladder and reached for the screws that held the copper dome clamped to its brass collar. It was almost identical to the dome in the bow. "No!" says he, near hysterical with fear, "'Tis death to open that hatch! You saw how the water came in from the crank-shaft. This would be worse. We'd be smashed in an instant."

"So what?" says I, "We're dead meat if we stay here, sure as taxes," I looked down as a thought came to me. "Cast that poor sod's lashings off and let him take his chance," says I, pointing at Brunswick and then I gave my attention to one of the big butterfly nuts and twisted hard. It was stiff but I'm a very strong man indeed and I soon had it turning.

"No!" says he again, "Do not touch…" Then his voice changed as he screamed at me in sudden hope. "Boswell!" he cried, "The lead keel! My brains were stunned and stupid. Let go those bolts at once and help me release the lead keel. God in heaven I forgot the damned thing!"

I was on my knees beside him in an instant as he rummaged for tools among the clutter thrown on the deck from the racks screwed to the hull. He found a brass spanner and fumbled for a great squared bolt, made of copper and sticking up out of the planking of the deck.

"There are four!" he said, "This one, this, this, and this!" He pointed them out where they stuck out of the narrow grating down the middle of the deck, "Each one must be unscrewed to drop the keel," says he, and jamming the spanner on the first nut he pulled hard to turn it. But nothing happened. He'd not got the strength for it.

"Let me!" says I, "Show me the way of it!"

"This way," says he, putting my hands on the long brass handle, "Counter clockwise! Pull, Boswell, pull! My watch is broken but I guess we have not more than ten minutes before the charge detonates!"

I got the first bold loose in quick time even though it was screwed home devilish tight and there was thick green corrosion where the nut sat against a copper washer set into the grating. But though I got the bolt turning, it wouldn't come out.

"She won't come out!" says I.

"Of course not!" says he, "The bolts cannot come out – there are collars on the shafts down in the hull, to keep the bolts in place. If we drew them out the hull would be breached. The bolts pass through the hull and into the lead of the keel. Each one is four feet long."

"Dammit," says I in dismay as I saw the thing in my mind's eye, "But the keel's hard against the bottom where it can't drop away from us, and the hull's pressing down on the keel. How can I unscrew the bloody things when the hull and the keel are jammed together?"

"But you can!" says he, "Can't you see it you fool? You must unscrew each bolt a little at a time, then each will act as a screw-jack and force the hull and the keel apart little by little. You will actually raise the hull on the four bolts until you push us clear. D'ye not see?" I did see. I forgave him calling me a fool and hauled away on each bolt in turn. By Jove it was hard work and the spanner was not fit for the job. It kept slipping and bruising the flat surfaces of the bolt-heads and so worsening its grip. Finally I threw the damn thing aside and used my fingers with the tail of my coat wrapped round the bolt-heads to give me a better grip. My fingers bled, the sweat streamed into my eyes, my muscles cried for rest, it was all so damned awkward. I couldn't get a good grip to use my full strength, and working as I was on a lump of metal flat on the deck, I couldn't even get myself in a comfortable position. And the water level inside was rising and no mistake. The bolt heads were well under water now.

"Hurry, Boswell, for God's sake hurry!" says Stanley. He was looking back towards the stern, imagining whatever fuse it was that he'd packed into his sub-marine mine. Nobody knew better than he how reliable it was and how likely to explode the powder on time.

"Try the bloody things yourself if you think you'd do it quicker!" says I, and he did too. But he couldn't so much as move any of them. Not even when he tried the spanner.

And then there came a creaking and a shifting of the hull.

"Faster! Faster!" says Stanley, and tried again to turn one of the bolts. "It's moving!" says he, for this time even he could turn it. We turned and turned and the hull shifted again. The first and second bolts suddenly turned free without resistance and the bow rose perceptibly. We cheered and thought we were free. But bolts three and four held and it was even harder to get at them, for the water ran down that end and my head was half under water as I worked. The bloody things were harder to turn too, for the upward lift of the bow meant that the vessel was at an angle to the lead keel and the remaining bolts were pulled to one side in their sockets instead of being free to move.

"How long've we got, Stanley?" says I, spluttering water, as I came up to breathe.

"I don't know," says he, lying. I could see it in his eyes. His damned clockwork must have been running late. I held my breath, ducked my head under and turned number three bolt again and again till it spun free and the bow lurched up another foot. I moved to number four bolt where the water was even deeper and at first I couldn't even find the bloody thing, for I was working blind. When my fingers finally closed on it, the bolt was rigid: the stiffest and worst of all. The steep angle of the bow was making the work impossible. But I ground my fingers against the metal, with the torn rag that had once been a coat-tail to help, and I squeezed and twisted like Hercules strangling the serpent.

I was failing. I couldn't shift the square of metal and a desperation was upon me. I roared aloud in my fear and anger, the sound lost in bubbles in the murky water, stained with all the dirt of the bilge. Then there came a distinct snick-clunk from down the length of the long bolt as it came free, and *Plunger* rolled and pitched and swayed and began to rise.

And that, believe it or not, was the worst time of all. Without the keel to ballast her she didn't know what was up and what was down, or even what was fore and what was aft. Stanley and I were on our heads one minute and our backsides the next. She rolled and rolled with drunken sickening motion. Water cascaded from end to end of her so you couldn't get a breath without half choking. Every last thing that was loose clattered and rattled about and the hull boomed and drummed each time something struck against it.

But in fact it wasn't quite the worst time of all. That came next.

It came with a fearful deep sound like thunder, and was the powder charge going off, and it rumbled and grumbled and beat deep inside of you under the ribs, and *Plunger* was jerked bodily upward and tumbled end over end like a half-smoked cigar tossed from a carriage window. The hull shivered and shook and the sea boiled around us. I saw white

118

foam through the scuttles in the bow and then blue sky for an instant as we broke water only to plunge back again and roll and roll, completely over and over.

I think I was conscious the whole while and hung on as best I could to stop myself being thrown about. But Stanley was limp and cold and bouncing from one end to the other of the vessel until I caught hold of him and wrapped an arm around him.

God knows how long It went on, but finally *Plunger* stopped her mad wallowing and merely rocked to and fro, half upright, with her upper dome about a foot above the sea. Stanley was unconscious but alive, Brunswick by some miracle was also alive and was even making himself known by groaning and vomiting. And I was alive too, so I suppose I can't complain. We stayed like that a while, with Stanley tucked under my arm and Brunswick feebly trying to untie himself, until there came a bump and a hail, and *Amiability*'s long-boat was alongside. They unscrewed the hatch, heaved it open and Captain Marlow shoved his head in.

"Ahoy!" says he, "Are all safe?"

"Aye," says I, "Get us out of this!" So Marlow wriggled himself inside *Plunger* which set her rolling again and damn near sank her as the hatch went under and the sea came in. But the boat's crew steadied her and Marlow and I handed out the injured men.

When I actually clambered out myself, into the hot sunshine and the fresh air, the relief and the joy of it was so great that I sat myself in the bottom of the boat, kept out of every man's way and held my face in the sun and breathed deep while the crew secured a line to the *Plunger* (she'd broken both her lifting lines) got her hatch shut again and steered for the brig, half a mile off on the other side of the bay. The long-boat was under oars and it was a heavy pull with *Plunger* in tow, but I was happy to sit in the sun and ignore what went on around me.

When we reached the brig, Stanley and Brunswick were hoist aboard and attended to by the second mate who was acting surgeon, having once been apprenticed to a horse-doctor in Germantown. This gentlemen let the pair of them a dozen ounces of blood each, which was his remedy for all ills. He came up to me with his lancet and bowl but I offered him the choice of getting out of my sight that instant or being knocked down on the spot. He chose the former.

Marlow bustled around and got me some rum and offered me the loan of his cabin and some clean clothes and his cot to rest in. I took him up on that and went below and slept, for I was exhausted and sick with *Plunger's* crazy motion. In fact I slept until next morning when I felt much better, and found Marlow's servant had laid out fresh water and towels and soap for me.

By that time they had *Plunger* hoist out of the water and secured amidships again. Incredibly, she was still sound and capable of repair, for the massively-strong oaken hull was intact and only minor damage sustained to her inside fittings. But she was useless without a new lead keel and her spar pincers had been snapped off and were lost. All this, and the fact that Stanley had just exploded the last of his mines, put an end to any hopes of raising gold from Morgan's Bay and there was a miserable air of gloom hanging over the brig *Amiability*.

I got Higgins up from the fo'c'sle where he was idling and told Marlow we'd thank him for the use of his boat and a crew to take us back to Montego Bay. I said I declared our partnership dissolved, and all further repairs to any metal ware would be on the basis of payment in advance in cash. Then just as Higgins and I were about to go over the side, with the longboat waiting, Stanley crawled out of the quarterdeck companionway looking like something the cat sicked up on the doormat. He'd dragged himself out of his cot to say goodbye to me. He swayed on his feet and blinked in the fierce sunshine.

"Mr Boswell," says he, "You saved my life, sir. I'd never have turned those bolts. I've not the strength." He staggered towards me in his shirt and breeches, barefoot with his hair hanging loose in wisps about his face. "Here's my hand, sir!" says he. "If ever you need a favour from Francis Stanley, you have only to ask."

I shook his hand and he smiled and got back a bit of his bounce. He pointed at *Plunger*.

"D'ye see my creation, Mr Boswell? D'ye see how she survived everything? And thus my designs are vindicated! You should know, sir, that I have been considering by what means this enterprise might go forward."

"Well and good, Mr Stanley," says I, "But you go forward without me."

"Ah!" says he and he nodded, seeing the look on my face, "So be it," says he, "But should you change your mind, then you'll find me here for a week or two. Aside from the clockwork, my mines can be duplicated aboard ship and I hope to improvise fuses with slow-match."

"Good luck to you, sir!" says I and imagined him already blown to pieces in his experiments. So Higgins and I went down Into the boat and headed for Montego bay and safety – or so we thought. In fact we'd have been safer with Stanley and his powder-kegs and live matches.

CHAPTER 15

*"Mr Boswell, the young gentleman who so closely resembles Sir
Henry, is a prosperous tradesman having his place of business in
Montego Bay. He may be found there by enquiry of any person."*

(From a letter of August 6th 1795, from Mrs Alice Powys and Mrs Patience
Jordan of Powys Plantation, Cornwall, Jamaica, to Lady Sarah Coignwood,
the King's House, Spanish Town, Jamaica.)

"Grievances, my Lord?" said Lady Sarah with a look of profound contempt
upon her face, "How could a tribe of black savages be supposed to have
grievances against His Majesty's Government?"

There was an air of embarrassment in the ornate, over-decorated reception room. Servants standing in attendance in powdered wigs and knee
breeches glanced nervously at each other. Lord Balcarras, in full dress
uniform with his sword at his side, squirmed as he sat with his aides around
him and a levee of the upper crust of Jamaican Society: the Bishop, the
Speaker of the House, The Lord Mayor, the Judges, the militia Colonels,
and last but not least, assorted assembly men and millionaires (the one
being the other in most cases): all these, together with their ladies.

Every last one of them was got up in his or her finest, most formal
court wear, irrespective of its total unsuitability to the boiling heat. And
all this for the benefit of she whose, stunning gown and glittering jewels
out-dazzled them all as she sat bolt upright with scorn in a shield-back
mahogany dining chair by Gillow of Lancaster (Lord Balcarras's own
furniture, shipped at great expense from England).

"My Lady," said Balcarras, "Like myself you are newly come out to the
colony and may not be aware of the formidable force constituted by the

Trelawney Maroons. It is no more than expeditious to listen to their ... ah ... ahem ... grievances."

A stirring went round the room and whispers passed behind hands. It was common knowledge that Lady Sarah was connected in the highest circles of London Society and was an intimate of the Prince of Wales and Billy Pitt. Thus, poured into the right ears, the tales she carried home could win Balcarras a Dukedom, or break him like a twig. Such was the power of petticoat politics.

Lady Sarah smiled sweetly, covering her boredom and impatience. She had no time for presumptuous natives, nor petty wars. She wanted a quiet, peaceful Jamaica to give her time for her own vastly important business. She wanted swift action by the military, to tread, beat, squash and pulverise the natives into quiescence.

"My Lord," she said, "I have no fear of these Maroons, for I trust in the protection of the English gentlemen present," (every one of whom instantly drew himself up, gazed sternly forward and pulled in his belly) as do all the ladies here today, for beauty must ever trust in strength." She swept her eyes around the room, and the ladies simpered and fluttered in support of her. "Nor my Lord," she said, direct to Balcarras, "Do I entertain for one moment the thought that within the noble breast of such a soldier as yourself, there could exist the least ... circumspection ... where the prospect of military action is concerned."

Balcarras ground his teeth and smiled as best he could. He was enough of the politician himself to know when he was beaten. Next day, August 3rd, he addressed the Assembly and roundly rejected the terms presented by John Tharp, Custos of St James's, on behalf of the Maroons. He furthermore declared Martial Law throughout the island and ordered the 83rd to march to Montego Bay and await his own arrival.

As he left the House, he was cheered on all sides, for every man loves a war when the soldiers will fight it and he doesn't have to go himself.

Among the crowd, Mr Custos Tharp threw his hat in the air, having got what he'd always wanted: the 83rd sent to save his town. The triumph of Balcarras was spoiled only by a heavy figure who fought through the press to attack his Lordship with his fists. Balcarras actually felt a blow on the side of his head, but it was misjudged and he turned to see a big, elderly man knocked unconscious by the butt of a soldier's musket. He did not recognise his attacker but learned later that he was Major John James, Superintendent General of Maroons.

Within days, the 83rd had arrived in Montego Bay to the cheers and rapture of the townspeople. In overall command was Colonel William Fitch, who had a thousand men of his own regiment plus another hundred of the 62nd. Also, under their commander Colonel Stanford, came two hundred cavalrymen with their mounts; men of the 20th and the 18th light Dragoons. This powerful force of regulars, together with the local militia put a total of over two thousand soldiers into the field against the Trelawney Maroons. All that was needed was their General, Lord Balcarras.

Such a movement of troops was too extensive for news not to get back to Trelawney Town, and when it did, it shifted the balance of Maroon politics right back onto the arms of Mr Vernon Hughes.

"See, my children!" he roared to a massed meeting of the young men, "See how the accursed forces of Beelzebub are descended upon us? What worth has a white man's promise? What worth has the word of Tharp, or Boswell, or Major John James?" They cheered him as loud as Balcarras had been cheered outside the House of Assembly. And that very night small companies of Trelawneys scattered in all directions to burn a farm here, cut a few throats there, and to rape and burn and slip away before any return stroke was possible. It was the Maroon way of war. A testing and a probing for the great attack on Montego Bay which every one of them now wanted.

In Spanish Town, Lord Balcarras read the horrifying reports of what the Maroons were doing and fell into indecision. He delayed his departure to Montego Bay and took council of his officers as to whether it would be best immediately to strike at Trelawney Town, or should he scatter his command to protect the island's most precious assets: the great sugar estates with their slaves and their stock and their buildings. He couldn't do both and so, for several days he did neither until eventually the decision was made for him.

For several days after her success in prodding Lord Balcarras into action against the Maroons, Lady Sarah Coignwood was herself becalmed with indecision, for she knew what she wanted but not how it could be had.

She'd come a long hard way in her quest for revenge upon Fletcher, the creature who so deeply disturbed her with his uncanny resemblance to her late husband, his natural father. These were deep and poisonous waters for Sarah Coignwood, throwing her into the same mad fantasies of revenge and torture and mutilation to which she had abandoned herself during the passage from England.

During this period, Mrs Collins and every other servant in Lord Balcarras's establishment came to dread the jingling bell in the servants hall that summoned one or another of them up to My Lady's room where she sat, in a loose silk wrap, thinking and thinking and thinking, because she knew now exactly where Jacob Fletcher was to be found. She'd even met people who knew him under his assumed name of Boswell, and she was unnerved by what she'd heard, for it seemed he had just exactly the same talent for money-making as his father. The fact served to feed and water the supernatural fear at the bottom of her mind that Jacob Fletcher was Sir Henry born again and returned to punish her for the torment she'd subjected him to in his first life.

These were impossible thoughts and Lady Sarah knew it. She knew it and feared it, because her lesser son Victor had been mad, even her Alexander had been far from normal and her own mother had been locked away for a while. But whatever might be the state of her own mind, Lady Sarah was a woman of iron will and was totally intolerant of weakness. But still, still, she couldn't quite shake off the unholy dread that Jacob Fletcher was something more than a mortal … though none of this altered to the least degree her resolution to kill Mr Fletcher in as unpleasant a fashion as might be contrived.

Finally she grasped the one inescapable fact shining from the mists that surrounded her. Since nothing less than personal vengeance would do, then she must get herself within reach of Mr Fletcher. She must go to Montego Bay. She must get close enough to cut with a knife, for this was not a matter that could be settled with the remote discharge of a firearm. So Lady Sarah sent for her maid, Collins, and laid aside the silk wrap and took the time to dress and present herself to best advantage. Then she sent a message to Lord Balcarras requesting the honour of a meeting with his Lordship, at his Lordship's earliest convenience.

She was swiftly ushered into a big, cool office with shaded windows looking out over Spanish Town's principal square and the shabby Government House. The sounds of people and horses came faintly from outside. Balcarras was busy with a couple of secretaries and an officer of regulars in his red coat and gorget. All stood respectfully as she entered and a chair was instantly found for her.

"Good day, my Lord, gentlemen!" she said.

"My Lady!" they said in chorus.

"How may we be of service to you, my dear Lady Sarah?" said Balcarras himself.

"My Lord," said she, "On behalf of the women of Jamaica I am come to beg that you should immediately place yourself at the head of your forces in Montego bay, and that you should attack the Maroons at their stronghold and so extinguish this menace forever."

Balcarras smiled, misled by the sweetness of her expression.

"My dear lady," said he, "There is much you do not know of this problem. I have many other responsibilities…" and here, her own impatience and arrogance nearly betrayed her.

"Lord Balcarras," she said, interrupting, "Should you not do as I ask then on my return to London I shall be obliged to report your vacillating incompetence to Mr Pitt when next I dine with him."

A gasp went up from Balcarras's attendants. Balcarras went white with anger and set his jaw defiantly. He was the King's first man on this island and wielded mighty powers. Lady Sarah instantly regretted the stupidity of her words. There were a thousand ways it could have been better done. She cursed herself for not being herself, and damned Jacob Fletcher to hell. But she stared steadily into Balcarras's eyes and never a flicker of her expression betrayed her confusion. And so: unjustly, unfairly and illogically … she won. Balcarras was faced down by her air of total confidence; confidence of the damage that she could do him by the political equivalent of a dagger in the back, and a poisoned dagger at that. Balcarras had no assurance that he would survive such an attack and the anger drained out of him and fear came in to take its place. So Balcarras wavered and dropped his eyes.

"Ah!" said Lady Sarah, reading the signs with immense relief, "And one other thing, my Lord. To secure my own personal safety, I shall accompany you to Montego Bay since the greatest concentration of military force in the island will be gathered about yourself."

"As you wish, my Lady," mumbled Balcarras, and by Saturday August 8th, Lady Sarah and Lord Balcarras were established in Montego Bay. His Lordship made his headquarters at the Town Hall inside the earthwork fort that had finally been completed, and Lady Sarah allowed herself to be accommodated in the house of Mr Tharp the Custos.

The abysmal grubby town was cram-full of the military and the people (feeling duly safe and protected) were crying out for a crushing blow against the Maroons.

However, once arrived in Montego Bay, Lady Sarah had no wish for the war to start. Her objectives were to find Jacob Fletcher and gain time to act against him. So it suited her to keep the town strongly garrisoned and safe against attack and she told Balcarras that things must proceed properly against the Maroons, who must be given stern warning and a chance to surrender. Balcarras, still nervous of what might she might say of him, back in London, responded with blood-curdling ultimatum to the Trelawney Maroons.

"You have forced the country which has long cherished and fostered you as its children, to consider you as an enemy," it said, "Martial law has in consequence been proclaimed." It went on to promise that unless the Trelawneys surrendered their arms to his Lordship by Thursday August 11th, then he would move against them at the head of his troops and burn their town about their ears.

Meanwhile, the instant that her bags had been unloaded into Mrs Tharp's best bedroom, Lady Sarah sent out Mrs Collins to ask after Fletcher. Then, having accepted Mrs Tharp's hospitality, Lady Sarah was then obliged to endure the company of that overwhelmingly-honoured lady, together with a goggling trio of her closest friends all dressed to their uttermost best. She gave them fifteen agonizing minutes and then pleaded the headache and retired to her room. There she received Mrs Collins who returned an hour later. Having achieved so much, the disappointment was bitter.

"'e hain't there, M'Lady," said Mrs Collins, "Gorn orf, 'e has. I found 'is shop – Lee an' Boswells – and made hinquiries. Gorn fishin' for gold out of a wreck in Morgan's Bay, along of a Hamerican gennelman, name of Stanley, what 'as new happer-atus special for the purpose, for working under the water ... M'lady?" The big woman stopped off short, for her mistress had gone pale and was swaying in her chair.

"The bottle! Bring it here!" said Lady Sarah, pointing to a long-necked blue bottle on the dressing table. Mrs Collins brought the bottle and Lady Sarah sprinkled a few drops of its contents on a handkerchief and held it to her nose. The room filled with the scent of lavender. Lady Sarah inhaled deeply and the fear slip away somewhat.

"Fishing for gold under the sea!" said Lady Sarah, "With apparatus special for the purpose? That's what you said, Collins?"

"Yess'm," said Collins, not understanding the unnatural fear welling inside her mistress. Not knowing how the combination of the pursuit of gold with some innovative mechanical device would have seized and fascinated Sir Henry Coignwood.

Lady Sarah made an effort. She sat upright and questioned her servant carefully.

"When is he expected back?" she said.

"Within the week, m'lady. 'e has business to hattend on the 11th. 'e'll be back for that. A dark gennelmun in the shop says as 'ow Mr Boswell – which your ladyship knows his 'is name – Mr Boswell his most particular with business meetings. Hain't never bin know to miss…"

"Shut you damned mouth!" snapped Lady Sarah with a ferocity that made Collins jump. Lady Sarah did not need to be told that Mr Boswell never missed an opportunity for business. She knew it as surely as she knew that he was never late, he never gave short measure, he could juggle figures in his head, he was a genius for making money, he was consumed with love for mechanism and he could bargain with the devil and come out ahead. She knew everything about him for she'd known him before. There was simply no denying it. The weed had sunk roots in her mind and was now a permanent fixture.

"Collins!" she said, when the wave of fright had rolled back once more. "You will find out where Mr Boswell lays down his head of nights to sleep. You will gain entrance to that place on the night of 10th August and you and I together will await the arrival of Mr Boswell on the 11th."

Mrs Collins was puzzled.

"Why yess'm," she said, "I knows where the cove lives already, m'lady. 'e has lodgings with a coloured woman, back of Rope-Walk street." But she hesitated, afraid of talking out of turn. She hesitated and pressed on, for her own neck was at hazard here, "But … beggin' yer pardon, m'lady … 'ow's it to be done? The details m'lady? An' 'ow's you and I to come off safe arterwards?"

There followed one of those rare occasions when the physical loveliness of Lady Sarah's exterior could not hide the warped disfigurement within, as she turned upon her servant with vile spite.

"Listen to me you great, fat, ugly bitch," she said, "I swear by the murders you have done, the abortions you have procured, and the hideous moustache upon your face, that if ever you question me again I will have you hanged and anatomised within the week. Do you understand me?" Mrs Collins cringed before the evil that burned within her mistress and never another word was spoken between them on that topic. Thus Mrs Collins never learned the full truth, which was that following the long months of unhealthy brooding over revenge, Lady Sarah's selfish, brilliant, narrow, cunning mind was now dangerously unhinged.

So there was no proper plan for dealing with Fletcher, only an irresistible desire to kill him at any cost. And there was certainly no plan for anybody '*to come off safe arterwards*'.

CHAPTER 16

Higgins and I left *Amiability* at dawn on August 10th, which was a Monday. Captain Marlow had the long boat rigged for sail under command of Laurence, the first mate and with a fresh on-shore breeze, we were in Montego Bay in a couple of hours where we could see that things were happening. For one thing, the harbour was full of transports including a huge, old 64-gun ship converted for trooping by taking out her main deck battery, and a number of merchantmen too, some of them fitted out for embarking horses.

There were also a couple of sloops flying Navy ensigns. That gave me a fright, but not half as much as it did Laurence and his men who were in mortal fear of being pressed, and it was all I could do to get them to beach the boat long enough for Higgins and I to scramble out. Then they bent to their oars like demented men, to get out to sea again. They were dead right too, for one of the Navy sloops sent a boat nosing after them, but they were too late and the longboat cleared the harbour and made sail for Morgan's Bay.

So Higgins and I trudged up the hot beach and into the town. It wasn't the same place that we'd left, and was bursting with soldiers: the 83rd foot, the 62nd foot and a strong force of regular cavalry, a scarce rarity in colonial warfare and a sign of the value that the home government put upon Jamaican sugar. The militia was out too and the town was more like Horse Guard's Parade than Montego Bay. They'd even thrown up a fort in the middle of the town, and Lord Balcarras (no less) had come in his majesty, up from Spanish Town, to be in command.

All of this was to counter the threat from the Trelawney Maroons, which it seemed had not gone away at all, but was come back with a vengeance. I sent Higgins to Lee and Boswell's to let them know we were back, and I went round to Sammy's House to get the news from him. But he was gone off into the interior to his wife's family, according to his neighbours. It seemed she was expecting their child and Sammy was taking no chances. He thought they'd be safer there if it came to fighting.

So I trudged back to Lee and Boswell's, feeling sorry for myself for having no Sammy Bone to share my adventures with. At the shop my people told me (with much glee and satisfaction) that the Maroons were to be rooted out at last by the good Lord Balcarras and his men and that they'd been given until the 13th to give themselves up into his power, which all Montego Bay hoped they would not do for it would spoil the fun something wicked (You see? What did I tell you? With 2,000 redcoats to do the dirty work, everyone else was itching for a fight). They also told me that old Major John James was in prison in Spanish Town on a charge of assault against Lord Balcarras, having got himself roaring drunk and attacked the Governor outside the Parliament. That was bad news and no mistake for I admired the fiery old buffer even if he was a bore with his arm wrestling.

Finally, I recall that they did try to say something about a grand English Milady who'd come up from Spanish Town in Balcarras's train. But I cut them off short for I was tired by then and short tempered and I had no interest in such frippery matters.

(At this stage, my lads, your Uncle Jacob would warn you to take careful note that not all things that seem unimportant may safely be ignored, and what a bloody tragedy it is that a man don't know when they can't be.)

In any case, I had a meeting that afternoon with a potential client who was seeking a planting attorney and I wanted to change my clothes to look my best. Maybe in the present emergency he'd not turn up, but he'd sent no message to that effect and I wasn't about to lose a piece of business. So I made my way back to the lane behind Rope Walk street and to Mrs Godfrey's house where I lodged. It was a big, neat, whitewashed wooden house on one floor in its own neat flower-garden with a picket fence around. It was set on its own with the nearest house some way off. I stepped up to the house, climbed the three stairs on to the big, shady piazza, with my boots booming on the planks ... and stopped. Something wasn't right. The house was silent. It was past noon, in the heat of the day, but there was no Mrs Godfrey, dozing in the shade of the piazza and no sound from the half-dozen children that played in and out of the house.

I paused for a moment, then shrugged my shoulders and took out my key. I thought they must all be asleep inside. Either that or they were gone to some friend's or neighbour's house. So I shoved the key in the lock and found the door unlocked. Suspicion prickled at the back of my mind, and fear too. I'd heard fearful tales of Maroon raids within a few miles of Montego Bay. What if they'd sneaked in here and done away with Mrs Godfrey and her brood?

"Mrs Godfrey?" says I with a great shout and darted forward. The house was black inside with the blinds drawn against the fierce sun and I could see nothing.

Chaos followed.

The door crashed shut behind me and I went down heavily as a rope snagged my feet. Something caught me a fearful blow across the back of the head and a blaze of sickening lights whirled round my head. I didn't quite go out but I couldn't move nor think straight. Then hands were plucking at me and turning me over and a woman's voice, high and shrill and mad, was spitting hatred into my ear and fists were belabouring my face. Other hands, rough and strong, ran a line around my wrists and round my ankles and hauled them tight.

"Hold him up! Hold him up to me! Give him here! *Give him to me!*" screamed the voice, transported into a passion of frenzy. The creature was drooling and sobbing with eagerness. Someone heaved me upright, so I was sat on the floor with my bound legs stuck out before me and my bound arms behind. Strong, heavy arms wrapped around my neck so I could hardly breath and fat legs wrapped around my waist so I was bound like a lamb for the butcher. I couldn't move a muscle.

With my head spinning and the breath stopped in my lungs I vaguely felt another shape plump down on my legs and reach out, ripping and tearing at my shirt. The insane sobbing voice was in my very face and then there came a couple of sharp stabs of pain in my chest and then … *Christ Almighty*! The most hideous sensation I have every suffered in all my life. I roared with agony and heaved and rolled to throw them off, but all I got was maniac laughter and the arms behind me tightened on my throat. Then the same quick, sharp pain and I screamed in anticipation even as there came the same ghastly torment.

With that, there was no longer just one foaming maniac in that stifling black room: there were two, and one of them was me. I kicked and fought and bit and twisted, with the primordial energy of a beast in its final extremity. I honestly doubt that a dozen men could have held me and my two enemies were bounced to all points of the compass. The smaller one was thrown off in a trice but the ape clawing on to my back kept hold until I got myself over on to my front, hauled my knees up, bound as they were, arched my back, and by main force heaved myself up and back to crash over backwards, crushing him into the floorboards under our combined weights – except that it wasn't a *him* at all for there was the unmistakable feel of pair of great, fat udders against my back.

I rolled clear the instant the thick arms fell slack and tried to get to my feet, but my hobbled ankles brought me over again. I struggled up again and with my eyes seeing clearer in the dark, I dimly saw a small, dark figure rush at me with a gleam of steel in one hand. I hauled mightily at the ropes round my wrists and they gave, but not enough and with no chance to parry to coming blow I ducked my head, screwed shut my eyes and butted low and forward at the figure. By God's grace the knife went wide and I caught her (for both of 'em were women) squarely in the middle and doubled her over like a snapped twig.

But the big one was up again and swinging at me with a cudgel. I turned and took it on the shoulder as she swung again. The cords on my wrists were giving way but she caught me under the left ear and half stunned me. The room spun again, there came a yell of wild glee and by God they were on me again, the pair of them. I don't think ever in all the fights I've fought did I feel quite the same unnatural horror at what those two demons might do to me should they get me down. I hopped and turned, terrified and desperate to keep my feet, but it was no contest with my feet bound and they heaved me over again. But then, even as I went down with a jarring thump, my hands came free at last and I could give it back to them, and give it with interest.

I knocked the little one spinning at a single blow and turned to the other who'd got her hands round my neck and was wringing away like a farmer with a chicken. All well and good, then, because I could play that game too! So what a jolly little throttling match we had there on the floor, just the two of us. We both had thick necks and big hands, but she was no match for me, especially when I was raging mad with fear and pain. I'm powerfully strong in the fingers and I crushed and crunched till the sweat poured from my brow and the thing in my hands was no more than coffin-meat.

When it was done, I heaved the great, limp mass aside and shook and shuddered with such horror as I never knew the like before. And slowly, as I came to myself and realised that the room was now bright lit, with the door swung open to let in the sun, and furthermore that I was alone and my other enemy long gone, I looked down at the dead face beside me and got another fright, because I knew her. And if I knew her, then I knew who her accomplice must be; that is to say her mistress.

The ugly, mannish face with its bristling moustache was unmistakable. This was Maggie Collins, who'd served Lady Sarah Coignwood at 200 Maze Hill Greenwich when I rescued Kate Booth from her clutches as the house burned down. Until that moment it had been my happy belief that my stepmother was burned to ashes in the fire, but now I knew different. Incredible as it seemed the woman was not only alive but had somehow tracked me all the way to Jamaica and come for her vengeance. I looked down at my chest and saw what she'd done to me. There were two small, neat rectangular patches of raw flesh weeping blood down my torn shirt-front. It puzzled me, because in those days I'd not seen the Afghans of India skinning their prisoners.

It's a simple thing: four shallow knife cuts to mark out a strip of skin, then a thumb-nail under one edge and a quick jerk to tear out the strip. The smaller the strips the longer the treatment lasts. I shuddered again. If she'd wanted simply to kill me, she could have done it ten times over, but it seemed that wasn't enough.

The thought of it brought on a fit of shuddering and I staggered outside and sat in Mrs Godfrey's rocking chair till it passed. Then I forced myself to go back inside past the fat corpse splayed out on the polished floor, to search the house for my landlady and her children. It was a horror to open each door for fear of what I'd find, but thank God they weren't there and everything was neat, and put away tidy. I could only suppose Mrs Godfrey had left willingly and taken the children with her. No doubt Lady Sarah blasted Coignwood had caused this, though I never did find out how, or where Mrs Godfrey went.[7]

I shut the door on Mrs Collins, and sat on the piazza, in the shade for

---

[7]   Many years later I was informed by sources in Jamaica that Mrs Godfrey and her family were paid off by Lady Sarah Coignwood, giving them money to retreat safe into the interior for fear of the Maroons, while Mrs Godfrey gave Lady Sarah a letter of explanation to Fletcher, which Lady Sarah destroyed. S.P.

a long time, occasionally helping myself from a jug of rum I'd brought out of the kitchen. I'd been taken aback badly and thrown over on my beam ends. I needed to think, to turn things over in my mind. The over-whelming threat was what Sarah Coignwood might do now? She only had to 'peach on me to the nearest magistrate and I'd be in irons bound for England, for was I not a notorious murderer and fugitive from justice? What's more, here I was with a woman strangled by my own hand. How would that look to Mr Tharp the Custos? In all probability Lady Sarah would be able to take her choice of a Jamaican or an English hanging for me! By George but I wished Sammy Bone had been there. Just to have a friend to talk to.

Finally, and with great sorrow I decided that I must cut and run again. It was bitter hard to abandon all that I'd built in Jamaica, but I couldn't see what else to do. That woman would never give up and she had the whole of the law and government of the island on her side. So it would have to be a boat. I'd steal a boat at night, something seaworthy, and rigged for sail but small enough for me to handle alone, and I'd head for America. But first I'd need some gear from the shop: money for one thing, as I had plenty of ready gold in the strong box. At least I could take that. And I'd need a sextant, charts, food, clothes and supplies. And arms too: pistols, a sword and powder and shot.

Once I'd made my plans my spirits rose, for it's indecision that brings pain and it's always better to *do* than to *dither*. No doubt the rum helped too. I reasoned that time was now precious and that I'd best move as fast as possible. If the law hadn't come for me yet then Lady Sarah hadn't sent them, but she might do so at any minute. So I locked up the house and set off cautiously to Lee and Boswell's.

As I got into the centre of the town I grew more confidant. Nobody paid me any heed except to greet me as ever they might. Soldiers marched by, a troop of dragoon trotted past and I noticed there was a general movement of people hurrying in the direction of the new fort round the Town Hall.

Something was afoot and no mistake, I could see the excitement in their eyes and the savage grins on their faces. But I kept myself to myself and came to the shop as fast as I could. It was shut and locked which annoyed me even in such a moment. What were my people playing at? If I'd had half a brain I'd have realised how much it was to my advantage for nobody to be there, but a man can't change his nature and I was cursing the loss of trade. Mind you, all the other shops were shut up, too. As I said, something was up.

But I unlocked the front door and slipped inside and went to get the things I'd come for. I cleared the strongbox and found a canvas bag for my goods, and got out the pistols and the dragoon sword I'd had for my visit to Trelawney town with Major James. I was just settling myself down in my back room, to wait until dark, when there came a thunderous beating on the front door, then the clang of the bell as it was pushed open.

"Come on m'lads!" says a loud voice, "It ain't locked and the rogue'll be in the back!" A rumble of swift heavy footsteps advanced and I leapt up, knowing my hour was come. There wasn't time to load my pistols. There wasn't even time to get out the back way. A sick fear was on me as I backed away from the door and drew the curved blade ringing from its steel scabbard. The door burst in and three or four redly sweating faces peered at me.

"Huzza for Boswell!" cries the first of 'em and turned to his mates, "Didn't I say he's the boy for some sport!"

"Well done old Boz!" cries another, "I see you've got your sixty rounds and bayonet sharpened!"

And they laughed and clapped me on the back. They were some of my militia-Officer customers. A few of the ones whom I'd been at special pains to make chums of, because they brought the most trade. They were in uniform and out for devilment, and each had a fair load of drink on board.

"'Tis the damned Maroons, old Boz!" says one of them. "That old villain Montague is coming in with a clutch of 'em to give himself up."

"Aye, says another. He thinks he'll get the King's mercy" And they all laughed long and loud.

"Hold hard there, boys!" says their leader, a Captain by the name of Wheatcroft. He frowned a bit. "His Lordship's ultimatum promises free pardons to those who render up their arms."

"Bah!" says one of the others, "That don't apply to blackamoors!" and he turned to me with a boozy grin, "Now come away with us Boswell," says he, "Put your sword away, for we've come out of our way on purpose to fetch you, for a sporting man who'd not want to miss the fun!" and they all laughed again and took my by the arms and hauled me off with them under the obvious misapprehension that I was even that minute getting ready to join the *fun* on my own behalf. They even shoved my sword in its scabbard, and stuck my pistols in my belt, for they were all armed themselves, in the like fashion.

Perhaps if I'd kept my head and thought of some clever excuse, I could have slipped away. But my brains were addled and my insides churned up, what with the horrid expectation of being captured, followed by the plunging relief. And then again, perhaps not. Maybe only actual bloodshed would've got rid of the bastards and I hesitated actually to kill them. And so I was swept along, leaving my preparations (and a small fortune in gold coin) in their sack beneath the counter where for all I know, they remain to this day.

Out we went into the street, whooping and hollering towards the fort where a great crowd was gathered. From what they yelled In my ear, it seemed that a couple of days previously, Balcarras had given formal notice to the Trelawney Maroons that either they surrendered themselves and gave up their arms by the 13th of August or he'd attack Trelawney Town with 2,000 men and burn it to ashes. Faced with this, Captain Montague and thirty-six chosen men of the Trelawney Maroons were coming into Montego Bay to give themselves up, to test Balcarras's promise of fair treatment. I suppose Montague knew he couldn't save his town any other way and so was taking this desperate measure, like the burghers of Calais in ancient times giving themselves up to the English army with nooses placed round their necks in a plea for mercy.

Well, judging from the mood among my gallant militiamen, and among the swelling crowd of Montego Bay citizens and soldiery of all kinds, Montague was wasting his time. They were out for a hanging at least.

There followed an hour or two of carnival fun and drunken amusements while the crowd kept itself busy awaiting Captain Montague. Fights broke out, pickpockets and hawkers plied their trades and eventually Lord Balcarras appeared his horse outside the fort, with an escort of Dragoons around him.

Among the officers clustered around him I saw my old friend Colonel Jervis Gallimore who'd tried to pay off Captain Mocho with pistol balls. The word ran through the crowd that the Maroons were approaching the town and that Balcarras was making a point of receiving them personally to dispense the King's Justice upon them.

Soon Montague's party could be seen advancing on foot with men of the 18th Light Dragoons riding on either side and a company of the 83rd Marching behind. A surge of excitement rose up among those around me and I took this as my chance finally to slip away from my companions. I was still in fear of being arrested at any minute and wanted only to get away. So I turned into the crowd and was free, but only for about half a minute because I walked slap into the arms of Custos Tharp himself and a posse of constables.

"Mr Boswell!" says he, with a puzzled, worried look on his face.

"What?" says I pretending not to hear him over the yelling of the mob, and tried to push past. But my muscles tightened as hands were laid on my arm.

"This is singularly embarrassing, Mr Boswell," says Tharp.

"I must be away, Sir," says I and dropped my hand to my sword. I looked about me. There were only three of them, besides Tharp and for an instant I considered cutting them down. But it was no good. There were soldiers everywhere.

"Mr Boswell," says Tharp, pressing close, "I know you to be an honest, straight dealing man, but …" The rest was drowned out in a roar from the crowd, and out of the corner of my eye I saw Montague and a body of Maroons around him, all armed. I recognised Whitfield among them. Tharp was shouting trying to say something. Bawling into my ear. I caught a snatch of it.

"…serious nature of these charges," says he, "and the dead body of Lady Sarah's servant…" The Dragoons horses were prancing about raising dust as the crowd pressed in, and the 83rd faced about and shoved the people back. Lord Balcarras was reading a paper to the Maroons. Montague and the rest were looking up at him anxiously. I couldn't hear what Balcarras was saying.

"So I must take you in charge, sir," came Tharp's voice, "For Lady Sarah Coignwood has powerful influence in England and even though I do not believe you guilty." The hands tightened on my arms. Yards away through the crowd I saw more soldiers appear, some of them bearing manacles. Montague raised his voice in angry protest. Some of the Maroons raised their muskets, the Dragoons closed in and belaboured them with the flat of the sword. A wild melee followed. The Maroons were overwhelmed by numbers and chained hand and foot. One alone avoided this treatment. Captain Whitfield cocked his musket, jammed it under his chin and stuck the big toe of his right foot into the trigger.

Bang! It was the only shot fired. Blood and brains flew up in a red mist and Whitfield sank.

"My God!" says Tharp, entirely blown off course from what he was trying to say to me.

"Did you see that, sir?"

"Yes," says I.

"They won't be chained," says he, "Tis worse than death to them."

" And what of me?" says I. He frowned and dithered.

"Dammit, sir", says he, "I have serious doubts in this case". He looked around him, dropped his voice and spoke in my very ear, "You will not believe this Mr Boswell, but certain rumours circulate in England about your accuser, this great lady, Sarah Coignwood. I know this for I have a sister who writes to me with the London gossip." He cleared his throat guiltily as a man does who feels he's said a shameful thing, and then he raised his voice and declaimed for all to hear, "And moreover, young Boswell, I simply refuse to believe you capable of strangling a woman!" He came to a decision, "Sir!" says he, "Will you give me your word to present yourself at the courthouse?"

"Willingly!" says I, resolving to collect my canvas sack from the shop and be out of Jamaica within the hour. He smiled and set a fatherly hand on my shoulder.

"Then though the charge be murder a thousand times over, I release you into the open custody of your friend Captain Wheatcroft," says he and my heart sank to my boots. "Wheatcroft!" says he and waved his hand to catch the bugger's attention. He then spent five minutes explaining to Wheatcroft who loudly protested the charges false and malicious, but I could tell by the look in his eye that he weren't half so convinced of this as Tharp was. But then I suppose he'd not had the benefit of Tharp's sister's letters to put him right about my witch stepmother.

Then Tharp and his constables departed and Wheatcroft took me off to the nearest tavern with his friends. They all affected to be jolly comrades and we sang the old songs and drank the old toasts. But they took my sword and pistols off me and kept their own handy. They were precious wary of me, and right to be so, for I was constantly looking for a chance to fell a couple of them and run for it, but never a chance did they give me. They even followed me out the back to piss against the wall, which I'd thought for sure would be my opportunity to run.

And when it got late and fellows were rubbing their eyes and yawning, Wheatcroft (who was a sharper brained 'un than he looked) sent for a set of leg irons and secured me with one leg on either side of an oaken pillar. He made a joke out of it, but he'd got me tight, none the less.

And so we spent the night in the Tavern and none of them went home for they were mustered on active service. In the morning they staggered down to the drilling fields outside the town, where their men (a regiment of planter volunteer cavalry) were bivouacked. They took me with 'em too since all of Montego Bay was closed down, shut up and suspended (including Mr Tharp's court of law), because the Maroon war was begun in earnest at last, and Balcarras was marching on Trelawney Town that very day.

CHAPTER 17

*"In the matter of this Boswell, or Fletcher - or whatever name
he goes by – I reject the accusations of the enchanting succubus
and attend only to the good, spoken universally of the young man
and – being foremost in this colony – I am resolved to do right by
him such that Madame may go hang."*

(From a letter of 10th August 1795 from Lord Balcarras, at Montego Bay,
Jamaica to his brother Charles, at Little Brook St, Hanover Square, London.)

Just before one o'clock in the afternoon of Monday August 10th 1795,
during the full heat of the mid-day sun, Mrs Tharp was resting on a day
bed in her parlour, fanning herself and idly flicking the pages of a copy of
Ackerman's Repository, that lavishly-illustrated magazine, a copy of which
was fresh out from England and no more than two months old. She was
trying to read, but her mind was on the stupendous military preparations going forward finally to extirpate the Maroon threat from the soil
of the colony. That and the unbelievable honour of entertaining Lady
Sarah Coignwood.

Suddenly there came a sharp rapping at the door: highly unusual at
such a time of day when sensible folk sheltered from the heat. She listened
through the thin, wooden wall and closed door, as a servant slowly went
to receive the visitor, and she strained her ears to catch the first sound of
the visitor's voice. Who could it be?

To her amazement there came the distinct sounds of a scuffle, a sharp
slap, a yelp from her maid, and a patter of swift, light footsteps vanishing
up the stairs towards her own best bedroom. At once there came a tapping
at her own door, which burst open to reveal her housemaid, Jemima with

tears in her eyes and a swollen cheek that was stinging from the blow she had just been given.

"Ma'am," said the girl, stunned with what had just happened, "Lady Sarah…"

"Yes?" said Mrs Tharp.

"She just came in, Ma'am!"

"Oh? You mean she'd gone out in the heat, without telling me?"

"Yes, Ma'am." Mrs Tharp considered this amazing lapse of etiquette. Perhaps this was how the great folk behaved? Mrs Tharp frowned in puzzlement. She did so wish not to appear … well … colonial in the eyes of her guest. "And she slapped me ma'am."

"What?" said Mrs Tharp, not wishing to hear.

"Here, Ma'am!" said the girl, indicating her puffed-up cheek.

"Nonsense!" said Mrs Tharp, firmly, "Get about your duties and let's hear no more of this!" So the servant went out and Mrs Tharp was left half perplexed and half fascinated and wondering what she would tell her friends.

Up in Mrs Tharp's best bedroom, Lady Sarah Coignwood tore off the thin cloak that was wrapped around her and threw herself face down upon the bed. She was wearing men's clothes: tight pantaloons and a shirt and her hair was wrapped tight in a scarf. There were blood-stains on the shirt.

She drove a clenched fist into her mouth to stop herself uttering a sound. She knew that just one squeak, one groan, one tiny yelp, would slip the leash of the hounds of hell and she would scream and scream and scream and scream. Instead, she screwed shut her eyes, kicked at the bedclothes, ground her teeth and wrung the sheets into knots in her hands. She threw herself from side to side and beat her head into the pillows. In short, and from the very depths of her being, she performed all the vicious rituals of an evil-tempered child under the horrors of a monstrous tantrum.

After some minutes of this she fell silent and ceased to move. But she did not feel better and she did not fall to the tears that a child would have used to comfort its self-pity, for Sarah Coignwood was not a child. Sarah Coignwood was a woman of outstanding intellect, profound cunning and vast experience. Consequently, no person in all the world knew better than she, in that moment, just how inexcusably stupid she had been in the manner of her attack upon Jacob Fletcher.

She knew that she had actually slipped into the pit. She had been mad, unhinged, deranged, insane. She vowed that never, never, *never*, again would she attempt so crass, so stupid and so hopeless an enterprise as a direct physical assault on the brat with her own hand. She shuddered at the memory of the encounter in the hot, black room, and sank her teeth in Mrs Tharp's patchwork coverlet, like a seaman biting leather to bear a flogging. She knew she could so easily have cut his throat, and knew that's what she should have done. But the pleasure of paying him off properly had been so great, and the pain of being stopped before she'd hardly started, was so unendurable.

And then there was the awful fright of the sheer, herculean strength exploding out of the bound and captive body. She'd never known a man so strong, certainly not the father! He couldn't have snapped ropes and thrown over Mrs Collins like a spring lamb. But worst of all, Sarah Coignwood was tormented with the realisation that having come so far and achieved so much, she'd then produced no better plan than to hit Jacob Fletcher over the head and cut him up with her own hands. All she'd achieved was to alert him to danger and get her servant killed. At least she assumed Collins was dead, for Lady Sarah had last seen her with Fletcher's massive hands locked on her throat.

Lady Sarah writhed under her own contempt for herself. She knew that she had been stupid, inept and totally deserving of failure. Such was the depth of despair to which she sank on that afternoon.

But the ugly mixture of flaws and talents that made up her personality included a limitless capacity for concentration on getting her own way, and once her greed was aroused it would stifle every other emotion within her body. The result was a ruthless crushing of any weakness or any contrary inclinations which might interfere with the fulfilling of desire. This was not self-discipline (of which she was incapable) but rather the absolute triumph of self.

In this case, self required that Lady Sarah be preserved unharmed at all costs for another and better move against her enemy. There was, for instance the remote possibility of a charge of attempted murder against herself. Unlikely, given Fletcher's condition as a fugitive, but not impossible. Not if he were as angry as she had been. So finally, she became calm and set her mind properly to work. Within an hour, she was dressed in her finery, smiling like an angel and descending the stairs to overwhelm Mrs Tharp and send for her husband.

Mr and Mrs Tharp were duly brought together and bowled over together. They listened (open-mouthed) to the tale they were fed: that Sarah Coignwood (continuing in Jamaica those charitable works to which her private life in England had been so devoted), had gone out discreetly with her servant to distribute small donations to the needy. That furthermore, on entering the home of a coloured woman by the name of Godfrey (to whom she had given certain monies to absent herself and her children to allow the use of her home for charitable purposes) Lady Sarah and her servant had been set upon by an escaped deserter masquerading under the name of Boswell, who was a notorious enemy come out from England for the purpose of an attempt upon her life. Tragically, the noble servant had purchased her mistress's escape with the sacrifice of her own life … and that the said Boswell must answer for this murder and other crimes too manifold to mention.

Having put Mr Custos Tharp into a dizzy spin, Lady Sarah insisted on the instant despatch of constables to recover the poor body of her murdered servant and the instant presentation of herself, before his Lordship the Governor, to secure the highest authority in the island for the apprehension of the malefactor, Boswell.

Mr Tharp roused slaves, servants and underlings to bring this about. The horrid murder in the house behind Rope-Walk street was duly confirmed and the news ran through Montego Bay as fast as tongues could wag. The crushed throat, squeezed by a giant's hand, seemed to annihilate any doubts as the absolute veracity of Lady Sarah's tale, and Tharp secured an interview with Lord Balcarras that very afternoon.

Ushered into Mr Tharp's own court room, now within the walls of the new fort and serving as headquarters to Lord Balcarras's military staff, Mr Tharp and Lady Sarah found the chairs and benches of the court, driven back to the walls to make way for desks and tables, papers and ink, maps and plans and a dozen red-coated officers, busy with the final details of the march on Trelawney Town which was to take place the next day. His Lordship rose as Lady Sarah approached and greeted her uneasily. He had much to do and the last thing he desired was an interview with this fearfully dangerous woman.

"My Lady," said he, bowing.

"My Lord," said she, smiling sweetly and on her most exquisite best behaviour. Every man In the room looked on in fascination, feasting his eyes on La Belle Coignwood's lovely face, round arms and voluptuous figure. But every man was equally fascinated by the struggle for control over the affairs of the island that was rumoured to be taking place between Lord Balcarras and Lady Sarah.

"I have heard disturbing news of an attack upon your person, My Lady," said Balcarras, "And you have my promise that every available resource will be concentrated on the apprehension of your assailant."

"Every available resource?" said Lady Sarah, and utter silence a upon the spectators as she insisted that the entire garrison be set upon the task of seeking out Jacob Boswell.

"Impossible my lady," said Balcarras, "Most of the 83rd are gone already, I have business here today with a delegation of Maroons coming in to surrender themselves," he paused and pointed to a window, "You can hear the mob assembling to receive them, even as we speak."

He was cut short by a torrent of words which Lady Sarah intended to be the definitive denunciation of Jacob Fletcher, whose fate she had now decided should be a legal hanging. In a single blast, she rattled off a detailed history of the life and times of Jacob Fletcher, alias Boswell, and his despicable attempt to usurp the inheritance of herself and her sons. She named Fletcher-Boswell severally as murderer, deserter, traitor, arsonist, thief, forger, savage, brute ... etc, etc, etc. It was an impressive and powerful speech. She preened herself when she was done and looked sidelong at her audience to note the effect of what she had said.

Before her, Lord Balcarras preserved a soldierly uprightness of bearing, though it was obvious that great emotions were at work within him. He fought to master his feelings while staring steadily at Lady Sarah as if unconcerned.

"By Hector, madam!" said he, at last, "As I am a soldier and a gentleman, I give you my solemn word that Mr Boswell shall receive everything that he deserves, and that I shall personally take care that the thing is done!"

Lady Sarah curtsied triumphantly. This was better. Much better. She had been madly wrong in trying to do the thing herself. Far better for Mr Fletcher to be put to a proper trial and then a proper hanging. She'd seen a hanging once and while it was (relatively) a quick death compared with what she had intended, it was ugly enough from the victim's point of view, while providing much entertainment for the spectators. She promised herself a good, close seat from which she could study every twitch and shudder.

She thanked his Lordship most humbly and allowed herself to be escorted forth by a young Lieutenant named Parker, whom Lord Balcarras specifically chose to entertain and protect her Ladyship while he, Balcarras, gave Mr Tharp particular instruction as the apprehension of Mr Boswell.

And so Lady Sarah exited stage left, happy in her ignorance that the great blast of accusation which she had directed at her victim, had in fact ricocheted badly inside of Lord Balcarras's mind. For his Lordship, burdened as he was with the responsibilities of a campaign, concluded that he'd had entirely enough of being told what to do by Lady Sarah. He further concluded that any man she so thoroughly damned, must have some good in him somewhere.

Consequently he spent some minutes of most interesting conversation with Mr Tharp who was indeed given particular instructions concerning Jacob Boswell, also known as Fletcher. Interestingly enough, Lord Balcarras found that Mr Tharp had similar opinions to his own as regards Lady Sarah, having acquired relevant information from a sister in England.

CHAPTER 18

On Tuesday morning, August 11th 1795 Lord Balcarras and his staff reviewed all the troops remaining in Montego Bay, which meant a company of the 83rd, left to guard the harbour with a detachment of tars and Marines out of the ships, plus the planter volunteer cavalry, which now included me, astride Black Tom once more, Wheatcroft having been thoughtful enough to seek him out for me.

Whether or not Wheatcroft knew it, by getting me in the saddle, he'd nailed me securer that he'd done with his leg irons, since every man in the regiment rode better than me, and they were all armed while I was not. If I'd stuck my heels in and tried to flee they could have taken their leisure in cutting at my head like a turnip on a broom-handle, set up for sabre practise.

In fact, Wheatcroft kept me by him and steered an erratic course between acting as my gaoler and treating me as the good friend that I had been. I could see he was embarrassed by the situation, and more than that, he was nervous, which puzzled until I realised why, having recognised all the signs. He was frightened. He was afraid of what might happen if it came to actual fighting. He was only a pretend soldier after all and perhaps he'd never been in action before? Who knows? But he was nearly pissing his breeches in any case.

"We shall have some sport presently, old Boz!" says he, with a sickly smile, trying to act bold, "Can't wait to get to it, can you my dear fellow?" Well as a matter of fact I was anxious for it to begin, because I was hoping some kindly Maroon would knock Wheatcroft over, once the fun really started and everyone else was too busy to bother with old Boz. And if the enemy didn't do it then I would, if only I could get my hands on him, which was going to be difficult on horseback.

As I pondered on these merry thoughts, the regiment lined up, with its horses shuffling and stamping as Balcarras and his staff went by. He caught sight of me in my blue coat and civilian hat mong all the uniforms, and he actually raised his hat to me and gave a smile, which was powerful odd. But he said nothing and rode past, running his eye over the planter volunteers, who weren't the world's smartest troopers. Then he visibly brightened as he rode past the lines of the 20th and the 18th light dragoons. They at least were turned out as cavalrymen should be.

And cavalry was almost all that was left in Montego bay, as the foot had marched earlier, to get into their allotted positions before Balcarras's deadline of August 13th. It was well planned because his Lordship was a professional soldier who'd seen service in the American war and was taking no chances with the Maroons. On that morning there was still the possibility that the Maroons would surrender, but Balcarras had split his forces in two, to make a hammer and an anvil to crush them if need be.

The anvil was Colonel Fitch of the 83rd with the bulk of his regiment: some nine hundred men who would form Balcarras's headquarters and stronghold at the small settlement of Vaughansfield to the south of Trelawney Town (the 83rd were already in place even as Balcarras was reviewing myself and the others outside Montego Bay). The hammer was to be the bulk of Balcarras's cavalry, based upon Spring Vale, to the north of Trelawney Town. On the morning of the 11th, one hundred men of the 62nd foot were in place at Spring Vale, together with over five hundred militia infantry where they were awaiting the cavalry to join them, that very day. The whole Spring Vale force was to be under the command of Colonel Sanford of the 20th light dragoons (on parade that day with Balcarras and his staff) with Colonel Jarvis Gallimore (he of the pistol balls) as Balcarras's second in command and adviser (God help him) on Jamaican conditions.

Now Balcarras made all this clear to the assembled men and beasts in a rousing speech, and concluded in the following words.

"Should the Trelawneys, despite the unprecedented magnanimity of my warning, not render up themselves by the appointed day then Colonel Sanford shall come down upon them from the north and drive them on to the bayonets of the 83rd, coming up from the south. I give you good day, gentlemen and ask you for three rousing cheers for our sovereign Lord, King George III!"

He was duly cheered and the parade moved off by companies with the dust rising in the hot morning air, with cheers and tears from the assembled population of Montego Bay, and that inevitable accompaniment to the movement of any large body of horse: the lifting of tails and the emptying out of dollops of dung upon the field of Mars.

I bounced off alongside of Wheatcroft and the volunteers who were astern of the 18th, who in turn followed the 20th. Black Tom was in an ugly mood and I'll not pretend I was in command of him. The beast snatched at the bit and continuously tried to get the reins out of my grasp, keeping station with the other horses only because he chose to.

And so we covered the twenty miles or so to our rendezvous with the 62nd and the militia, at Spring Vale. It was an agonising ride for me and each time we stopped to rest it took all my courage to dismount, anticipating of the agony of getting up again later. Meanwhile, Wheatcroft and his brother officers complained about the weather.

"If we don't look sharp we'll lose the bastards!" says Wheatcroft.

"Aye!" says another, "Look at that sky. We'll have the rains before long and all the roads turned to mud and the Maroons up in the hills." They were boorish company even at the best of times, but on that day I was sunk in gloom for the further we pressed on inland, the further I was taken from my natural line of escape: the open sea. But late in the afternoon, just outside Springfield, where Balcarras and his personal escort were to part company with Sanford (the former going to Vaughansfield and the latter to Spring Vale), I got sent for by the Olympian company of gentlemen who were in command of us up in the van of our formation.

A young cornet of the 18th came clattering down the road, with sword and accoutrements flapping at his side and reined in beside myself and Wheatcroft in a shower of dirt. He spun his horse round high up on its stern legs, all fancy-fashion with a whinny of protest and the for'ard limbs thrashing the air. In his fur-crested helmet and tight frogged coat he looked down his regular army nose at Wheatcroft and saluted with minimal courtesy.

"Good day to you sir!" says he, "I'm Beeston of the 18th," he looked at me curiously, "His Lordship's compliments and Mr Boswell is to be released into my custody and taken to Colonel Sanford without delay."

Wheatcroft didn't like that one bit. He didn't like Beeston's cavalier manner and he didn't like being ordered about, in front of his men, by a boy with a face as smooth as a girl's. He blustered a bit and looked at his cronies for support. But he knew it was no go and took refuge in form.

"Mr Boswell," says he, turning to me all solemn, "If I release you into this gentleman's custody, will you give me your word to act to him as you would to me?"

"With all my heart!" says I, with total sincerity, and added a little dig, partly to put salt on Wheatcroft's tail but mainly for a more serious purpose. "Especially, sir," says I in a loud clear voice, "Since you know that I am an innocent man wrongly accused by the trumped up falsehoods of dishonourable persons!" He blushed at that and dropped his eyes. Serve him right, the swab.

Beeston followed this and his eyebrows shot up. I don't know what he'd been expecting of me but I assume it was the sweating, cussing, boozing manners of a Jamaican Planter. Instead of which, he found me affecting the style and manner of a gentlemen with all my might: a thing I can do very well when I choose to.

(The thing is, children, that with young Beeston's arrival, your Uncle Jacob had sniffed a sea change in his circumstances, and he cannot impress upon you too strongly the importance of making a good impression at first sight, since most folk are far too lazy to change their minds thereafter.)

"If you'll follow me, Mr Boswell?" says Beeston and set off and a smart canter towards the head of the column. That was the worst part for me. There could be no holding back, for gentlemen are supposed to be able to ride. So I kicked Black Tom with all my might and suffered the torments of the damned as the great monster shot forward and pounded after Beeston's sleek little mare. Then, since Tom was hung with all his tackles, I'd guess Tom was following the mare rather than obeying me, but for whatever reason, up to the front we went and Tom stopped when Beeston stopped thanks to my hauling on the reins fit to pull his big ugly head off.

And there was Lord Balcarras, splendid in scarlet and gold lace, with a plume in his cocked hat and a thousand-guinea Mameluke-hilt sword at his side, his officers around him, and the standard bearers behind him: a Union Flag and the colours of the 20th and the 18th. To my surprise I noticed there were some shifty-looking mulattos riding along with the officers, and even more surprising there were a couple of Maroons trotting along beside them.

At once, a dozen sharp, hard faces looked me over, among them Colonel Jarvis Gallimore, who to say the least was unfriendly. I realised that I'd been the subject of discussion. Then an aide leaned across to Balcarras and said something to him, including the word *Boswell* which I plainly heard. Balcarras nodded and turned to me.

"Mr Boswell," says he, "I'll be brief, for events are proceeding even as we ride. You stand accused of certain crimes."

"Falsely, my Lord!" says I.

"Sir," says he, calmly, "I am entirely unconcerned with your personal affairs. That is a matter for the courts. But interrupt me again and it'll be the end of you. Do you understand?" Pompous bastard. But he was at the head of an army.

"Yes, my Lord," says I carefully.

"Mr Boswell, you are a man of mystery," says he, "I am told that, although consumed with a preoccupation in trade, you are an adventurer who has seen service and seen powder burned. You are furthermore possessed of considerable expertise in dealing with the Trelawney Maroons."

That gave me jolt, I can tell you. What *service* was he talking about? I got the nasty feeling that much, much more was known about me that ever I'd imagined. He even said the name Boswell with a touch of irony.

"And therefore," says he, "I am conscripting you as adviser to Colonel Sanford, who has asked for you as an informant upon local conditions." I looked again at the officers around Balcarras. They were staring at me curiously, and Sanford was nodding like a Jack-in-the-box.

"The case is, Mr Boswell," says Balcarras, that my scouts," he indicated the two Maroon renegades running along behind, "my scouts inform me that the Trelawneys have resolved to defend their town to the last and refuse all surrender. The women and children are hidden in the cockpit country and the men are taken to the hills. All possibility of peace is thus ended and I shall move against them tomorrow. You will go with Colonel Sanford, Mr Boswell, when he sweeps the ruins of Trelawney Town to drive the Maroons into the arms of the 83rd. You will give him your best advice, sir." And then to my great surprise, he smiled and added, "I am better informed than you know, Mr Boswell. Serve me well and you have little to fear." That's what he said. Those were his words. Though I'm damned if I knew what he was driving at.

"Aye-aye, sir!" says I, in my confusion and the swab laughed loudly at those seamanlike words, and slapped his thigh.

"Good man!" says he.

Shortly after that the main body parted company with his Lordship. He and his staff turned off and headed for Vaughansfield and the 83rd, while Sanford with nearly five hundred sabres, rode on to Spring Vale to join the 62nd and the militia. By nightfall, everything was set for the final extinction of the Trelawney Maroons. Mind you from Springfield onwards, our outriders had been in contact with Trelawney scouts and there was an occasional pop-popping of gunfire: carbine against musket, until we came into camp at Spring Vale. Three of our men were wounded but none seriously.

That night Sanford had me to dine with his officers and pumped me for all I knew of the Trelawney Maroons. He was a highly-intelligent officer; active-minded and vigorous and as good a light cavalrymen as could be. Finally, before we laid ourselves on the ground to sleep, Sanford took me aside.

"You're a young man that fortune smiles upon," says he.

"Eh?" says I, "I mean, what?" He grinned.

"My Quartermaster will see you supplied," says he, "Blanket and field kit, sword and carbine. Or would you prefer a brace of pistols?" This was loose treatment for a man supposed to be a prisoner! But I spoke up fast before he should change his mind.

"Pistols, thank you Colonel!" says I, for a carbine's an abomination: too short to be a proper musket and too clumsy for a hand-to-hand fight.

Next day, Wednesday 12th August, Sanford had us up and paraded before dawn: just over one thousand men almost equally horse and foot. As the sun rose, he made a point of reading Lord Balcarras's orders aloud to the assembled ranks.

The plan was for us to come down upon Trelawney Town from the north and engage the Maroons. Sanford was then to occupy the New Town half of Trelawney Town, having driven the Trelawneys through the narrow defile that led to the Old Town.

Simultaneously, Balcarras would come up from the South with the 83rd and take Old Town. The Trelawney Maroons would then be trapped and defeated. The whole plan was timed by the watch and I could see no fault in it. Even Major James had said the Trelawneys couldn't stand fire in a set-piece engagement with disciplined troops, not even with numbers on their side, and tomorrow they'd be outnumbered two to one, with no option than to fight since they would be defending their homes and families.

What's more, with such a powerful force of cavalry on our side, there was every prospect of a mass slaughter if the Maroons broke and tried to run. The Dragoons among our troops were relishing this opportunity, for the finest dream of your regular light horseman is to put broken infantry to the sword. They'd had the grindstones busy in Montego Bay in eager preparation putting a razor edge on the two-inch wide, curved, stirrup-hilted blades that now hung ready and waiting in their steel scabbards. Indeed I had one, myself courtesy of the Quartermaster of the 20th light. But I wasn't looking forward to the battle quite so much.

In the first place a battle is a damned good place to get yourself killed and I would advise you youngsters to exert yourselves to your uttermost endeavours to avoid ever taking part in one. In the second place, I was wondering just exactly was happening to myself. Was I now a prisoner awaiting trial for wringing Mrs Collins's neck? Or was I not? What had Balcarras meant by '*serve me well and you shall have little to fear*'? and just how much did he know about me?

I worried these thoughts in my mind while Black Tom pounded my arse all the way to Trelawney Town. I was up in the van again, riding with Sanford and Gallimore (who'd finally brought himself to acknowledge me and talk reasonably civil). Like Balcarras, Sanford had some Maroon runners with him and these were out ahead with our own scouts. They weren't renegade Trelawneys as I'd thought but Maroons from distant St Elizabeth. They had no love for the Trelawneys and were ready to sell their services for gold, and it was from one of these gentlemen that we got our first nasty shock. He came bounding back up the road towards us, leaping over stones and ruts and halloing loudly.

"Colonel-sir! Colonel-sir!" says he, "Dem Trelawneys dey burn de town, sir! All in smoke. They took to de hills, sir!"

We were moving up rising ground at the time, with a thick growth of trees ahead, but as we came to the crest and followed the road round a bend, we could see for ourselves. A few miles ahead a great column of smoke was rising from the direction of Trelawney Town.

"They burn de town, Colonel-sir," says the man, scampering beside

Sanford's horse. His eyes were big with the horror of it. The Trelawneys had done what the Russians later did before Boney's Grand Army: they'd destroyed their everything rather than see it taken by the enemy. "All de womens and chilluns gone to de Cockpit country, sir," says the Maroon, "An' de mens done took to de hills!"

"No matter!" says Sanford, "I shall follow my orders none the less. There may still be a force of Maroons waiting to challenge our approach."

So we pressed on until we came within sight of the New Town half of Trelawney when the Infantry manoeuvred from column Into line and were ordered to load and stand fast. From Spring Vale to New Town was about an hour's march at an easy pace to keep the men and horses fresh. So it was still early morning as we watched the fires dying in the ashes of what had been half of the Maroon stronghold. It had never been a grand place and now it looked desperately miserable. Our scouts went forward and picked over the remains and some of them even managed (as soldiers will) to find something worth looting. But there wasn't much. One fellow picked up a prayer book which he thought had gold at the corners of the covers, but it was only brass. I saw it because once the scouts had declared the ground safe, I was ordered forward with Sanford and Gallimore for a reconnaissance.

There wasn't much to see, and apart from getting the stink of wood-smoke into our clothes and hair we didn't achieve much by shuffling through the ashes. And as for the Maroons themselves, there was no mystery as to their whereabouts. Between New Town and Old town there was a range of great hills, going up to a thousand feet. Up on these steep slopes, well out of musket range, the Maroons were present in great numbers. We could hear them yelling insults and waving their cutlasses and firearms. They were blowing on conch shells too: a deep booming notes that carry like a bugle-call.

Down in the ruins, I felt exposed and liable to be picked off by a sharpshooter. The fact that we couldn't see any of them nearby, didn't at all mean they weren't sneaking down to take a pot shot. Maroons could hide behind a pebble or a blade of grass. But Sanford ignored any threat and took his time and came to his conclusions.

"We shall occupy the provision grounds, there," says he, pointing to an area of level ground where the Maroons had grown their food, "That will give maximum advantage to our musketry should the enemy come upon us, and prevent our being surprised. Our scouts will pass through the defile to Old Town and advise me of Lord Balcarras's arrival. We shall then effect a junction in Old Town."

In other words he was at a loss as to what to do next. The Maroons weren't acting according to plan. They'd been expected to come out and fight, and now they were hiding up in the hills where we'd be led a merry dance and lose men in scores, should we be foolish enough to chase them. So we rode out of the ruins, and took our station on the provision grounds as our Maroon scouts went forward.

"Got to admire the bastards for pluck," says a planter volunteer looking at the scouts, "Shouldn't like to be in their skins if the Trelawneys catch 'em."

"Shouldn't like to be in our skins if they catch us!" says another and there began a most unpleasant conversation on how Maroons dealt with prisoners; a conversation that I chose to ignore.

So there on the provision grounds our five hundred foot and five hundred horse, waited out most of the day. As the hours passed, food and water was brought up from the commissary wagons, the foot were allowed to take off their packs, and the horse dismounted. All the while the Maroons could be seen like busy ants shifting about up in the heights and calling and waving. But they showed not the slightest inclination to come down and fight. Then, late in the afternoon, Sanford got fed up waiting.

"Gentlemen," says he, to his officers, "I am convinced these fellows constitute no threat," he waved at the Maroons with the small telescope he'd been using to study them, "However formidable they are by repute, I see they have no stomach to engage formed bodies of troops. I am therefore inclined to pass through the defile into Old Town and join his Lordship, whom we must presume is delayed."

There was a busy argument at that, and some of the planter volunteers were firmly against going through to Old Town, but the regulars sneered at this as a lack of spirit and things were evenly balanced. Then Sanford picked me out, despite the fact that I was trying to hide at the back, for I'd no real idea of what was best.

"Mr Boswell!" says he, "We've not heard your voice in the matter. What would you advise?" Pressed with the need to declare something, and since the way to Montego Bay and the sea, lay through Old Town, I gave them Major John James's view on the inability of Maroons to face disciplined musketry.

"And he knows them better than any man alive," says I.

"My own view precisely," says Sanford, "Gentlemen, we march!"

The troops were delighted at this, for they'd lost all fear of men who pranced about the side of a hill and hadn't the stomach for a fight. And they were fed up with doing nothing besides. But as soon as they heard the news, the maroon scouts instantly deserted, even though this meant formfitting every penny of their pay. And that wasn't good news. Not good at all.

CHAPTER 19

As soon as the redcoats had got their packs on, there was a rolling of drums, colours were unfurled, and with the 62nd in the lead the infantry stepped out for the short march into Old Town. A small band of fifers struck up *Tom Tom the Piper's Son* and the men sang along with the tune. In front of them rode the 20th and the 18th with Sanford, Gallimore and myself, and bringing up the rear was the planter volunteer Horse.

The Maroons rose to their feet as one man, the minute we marched off and you could see the little figures up above, pointing and calling to one another. Then an odd thing happened. They all disappeared. One second you could see them, and the next they'd dropped out of sight and gone to ground.

Tom, Tom the Piper's son,
Stole a pig and away he run!
The pig was eat and Tom was beat,
And he went howling down the street!
Rum-tum-tum
Rum-tum-tum,
Rumatum-rumatum,
Rum-tum-tum!

Through the ashes of New Town we went in grand style and the front rank of the 20th passed into the ravine that lead to Old Town. It was about half a mile long, with a track some twenty yards wide at the bottom, and steeply shelving sides that went up and up on either hand. The slopes were well covered with boulders and short stumpy bushes and long grass.

The 20th's scouts dug in their heels and put their horses to the slopes on either side. With a scraping of hooves, the animals laboured up and fanned out, looking for an ambush.

Rum-tum-tum,
Rum-tum-tum!

The 20th were entirely in the ravine and the 18th followed. Sanford and I and the other officers were with them. Not a Maroon was there to be seen. Not anywhere and I was looking hard, believe me.

I looked back down the column and saw the 62nd follow us in, the men still singing. Then the militia infantry were in and the planter volunteers, and the whole thousand men of us were stretched out along the bottom of the ravine: stretched out and crammed in. Muskets were shouldered, carbines hanging on their slings and swords sheathed, and most every man was cheerful.

What happened next came with shocking speed. There was a blast of conch-shells and Maroons stood up in their hundreds all around us, not more than a dozen yards from the track. How they'd got so close without our seeing them is little short of magical, but by George they'd done it. About twenty of them, ten on either side, were clustered about Sanford and his staff. Without a word. they ran forward until their musket barrels were mere feet away from us and fired together in a volley. I suspect I owe my life to the fact that I was the only man in that group not in a red coat, and a plumed hat, for damn near every man who was, got blown out of the saddle in a cloud of white powder smoke.

B-B-Bang! Roared the twenty muskets and the column lost its senior officers in that single, well planned instant. Sanford went over with a ball in his side and half his jaw hanging in a rag of red meat. Black Tom screamed in fright and reared high in the air, as the hot powder grains burned his skin and the muzzle-flashes scorched his eyes. He kicked and bit in all directions, bowling over two or three Maroons even as they tried to reload. One got his big hoof square in the face and was a dead man for sure.

I fought to stay aboard him, and saw the astonishing discipline of a Maroon attack: these people who we'd supposed unable to face formed troops. They were delivering vollies *down the length* of the column, so every musket ball must strike at least one man. They were formed up into companies of twenty to thirty men posted at regular intervals down the ravine. First the company nearest the head of the column would run in and fire, close as could be to our men, then the next would run and fire, then the next and the next, like a man-o-war giving a ripple broadside. That way they kept up a continuous fire and didn't get in each other's way.

And all the time their best marksmen were darting up and down the column, acting extempore to nip out any remaining officer or sergeant who looked like rallying his men. These men were simply without fear. They ignored their own fire or anything directed back at them, and their method was simplicity itself. The Maroon would mark his man: some poor devil of a lieutenant or a colour sergeant, bawling at his men to stand firm and give fire, the Maroon would run in close as he could get and ... Bang! The victim was dead meat.

The effect was devastating. Deprived of their officers, packed together like rats in a pit and with comrades falling on either side, the 62nd and the militia reeled and staggered and fired aimlessly at targets they could barely see. The Cavalry weren't much better. They drew swords and tried to charge up the steep sides of the ravine, but it was useless. The slope was too great and the nimble-footed Maroons moved faster than the Dragoons. A horse makes a fine target, too, especially when it's staggering and sliding and stumbling, so the screams of dying horses rose over that of the men and wildly kicking animals tumbled over on their riders and rolled down into the chaotic ranks on the path, confounding confusion still further.

By dint of brute force, I got some control over Black Tom and turned him forward to the far end of the ravine and safety, but just as I was about to urge him on, there came a great rush of men from behind me. The redcoats had broken and were running in panic all around me. Some were even throwing down their muskets and casting off their packs, all the better to run. Tom kicked out madly again as the bodies pressed against him and shoved by. One man tried to meet his black hide with a bayonet, but down he went with a hoof in his chest.

Then Jarvis Gallimore was at my side, with his sword in his hand, fighting to control his own horse and yelling something at me. Such was the din of screams, gunfire and cries around me that I barely heard what he was saying, but he pointed with his sword up the side of the ravine and bellowed at me to:

"Follow or be damned you bloody shop-keeper!"

159

They'd missed him when they killed Sanford and now he was charging the slope with his sword extended, stiff-armed in the approved manner. And then I saw what he was after.

Standing with his head thrown back and a big black book in one hand, was that infernal swine Vernon Hughes. His long, gaunt figure stuck out like a nine-inch nail in a table-top. His white hair streamed about his face and he was clearly in the upper reaches of ecstasy. He was waving his arms and mouthing words at the sky and I supposed the bugger to be praying.

No doubt he thought his longed-for slaughter of the whites was that very day commenced. Gallimore was out to kill him, and in that instant it seemed a jolly fine thing to do, so I kicked away at Black Tom and made to follow Gallimore. But Tom had other ideas and wouldn't go, and drawing sword while mounted was damned near the limits of what I could achieve, so round we went in a tight circle, knocking down terrified soldiers left and right, with Tom rolling his eyes and me tugging away at my curved blade.

As I came round again, I saw Gallimore's arm go up, bend at the elbow, and then sweep down with his glittering sword. But Maroon muskets went off close by and Gallimore's horse foundered under him. I lost sight for a moment as Tom went round again, and then suddenly my sword came free, and Tom decided that we were going up the side of the ravine after all. Two or three strides of his long legs and we were in the middle of Gallimore's last stand. Maroons had pulled him from his fallen horse and were hacking at him with their cutlasses. He was already a lost man.

His sword was gone and his two arms were off at the elbows where he'd lifted them in protection, and blood spouting from the stumps. He roared and bellowed as a blade, swung by a muscular brown arm split his face from brow to chin, and choked off short as another blow finished him. Vernon Hughes had pitched in beside the Maroons and was jabbing away at Gallimore with his own sword, and without much effect but screeching in triumph with every stroke.

Taken by surprise, one Maroon was knocked spinning by the arrival of Tom's heavy chest and I caught something a heavy cut with my sword. I think it was a Maroon but I ain't sure, and it could have been Gallimore's horse. I'm a strong and dangerous swordsman on land or with a solid deck under my feet, but it's a damned hard art to master, is sabering a man from the back of a horse.

Then Vernon Hughes caught sight of me and I'm sure the swab recognised me for he screamed out something about,

"Beelzebub," and "Profiting by the traffic in death," and he took a fearful swing at me with Gallimore's sword, but he bodged his stroke worse than I'd just done. He stumbled and spun round as he all but missed me and Tom, connecting with just the utmost tip of his blade which nicked the horse's neck and threw him into a madder rage than ever. But my blood was up too and I took a swipe at Hughes as Tom snorted and bucked and tried to get all four feet off the ground at once. But Hughes came on again, and missed again staring at me all the while with his round, maniac eyes.

And so the clumsy pair of us bodged about hacking and slashing: a coin's toss as to which of us was the worst at it. But finally I got in a good one. A really corking swing with all my weight behind it, that smacked home, fat and beefy alongside of his neck. The blade sliced through his collar bone, and deep down into the chest. Down he went, the filthy, screeching, lunatic bastard, dead before he hit the floor! Best possible thing for him if you ask me, as even Jesus would agree, and a damned shame it'd not been done to him years ago.

But that was all that Tom and I saw of the battle in the ravine, because Tom decided we'd had enough and he put down his head and charged for freedom. By good fortune he was pointing the way I wanted to go and so we forged through the wreckage of the 62nd foot and the militia: the dead and the dying, the brave and the cowardly, those fleeing in panic and those who spat on their hands and turned to fight.

Thanks to Tom's size and strength, we came safe out of the ravine at the head of a rabble of horsemen and some soldiers who were keeping up by hanging on to the stirrup leathers of those who'd allow 'em, though there were horseman who turned to the sword and hacked the poor devils off, being determined in their panic that nothing should slow down their escape. Once through the ravine we came into the Old Town: a burned out wreck just the same as New Town, and found Lord Balcarras and the 83rd nowhere in sight.

Since the Maroons didn't pursue us beyond the ravine, there was a recovery of sorts on the far side of what was left of Old Town, and the few officers that had escaped the Maroons, knocked their men together. One Captain of the 62nd especially distinguished himself and had those of his men who'd got away (about half, as far as I could judge) form ranks and stand with commendable steadiness as an example to the rest.

But it didn't last. The whole column was shaken and by what had happened and at least a third had been killed or wounded. Few people today have heard of the battle of Trelawney Town but it must be one of finest thrashings that British troops ever took from so-called savages.

And it wasn't over yet, neither. Despite the 62nd's example and a half-hearted forming of ranks by the rest, there was a general and inexorable movement towards the road that lead to Vaughansfield, down which road Lord Balcarras must surely be coming with the 83rd. It was only two miles to Vaughansfield, but it was late in the day and it would soon be dark, and those who knew the Maroons had told those who didn't that there'd be sneak attacks and throats cut once the sun went down.

The few officers left could not hold back the men and there followed a barely-controlled rout along the road as the remnants of Sanford's column scuttled away with their tails between their legs. It crossed my mind once or twice to take command. I could have done it too because I have all the necessary qualifications in my two hands and strength. I don't need no gold lace nor a gorget.

But why should I do it? Why should I fight the Maroons? The best that Jamaica now held for me was the certainly of a trial for murder and the possibility (only the possibility mind) that I might get off. No, I was heading up the road to Vaughansfield and Montego Bay harbour.

The last thing I saw of Trelawney Town was that not a Maroon was in sight. They'd disappeared again and I wondered where they were gone. But I didn't wonder long. The road to Vaughansfield ran through thickly-wooded country and the moment the trees and the undergrowth closed in, those demons were at our heels again, probably having placed men in ambush on the road well before the attack in the ravine, so they were waiting with hit-and-run fire as we came.

There couldn't have been many of them at first, and it was just the occasional shot, always taking effect: a man dead or screaming with a smashed limb. But soon the firing grew fiercer and I suspect men were coming up from Trelawney Town to join in. The only thing that held back the column from a headlong flight was the fear of being out in front alone, with the Maroons all around. So we stumbled along, with men firing away their ammunition into the trees and hitting nothing, while the Maroons killed us in ones and twos as they pleased.

Finally two things happened at once. At long last the drums of the 83rd could be heard coming down the road, and the first torrential rains of the season came battering down upon our heads.

Tap-Tap! Ratatat-tat! The side drums around the bend ahead, caused a glad cry to rise up from the half-crazed, disordered mob of mixed-together horse, foot and stragglers all around me. The hope of rescue surged within them and their eyes widened in joy. In an instant, they broke forward, swarming over their few officers and poured stumbling and sliding forward under a darkening sky, sodden wet and shining grey and silver in the little light that remained.

Tom went forward with them, biting and kicking all the way to clear a space around him and leaping to catch up those who were ahead (I'd kept him as near the centre of the rout as could be, reasoning this to be the safest place). Muskets were still banging and flashing in numbers from the wet, gleaming bushes and men were going down under Tom's hoofs either shot or simply unfooted in the churned-up mire that had been a path but a few minutes ago. What's more, the Maroons were getting bolder and you could actually see 'em now: naked muscular figures, wet and slick in the stinging downpour, as they darted out singly from the undergrowth to butcher some poor devil with a couple of slashes before leaping for cover again.

Round the bend we ran, howling and staring, and slap into the 83rd's light company extended in open order with firelocks at the ready. They were bowled over like skittles and driven back upon the main body, coming on six abreast, shoulder-to-shoulder at seventy-five paces the minute. For a second I saw the impressive regularity of the long lines of steel-tipped musket barrels, rising vertically in a great hedge, and then it was all knocked to a bugger's muddle as our rout smashed into their steady advance.

I can't pretend to give a clear account of what happened next. For one thing it was getting darker by the second, for another the rain come down so heavy that you could hardly think, but mainly the jumble and press of men was so tight, and the struggling and fighting so universal that only disjointed impressions remain.

"Where was you y'bastards?" screams a soldier of the 62nd seizing a corporal of the 83rd by the throat.

"Waitin' on 'is fuckin' Lordship!" cries the corporal, and smashed his fist into the other man's face. "Fell orf of a fuckin' log, makin' a fuckin' speech, an' stove his fuckin' head in!"

(And that my lads is exactly what had happened and is exactly the way great events are sometimes decided. Not by grand acts of policy but by some silly devil slipping in a puddle and stunning himself. At least Balcarras survived.)

Then the Maroon fire cracked and banged again, up and down the road and I saw some of the 83rd, here and there, with a semblance of order try to return fire. But their muskets were drenched and the locks snapped uselessly. Not one in ten gave fire. God knows how the Maroons kept their powder dry. I suppose they were more used to the rains than our men, and perhaps they had more shelter under the trees.

In the awful confusion the planters and the militia simply fought to get away, but you could see the 83rd and the 62nd trying to load sodden firelocks under their blankets or torn-open tunics. Anything for relief from the rain. Tom stamped and pranced and suddenly we were at the roadside with the foliage brushing my head. Out leaped a Maroon and up came his musket to shoot me dead. Flash-bang! But Tom reared up and the ball whizzed by and Tom jerked his head down and forward like a striking snake and bit the wretch in the belly.

He screamed in agony and Tom swung him from side to side and I cut at him with my sword, every time I got a chance and between us, by the time we were done with him, he was the deadest Maroon in Jamaica just you believe me! Then there were more bangs, more flashes, more screaming, more rain, near total darkness and Black Tom decided he'd had enough. He dropped the Maroon and charged flat out down the black-dark road tearing through everything, man or beast that stood in his way. For a while there were bone-jarring collisions and the beast stumbled fearfully once or twice and screamed like pig at the butcher's. I hung on by blind faith, and then he was clear.

The ghastly rout faded behind us and the only sound was the regular pounding of Tom's hooves and the unremitting hissing of the rain. I could see next to nothing, I threw away my sword the better to hang on and the pair of us were in Black Tom's hands, or rather his feet, for it was him that was in charge now, and not me. He galloped all the way home as far as I can recall, and I've no idea how long it took. I had no watch nor could I have consulted it if I'd had one. The simple fact is that we on the road just as long it takes an exceptionally strong horse to cover a dozen miles at his best speed, and you can work out for yourselves how long that takes.

He didn't stop till he came to Montego Bay and the door of his own stable in the yard at Mr Prescott's the Farrier, whose pride and joy Tom was. Once I was sure the beast had really stopped, I eased myself off him at got well clear of his hind legs. Tom shuddered and snorted as I made fast his reins by a clove hitch to a nearby rail. His breath blasted out from his nostrils. His mad eyes rolled white around the edges, studying me and he let fly with a vicious kick. But I was expecting that and he missed. He didn't try to bite though, by which token I knew he wished me personally, no more special ill-will than he did all of mankind in general.

I was so tired that I crawled into the shelter of a barn and slept for a while in a corner before the storm woke me and I hobbled away through the night, looking enviously at the lights in Mr Prescott's windows and made my way down to the harbour. At first I'd hoped to get into Lee and Boswell's for my things, but to my intense disappointment it was obvious that I'd slept too long, and I was now very far from being the only man home from the disaster at Trelawney Town.

Riders were going up and down the town, doors were opening and lanterns waving. Even at night in the pouring rain, the town was coming alive. There were even soldiers about: those of the 83rd who'd been left to guard the town. There was fear in the air too.

"The town's lost!" says a quavering voice, calling to a neighbour, "Balcarras and all his men are killed and the Maroons are risen. The slaves are joining them!"

"I'm for the harbour!" says another voice. "Before the Maroons come upon us. Bring your family and I'll take 'em with mine, in our boat. But none else mind!"

"God bless you!" says the other "We'll come at once!"

"Be quick!" says the first man, the terror coming upon him.

I stood in the deep shadows, soaked to the bone and decided that time was short. I headed straight for the harbour at a run. I didn't know if the Maroons were indeed coming, but I didn't intend to find out. I resolved, at any cost, to beg, fight, threaten or steal my way aboard a boat and trust to fortune once at sea. One way or another it was farewell to Jamaica.

CHAPTER 20

If I'd paused for thought I'd have gone back once more to Lee and Boswell's for my goods and my money (especially my money) left where I'd laid them. But I didn't. I was tired and aching from my adventures on horseback and I was confused too. Was I under threat of recapture or was I not? What had Balcarras meant with his hints of assistance? Was I being looked out for by any of the soldiers and other armed men staggering about in the mud that night, under the streaming rain? Perhaps they'd plenty else to think about with the Maroons about to fall upon Montego Bay, or perhaps not.

But I certainly wasn't going to find out the hard way, so I turned up my coat collar, pulled my hat around my ears and headed for the harbour. The town was in a terror and no mistake. Hordes of people were trying to get into the fort; whole families, mainly blacks, with their bundles of possessions. But the fort was already cram-full of humanity and the gates barred against newcomers. I kept clear of this and passed them by, hiding my face and glad of the dark. But I heard the ugly cries of anger, and the pleading and crying out of those outside the walls. There were screams too, as those inside fought to keep them from scaling the gates. It sounded as if some brisk work with the bayonet was under way.

I hurried on faster and left the fort and the town centre behind. At the big splendid bay that gave the town its name, I kept away from the wharves for I guessed that's where I'd be most likely to run into the Royal Navy. The transports anchored in the bay with its accompanying warships would likely use the wharves as landing places for their boats. Also there were a few wooden shacks by the wharves which the Excise men and the Harbour Master, dignified with the name of offices.

I was right, too. There was another crowd of desperate folk at the wharves, trying to get out to the ships, and a line of marines and seaman holding them back. It was the same as what was going on at the Fort, and a ghastly thing it is too. I've seen the like many times since in many other places where the people are terrified of something unspeakably terrible that's about to fall upon them, and they're desperate to escape it, and to get away by any means, and not be left behind. In this case it was the Maroons, but it could be Cossacks, a Zulu impi or Jappo Samurai that's *coming*, and the result is the same, and the special horror of it is the ordinary little folk in their terror, the which is a more shocking thing to see, even than broken soldiers.

And if you don't believe me, then I'd ask you to think of your old grandmother, or the fat gentleman with a bad leg who lives next door, or your grocer's pretty young wife with her babies wrapped in a shawl and them bawling their eyes out. Think on the likes of them, my jolly boys, in the black night, in the heavy rain, with strong young men beating 'em back with musket-butts so's they can't get into boats that are already overladen and full.

There was no way through there, even if I could risk facing the Navy. So I hurried away to where the fishermen hauled their boats up on the beach, safe from the tide. The rain eased off at about that time and the smell of the sea was powerful strong and the taste of salt and seaweed was in my mouth.

But here were the boats! And men busy heaving them down to the water on skids, all of them blacks of one shade or another, and you could hear their deep voices chanting the time as they threw their weight together to shift the stubborn weight of the timbers. Waiting beside the men were groups of women and children and old folk: the families of the fishermen.

"I'll give a hand!" says I and shoved forward towards the nearest boat. I took a heaving line and was about to pull, when a couple of men stepped forward and shoved their faces close to mine. They were standing guard and each had a heavy cutlass in his hand and death in his eyes. The other men never even stopped in their chanting as they drew the boat down to the sea, foot by foot, like Egyptian slaves dragging a block to build a pyramid.

"No, Cap'n!" says the first man, a big chap with greying hair. The other looked like his son. "You go 'way Cap'n and you don't come to no harm! Only *we* families in dis boat: see?" He jabbed his thumb at his womenfolk and nippers. There weren't room for me, that was clear. I hesitated and they raised their blades. I was unarmed and there were two of them. I dropped the line and stepped back.

This looked grim and I thought of the pistols left at Lee and Boswell's. Should I go back for them? Would there be time? The boats were half-way down to the water by now. And what if I had the barkers? Could I force my way aboard and stay aboard? I'd most likely get a knife in the back the moment I dropped my guard. So I was going from boat to boat, not knowing what to do when there came the sound of feet pounding the sand and a file of soldiers came round the black shape of a steadily-moving hull.

"You there!" cries a voice, obviously an officer, "Halt!" I turned to run but that's not easy on soft sand, especially when a man's as tired as I was. To tell the truth I hadn't the heart to run, anyway. For where should I go? And so, they had a ring of levelled bayonets round me in an instant.

"Fletcher!" says the officer, a young Lieutenant of the 83rd, "You are Jacob Fletcher, known as Boswell." It wasn't a question, it was a statement. The lad looked excited and pleased with himself. I must have been longer hiding in Montego Bay than I'd thought, for not only had the rains stopped, but the dawn was coming up and I could see the expression on his face. Over his shoulder I noticed that one or two of the boats were into the surf. They were raising up the women and children to get them safe aboard before shoving off. My chance of escape was slipping away.

The officer looked back towards the wharf and the customs house. He was waiting for something. His men grinned at me, as men do who've caught a prisoner and are pleased with themselves. There were only four of them and maybe their muskets were soaked by the rains. If so, I might chance snatching a musket and setting about them. But I saw the greasy rags freshly cast off the firelocks. They'd kept their priming dry as good soldiers should. I sighed and sat down in the sand. Boats were now leaping out over the waves, to the pull of their oars.

Then there came a scrunch, scrunch, scrunch of footsteps and I looked up to see a truly amazing sight. Stepping across the sand towards me came a procession of slaves carrying a train of luggage, a file of ten redcoats to keep them from running, and at the head, somewhat bedraggled by the recent rains but still every inch the grand English madame, came my stepmother, Lady Sarah Coignwood. I leapt to my feet on the instant and my four guards stepped back and cocked their muskets.

She glared at me and I glared back. By George it gave me a nasty turn to see her. The last time I'd set eyes on her had been in London over a year ago when I thought I'd seen her shot through the skull and fall dead at my feet. But if I took a fright, then so did she, only more so, I'm pleased to say! The fact is that the creature not only hated me for running a cutlass through her eldest son (dirty, murdering, foul-minded, back-stabbing, shirt-lifter that he was) but she thought I was my father re-incarnated, would you believe, because I look so like him. Well I'm his natural son, ain't I? What did the spiteful cow expect?

Well, she took one look at me and all the fancy airs vanished and she damn near fainted. She staggered and went corpse white and her hand went up to her mouth. Serve her right, damn her. I only wish the sight of me had turned her to stone.

But here's the rub. Call me a garlic-breathing Frog, if I ain't forced to admit that she was a splendid bitch. By God she was! Some lovely women (like Katy Booth) have a fairy look to them, that appeals to a man's finer thoughts so he dreams of romance and poetry and wants to set the lady up on high to worship her. All well and good, but other women have an entirely different look about them that sends a man hot under the collar and fills him with the desire to grab hold of the bouncy bits and tumble her into bed. And that, my lads, was what Sarah Coignwood had to a most incredible degree. That was the source of her power over men.

She recovered her poise before I did, too, damn her.

"Ah!" says she, "Well done Lieutenant!" She wrenched her eyes off me and peered at the boats. One was still not yet launched.

"You will commandeer that craft at once!" says she, "Send those fellows," she waved her hands at the men guarding her luggage porters.

"Set to it!" bawls the Lieutenant, who was all too clearly under madame's power and bursting to impress her at all costs. The men set off. fast as they could and stopped the boat with levelled muskets, just as its bows were getting wet. The baggage thudded into the sand the instant the guards left, as the porters took to their heels along the beach.

"My lady," says the Lieutenant, looking doubtful, "Cannot I persuade you even now, to abandon this course and take a boat out to the fleet?" He pointed to the waiting vessels anchored in the bay. "In your case there could be no impediment to your being taken aboard." She smiled and silenced him with a soft gesture, laying her hand upon his arm. You could see the poor devil melting into his boots at this.

"Duty forbids!" says she and pointed to myself with a disdainful finger, "Only the hand of Providence could have contrived the chance that caused me to recognise this monster, as I was in the very act of entering a boat to go out to the fleet." She was telling the simple truth, I could see it. If she'd only looked the other way she'd have missed me. "And so," says she, "I knew it my duty to personally apprehend Mr Fletcher, and take him in charge."

"But my lady," says the Lieutenant, "His Lordship commanded me to secure your safety. He said…"

"Dear boy!" says she, "But I shall be safe! For you and I, and some of your men, shall take that boat," she looked at the fishing boat with its ring of redcoats, "And we shall go out to the flagship where I shall be received into the safe protection of the Navy, and Mr Fletcher shall be chained in irons among the filth of the lower decks, where he belongs." She looked me in the eye and smiled a fierce unnatural smile, "Until such time, I pray, as we shall see him hoist up off his feet to decorate the *yard-beams*, or *crossed-arms* or suchlike apparatus," says she affecting a disdainful ignorance of naval parlance.

And by George, that's just what she aimed to do, and no mistake. She had the soldiers jumping in double time. With the officer yelping like her poodle, they charged down to the sea. Four men were set on me, prodding with bayonets to keep me moving, and under orders to slay me on the spot should I show fight. The buggers drew blood with their jabbing and there was not a thing I could do.

Five men were sent back for the train of baggage, while the rest covered the boat's people with their firelocks. There was a deal of screaming and yelling at this stage, and jabbering and waving of arms from the skipper, stood at the tiller, and from the boat's crew, standing by to launch, and from the women and little-uns already embarked. They were full of terror of the Maroons and wanted to be away out to sea, and the whole circus of 'em cried out that there was no room in the boat. But the Lieutenant bawled a command and a thundering volley of musket shots over their cringing heads, filled the air with white smoke and convinced them that there was room after all.

The soldiers plied their ramrods, Lady Sarah was hoist up over the high gunwale, her luggage followed, the Lieutenant clambered up over the knapsack of the bent-double back of one of his men. I was forced to climb aboard with muskets at my back and the Lieutenant's pistols in my face. Three more redcoats followed us into the boat and the fisherman cried and protested afresh that we should be swamped, and we'd all be drowned.

"Then out with them!" cries that she-devil, meaning the fishermen's families, "You!" says she to one of the soldiers, "Throw them out!" The redcoat gaped at his officer and at the screaming women. Round the boat, the fishermen roared with anger and pulled their knives and cutlasses. Bang! A redcoat fired and missed and swung with his musket-but. A general fight broke out around the boat.

But ... Boom! Boom! Came the sound of heavy guns from the direction of the town, and a sudden rolling volley of small-arms fire. A thick wave of fear rolled down the beach and over the boat.

"Maroons! Maroons!" cries everyone.

"Launch de boat!" cries the skipper.

"Launch the bloody boat!" cries the Lieutenant. The fighting snuffed out instantly, blacks and redcoats heaved together. The boat ground forward over her rollers. Men splashed thigh-deep in the salt sea. The morning sun fell hot upon us. Powder smoke rose over the town. The boat took to the water. Her bows swung up to ride the first wave.

The fisherman scrambled aboard, nimble as monkeys. The soldiers tried to follow, in their heavy coats and weighed down with their packs. Some got aboard but the fishermen beat savagely on the fingers of the others, as they fumbled for the gunwale, and clumsy as they were and weighed down by their kit, they were left wallowing in or out of their depth as the fishermen bent to their oars and drove us plunging out into the bay. For honour's sake, the young Lieutenant made a show of bawling at the fishermen to go back for the men left behind, but they simply ignored him, and the other redcoats were so anxious to be off that they managed not to notice their mates wallowing in the surf. So the Lieutenant sighed and damned, and learned a bit about himself, and gave it up as a bad job.

The bows and the waist of the boat were crammed with the fishermen and their families, all busy making sail. The stern was full of the skipper, Lady Sarah, her baggage, myself and the Lieutenant and the three of his men who'd got aboard. They staggered about and grabbed at one another in the unfamiliar, bounding boat and eventually sat down, looking nervous.

But they kept hold of their muskets and kept 'em pointing in my direction. And the Lieutenant even checked the priming on his pistols and poured dry powder into one, which he wasn't happy with.

"You! Boatman!" cries Lady Sarah, "You will go that way," she pointed to the old 64 that was the flagship of the-squadron. It was about half a mile off on our larboard beam. The skipper grumbled and cursed and wanted to be away to Port Antonio which he declared to be safe from the Trelawney Maroons, but the Lieutenant stuck a pistol in his ribs and gave him his orders sharply. The skipper sniffed the wind and eyed the set of his sail. The breeze was fresh and we could be alongside the flagship in a matter of minutes, and then I'd be precisely where that woman had said, viz: in irons on the lower deck, awaiting a Navy hanging.

But first the boat would have to come about on the other tack. I looked at my guards and hoped they were as unused to boats as they seemed.

"Stay-shuns!" says the skipper and his crew readied themselves for going about. He edged her a little closer to the wind, till the sail was taught and full and the boat running smartly through the water heeled well over on the larboard tack. I watched him make his judgment, and put down the helm.

"Helms-a-lee!" says he in a high sing-song note. At once there came a thundering of canvas as we came through the eye of the wind and a swinging of the boom and a rolling of the hull as she came over on to the opposite tack, nearly putting her lee gunwale under in the sharp smartness of the manoeuvre. At the very most, I was now only five minutes from the Navy's power and the Navy's vengeance. They'd stretch my neck without a doubt.

But the deep rolling of the vessel and the suddenness of it, so easy and familiar to seafaring men, were fearfully alarming to landmen. The Lieutenant and his three redcoats gasped, grabbed out for hand-holds and slid or stumbled to leeward. So did Sarah Coignwood. The fight was short and nasty. One of the soldiers had his bayonet in his hand for just such an emergency and he nearly had me, the rascal, while I was busy trying to clap the heads of his mates together. But I was half on top of him at the time and, by God's mercy, I managed to get my knee on his grapes and crushed 'em into the hard timbers of a thwart.

"Aaaaaaah!" he screamed, and the tears spurted from his eyes. Bang! Bang! Went the Lieutenant's pistols, as he let fly, scorching the back of my neck with the flash of the first and nailing one of his own men through the elbow and into the chest, with the second. Then he and that vile woman tripped over one another as they leapt at me, just as I finished pounding the last man senseless. The Lieutenant had his sword drawn and La Belle Madame was levelling a neat little silver-mounted pistol.

He was a trained man, and tried to shove her aside, the better to steady his blade for a lethal thrust (and all credit to him for his calmness in action) but La Belle Madame wouldn't have it. She shrieked with rage, cursed him foully, and actually bit his arm to make him let go and get out of her way! And so, what with their confusion and the motion of the boat, they clashed and tangled and went over into my very lap. All I had to do was seize each head swiftly by the hair, jerk it up from the bottom of the boat, and ... Thud! Thud! All was quiet again.

And now, you'll think me boastful. You'll disbelieve I overcame four men unaided. But why not? Couldn't *you* beat four children at fisticuffs? Well, so it is with me and four ordinary men, and I claim no credit for it. I'm just too strong. So, if ever you get one like me under armed guard, then instantly shoot him dead while you've still got the chance.

As I sat in the bottom of that boat, with red coated bodies all around and under me, and one silk-clad woman, I looked up at the skipper and his crew and his women and children and fumbled for Sarah Coignwood's little pistol, and the Lieutenant's sword. They were gaping open-mouthed and wondering what to do next, and the boat was bouncing along with a fair turn of speed and her bowsprit pointing at the ensigns of the anchored squadron. That wouldn't do at all.

"Belay that course!" says I with a mighty roar, "Bring her about and steer for Port Antonio!"

"Aye-aye, Cap'n!" says the skipper, with a grin, "Hands to stay-shuns!" and he brought her back on her original course, northwards out of Montego Bay and around to the east, to follow the coast to his destination a hundred miles away. They even raised a cheer for me and never a drop of need was there for me to use the weapons I'd taken up. They were going where they wanted after all.

But I wasn't going with them. Their course took them by Morgan's Bay and the good ship *Amiability* where Mr Francis Stanley owed me a great favour. What's more, with the defeat and rout of its main body of white troops, the island of Jamaica was about to descend into an orgy of rebellion and bloody murder. At least, that's what I was going to tell

Stanley. Whatever might truly be afoot[8] my plan was that Stanley should thank me for the warning and be only too grateful to up anchor and head for America, taking me with him.

So I gave the skipper his orders and he agreed willingly. Meanwhile his crew were busy with the redcoats, emptying their pockets and pilfering their kit. Fair enough, I thought, but then they got ready to heave them over the side.

"Avast there!" says I, as the first one went over, for I couldn't have that and was obliged to step forward and knock down the fellows who were dragging the Lieutenant's limp form to the gunwale. I hoped it was the dead 'un who'd gone over, but it wasn't. He was still in the boat. So I kicked the skipper and made him put about and go back. But it was no good. We found the redcoat all right, but he was face down and drowned. So we left him and set course for Morgan's Bay once more. I was furious with the fishermen and knocked a few more down, to screams and tears from the women, but I couldn't see helpless men treated like that, now, could I? I wouldn't let the fishermen break into madame's baggage either, just to show who was master.

By the time we reached Montego Bay, the Lieutenant and the surviving redcoat were sitting in the bottom of the boat, holding their heads and moaning weakly. I considered binding them, but I'd got their weapons and they were in no fit state to give trouble without them. Her precious ladyship was still unconscious, though unfortunately she was breathing steadily and what with that and the disarray of her garments, her breasts rose and fell most interestingly, damn her. In fact the fisherman began to show an altogether unseemly fascination in the phenomenon and I had to order them about their business.

As we came alongside of *Amiability* I saw the *Plunger* stowed amidships and the longboat secured astern. No diving was under way and the crew lined the rail looking on curiously. Stanley and Captain Marlow waved and hailed me in the most cordial fashion, as we came under their quarter.

"Boswell!" says Stanley, "What is it, my boy?"

"Slave revolt," says I, "Jamaica is lost and the garrison slaughtered! We

---

8   Jamaica was spared any greater disaster. The Maroon attack on Montego Bay was weak and poorly led. The fort stood firm and there was no general rising of slaves, since they took no common cause with the Maroons. Lord Balcarras recovered from his fall, reformed his troops and prosecuted a successful campaign against the Trelawneys. S.P.

must be away at once, before they come after us. Every other vessel in Montego Bay is taken, and all the island knows you are here with a cargo of gold. We must expect pursuit within the hour!"

Well, I had to tell a good tale, didn't I? I wanted to be over the horizon by nightfall. It was America for me.

"Jehovah!" says Stanley.

"Tarnation!" says Morley, and thumped the rail with his fist, "Get aboard, Boswell and bring your people," He turned at once to his first mate, "Mr Laurence!" says he, "Make ready for sea! All hands!"

"Best slip your cables, Cap'n!" says I, "We've little time. They're bound to come for the gold."

"Are you sure?" says Morley, for he'd four anchors down and anchors and cables come expensive.

"That I am, air!" says I and hauled myself up the side by the line they'd lowered and clambered over the rail. Unfortunately, things then got deuced awkward.

"But your people, Mr Boswell?" says Stanley, "And I see a lady among them!"

"Ah…" says I floundering for words. What I wanted to say was "Leave 'em rot!" but I couldn't say that, could I? Morley peered at the red coats in the boat and misunderstood my embarrassment.

"Bring 'em aboard, Mr Boswell!" says Morley, "I see those gentlemen are in your King's service, but the damn war don't count not at all." He placed a reassuring hand on my arm, "Sir," says he, "I'd not leave a dog behind in such a case!"

"Ah…" says I, again. I didn't want any of 'em aboard, but what was I to do? So I said nothing and stood back as Morley's crew hauled the unconscious Lady Sarah aboard in a sling, followed by her luggage and the two soldiers, while Morley (who'd not leave a dog behind, remember?) told the black fishermen to haul off before round shot was dropped through the bottom of their boat. Then *Amiability* was got to sea in record time, with the lookouts straining their eyes for boatloads of blood thirsting slaves, and a stand of pikes and muskets made ready round the mainmast, and finally they slipped just three anchors, bringing one and its cable aboard, so *Amiability* should have a hook to drop next time she made port.

As we cleared Morgan's Bay, the Lieutenant (Parker was his name) came to himself, blurted out much unfortunate information about me and demanded that he, I, Lady Sarah and the redcoat be set ashore at Montego Bay. A furious argument followed. I repeated my tale of revolt and massacre. He declared he'd not abandon his regiment. I said his regiment was lost. He called me a liar. I described the disaster at Trelawney Town. He was visibly shaken, as were Morley and Stanley. But Parker stuck to it and hammered on about duty and going ashore. At this, Captain Morley stamped his foot and ordered the cutter slung out, declaring that any dang fool that wanted to go ashore, might do so at once, but that no man should go by force.

So the two soldiers got into the cutter for the pull to the distant beaches of Jamaica. The sea was moderate and a few hours work for seafaring men would have seen them safe ashore. Whether landmen could do it was another matter. Morley had a couple of muskets and some food and water handed down, and warned Lieutenant Parker to keep the sun on his left, to steer a course southward to the island. And so we parted with a final threat of retribution upon me from Parker, and myself keeping mum, since the less said the better.[9]

And so began one of the oddest voyages I've ever suffered. Round the eastern tip of Cuba, through the Gulf of Florida and northward up the American coast past Georgia, the Carolinas and Virginia. We put into Charleston for supplies and new anchors, then onward, past Pennsylvania and New York and finally into Boston after forty days: a slow passage and a damned miserable one, because that bloody woman split the ship in factions and caused the death of two good men.

So it was an ugly voyage. But Boston was worse.

---

9   Lieutenant (later, General Sir Rodney) Parker and private Simons, 83rd Foot, made safe landfall and eventually re-joined their regiment. Later, in a letter to the 'Times' newspaper in 1823, Sir Rodney accused Fletcher of wilfully abandoning him to the sea, giving an account of these events markedly differing from Fletcher's. The scandalous details of Fletcher's subsequent assaults upon Sir Rodney, first at the Opera House and later in Bow Street Magistrate's Court, are too well known to merit repetition. S.P.

CHAPTER 21

*"I know, and the Almighty Being knows, that ever and always I
did what I might in pursuit of my duties and had not I had under
my hand such a pack of rascals and mutineers, and had I not been
so ill served by the treachery of my own officers, then I should have
made as good a career as any man in His Majesty's Sea Service."*

(From a letter of 19th June 1794, from Captain Lewis Gryllis, His Majesty's
Frigate *Calipheme* off New York, to his father in Portsmouth.)

At 10 a.m. on the 15th of September 1795, with the wind steady from
a point north of east, the British 18-pounder, thirty-eight gun frigate
Calipheme, under the command of Captain Lewis Gryllis, being in lati-
tude 41 degrees 12 minutes north, longitude 69 degrees 2 minutes west,
proceeding northward off Nantucket Island, sighted a strange sail standing
towards her.

At 11.30 a.m. the stranger, which proved to be the French, 12-pounder,
thirty-two gun frigate *Mercure,* Captain Jean-Bernard Barzan, hoisted the
colours of the French Republic and hauled to the wind. *Calipheme* instantly
replied with the Union Flag, tacked and stood towards the enemy, then
bearing on her weather bow.

A chase developed which continued for several hours with a steady
advantage to *Mercure* such that *Calipheme* fell astern of her, until four
p.m. when *Mercure* came about and fell upon the British ship with the
evident intention of bringing her to action.

Captain Gryllis stood on his quarterdeck, with his officers looking
to him for leadership, and he trembled in sick horror as the Frenchman
thrashed towards his ship with the ocean foaming under her bow. Her

every sail shuddered on the edge of the wind, but she forged onward and Gryllis saw that he was going to be wrong. Oh dear God in heaven! He was going to be wrong! He'd thought the Frenchman couldn't cross his bow. He'd got his starboard battery manned for a broadside exchange as the French ran past. And he was wrong because *Mercure* was bearing down with the obvious intention of discharging her larboard battery, right down the length of *Calipheme's* deck in a deadly raking fire.

"There, sir!" screamed Bantry the Sailing Master, as doom came down upon them, "Didn't I say she *would* rake us by the bow? And didn't you say she *couldn't*? By God, Sir, but I hope you're pleased with yourself… you … you …" and the ingrained habits of a lifetime's discipline sundered and foundered, as Bantry hurled the foulest insult that he knew, directly at his Captain, upon the quarterdeck, in the full hearing of all those present: officers, mids, tars and marines, "You *no-seaman*, you!"

"What? What's that you say?" cried Gryllis, his eyes bulging from his white face, his prominent teeth shining from his fat lips, and his wispy red hair fluttering from under his hat. Tears started from his eyes and he blinked, as he tried to face down the fierce, hard officer glaring at him in such contempt.

Gryllis was not a bad man. He was a kind husband and father. He was a scholar, fluent in Greek, Latin, French and Spanish. He would have made a fine teacher, or a librarian, or a writer of serious books. It was his curse to be the son of a Navy family whose friendship and influence with the Howe clan had placed him where he was, without ever wondering if it were wise to do so. This powerful influence had made Gryllis a Lieutenant at nineteen, a Captain at twenty-eight, got him command of *Calipheme* and sent him out with Rear Admiral Sir Brian Howe's America Squadron to keep the Yankee privateers in port for the *False War* now in its second year. Gryllis had done his best, but without aptitude or the least inclination towards the tough, brutal life afloat, he'd varied between overindulgence of his crew and over-use of the lash when they frightened him with their surly insolence.

Thus Gryllis feared and despised his men and subjected them to the horrors of unjust, arbitrary tyranny. He knew they were dangerously near mutiny and he thought they were scum. But they were not. They were no worse than many another ship's crew in the King's service. What Gryllis could not know was that their genuine and obvious contempt for him, was a direct recognition of his unfitness for command. They'd have stood the floggings from a hard man who was hard *reliably*, and they'd even have preferred such a tartar to a weak Captain. But Gryllis's regime had left every man aboard not knowing on who's back next, the cat would fall. And to Gryllis's deadly peril, that included the marines who'd been flogged along with all the rest.

Gryllis was ignorant of this, but he knew that it was only due to the professional competence of the Master and the First Lieutenant that the ship functioned at all. And now the Master was denouncing Gryllis before the entire crew.

"Sir," said Gryllis in a quavering voice, "I will re- re- m-mind you ..." But Gryllis's voice cracked with emotion and he stammered over the word and speech dried up on his lips.

"Swab!" said Bantry, and all along the gun-deck and up to the mastheads, and down to the orlop, the whispers ran, to take this juicy piece of news from man to man.

But nobody had time to relish the news for its arrival preceded only by seconds, the arrival of *Mercure's* broadside as she shot across *Calipheme's* bows. A thundering bank of smoke poured from the French 12-pounders with lances of bright flame, and the shot that smashed and tore and shivered their way from stem to stern. Guns went over. Rigging parted. Timbers split. Tumbling splinters whirred through the air, longer than a man and razor-sharp. Flesh tore. Blood spouted. Men shrieked in pain and fright.

Aboard *Mercure*, Capitaine de fregate Jean-Bernard Barzan snapped his fingers and roared with joy as the Englishman's bows sped closer and closer. The Rosbifs were tricked and beaten.

"Mes enfants! Mes braves garcons," cried Barzan and pinched the cheeks of his officers. He pulled their noses and slapped their backs. They laughed in their joy and their love of him. He leapt down the companionway to the gun deck and called for three cheers for La France, La Mercure and La Liberté.

The men turned from their guns and lifted up their voices in three bellowing barks, in time to Barzan's waving hat. They grinned and called to him and waved, and Barzan ran from gun to gun with a word for each man, because he knew the names and nick-names of every soul aboard, and they knew him.

They knew he'd gone to sea as soon as he could walk, and that he'd served in Louis Bourbon's navy before the freedom of 1793. They knew that Barzan (a humble seaman) had been raised up high in the new Republican Navy and they knew how much he deserved this. There was not one thing they could do, that he could not do better, whether it be bending a sail, splicing a rope or training a gun. He was a splendid seaman, he fought like a dozen devils and, above all, he possessed the gift to inspire men to follow where he led.

What did it matter if he could not read nor write, nor fiddle with a sextant and charts? There were others to do that for him. What did it matter if he never bathed nor washed? They loved him all the more for that. What did it matter if he got drunk? Would not any man do the same, given the chance? What did it matter if he worked them like horses? He worked himself still harder.

And Barzan had worked them hard indeed. He'd worked them incessantly, ever since June 29th when *Mercure* had broken out of the Brest Blockade with the three other frigates of Contre-Amiral Vernier's squadron. As every man knew, the squadron's mission was to find Sir Brian Howe's America squadron and defeat it. This would free the Americans to resume their war of commerce against the British. It would impress the Americans with French sea-power and would reinforce the diplomatic efforts being made in Washington to secure an active American participation in the war, securing for France the limitless resources of that mighty continent: grain, timber, cotton, tobacco, and mineral wealth beyond computation.

In the two-and-a-half months since Vernier's squadron had been out on the broad Atlantic, his ships had enjoyed the invaluable opportunity to work up their crews and become fully proficient. It was an opportunity that the Rosbifs seldom allowed the French Navy, and no ship in the squadron had profited better from it than *Mercure*.

On arrival off the coast of America, Vernier had recognised the greater proficiency of *Mercure* by giving Barzan a roving commission to scout ahead of the squadron with the intention of contacting separated elements of the British squadron and luring them into action with the main force. The British were known to be using their ships individually, to cover the long eastern seaboard of the United States, since the new United States Navy's sole warship, the heavy frigate *Declaration of Independence* (thirty-six 24-pounders) was still undergoing repairs in Boston harbour after damage sustained in an action five months ago, when *Declaration* claimed to have sunk the British frigate *Phiandra*.

Hence Barzan's tactics on sighting *Calipheme* at ten o'clock on the morning of the 15th September, when, contrary to all his inclinations Barzan immediately changed course, seemingly running away from the Rosbif, but heading for where Vernier's squadron lay in wait to bring the guns of four French frigates against the single enemy.

Thus *Mercure* made all plain sail and led *Calipheme* in chase until four in the afternoon, and every minute of the way with Jean-Bernard Barzan cursing and frowning and pacing his quarterdeck and his officers wagering on how long it would take before he threw his orders to the winds and backed his topsail to let the English catch up for the fight that Barzan was longing for.

"Merde!" said he finally, and growled at the helmsman, "La barre an haut!" put up the helm! No other order was needed. His men knew what was wanted and ran to wear ship and bring her on course to engage the English. As always aboard *Mercure* the men gave their utmost. Punishments as such were never needed, for those perceived to have let down *Mon Capitaine* received summary justice from their own mates below decks.

Half an hour later, with his officers dancing with glee around him, Barzan took his ship across the bows of the enemy, shaving the wind with his sails closer than any other man would have dared, and saw his gunners fire into the broad round bow of *Calipheme* with its gleaming gilt figurehead, jutting bowsprit and massive anchors slung to the catheads on either beam. Pop-pop! Went the enemy's bow-chasers but otherwise not a gun answered as *Mercure* passed within sight of the enemy's larboard battery, which the Rosbifs had not even manned. Thus Barzan's attack had been perfect and the English completely deceived.

"Encore une fois!" roared Barzan and stabbed his arm to leeward. The helmsman spun the wheel, the sail trimmers leapt to their work and the *Mercure's* 800 tons of timber, hemp, canvas, iron, men and stores heeled heavily under bulging sails as she came round to larboard to cross *Calipheme's* stern and hit her again from the worst place of all: straight through the stern windows. This time the move was only partially successful, for it was done so swift and smart that not more than a quarter of *Mercure's* gunners had reloaded as Calipheme's stern came under their sights. But half a dozen round shot smashed through Captain Gryllis's cabin windows and sped, killing, maiming and destroying down the whole run of the open gun-deck.

And now the British got their chance. Gryllis was frozen in horror but Mr Bantry called for the wind to be spilled from the topsails, so *Calipheme* should not outreach the Frenchman coming around for a broadside to broadside duel on Calipheme's starboard beam, where her gunners were ready and waiting.

"Twelve pounders!" bawled Bantry at nobody in particular, as he saw a spent French shot, hot from the gun, embedded in the mizzenmast, "Now ye buggers: give 'em our eighteens!" After a fashion, *Calipheme's* gunners replied. But they'd been heavily knocked about by *Mercure's* shot. Four guns of the sixteen were thrown over and thirty men killed or injured. *Calipheme's* people never had been fired with enthusiasm and now they were losing heart. A ragged broadside thundered out, poorly aimed and largely ineffective except for the blessed protection of the huge rolling bank of white powder smoke that screened her till the wind took it away.

Mercure's gunners loaded and fired steadily from an untouched gun deck which had not taken a single hit or casualty. They pounded *Calipheme* with shot and they aimed low, into the hull, according to Barzan's drill. For Monsieur Le Capitaine had no time whatsoever for the prevailing French practise of aiming high to dismast and disable. It was *Englishmen* that Barzan wanted to kill, not ships. Had there been an ounce of justice in the cosmos then Barzan should have won the victory he deserved. But there is not, and he did not.

Two things snatched victory from Barzan's black-nailed, calloused hands. First, the wind freshened and came round to a point south of west and second a couple of lucky shot from *Calipheme* knocked his foremast to a stump twenty feet up from the fo'c'sle and parted his main stay.

Being to windward and slightly ahead, and with sails undamaged, *Calipheme* felt the wind first and was nearly taken aback. But a skilful hand at the wheel brought her round to starboard to get the wind on her beam and fill her sails. And that same skilful hand ensured that she kept right on turning, around the Frenchman, until *Calipheme* was heading northward again, with the wind on her starboard quarter enabling her to run from her enemy at her very best speed.

Jean-Bernard Barzan tore his hair and swore fearfully when he saw the Rosbif run.

"Pas juste!" he cried, "Pas croyable!" He hated the English as deeply as any man but he knew it was unknown for them to run from the fight. So damn them! Damn them all! But he wasted no more time and dashed among his men, the better to encourage them to cut away the wreckage and get *Mercure* under way to catch the cowardly English.

Gryllis's quarterdeck survived the first raking broadside from *Mercure*. It survived the second, incomplete, attack from the stern. But the first broadside from *Mercure's* guns, when the two ships were laid alongside, brought Armageddon. Bantry and the first Lieutenant were killed outright and the Lieutenant of Marines lost most of the meat of his thighs as if by a surgeon's knife. He howled like a child and fell in his own blood. The bulwark was stove in and the quarterdeck carronades dismounted. Gryllis was untouched. He was not so much as stained by the smoke. He was untouched but he was broken.

He stumbled through the chaos and found a fire bucket. He plunged in his hands and threw cold water over his face. He stood up and looked down into the gun-deck. Some of the guns were firing, others blown crazily out of their carriages and laid among their own wreckage on the splintered deck. Here and there men were laid down upon the deck with their hands over their ears. That's cowardice, thought Gryllis.

His mind flickered upon Article XII of the Articles of War, the one dealing with cowardice or neglect of duty in time of action. He strained to remember it … "Every person in the Fleet, who through Cowardice, Negligence…" He could remember no more, but he was sure that the prescribed punishment was death, without option of mitigation to a lesser penalty. He sighed, knowing what he must do to those wretched fellows.

"Captain, sir!" said a voice at his elbow. Gryllis turned to see a common seaman at his side. The man spoke again but a booming discharge of heavy ordinance annihilated all other sound and left Gryllis's ears ringing. Then the enemy fired again and shot came shattering and crashing into Calipheme's hull, killing and rending and tearing.

"It won't do, sir!" said the man, "The men won't stand for it," he pointed at the gun deck where still more men were running from the guns. There was a fight at one of the hatchways where a marine sentry was vainly trying to prevent men from running below to abandon their duty in the face of the enemy. Then the marine fired, shooting one man dead. The sound of the musket was lost hopelessly in the background of cannonading as the marine was lost in the flood of angry knives and fists and cutlasses.

"There sir!" said the seaman, "You must haul out of the fight, sir. It is imperative. You have no other option."

"No other option?" said Gryllis. He was not merely repeating the man's words. He was expressing his surprise at the educated voice and the choice of words. Gryllis noted that a number of others stood with this man including some of the most rascally recidivists aboard. Gryllis vaguely recalled the leader as being one who'd enlisted to escape a charge of debt. A solicitor by all accounts, and a member of one of the notorious Corresponding Societies that had supported the French Revolution. But there were so many men aboard, that who could recall any one among the ugly-faced hundreds?

"What?" said Gryllis.

"I do most strongly recommend…" said the ex-lawyer, but he got no further, for a dozen or more men came pounding along the gun deck and up the quarterdeck companionway, led by a young Midshipman named Parry.

"Sir," says Parry, "Mutiny among the fo'c'sle hands."

"Mutiny?" said Gryllis, and a great fear drained the manhood out of him.

"What's this?" said Parry looking death at the solicitor and his followers. There was a second's pause as the two groups of men took the measure of each other and then, even as French guns fired into *Calipheme* once more there was a brief savage fight, Briton against Briton, all around Gryllis. Blades flashed, pistols roared and men died. Reinforced from the gun deck, the mutineers won and Gryllis found himself bundled below into his own cabin with Parry and the loyal hands, including the Purser, the Chaplain, the Bosun, the sergeant of marines and the last surviving Sea Service Lieutenant, Mr Mountjoy whose leg was broken and bleeding from severe wounds.

Up above, Mr Westley, late of Westley and Pevensey, solicitors of New Bond St, took command. The quartermasters at the wheel accepted his orders without question as did the great bulk of sail trimmers and all those left on the gun deck. Of a ship's company of 260 men and boys, only about 50 remained loyal.

It was Westley who ordered the ship out of the fight, taking advantage of a sudden shift of the wind. But it was one of the quartermasters, the most experienced seamen among the mutineers who declared that their best course now was to run before the wind and so hope to escape the French.

So *Calipheme* ran, and ran so effectively that she nearly left *Mercure* below the horizon: nearly but not quite. For *Mercure's* people achieved wonders of swift and strong repairs. They spliced and mended, and raised a jury fore-mast and got their ship under way as fast as any Royal Navy crew could ever have done. She hadn't her best speed any longer but, with her splendid crew and efficient officers she never quite lost touch with her enemy.

Aboard *Calipheme* a Sea-Committee was convened on the quarterdeck with all hands present, save only those absolutely needed to keep the ship ahead of the French, and of course, those locked below decks. Very much under Westley's Influence (as the only educated man among them) this committee duly elected Westley Captain by show of hands and listened to what he had to say.

"We are marked men," said he, "and there is no return for us to England. The Navy will never forgive us and they will never forget us."

"Better'n livin' under that bastard Gryllis!" cried a voice.

"Aye!" they cried.

"Up with him and flog him!" cried another.

"Aye!"

"Flog-him-be-buggered," cried yet another, "*Hang* the bleeder!"

The roar of cheering took all Westley's skills to control.

"No!" he cried, "No! No! No! Kill him and we're all dead men. But if we let him live, him and the other officers, then there's some chance that some of you … and only *some* mind … might hope to be let off a hanging. You can claim you were forced into it. Claim anything you like. But kill Gryllis and you're all dead men."

"So what we gonna do?"

"We shall take the ship into an American harbour and hand her over to the Continental government. They'll be more than grateful for a new frigate and they'll take us in. What's more, America is a new land,

and a free land, where those of you with any sense, will make a new life. You've all seen what England has to offer: a bloody back, stopped grog, and a man set over you that's not fit to swab decks. So who's for America?" They all were, and they cheered wildly. Westley turned to one of the quartermasters.

"What is the nearest American port?"

"Boston," said the quartermaster.

CHAPTER 22

Amiability was about one hundred feet long, and of two hundred and fifty tons burthen, which was large for a two-masted vessel. Without doubt she'd have sailed better if ship-rigged with fore, mizzen and main. She suffered badly from the great size and awkwardness of her mainsail, set well forward, brig-fashion, on a gaff and boom. This was her principal driving sail and to my mind, it was too big, tending to push her bows under, making her a wet ship and a lumbering one.

But of course, the reason why this rig had been chosen, was to give as large a space amidships as could be contrived, for the stowing of Mr Francis Stanley's *Plunger* with the tackles to sling it out and over the side. So for this reason, *Amiability's* sea-keeping qualities were compromised and she was quite remarkably slow and unhandy for a Salem-built, Yankee vessel. The dead weight of *Plunger* didn't help neither, for it spoiled her ballast and made her roll. So *Amiability* was a sickly ship with a heavy motion that caused even hardened seamen to cast up their dinners from time to time. But that wasn't why the voyage from Jamaica to Boston was such an exceedingly unpleasant business.

The reason for that was five-and-a-half feet of evil incarnate: Lady Sarah (La Belle) Coignwood. And if there's one thing I regret in my life then it's the fact that when I got my hands into her thick, lovely, perfumed hair, and I slammed her brow hard into the deck of that Jamaican fishing boat, then it's a tragedy that I didn't lay on a damn sight harder.

But I didn't, did I? Nor could I have, for great beauty in a woman is a terrible thing. It blinds a man from what lies within. It makes a man act like a fool and make a spectacle of himself. Thus she was at it the moment she stirred out of her stupor. I have a strong suspicion that she timed her moment too, because *the poor lady* waited till Morley's got her down into his cabin, laid out in his own cot, with most of his crew pressed in behind, goggling at her, and myself hopping from one foot to another wondering what to do. I knew what would happen the moment she woke up, and by George didn't it just!

Morley, Stanley and I were round the cot (it was one of the swinging kind, suspended from ringbolts in the deck head) together with Morely's first mate who fancied himself a bit of doctor. This gentleman was busy patting madame's hands and wringing out cloths to cool the ugly bruise swelling across her brow. Her gown was half open at the neck and eyes were darting all over her. Even mine, I suppose.

Then the red lips parted, the white teeth shone, and the great lashes swept up to open the gorgeous eyes. She somehow contrived a look of the utmost innocence, like a lovely child that finds itself lost and turns to some stranger for help. She smiled at the faces around her, then gasped in horror and clutched at Morley's heavy paw and made the most fetching attempt to hide behind it. Note that well, incidentally, she had to reach over the first Mate to get at Morley. She wasn't wasting her time on underlings.

"Sir! Sir!" she cried in a voice that would have melted the heart of a stone statue, "If you are a Christian I beg you to protect me from that man. In God's name do not leave me alone with him."

And there you are, my jolly boys. I'll ask you to guess whom she was pointing at, and the effect was terrific. Every man edged away from me and looked at me as if I'd suddenly grown horns and cloven hooves. Damn the woman, they were her men already.

"Belay that!" says I, "You don't know her! You don't know the tricks that bitch has played on me."

"Save me! Save me!" she cried, and tears sprang from her eyes, "Oh God help a poor woman alone!" Up came one dainty hand to shield her eyes while the other clung to Morley like a limpet. I had just sufficient wit to retreat. No words I could utter would have helped. She was so much my master at the game she was playing that all I could do was run away. But I caught Stanley by the arm as I went, and dragged him with me. Out of the cabin we went and I shoved him through the press of curious hands and towards at the companionway up to the quarterdeck. But he turned to stare at me.

"Boswell," says he, "What did she mean? Who is that woman?" He was curious, not worshipping like the rest. So there was hope.

188

"Up!" says I and heaving Stanley bodily off his feet and placing him half way up the rungs. I clambered after him and we came out just aft of the wheel. The helmsman darted a look at us as we went to the stern rail. He'd heard madame's cry for help and his eyes were as round as pennies. The few other tars left on deck looked much the same. They all knew something was up, and they knew it involved the stunning goddess who'd come aboard. I cursed 'em for idle dogs and gave 'em the toe of my boot where it did most good.

"Stanley," says I, steadying myself against the heel of the deck and the steady breeze. Jamaica was still clear in sight astern over the swelling waves, and the tropic sun was fierce. "Stanley, you said once you owed me a favour."

"Aye," says he, carefully. He was suspicious.

"I saved your life, did I not?"

"Aye," says he, paying a little more attention this time. He was remembering our last voyage in *Plunger*. Good! I pressed my advantage.

"You'd have drowned without me, would you not?"

"Aye."

"Then will you give me the chance to explain myself?"

"I'll hear you, Boswell," says he. "I owe you that."

"Well," says I, "In the first place, I ain't Boswell ... I'm Fletcher ..." And I gave him the story of my life. I gave it to him as quick as I could and I gave him the truth of what the Coignwoods: Alexander, Victor and most of all Lady Sarah, had done to me.

There is not the slightest doubt that I owe my life first and foremost, to the fact that Francis Stanley believed me, which he did because he was grateful to me, but also because he was a sharp 'un and he picked me up on a number of points, to see if my tale held together, which it did seeing as it was all God's truth. And there was something else too. It's my guess that Stanley didn't care for women, and was therefore invulnerable to madame's charms. Don't get me wrong: he wasn't a mincing macaroni, but I'm sure his desires lay elsewhere than in women, or even men for that matter, and so he stayed on my side.

Morley and the most of the hands came up on deck while we were talking and I got dirty looks from every one of them, Morley himself most of all, which was a true omen of what was to come, and a damned shame too. Morley ignored Stanley and me after that, and got on with his duties.

When it came time to cast the log he stumped up to the stern rail with a ship's boy carrying the big spool of line and another with the sand glass and he pointedly refused to acknowledge me, although he was within six feet of where I was bent in conversation with Stanley. He barely even nodded at Stanley himself, who was his friend of fifteen years.

"D'ye see?" says I to Stanley, when Morley had gone, "That's her work."

"And do you really think she'll try to kill you?"

"Never a doubt of it," says I.

"Leave James Morley to me," says Stanley. "We've not been shipmates all these years without trusting one another," and so he tried, and so he failed. Stanley did his very best to argue my case to Captain Morley but it was not a jot of good and only widened the split between the two friends. Stanley had more success in other quarters however. Many of the crew had served with Morley and Stanley for years and some of them were ready to take Stanley's assurance of my good character. The result was a splitting of the crew into two parties: hers and mine.

Of the nineteen men and six boys in the crew, eleven, including Morley himself (and all six boys for what they were worth) took Lady Sarah's part. That left me with nine men including myself and Stanley. At first things were merely unpleasant, with curses and evil glances, and messes broke up and reformed along new lines. That lasted for about a week as *Amiability* made her way slowly through the Caribbean and headed for the Florida peninsula.

Lady Sarah had the advantage of her full wardrobe of gowns and trimmings from the trunks and cases she'd brought with her. This panoply of dazzling silks and satins she used to utmost effect, parading about the ship in a different outfit every day. In the absence of a lady's maid she had the youngest ship's boy to help her get into these creations and this young gentlemen was the envy of the ship.

The tars were simply blinded with wonder, even those loyal to Stanley. They'd never seen anything like it, not up close anyway. She had a good word for all except me of course, whom she always cowered away from as if expecting a blow. She even had me wondering, once or twice, whether I should apologise to her, if you can believe that.

The tale she put out, like all good lies, was carefully close to the truth. She acknowledged me as the bastard son of her late husband, and claimed I had killed both her sons (it seemed Victor Coignwood was dead along with his brother – that was news to me, and damned good news too) and now I was trying to kill her to get my father's money. She told 'em that, and all the rest about my being a deserter and wringing old mother Collins's neck. I damn near laughed aloud when Stanley told me of her description of Collins though. The old sow was transformed into a blushing virgin of sixteen, placed into Lady Sarah's devoted service by her mother, an old retainer, who will now be broken-hearted at the loss of her only daughter … etc, etc.

The trouble was, she told her tales so well, and she was so damned lovely that she was winning hearts every day and I began to doubt the men who were taking my side. And then, once I had nobody to stand with me, I imagine I'd have got a knife in the ribs or a blow from behind and be pitched over the rail nice and quiet. That or the like.

But something prevented that, and it was madame's own fault too. It was Captain James Morley. He fell in love with Lady Sarah. He fell really seriously in love, like Romeo and Juliet, and him a married man in his forties with six children and one on the way. It was comedy and tragedy all in one.

You could see the poor devil following her round and making a fool of himself dressing up in his best coat, and shining his buttons, and plastering down his hair with grease. He even got some flour from the cook so he could powder his head for dinner.

He bodged the powdering and looked like a scarecrow, but she complimented him and fluttered her eyes over the table and laid her hand on his, and laughed at his ancient jokes. Stanley was there and told me about it. He said it made him sad to see a fellow so deceived, for Morley was a rough-faced tarpaulin with coarse manners and a plug of tobacco forever working in his cheek. Only an idiot could have imagined that a woman like La Belle Coignwood could be drawn to him; an idiot or man made idiotic by love.

The counterpoint to all this dalliance, which she encouraged furiously, was that Morley began visibly to work himself up to an attack upon me. Of course it was her that put him up to it, and of course she continued radiating sweetness and flowers, but he was her creature and it was he that was going to do her dirty work. She sneered at me once or twice when nobody was looking, with a nasty look of triumph on her face.

I saw what was coming, days in advance, and did all that I could to avoid it. So did Francis Stanley. He tried to talk sense into Morley and got

191

knocked down for his pains, on the quarterdeck in full view of everybody. That brought a stunned silence over the ship, for all hands knew what friends the two had been, and it brought a few of the hands over to my side. But poor Stanley had to go below with the tears in his eyes. I think it was more in sorrow than hurt, but by Jove he was in a state.

For my part I kept out of Morley's way as best as I could contrive, which is pretty hard on board a brig on the open sea. I spent as much time as I could on the fo'c'sle, and when on some pretext or another, Morley came for'ard, I was as polite to him as ever I knew how to be. But it didn't stop him cursing and abusing me and it came to a head as we were passing between the Grand Bahama and the tip of Florida. That day, after breakfast, Morley came on deck with a cutlass at his hip and another in his hand. He walked straight to the fo'c'sle and up to me. You could smell the drink on him a cable's length upwind and he was white with anger.

"You there," says he, "Y'darnned limey bastard! Will ye fight like a man or do I have to chop you like the cowardly, murdering swine y'are?" Over his shoulder I could see her, standing close enough for a good look and with her big eyes alight with excitement.

"I'll not fight you, Morley," says I and turned my back on him, "And I don't think you're the sort to strike down an unarmed man." My heart was beating heavily, but I looked out over the bowsprit under the swelling jib sail, and studied the waves. You could even see the coast of Florida as a dark line on the larboard bow.

But there came a ring of drawn steel and something hit me a fearful whack about the left ear. I spun round thinking he'd killed me and raise my hand to feel for the deep slash In my head. But no, he'd caught me with the flat of the blade.

"Now will ye fight?" roars Morley, and threw a naked cutlass at my feet. He was bent forward with his blade raised and trembling with the passions that were driving him on.

"You can't fight me," says I desperately, "I'm a King's navy man-o-war's man. I'm a trained man. It'd be murder." It was true too. He was a tough man but no match for me. I was younger and faster and had the longer reach, and I'd seen a sight more action that he had. Put at its most brutal truth, I'd killed men before and he hadn't.

Swish! He raked his point down my cheek and though I darted back he drew blood. I knew then I'd have to fight him. Either that or be butchered.

"Fight!" says he, "You damned killer of women! You thief and bastard, you!" I looked down and the cutlass, where it lay on the deck.

"You'll kill me 'f I touch that!" says I, for I'd have to bow down before him to pick it up. As I'd hoped he stepped back two paces.

"There!" says he, "Take up the blasted thing and defend yourself."

There was nothing else I could do. I snatched up the weapon and raised it as he brought down his blade in a terrific swipe that would have cleft me to the chin had it landed. But I caught the blow and leapt clear. He was no swordsman but he was full of hate and waded in with mad abandon swinging left and right.

Clash! Clang! Clash! The blades sparked and rang as I gave ground. In such a case there ain't no question of simply defending. Not for me anyhow. I've faced swordsmen (Alexander Coignwood being a prime example) that were so clever as to be able simply to parry a man's cuts and thrusts till he should wear himself out. But I'm not like that. Not by aptitude nor by inclination. I'll always avoid fighting if I can, but if a man tries to kill me, then I try to kill *him*, and I go at it hammer and tongs.

And that's just what I did to James Morley. And so I caught him on the right-hand side of the neck, which if you're interested is where most death strokes fall in cutlass fights between right-handed men. A navy surgeon told me that, and he ought to know. Marlow went down with his throat chopped to the bone and closed his eyes in seconds, even while the blood was still spouting and jumping out of the big severed vessels.

"Dammit!" says I and flung my cutlass over the side with all my might. I was panting and sweating with the fright and the shock of mortal combat, and with disgust besides, and more than that too. I was filled with sorrow and shame, for not if I live to be a hundred will I cease to regret killing that poor bugger. He was a good seaman and a decent fellow with a family and dependants. He was put up to a fight that was none of his making, and moreover a fight that held little chance of winning. I'd even go so far as to guess that what madame had tried to do was persuade Morley to kill me on the sly, only he wouldn't stoop to that. I think that to be the case since it's exactly what she tried next.

But as Morley died with a ring of his own astonished men around him, I saw her shrug her shoulders, turn on her heel and go below, no doubt to plot and plan.

Meanwhile, Stanley came up and led me off to my cabin down below, so I could sit and be quiet a while. Nobody stood in my way and nobody tried to stop me. The crew were as stunned as I'd been by their Captain's behaviour and if anything it swung opinions my way again and to madame's disadvantage. For one thing, Morley had been the only navigating officer worthy of that name. Stanley knew the theory but had never practised it and the first Mate should have known how to plot a course, but had to admit he didn't.

And so, my jolly boys, that left your Uncle Jacob to con the ship home to Boston. Stanley took command, as part owner of the vessel, but I kept watches and served as Master. It was even me that entered up his epitaph in the ship's books. I put his death down to "...*insanity consequent upon tropical fevers, occasioning an attack upon my person which I was obliged to defend myself against, with deadly force.*" But I let Stanley read the service over him when we slid him over the side under the Stars and Stripes. It wouldn't have been proper for me to do that, now would it?

For the rest of the voyage, including three days in Charleston, madame kept away from me and I kept away from her. Thoughts of heaving her over the side one dark night were constantly in my mind. Having been forced to kill one thoroughly decent man, the business of extinguishing Sarah Coignwood wouldn't have weighed with me not a trifle. So I'd have done it, given the chance. But I never got the chance. She must have guessed what I had in mind and took to keeping one or another of the boys with her all the time. She made play of this by dressing them up in turbans and finery, like black pages in her London salons, and the nippers were spoiled something rotten in the process. But they never left her alone, so unless I was prepared to do away with one of them into the bargain, she was safe.

But she did launch one further attack on me.

She did just what I was so much longing to do to her. Or she tried to anyway. We picked up three fresh hands at Charleston, including a first Mate who knew his business. One of these men was a big, handsome fellow with a touch of Spaniard in him. His name was Gomez or Sanchez or something-ez. He took to madame on sight, and I think she to him. They certainly spent time together, whispering to one another.

And there's another example of the woman's devilish cleverness. Any other female who so openly consorted with a hand before the mast, would have been seen as a tart and a whore by the ship's people. But not madame. She managed somehow to have it both ways. Mind you, the hands did press their ears to the deck over the great cabin when she entertained Gomez, to listen to the sport. At least they did when I wasn't on deck, because it disgusted me and I'd not permit it.

By the time we were off Virginia the weather had changed. The hot tropics were long astern of us and the September sunshine was warm but it no longer hit you on the back of the neck like it did in Jamaica. And some of the nights were strikingly chill to men who'd got used to Jamaica. As a result I took to wearing a thick pilot-coat when I came up on deck at night.

On the night of September 13th off Norfolk. Virginia, I was on deck at the stern rail peering into the wake, listening to the wind in the rigging and the creak of big mainsail boom and enjoying (as far as ever you could in that ship) the steady motion as *Amiability* rolled northward at her slow pace. Very dimly, the lights of Norfolk glimmered far away on the larboard beam. It was a clear night with fair weather and steady wind.

At about one in the morning shore time, I heard the new first Mate, who was on watch, tell the helmsman he was going to the piss-dale to relieve himself. The Mate made a joke about having drunk too much grog and the helmsman laughed but I assume he kept his eyes on the compass in the binnacle and the mast-head wind vane. There was a lookout in the maintop, but he couldn't see where I was standing for the swell of the mainsail was in the way.

At that moment I was alone at the stern rail, with no man's eyes upon me. I was deep in thought about what I'd find waiting for me in Boston. It suddenly occurred to me to go and ask Stanley about the Cooper family, a tribe of powerful merchants I'd been heavily involved with on my last visit to Boston. How they received me could be crucial to my future. I wondered how they were. I turned to go and wake Stanley …

A dark figure was running forward, barefoot and silent. A long knife gleamed in his right hand, held low for an upward thrust: under the ribs and into the heart and lungs. I gasped and jumped aside. He missed his stroke by a split second and the blade sliced the cuff of my coat as I raised my arm. It was Gomez. No other man in the ship had a moustache. His teeth snarled and he leapt at me again. But I jumped back and a phrase of Sammy Bone's sprang to my mind.

"If you've got to fight a knife unarmed, lad, your best defence is your coat. Get it off and wrap the thickness of it about your arm as a shield."

I wrenched off the pilot coat, starting the buttons out of their threads and spun the material round my left forearm, just as Gomez came in again. Sammy's ruse worked. The blade sunk harmlessly into the thick worsted. But Gomez whipped it out and danced round me looking for an opening. He was nimble and clever and confidant. I dared not cry out for help for fear that an instant's loss of concentration would give him his chance. Jab! He came again. I caught the blade and tried to catch him. Once I got my hands on him, God help him! But I missed. Jab! Jab! Jab! Again, and again, and again. He was like a dancer, poised on the balls of his feet. He had me hemmed in against the corner of the stern rail and the starboard bulwark and I still didn't dare cry out.

But someone else did. The Mate was buttoning his breeches and turning back to the wheel.

"Avast there!" says he, "*Alllllll hands*! *Alllll hands*!" and he grabbed a belaying pin and ran forward.

Gomez turned in fright and I kicked him with all my might. I missed his stones but caught him on the left kneecap and knocked him spinning. Down he went and I swung my foot again, and he grunted heavily as the air drove out of his chest. He was a hard bastard and no mistake, and he still struggled up with the knife in his hand and stabbed at me again, but then the Mate joined in and fetched Gomez such a mighty clout across the skull with the heavy oaken pin, that you could hear the bones breaking Inside.

This time I ascribed the attack to "…*Malice and mutiny consequent upon excessive use of strong drink smuggled aboard at Charleston*." And this time I read the service, but we put no colours over the body for we thought he deserved none.

And that was madame's last attempt upon me during our passage to Boston. On Sunday 20th September 1795, I took *Amiability* in through Broad sound, with Deer Island on our starboard beam and passed between Governor's Island and Cattle Island down the main channel into Boston. It was Stanley's home so he knew it well, and I remembered it too. The seaway was as busy as I'd seen it in March and April of the previous year, with ships of all kinds coming and going. And from the North Battery, down past the Long Wharf to Windmill point, there must have been over four hundred ships anchored.

This was Boston as I'd known it: one of the principal seaports of the American republic, and one of the richest. It was a town built on mercantilism and seaborne trade. All of this I had been expecting, but there was something else in Boston harbour. There was something that had every man jack pointing and getting up into the rigging for a better look and wondering what was going on.

For anchored three miles out from Boston, in the area bounded by Deer Island, Spectacle Island and the north of Long Island, there were three frigates. One, and by far the biggest, I recognised, as I'd served on board of her. This was the United States Navy ship *Declaration of Independence* mounting a massive battery of 24-pounders. Of the other two ships, one flew French colours and the other flew a plain red flag at each masthead. In those days, before the great mutinies at Spithead and the Nore, I had no idea what the red flag meant. Each of the three stood at the tip of an equilateral triangle with sides a mile long. They seemed to be guarding one another.

CHAPTER 23

"… but I gives no heed to foul rumour, and I disbelieves that
any son of mine would consort with the British by laying his ship
alongside one of theirs in any cause other than cannonading,
and I knows that when next we meet you will put all to rights,
explaining everything."

(From a letter dated only as 'Monday' to Mr Patrick Gordon, from his
father Absalom Gordon, Shipwright of Pawtucket, Massachusetts.)

In the late afternoon of Sunday September 20th the fast schooner
Nancy Ellen was running south under a press of sail, down the coast of
Pennsylvania, heading for a rendezvous off Delaware Bay. She was long
and low, rigged fore-and-aft on two masts with a topsail on the foremast
and with jib and flying jib to the bowsprit. She was a fine, deep water
vessel, fit to sail the world around, and with the wind steady on her
quarter and she was forging along at eleven knots: a cracking speed, but
she could do a damn sight better than that under ideal conditions. She
was built for speed and she was three days out from Boston, looking
for a friend. She had already been elsewhere to alternative places where
that friend might be found, but he was not there. This time, however,
she was in luck.

"Ahoy deck!" cried the lookout In the fore-top, "Man-o-war topsails
in sight!"

"Where away?" cried the Master, Mr Patrick Gordon, at the helm and
steering by the long tiller. He was a small, slim, clever young man, bred
up to the sea, and with a reputation for being ready to do anything for
money. In his home port of Boston, he was well known and liked by all

those persons who never found out some of the things he actually did, for money.

"Bearing on the bow!" called the lookout, "British colours!"

Within the hour, and just as the sun was sinking over the shores of the vast American continent, *Nancy Ellen* hove to upon the darkening ocean alongside of His Britannic Majesty's frigate *Diomedes* of thirty-eight, 18-pounder guns: the flagship of Rear Admiral Sir Brian Howe's America squadron. *Nancy Ellen* swung out her boat for the short journey, made fast under the frigate's lee quarter and Gordon was brought on board of the Britisher.

He looked eagerly in all directions with intense professional curiosity at this huge ship, the biggest he'd ever been aboard in all his twenty-one years. He whistled to himself at the gleaming cleanliness of absolutely everything: the white decks, the brass, the copper, the lines of great guns, the men in their neatly uniform dress, the immaculate setting up of her rigging. The busy, smartness and seamanliness of everything. And then there was the enormous crew: hundreds of them! And the officers tricked out like gods in their glittering gold lace and tall hats.

He was so fascinated that he failed to notice, or more likely never appreciated the fact, that they didn't pipe the side for him. He was a master mariner after all, and deserving of that honour. But Mr Gordon was engaged in a business that his own government would despise as treachery, which opinion was thoroughly shared by Sir Brian Howe (younger brother of Admiral of the Fleet, Lord *Black Dick* Howe), who despised anything even sniffing of espionage or secret agents. So the good Sir Brian might use what means he was forced, by circumstance, to use, but he damn well wasn't going to render any honours in the doing of it!

A tall officer approached Gordon, who was gazing in rapture at the great masts and their mighty yards. He doffed his hat and looked down upon the young man.

"Good evenin' t'ye, sir!" said he, "Might I ha' the pleasure o' knowin' y'r name?"

"Patrick Cordon," said Gordon and shook the other's hand vigorously. He was surprised to note that the British officer's hand (unlike his own) was soft and smooth. He grinned at the British accent, too, which he'd never heard spoken except by common tars who sounded altogether different. This aristocratic-looking officer seemed to bite out the middle of his words and not speak them naturally at all.

"If y'd be s'good as t'foller-me, sir?" said the Englishman, "S'Brian's awaitin' ye, below."

An hour later Gordon was back aboard his ship, racing north, home to Boston. He was the better off by a tidy sum in British gold. The head on the coins was that of the same King George that Gordon's father had fought against, but gold was gold. The only pity was that half would have to go to a certain Mr Ratcliffe in Boston who'd contrived all this. But without him, there'd have been no gold for anybody, and a very nice piece of business it was too, except that Gordon came away with no good opinion of Captain sir goddam tight-assed, Brian Howe who'd been only too ready to snatch up the information provided by Gordon, but had treated him with calculated rudeness.

Even as Gordon was complaining of this to his crew, Sir Brian was holding a council of war in his great cabin. His Captain, his Master, his First and Second Lieutenants, and his Lieutenant of Marines were present as well as his Chaplain, Mr Millicent whose opinions Sir Brian respected for his sharp intellect and great learning.

It was the Rev. Millicent who was first to recover from the shock of what Sir Brian had just read out to the company, from the report that the young Yankee captain had brought on board from Mr Ratcliffe, the British secret agent in Boston. Millicent looked around the table at the stunned faces of the ship's officers. Millicent himself was surprised by what he'd just learned, but the others were reeling under a mixture of shame, disgust, disbelief, fear and anger.

"Are we to believe, Sir Brian," said Millicent, "that a British frigate of thirty-six guns has run from a French frigate of thirty-two?"

"Gryllis!" growled Howe, and the rest nodded in understanding. Gryllis's limitations were no secret. "But his father is my friend, gentleman," said Howe, "We served as mids together," He sighed, "What was I to do?" They nodded again, this time in sympathy, since the obligation to advance the kin of one's friends was as deep and natural to these men as the sea upon which they served.

"And now he has lost his ship," said Millicent, "Sent ashore by the mutineers, who are actually in negotiation with the French ... *the French*!" he uttered the words in totally profound, totally English, total disbelief and disgust.

"Yes," said Howe, "The French Consul has been out to the ship and offered amnesty to all hands and a large sum of money to each, if they will hand over the ship to the French vessel." He paused and looked down at the papers on the table, "This Captain Barzan of the *Mercure* seems an active fellow."

"Damned Frog!" said somebody.

"No, sir!" snapped Howe, "Damned *Englishman* for running from the Frog!"

"Indeed, Sir Brian!" said Millicent, "The effect could be incalculable," He pointed at the report, "Our man says that Captain Barzan is a revolutionary of the deepest red hue. Should one such as this, not only beat a British ship, but persuade her people to come over to him, and this before the very eyes of the Americans..."

"Then all our work is in vain!" said Howe, "The sum total of these months of dancing around the blasted Yankees and never taking a prize, and being so damned careful of 'em, just to keep 'em out of the war? Then all of that is wasted, for if the French can do such a thing, then nothing on God's Earth will stop the Yankees coming in on their side. They'll believe the French are the new force in the world and we are the old."

"Thank the Lord the Yankees have no navy to speak of," said the First Lieutenant, "Should they throw in with the French there's little they can do to harm us."

"Pah!" said Howe, "You're wrong, sir! I invite you to consider this country," he waved an arm in the direction of the great, dark continent away on their larboard beam as *Diomedes* sailed northward in the night, "Naval supplies to uncountable profusion! Great harbours to provide safe havens! Timber, cordage, tar, and now they've even got foundries and iron-masters to cast cannon! The Yankees have all the skills to build a fleet, should they chose to do so, and they're as good seaman as we are, with a pluck and determination equal to our own, and we'd be fighting on both sides of the Atlantic!" He glared at the unfortunate officer, "By God, sir, they could tip the scales in favour of the French. Dye not see that? It is worth any sacrifice, and any price to keep the Yankees out of this war!" The First Lieutenant shrivelled in his chair and wished himself elsewhere.

Howe paused and looked at his at his followers, they were miserable enough and it was time to put heart into them,

"Don't be such dull fellows, gentlemen!" he said with a smile, "The solution lies in our own hands. We shall proceed to Boston harbour and then we shall see what can be done by means of a cutting-out expedition."

CHAPTER 24

Two of the three frigates had recently been in action. The Frog had lost her foremast and was making do with a jury rig, while the other was peppered about the hull with shot-holes and her rigging was damaged too, though no effort seemed to have been made to repair it. The odd thing was that *this* ship was British; every line of her said so. But in that case, why the slovenly look of her? And what were these red flags? All three frigates had springs on their cables so as to be able to swing their broadsides in any direction, and each looked as if it were waiting for one of the others to move.

It was all very odd, for while we were only *supposed* to be at war with the Yankees, we were bloody well most assuredly at war with the French! So why didn't *Declaration* and the Frog, just pitch into the Englishman and batter him mastless?

We learned some of the answers when we worked our way carefully through the bustle and noise of the great press of shipping, and anchored off the long wharf. For then, a boat came out with the Harbour-Master's people and the Excise, to run the rule over us. *Amiability* was well-known in Boston and so was Francis Stanley. So, it seemed was Stanley's business in Morgan's Bay, Jamaica.

"Francis!" cried the Excise man, in his smart uniform and cocked hat, "How's the fishing?" He winked at Stanley to show what a sly dog he was. "You know these fellows, I don't doubt," said he, introducing the two other officials, and Stanley replied by introducing me: giving my true name which made me jump, as I'd grown so used to hiding it.

"Good day, to you, Mr Fletcher!" Says the Excise man. He looked me up and down and I got another fright. "Fletcher?" says he, "I know the name, sir! Though I don't just place the connection." But I stepped in promptly with a question to change his tack, being most unwilling to discuss my past doings in Boston.

"Those ships, sir," says I, pointing at the three frigates where they lay glowering at one another, "What is happening?"

"Aha!" says he, with a fat grin, "You mean you've not heard?"

"No," says I, and all the hands edged closer to hear what he would say.

"Why, sir," says the Excise man, "Them there is the French *Mercure* of thirty-two guns that three days ago, chased the British *Calipheme* of thirty-eight guns, all the way up the coast from Nantucket and sent her running into Boston, with her tail between her legs."

"*What?*" says I, in a strangled voice, "*A British Frigate ran from a blasted Frog?*" I couldn't believe it! I'd no love for the Royal Navy[10] but I knew how good they were at their trade. Everyone knew that. It passed beyond belief that a British Captain would run from the Frogs, even against superior force let alone from a weaker ship. Your average frigate Captain would give his eyes and limbs for the chance of a single-ship action. But the Excise man was looking at me with his head on one side.

"You'd be *Bridish*, yourself I take it, from the sound of your voice?" says he.

"No," says I quickly, "I'm an American Citizen, sworn before a Magistrate in your own city." It was true. I took citizenship last time I was in Boston.

"Ah!" says he, less than fully convinced.

"But what are they doing now?" says I looking at the tall masts three miles away down Boston sound.

"Well, Mr American Fletcher," says he, "First of all the big 'un is our own *Declaration of Independence*, God bless her, the which is there to keep an eye on the other two. The *Mercure* is French and is there to keep an eye on *Calipheme* which is there for discussions with the Consul of France, to hand over the ship to that country's government?"

"What?" save I, yelping as if a red hot iron had been run up my breech, "*Go over to the Bloody French*? Never! Never, never, never! What's her bloody Captain thinking of?" The Excise man laughed.

"That poor damn lubber's piping his eye over a bottle of rum in the New Prospect tavern," he jabbed his thumb shore wards, "His crew turned him out of the ship day before yesterday, along of those who'd go with him."

---

10   False! Fletcher loved the Navy to the deep of his soul. S.P.

"Oh," says I, "There's been a mutiny. Now I understand." It was a relief, because otherwise the world would have been stood on its head. I resolved immediately to keep as far away from *Calipheme* as ever I possibly could. She'd taken the Angel of Death on board when she dealt with the French, because now the Navy would hound her people to the ends of the earth. And besides, since I couldn't go home to England, what was any of this to do with me?

"Well," says I, putting the thought into words, "That's something for the British to worry themselves about. I don't see as an American need be concerned."

"Aye, sir," says the Excise man, "And I can see that not a drop of British sentiment lies within your bosom!"

"Quite so, sir," says I and somebody sniggered who, to his very great good fortune, I never spotted. Meanwhile, the Excise man turned to Stanley.

"Now, old friend," says he, "Enough of the politics, let's just cast an eye over your papers and let you get to your berth." His two companions smiled genial as could be and we all went below together. This was special treatment indeed! The natural way of harbour officers is to make a Merchant Skipper come to them, and it ain't many Excise men that makes it quite so plain that they're resolved to find no contraband, before even the search commences. Not that there *was* a search, and it was obvious that someone's palm had been well greased for the courtesy.

(Excise men? Damn them! Damn them all! For what's the use of 'em say I? Other than to interfere with the free passage of goods which is the life's blood of commerce and the foundations of civilisation. Any man with a grain of sense knows that the world would soon become a better place if a dozen of Excise men could be hanged every day of the week, and two dozen on Sundays.[11])

Once we were crammed into Stanley's tiny cabin, a bottle and glasses were sent for and we all sat down.

"Where's Cap'n Marlow?" says the Excise man, looking round the

---

11   Fletcher had many prejudices, all of them powerful and deep rooted. But his hatred of the Excise service was extreme. The explanation for this lies in the history of the Mexican emeralds, later in his memoirs: a bloodstained tale of iniquities bringing little credit to Fletcher himself. S.P.

narrow space, crammed with Stanley's junk. "And ain't we good enough for his cabin?"

The three of them laughed, but Stanley looked miserable.

"A lady passenger has the stern cabin," says he, "and as for Marlow, the poor fellow went mad and had to be subdued, and so he died." That was the tale we'd agreed on, to spare his family the truth. But even that was bad enough and the three Bostonians shook their heads and raised their glasses to his memory.

However, once we got up on deck again, there was Madame La Belle waiting for us by the main hatch, with the tars swinging her trunks and valises up out of the hold. She had a ship's boy beside her, done out in a turban and silk drawers. The little blighter had even washed his face. God only knows how many different rig-outs she'd got in those damn boxes and here she was in a fresh one. I'm no hand at describing ladies gowns, so find yourself a ladies' illustrated journal for the period, if that's your taste, and look at the silly creatures in the latest fashion plates.

But much as it galls me, I have to admit that the blasted woman looked absolutely gorgeous. And it was all simple stuff too. Not like the stiff, elaborate gowns that most of 'em were wearing. Simple but damned effective. I sighed and stood back out of the way while the Excise man and his mates, stopped dead in their tracks, threw out their eyes on stalks and snatched off their hats in unison. I couldn't win any sort of exchange with the woman, and I knew it. Fortunately she chose to ignore me.

"Good day, gentlemen!" says she in a clear confidant voice.

"Mumble, mumble," said the three, overawed, and bobbing and bowing as by instinct. She'd got 'em already. She could have asked 'em to jump over the side and they'd have done it. She advanced towards them and extended her hand, palm downward to the Excise man, whom she'd spotted as superior man of the three. He attempted the impossibility of bowing, kissing her hand, and stuffing his hat under his arm all at the same time. The hat dropped, the fellow stumbled, his companions gaped. But Madame, smiled graciously.

"I am Lady Sarah Coignwood," says she, "I am a subject of His Majesty King George III of England, under whose laws I hold powerful interests, properties and authorities. Considering the situation that exists between our two countries, His Majesty's Government would consider it to be of the utmost importance that I be conducted without delay, to your head of civil government," she paused before demanding, "So who might that person be?" By George! She had the three of 'em hanging on her words and wringing their hats in their eagerness to please her.

"The head of our government? Why, ma'am, that'd be the Governor, at the State house on State Street." says one of them.

"No, ma'am," says another, "By rights it must be The Committee of Selectmen at Faneuil Hall." They commenced to argue the point, but the witch raised her hand as if to chide infants in the schoolroom, and drew their attention to something far more important than the civil administration of the city of Boston.

"I am addressed as *My Lady*," says she, and they all repeated the words and nodded like good boys.

"Milady, Milady, Milady."

"Furthermore," says she, "And they all stood up straight to pay attention, "I shall require assistance with my luggage." They started forward like greyhounds, "And!" said she, stopping them with a glance, "I shall require appropriate protection since there are present, certain monies and other valuables."

"Yes Milady!" says the three and conferred together. I couldn't hear everything but I caught the words "Constables? Militia? Dragoons?" and two of them were bowing their way over the side, down into their boat.

Half an hour later, during which time madame kept the Excise man and the ship's people entranced with her conversation, there arrived on board a Mr Thomas Edwards, representative of the Committee of Selectmen who ran the city. This gentleman puffed and blowed with self-importance and with republican determination to put some damned English Lady in her place, what with titles and powers that didn't mean nothing at all, not here, not in Boston by crackey! And then ... and then ... down he went with all the rest, bowled over at the first assault of Milady's charm.

So that was her magic carpet to the uppermost levels of Boston society. Off she went with stevedores hauling her boxes and a troop of horse in escort. We saw it from the rail of our ship, and we saw the crowds that gathered around her. By all accounts the bitch was soon installed in the town's best lodging house in Summer Street, and kept so busy swanning around salons and wearing out bed-linen that she had little time to devote to me. So I thought at the time, and by George but I was wrong.

Once we'd cleared the formalities at the long wharf, Stanley had me work

Amiability northward and round the mass of wharves and jetties that made up the eastward side of Boston, towards Hudson's point and the great bridge running across the Charles River, where he had property of his own. On the way we passed Hart's yard where the new Yankee frigate *Constitution* was building, though there was little to see for she wasn't much more than a keel, with a few ribs raised and a great stack of timber standing by.

Finally, we made fast at Stanley Wharf, and Stanley and I went down the gangplank, along the timber pier, and into the big fenced-in yard full of brick and wooden buildings of all kinds: sheds, offices, a warehouse, and wonder of wonders, an actual engine-house with a tall brick chimney, where there was installed the very latest in Boulton and Watt beam engines, brought out from England. This monster could have driven a manufactory full of machines with hundreds of hands to serve them. And here it was in Stanley's yard with but twelve men and boys employed! It was there for him to study, if you'd credit it: to study and improve upon.

And finally, there was a little cottage in a miserable scrap of garden, with dying plants fighting a rear-guard action against the weeds that strangled them and the cats that came to drop dung. This was where Stanley lived. He was a bachelor with no family.

Mr Francis Stanley was an odd 'un in many ways. As I've already said, he'd no interest in women whatsoever, and if his inclinations turned elsewhere, then he kept 'em strictly to himself though I suspect he had no interest in worldly comforts at all. For instance he lived *over the shop* surrounded with the tools and mechanical tinkering's which were his life.

But he went a lot deeper than that. He was a very clever man indeed and far more than he seemed. He once showed me his private study where he'd got correspondence from all the known world of natural philosophy. I saw letters from Benjamin Franklin, the Yankee who invented electricity, from John Dalton the Quaker who invented atoms, from some damned Frog called Lavoisier who invented chemistry, and from a German called Herschel who invented whole moons and planets.

There were lots more besides, some of them years old, and all of them on matters of natural philosophy that would make your head spin: galvanic conduction, the orbits of the moons of the planets, the theory of the atoms, and something called *phlogiston* (which Stanley said was rot). And then there was his attitude towards money which was something powerful peculiar. He got round to that the first night we were ashore.

He still felt he was much in my debt, and so he offered me a bed in his house. Having nowhere else to go, I was grateful, since I needed to find out how the land lay in Boston before I took any risks. So the first night we spent under his roof, I wanted to pump him for information, but I got a confession instead.

He had one old manservant to look after him, a half-Indian by the name of Joe, and once we'd finished the appalling meal that this gentleman laid before us, and Stanley had packed him off to his bed, he drew up a couple of chairs to the parlour fire and got out a stone jar of some fire-water Yankee spirit. And so we sat in the firelight taking turns out of the jug with tinned mugs and he opened up his heart to me.

"Fletcher," says he, looking into the embers, with the red glow on his face, and the shadows all around, "There's a thing I got to tell you."

"Oh?" says I.

"Morley and I were parties to a crime that I believe the Lord has punished with Morley's death: *I shall smite the unrighteous, sayth the Lord*," he murmured, "So says The Book!"

"Does it?" says I.

"There's a guilt upon me, Jacob," says he, not hearing me at all, "There's a thing I dared not mention aboard ship, with that woman poisoning minds such that none might be trusted."

"Oh?" says I, for I thought he and I had talked over most things in a forty day's voyage. It's only natural.

"No," says he, "I dared not speak then, and by heaven I'm shamed," he looked at me as miserable as an undertaker when the condemned man is reprieved, "I'm a common thief", says he,

"Good Lord!" says I, trying not to laugh, "Surely not?"

"Yes!" says he. I had to bite my lip hard, for by the look of the little squirt, he'd not have got away with anything more than pinching a penny off a blind beggar's plate.

"And what was the extent of this theft?" says I solemnly.

"Over four hundred and sixty thousand pounds sterling," says he, "in British gold."

He sat staring into the fire.
I sat staring into the fire.
He nursed his guilt.

I hesitated.

"What?" I thought, "Did he say four hundred and sixty thousand pounds? No! He couldn't have." I turned and looked at him, "How much?" says I.

"The better part of half a million pounds," says he. I was taken flat aback and astounded. Such a sum was vast beyond belief. It would have bought most of Oxfordshire, with Blenheim Palace thrown in. It was a colossal, enormous fortune. I could barely believe it.

"Where'd you get such a sum?" says I.

"From the wreck," says he, "From the *Brigand*."

"Wait a bit," says I, "She didn't have nowhere near that much on board, it was thirty thousand pounds, wasn't it?"

"No," says he, "The amount was falsified by all parties to discourage adventurism."

"Adventurism?" says I, "What's that?"

"Theft," says he.

"Didn't damn-well work then, did it?" says I, "So how much gold was embarked?"

"Two million pounds."

"Jesus Christ!"

"I wish you'd not use the sweet name of Jesus as a cuss word," says he.

"Well how did you do it?" says I.

"By trickery," says he, "We were months at the work before you came aboard, and had already emptied the strong-room."

"What?" says I, "But you showed me the bloody thing and you tried to blow it open."

"No," says he, "I showed you the spirit room and led you to believe it was the strong room."

"Did you, by Jove!" says I.

"Yes," says he.

"But you said you'd kept this secret," says I, "And the whole of your damn crew must know, and the damn boys too! It'll be all over Boston by now."

"No," says he, "It was a deception twice over. Once on the British and once on the crew."

With that he set to and told me the tale. It seemed that once a month a navy cutter had come out from Kingston, to take off any gold raised by the salvors, for safe delivery at Dean Barlow and Glynns of Kingston. This ensured that great quantities of gold were not accumulating on board of *Amiability* where they might have tempted the salvors to cut and run with the loot.

Once a month, then, the navy took delivery of the gold, which was entirely in minted coin, and sealed into boxes by Dean Barlow and Glynn's London Counting house, in lots of one thousands, two thousands, five thousands and ten thousands, this being the normal practise of that Bank. In addition to this, the Navy also took away coin in boxes supplied from *Amiability's* stores, for loose coin, out of stoved-in Dean Barlow and Glynn boxes. Only Stanley and Marlow had keys to *Amiability's* strong room and, once a month when the Navy came, they'd take the Navy down to the strong-room and make a good show of delivering up what was in there and getting a signed authority to keep their agreed percentage. What they didn't tell the Navy was that about half the gold had already been removed by Stanley and Marlow through a hidden port at the after end of the strong-room, which opened into Marlow's cabin, and all smartly carpentered so nothing showed.

It was simple in execution and very clever, because they kept the Great Law of theft, which is don't be greedy. They never tried to keep the lot, or even most of what they got, and kept feeding the Navy with large amounts of gold, which kept all parties happy. Furthermore, they kept the crew happy by divvying out each man his agreed share of *Amiability's* fifteen percent, every month on *Navy Day*. But there was one other element to the plan, and one that troubled Stanley most of all.

"Trust!" says he, with a sigh, "The thing could never have worked without their trusting me," he turned his face towards me, and I saw tears in his eyes, "They trusted me, my boy! Had they placed a man aboard, and kept tally of what was brought up, then I don't see how the thing could have worked. But they knew me by reputation as an honest man, and I suppose they were grateful to recover any part of their great loss."

"Jesus Christ!" says I.

"Please, Jacob," says he, looking pained.

"My apologies, sir," says I, to one of the greatest criminals in the history of crime.

"So where is the money now?" says I.

"In the ship," says he.

"And who *knows* it's there?"

"You and I, my boy. And with poor Marlow's death, no other."

There followed a long silence while both of us thought this over, and such a tumbling torment of ideas fought for life in my brain as I could not pretend to remember accurately nor report clearly. I'm a man that prides himself on his ability to create wealth, and build his own way. But here was a temptation (like the Coignwood Inheritance had been) that would rob me of this joy, forever … or would it? Perhaps I might build still greater: huge Fletcher enterprises spanning the American continent? Vast Fletcher manufactories in New York, Boston, and Philadelphia, blazing with light as the whirling machines work without cessation through the night? I dreamed on: why not *Fletcher town*, Massachusetts! Why not *The State of Fletcher*? Why not *The Free Republic of…*

"And so," says Stanley, "at length, I don't see as I've no option than to attempt to make good my crime,"

"What," says I, for here was another twist to the tale, "What do you mean?"

"You don't for one moment imagine that I did this thing for personal gain?" says Stanley, looking shocked, "Even if I weren't a God-fearing man, I've already got all the money that I'll ever need." And that was probably true. He was a man who could afford to bring a steam engine across the Atlantic as a toy for playing with.

"So who drove you to it?" says I.

"The Congress," says he, "Or agents acting for it. I was asked to do this thing as a patriotic act, to strike a blow against our British enemies. But more than that, our country has not bullion nor coin sufficient to support the great increase in trade that is daily occurring." That was also true. The Yankees were so short of coin that they were paying men in musket balls on the frontier.

"I've already started to make good, though," says he, with a weak little smile such as a spaniel might give, having shit in the kitchen and been caught trying to bury it in the hearthrug. "You'll have noticed the Excise officer, who came aboard today?" says Stanley.

"Yes," says I.

"He was more than he seemed, Jacob! When he and I were alone, I told him that the British watched over me too closely for our plan to be enacted. And he believed me too because he trusts me, so now I have deceived the Congress too."

212

"So what in heaven's name do you plan to do?" says I.

"Give it back!" says he.

"But Jamaica's in flames, man!" says I, "Your clients have probably been skinned and eaten by the bloody maroons!"

"Then I will return the money to England."

"But you're at war with bloody England!"

"And that's just why I need your help, Jacob!"

"Eh?"

"Yes!"

"Why?"

"Because you are an honest man, with a mighty talent for business and money." He looked at me all solemn and shook his head, "I doubt that you know just how exceptional your talents are in this direction," says he. By Jove he was wrong there! But I didn't interrupt him for he was in full flood. "And so," says he, "I want you to do what I can't do for myself. I want you to take charge of this great fortune of money, and place it with the banks or whatever, you'll know the way, so the money gets back to its rightful owners. I believe that it can be done, but I don't know what levers must be worked to set the machinery in motion."

And so a great happiness and a great peace descended upon your Uncle Jacob. I could see the way ahead. I could have everything.

"I'm your man, Mr Stanley!" says I, and we shook hands on it.

CHAPTER 25

*"Rising over all artistry of Greece and Rome, our fair Boston –
Athens of the West – summoned the nine muses to receive La
Belle in such splendour as could not be found in London, Paris or
Vienna, and engineered with such speed as could not be matched
by Hermes, messenger of the gods."*

(Cutting from 'Boston Monitor and Reporter' presumably of September
1795)

Within two days of Lady Sarah's arrival, a grand welcoming ball was
held in Faneuil Hall for Lady Sarah. After vicious in-fighting between
the Town and the State authorities, the Town won since the State House
was less suitable for a reception on the scale planned, than was Faneuil
Hall. Every person of notability, was invited. The press was intense, the
heat was unbearable, the carriages jammed the streets, the music was
continuous, the food was lavish, and ladies fought like the savages of
great unexplored interior, to get close enough to La Belle Coignwood to
feast their eyes upon her gown.

As a concession by the Town to the State, Lady Sarah was led in jointly
by Governor Sam Adams and by Deacon William Boardman (who'd won
the ballot among the nine Selectmen).

The ball was a tremendous success. It was also an occasion which entirely
changed the life of Captain Daniel Cooper. In his full dress with gleaming
bullions at his shoulders and gold lace twinkling against the navy blue,
Cooper looked every inch a man and a Sea Officer. Together with his Uncle
and Aunt, he was duly presented to Lady Sarah whom he found deep in
conversation with Mr Paul Revere, a broad-faced over-dressed, 60-year

old with extensive manufacturing interests and the reputation of being the biggest bore in Boston, as well as being not quite the thing socially.

"Captain Cooper!" cried Lady Sarah, "How good of you to come," she smiled at Cooper like the glory of mid-summer sunrise. She extended her hand to him. She focussed her artillery upon him. She pounded him into rubble. And she did it in three seconds flat.

Cooper took the hand and there was not one other thing in the great, hot, jam-packed chamber apart from the hand and the arm and the lady. His Uncle, his Aunt, Mr Revere, and everything else vanished into smoke. For Daniel Cooper, clever and devious man that he was, and a full Captain US Navy (and all this at 25 years old) was a virgin and afraid of women.

There had been certain experiences in the past during which, because of such nervousness as any young man might suffer, he had consumed large quantities of drink to bring himself to action, and succeeded only in rendering that action impossible. And so he now believed himself no man at all and was deeply shamed by it, and directed his energies ruthlessly into other directions to compensate. Hence his success, hence his failure.

By what stages Cooper and Lady Sarah escaped into a dark and uninhabited corner of Faneuil Hall, Cooper never remembered. But some things were branded into his mind for ever: the sweet goodness of the lady, her gentle modesty, her poignant story of the loss of her adored husband, the tragedy of the death in action of her noble son Alexander (a Sea Officer very much like himself), the further blow of the murder of her adored younger son, the poet and writer, Victor Coignwood. And through all this like the serpent that wound around the tree of paradise, was the black-hearted malevolence of Mr Jacob Fletcher.

And most of all, with a hot pulsing shame and yet with eternal delight, Daniel Cooper remembered what had happened in the semi-dark of one candle.

"Sit beside me, dear boy" she had said, drawing him next to her on a great upholstered couch. No other person was present. And SHE was beside him. Her gown was of some new kind that all the other ladies of Boston were copying, and that showed the lines and curves of a woman's body most indecently. Not that she herself was anything other than the very model of chastity. Indeed, Cooper knew that the thoughts pounding through his body were entirely of his own base origination and that she would respond in shock and horror did she but dream of what he was thinking as he gazed into the smooth, swelling bosom glowing in the candle-light.

She spoke to him as a mother would, for she was older than he, and that too weighed upon him, and yet she looked like no man's mother that he'd ever met before. Oh God, it was agony, but agony a man would run towards and not away from.

"There is much I must tell you, my boy," she said and explained about the gold that Jacob Fletcher had stolen with the help of Francis Stanley. She explained how Fletcher had goaded the Captain into a fight and killed him. But Cooper was not listening properly. He was inhaling the perfume and moving closer and not even wondering at the fact that what he had thought moribund within him, was rising and straining into erect and fighting trim. He could bear it no more and placed a hand upon the round thigh beneath her thin gown.

"Sir?" she said, "What does this mean?" The words were stern, but the thrust of her shoulder, the move of her head, the raising of her hands, supposedly in admonition but in fact to expose the bosom still further, all sent a different signal.

"Sarah," breathed Cooper, "I love you," and he sank one hand down into the warm deep recesses of her gown and seized a full round breast.

"Oh sir!" she gasped, "No! No! I beg you." She fell back raising her arms above her head and closing her eyes, "Oh no! Oh no!"

She said "No" when he tore open the gown. She said "No" when he slid his hands all over her. She said "No" when he rubbed his face into her breasts and between her thighs. She said "No" when he proceeded to throw off his clothes. She said "No" when he leaped upon her. "No, no, no," she said and could hardly stop from laughing.

Afterwards she wept so piteously that Cooper would have hung himself had only he been given a rope and a beam to tie it to. But these facilities were denied him. Instead, with Cooper sunk fathoms down in guilt and with his mind in a most excellently plastic state, some new directives were implanted deeply within it. It was not done by threat of Legal action. It was not done by blackmail. It was simply a matter of what a decent man should do to pay back a beautiful, good and wonderful lady whom he had wronged, defiled and insulted.

The directives were all to do with Mr Jacob Fletcher. Mr Fletcher was to be denied all opportunities for his pernicious business activities in

Boston. Mr Fletcher was to be denounced to the American authorities as a British spy, or to the British as a deserter and murderer: whichever would get his neck stretched the sooner. Best of all, direct action should be taken against Mr Fletcher personally.

Drunk on wine, guilt, lust and Sarah Coignwood, Captain Daniel Cooper promised to do all this to the best of his ability.

CHAPTER 26

Over the next few days I acted fast. I had to. Boston was a fine, rich town of over twenty thousand people, but it was only a mile across and small enough for word of me to get around, should people take note of me, which inevitably they do because of my size. And it was vital I got myself shipshape and Bristol fashion before the man I wanted to do business with, should get the wind of me.

First I borrowed some cash off Stanley (of which he did indeed have plenty) as I needed to splash it about, and using any of the British gold would blow our gaff in double quick time. Between the Monday and the Wednesday of that week I got myself some proper clothes: dark broadcloth and sober shoes, and stocked up on clean linen and got myself properly shaved. I got proper lodgings too, for I couldn't work out of Stanley Wharf, and to tell the truth his dismal little house brought the blues upon me, as the Americans say. I picked out a suite of first-floor rooms in a smart new, brick-built terrace on the West side of Congress street, near Salter's court. This was a splendidly busy place with the hum of commerce about it, and it put me a few minutes walk from the State House and from Market Square, the very heart of merchant Boston.

My landlord was a serious, fat little gent, by the name Poole; quite young but a man of some property, who made clear that no *Shenanigans* were tolerated and a month's advance rent required in cash. He named a figure and I knocked it down a bit, for it ain't constitutionally in me not to bargain, but I didn't try too hard, for I wanted him sweet. I let him charge me for meals too, which I knew I could get cheaper in a chop-house, but it was necessary.

Finally, I took the risk of going round the town and enquiring, discreet as I knew how, about one Ezekiah Cooper and his nephew Daniel, the same Captain Daniel Cooper, United States Navy, now in command of the frigate *Declaration of Independence* anchored out by Long Island. The Coopers were one of the great merchant clans of this merchant city. They were in everything from the slave trade, to ship-building, to imported fine china from Staffordshire. Thus Daniel Cooper and his Uncle Ezekiah were into every shade of Boston politics, while Daniel's father was a Congressman, sucked up like a leech to President Washington and the Federal Government. All-in-all they were just the clever rogues I needed for Stanley's plan. I knew this as I'd been precious close to the Coopers when I was in Boston, from March to April of the previous year.

In fact I'd done a deal with Uncle Ezekiah, to train up the gunners on his nephew's ship, and teach them British drill. They got me Yankee citizenship papers and a sort of honorary Lieutenancy in their navy, and put $5,000 in the bank in my name for when I should return. But I got fed up with the twisting double-dealing of young Captain Daniel and abandoned ship in mid-Atlantic to be picked up by the British ship that Cooper was fighting at the time.

So there you have it, my jolly boys. They'd reneged on me, I'd reneged on them, and I wasn't at all sure how they'd greet me. But I knew for sure that they'd freeze me out of every bank and counting house in Boston if I didn't make my peace with them and so I had to try. And to tell the truth, there was one other reason I wanted to get back among the Coopers. That reason was Daniel Cooper's housekeeper: a six-foot tall black girl by the name of Lucinda, with a figure like an hour-glass and the longest legs in the Americas. She was someone else I'd met last time and was eager to meet again.

So, come the Wednesday, I sent my Landlord's parlour-maid, round to Uncle Ezekiah's offices at the corner of Exchange and State street. There she delivered a letter to Mr E. Cooper (strictly private and personal for his eyes alone). She had to wait over an hour before the humble paper was presented to the great man. But eventually a senior clerk came running down the stairs from the Sanctum Sanctorum on the first floor, and thrust a letter into the girl's hand where she stood waiting by the Porter's Lodge, inside the front doors.

"See here, girl", says he, "Put this into Mr Fletcher's hands directly, now! D'you understand?"

She told me that later, and quite a lot later too, because I was out the

219

door behind her the moment she left and into a coffee house on the corner of Bath street where I got myself a seat by a window that gave look out down Congress street so I could take warning if the Peelers were set on me. So I stayed there all day reading all the journals and newspapers ten times over. They even had London and Paris papers in there, and there were actual Frogs about too, gabbling away bold as brass in their vile lingo, as if they were safe at home. Disgraceful, and a nasty sign of the Froggish influence in America.

Eventually, I saw the girl come back, but I stayed at anchor until dusk. Then, when I felt reasonably sure that Cooper hadn't turned out the constables, with chains and cudgels, I went back to my lodgings.

There, the girl gave me the letter of reply, which was an invitation to visit the Coopers at Daniel's house in Tontine Crescent, on Franklin Place. The invitation was for eight o'clock that very evening. I hauled out the new silver watch I'd bought. The time was past ten. I took up my hat and a stout stick, locked the door of my rooms and went downstairs. Poole stuck his head out into the corridor as my feet rumbled down the stairs, for it's hard to tread light, at my weight.

"Going out, Mr Fletcher?" says he with a frown, "At this hour?" From the look on his face you'd have thought I was pissing on his head from the upstairs landing.

"Urgent business, sir!" says I, "Vital matters of state!" Silly bugger; I think he actually believed me.

Boston was well-lit even in those days, and it didn't take me long to walk the few streets to the elegant crescent of houses where Daniel Cooper lived. Last year the south side of the street had still been mud and builders' clutter. But now it was done and finished and the whole thing looked like something magically transplanted out of the smartest square in London.

I knocked on the Coopers' door hoping to see Lucinda, but a black butler answered instead. This was a new fellow, not the man they'd had last time. He looked me up and down, measuring me against his instructions.

"Mistah Fletchah?" says he, with the bearing of an earl at a levee.

"Yes," says I.

"Yo ah expected, suh!" says he, and he led me through the familiar hall, to the drawing room and threw open the double doors.

"Mistah Jacob Fletchah," booms this noble minion, "Lately an acting-officer of the United States Navy!" And to that resounding announcement

I went into the splendidly furnished room, crammed with every conceivable luxury of glass, brass, silver, gold, yew, teak, porcelain, brocade, silk and ivory, and polish; especially polish. Some would say the pudding was over-egged, but that's how the Coopers liked it.

And there they were, stood before the fire, beaming and smiling their dear, honest, little hearts out: Uncle Ezekiah Cooper and Captain Daniel Cooper. Uncle Ezekiah was in his middle fifties and thickening impressively at the middle. He was dressed in a suit of black silk with a formal white wig on his head. Diamonds flashed here and there about him: on cuffs, buckles and buttons.

Captain David wore his Yankee Sea-Service coat with a pair of epaulettes. It was a stained and faded garment that had obviously seen wind and weather from the quarterdeck. He looked fit and sun-tanned. You could see the family look about them in the thin, straight noses, the clever eyes and the long upper lip that always gave them a serious look. But tonight they were all smiles.

"Well, my lads," thinks I to myself, "I know what you've got the scent of to be so uncommon friendly."

"Jacob, my dear boy!" cries Uncle Ezekiah.

"Fletcher, old fellow!" cries Daniel, and they surged forward and took turns at pumping hand.

"We thought you dead!" says Daniel, "We rejoice to see you alive!" The joy shone from his honest eyes just as if he'd not ordered an 18-pounder stern chaser fired at me as I pulled away from his ship last year. But best forget that.

"Not at all," says I, "I was blown overboard during the action and had to swim for my life. By chance the British picked me up, and after many adventures, here I am returned!"

"Wonderful!" says Uncle Ezekiah, "You must tell us everything my boy. We rejoice to have you back among us!"

And so we sat down together like the old friends we'd all decided to be, and told one another just enough about our doings to keep the conversation flowing nowhere in particular. I told them about the shocking state of affairs in Jamaica. They told me about the shocking state of affairs (no-war, no-peace) between King George and the Yankees. I asked after mutual acquaintances. They told me. They smiled. I smiled. They offered French brandy. I accepted. And neither party raised the topic that had brought us together. All of which was a very reasonable way to begin a negotiation. One piece of small talk sprung a real reply though.

"I saw the old *Declaration* out in the bay, Captain," says I, "Is she repaired from the battle of last year?"

"Mostly," says he, "She'll stand a press of sail aloft and the worst is made good below." He smiled confidently, "She'll face Howe's *Diomedes*!" then he blinked, and cut himself short, "If need be," says he, and his eyes flickered to Uncle Ezekiah who never moved a muscle of his face.

"Howe?" says I, "Not Black Dick Howe?"

"Daniel refers to Rear Admiral Sir Brian Howe," says Uncle Ezekiah, "Who is in command of four British frigates out here to watch over us. We'd not feel safe without them!" says he, and they laughed at his little joke, "More brandy old fellow," says Daniel, "By Cracky but it's good to see you!"

But it was too late changing the subject. He'd already said too much. I already knew there was a mutinied British ship off Boston with a Frog waiting to snap her up. Now I knew there was a British Squadron in the offing, and that could only mean they were coming in to set things right. That's just what the Navy would do. They'd either cut out the mutineer or burn her, or die in the attempt. And so, *Declaration* was waiting to prevent them from doing such a thing inside of American waters.

You see? What did I tell you? The mark of death was on *Calipheme* and I wanted nothing to do with her. I was only too happy to let the matter drop.

So we fenced about for a while and eventually we three sat looking at one another, pleased with ourselves and we stretched our legs out to the fire and swilled the brandy round the glasses. And then it was time to begin.

"Well, sir," says Uncle Ezekiah and pulled my letter out of his pocket, "Here's an interesting epistle that you've sent me. And an interesting calling card." He unfolded the sheet of paper and shook out a shiny new guinea, "You say you've some more of these, Jacob," says he, "and you'd be grateful for my advice in a piece of work concerning them," the smiles were gone now, and Captain Daniel leaned back while Uncle Ezekiah leaned forward. So I stuck my hand in my pocket, brought out another guinea and tossed it across to Uncle Ezekiah. He took it like a dog snapping a piece of meat.

"I am acting for a party who has acquired a number of these," says I, "It's a large number and he wants the value of 'em shifted across to

England. It might be that the Cooper Interest, can help us do this and it might be that some small expenses could be paid to the Cooper interest in recompense."

"I don't see as how as such a thing could be done," says Uncle Ezekiah, shaking his head solemnly, "Not without enormous costs." And away we went at a cracking pace. It was one of the most thrilling moments of my life.

You see, I'd proved over and again that I could make money in a face-to-face, market-trading sense. I knew too, that I could run a good, middling business like Lee and Boswell's and my other enterprises on the side. But now I was breaking new ground. I'd no direct knowledge of this Rothschild world where the value of money slips across frontiers and oceans, by way of a sealed paper with the proper signatures on it. A world where a letter from Boston would be honoured by a bank in London, or Prague, or Paris or Moscow, by a payment in gold.

But Uncle Ezekiah knew that world. I could tell from the first seconds, and the game for me (which is what made it so exciting, and why I was doing this for Stanley at all) the game for me, was not to let on how little I knew, so as not to get skinned and boned by the sharp-toothed rascal!

So we talked for several hours, the servants brought in sandwiches, and most of the night passed by. Just before dawn I left Tontine Crescent with my head aching with new knowledge and a very passable compromise agreed with the Coopers.

I'll spare you the details for they were fiendish complicated, but what it boiled down to was that the thing could indeed be done, even with England at war with America and with the French! It would take a good while to complete the manoeuvrings, but the cash would be shifted by devious routes, and the great bulk of it would end up in London to the account of Dean Barlow and Glynn with any letter of apology or explanation that Mr Francis Stanley cared to write. There would of course be generous expenses and fees for numerous interested parties along the way, for otherwise they wouldn't have done it, now would they?

And upon this subject, you youngsters should take note that no workman worth employing can be had cheap and that goes ten times over for the fraternity of Hebrew bankers (men with brains big as mountains), who alone had the skills to do what we needed. But look what you get for your money! For one thing, these gentry knew how to make the money grow, by loans and investments upon short term, and thus a considerable degree of what got took out, was took not from the capital itself, *but out of the profits that got made out of the capital*. It was a wonderful, wonderful world and I was intoxicated by it.

Back at my lodgings I slept a couple of hours and then went to see Stanley to tell him the good news. It was then Tuesday afternoon September 29th and Stanley's been busy himself by then. All the gold was out of the ship and stowed away safe under a flagstone in the cellar of his cottage, and all the dust re-scattered to make it look like nobody'd been down there for centuries. He was a wonder at any sort of trickery like that.

He was still miserable because he'd been round to see Mrs Marlow who'd sat the children out in rows to hear what had happened to dear Papa. So he snivelled a bit over that, said how he'd look after Mrs Marlow so she'd never want for nothing, and I looked at my boots and sighed a few times, and I damned that bloody Coignwood woman a few times more.

And then he cut up a bit rough over the expenses that would have to be paid out, to get the gold back to England, and he said it was naked robbery (fine sentiment from the likes of him!) and he'd not have it. But he saw sense in the end, for what else could he do? So we parted on good terms and I agreed to keep him informed as the business moved forwards.

Then I went back to my lodgings for a proper sleep and didn't wake up until I was disturbed by the arrival of two old friends, one extremely welcome the other extremely unwelcome.

CHAPTER 27

"The continuing unmarried state of my nephew troubles me. You know how hard I have laboured to effect alliance between him and some girl of good family, yet now I am reduced to wishing him hitched to any female that breathes, howsoever low, sooner than suffer gossip to the effect that his preferences turn unnaturally."

(From a letter of 29th June 1794, from Mr Ezekiah Cooper of Boston, Massachusetts, to his brother Ephraim, United States Congressman, at Philadelphia, Pennsylvania.)

Thump! The distant sound of the front door came to Ezekiah Cooper and his nephew, Captain Daniel Cooper, where they sat blinking with tiredness in the splendid drawing room of Daniel's house in the Tontine Crescent. The two men were exhausted with the effort of concentration they had been put to over the last few hours. For a few minutes they sat staring at one another, then Uncle Ezekiah stirred as a candle guttered out in an elaborate silver mount, on a table at his elbow. It went out and sent up a thin plume of smoke. He wet his thumb and forefinger and snuffed the wick.

"That was a most remarkable young man!" said Ezekiah, "Never in all my years have I met any man with such a gift for business."

"Huh!" said his nephew, "You don't know him as I do!"

"D'ye know, Daniel," said Uncle Ezekiah, "When he came in here tonight, I looked at the size of the creature, and I remembered what you'd told me about the strength of him, and how he scared the daylights out of your crew."

"Huh!" said his nephew.

"And I said to myself, Ezekiah, you're lucky to be meeting Mr Fletcher on *your* ground and not *his*!" Uncle Ezekiah laughed and shook his head, "But did you just see the speed of him? Did you see him catch me every time I tried to gain some trick over him?"

"Oh get the hell over with it, Uncle!" said Daniel, "So you think the bastard's something damn special, do you?"

"What?" said Uncle Ezekiah, for oaths were not at all his nephew's style. Not in the drawing room.

"What's gnawing your bones, boy?" he said, "And just so's you'll know, *yes* I do think Mr Fletcher is something damn special! D'ye know, boy, it enters my mind to suspect that Mr Fletcher didn't know nothing about banking and shifting credit, before he entered this room, and yet in five minutes he was talking to me as an equal."

"Oh, don't talk such damn rubbish!" said his nephew, "The fellow was drawing you on! He's a practised expert. I saw it at once," he sneered, "All that damn pretence about not knowing! All those damn polite questions! I thought better of you, Uncle!"

"You saucy rogue!" said Uncle Ezekiah, jumping up in his chair and slamming his fist on the arm, "You mind your damn manners, boy!"

"God's prick!" said Daniel, "The bastard's a…"

"Shut your mouth, boy!" said Uncle Ezekiah, furious and amazed. He struggled to his feet and pointed accusingly at his nephew where he slumped in his chair, "You keep your damn cussing for your damn ship where it's appreciated. I'll have you remember who controls your money while your father's in Philadelphia and I'll have you give respect! By Jove I never heard such language from you."

Daniel shrunk into his chair and chewed at his nails. He seemed to collapse in upon himself, the tarnished epaulettes on his weather-beaten coat, folding in towards each other as he sank back.

"She told me…" he said, beginning an explanation.

"She!" cried Uncle Ezekiah, "That woman! That damned English Ma-Dame! What is she to you, boy?"

"Didn't she tell us about Fletcher?" said Daniel, "Didn't she tell us he was in Boston?"

"So what?" said Uncle Ezekiah, "I already knew he was in Boston. He was asking about the town for me." Ezekiah banged open a glazed door in a yew bureau-bookcase, and dragged out a bundle of letters.

"Listen, boy!" he cried, peering at the first letter in the fading candle-light, and running his finger over the paper. He read aloud, "…a young man, English by his voice, and of formidable appearance, was at my counting-house desk today, asking after yourself. He had the manner of one used to command and left my unfortunate chief clerk in a state of nervous alarm…" Uncle Ezekiah looked up and caught his nephew's eye, "There!" said he, "Who'd that remind you of, eh? The sort of man that leaves a poor pen-pusher shaking in his shoes?" He waved the bundle of letters, "And here's another half-dozen of the same, from friends who wrote to warn me."

Daniel Cooper squirmed in his chair and sulked.

"I'll admit you knew he was here," said he, "But didn't she tell us he'd been with Stanley and Morley, raising gold from a wreck? You didn't know about that did you Uncle?"

"No," said Ezekiah, "but it don't count no-how, for I knew he was looking me up for some piece of business or other."

"Business, you say? You don't know the conniving bastard that he is!"

"Lay off the cussing, boy!" said Ezekiah, "I'm warning you. And anyway, just what *did* he do aboard that ship of yours, last year?"

"He humiliated me before my men!" snapped Daniel.

"You mean he was better at your trade than you were!"

"Yes!" cried Daniel, "Just as he was better than you at yours in this very room tonight!" Uncle Ezekiah sneered and shook his head. He eased himself back into his chair, puffed out his cheeks, clasped his hands together behind his head, and stuck out his legs. He thought for a few seconds, then spoke.

"No!" said he, "It won't do, boy. Last year you told me it was Mr Fletcher that trained up your gunners to fight the British. You said that without him, you'd have lost the fight. You said you didn't like his rough methods, but that you'd have lost your ship without him!"

"But he abandoned me!" said Daniel, "I caught him leaping out of the stern lights of my cabin. And then he stole a boat and pulled for the Britisher we were fighting!"

"No doubt!" said Ezekiah, "But only because you twisted him first! You told him he'd not have to fight against his own people, and then you took him into action against the first British ship you found!" Daniel Cooper's eyes narrowed with anger as his uncle hammered home his point, "Fletcher had plenty to come back for," says Ezekiah, "$5,000 dollars awaiting him in the bank, and your housekeeper, Lucinda that he was humping on the sly and thought nobody knew about."

"Uncle!" cried Daniel, blushing to his collar, "How dare you suggest I'd permit such a thing in my house?"

"Bah!" cried Ezekiah, "Don't pretend you never knew! And anyhow, just what did you get up to with your friend Lady Sarah Coignwood, that was so almighty friendly to you at Faneuil Hall?"

"How dare you, sir?" gasped Captain Daniel Cooper, "That Lady is a noblewoman of the purest blood. She could never stoop to anything that was base or mean," and he sweated and gulped and fumbled for words, sunk deep in a pit of shame and rage and agonized embarrassment, "Why… why sir, I'll have you know that she is … is… as far above … that … that is to say I what you *suggest* … as … as angels are above m-mortal m-m-men"

"Is that so?" said Ezekiah, with a snort of laughter, "If you believe that, boy, then you're a bigger damn fool with women than even I believed you to be!"

"Meaning precisely what, sir?" cried Daniel.

"Meaning precisely what I said, sir!" cried Ezekiah.

"Which is what?"

"Which is what you *know* that I mean!"

"Which is *what*?"

"Which is that you don't know what a woman's for and you've never had the wit, nor the will to find out!" By this stage, with an unspoken, unmentioned family secret dragged brutally out from under its covers, where it had lain hidden for many years, both men were shouting at the tops of their voices and had entirely lost their tempers.

Much more was said on this sensitive matter and cruel words were exchanged which afterwards would be regretted. The quarrel grew. The quarrel developed. Mr Jacob Fletcher was examined. Lady Sarah Coignwood was examined. Captain Daniel Cooper's fitness to command a ship of war was examined, likewise his fitness to call himself a man. Mr Ezekiah Cooper's fitness to handle money was examined, likewise his fitness to call himself a kinsman and a Christian.

And every word of this raging, roaring debate was followed with gleeful fascination by Captain Daniel Cooper's servants, who crept along the corridor for the free entertainment. They didn't even have to press their ears against the drawing room doors.

And so they picked up much valuable gossip and it is a great pity that having missed the earlier part of the conversation, they missed entirely the overridingly important fact, that despite the many angry words spoken, the balance of power between uncle and nephew remained with the uncle, and that the uncle was firmly resolved to deal straight with Mr Jacob Fletcher, whom he liked and respected and admired.

CHAPTER 28

Booom! I was awakened in my bed in Mr Poole's house by the deep voice of a heavy gun. It roared and echoed, and all the windows of the town shivered in fright. After a few minutes it spoke again, and then again. Three rounds, slow and steady: an alarm signal from the North Battery, calling the people of Boston to arms. For the North Battery looked straight down the channel to the Broad Sound and out to the open sea. And something was coming in from the sea, heading for Boston, that the North Battery did not like.

The guns had me awake, but it was the clamour and the voices outside the house that got me out of bed: the running feet, the clattering horses and the shouts. I even heard the rolling of a side drum somewhere far off. I washed myself and dressed fast as I could, trying to cock an ear to what was going on outside, and then there came a knocking at my door. I opened up, in my shirtsleeves and a towel in my hands still drying myself. It was Mr Poole, popeyed, red-faced and gasping from his ascent of two flights of stairs.

"Mr Fletcher! Mr Fletcher!" says he, "Tis the British, sir! They are come down upon us to burn the town. Fly for your life!"

He poured out lots more of this, but he was wetting his breeches by then, and making little sense. So I thanked him, shut the door, and finished my dressing. Then I clapped my hat on my head, buttoned up my coat and went out to see what was happening. I was praying that he might be wrong. The last thing I wanted was the dead embers of this war brought to life just when my business interests had taken such a dramatic leap upwards.

I followed a press of people making their way to the Long Wharf and the sea. It was like Montego Bay all over again: a town in a commotion

230

from an approaching enemy. And yet it wasn't the same at all. There was more anger about than fear, and when a company of foot went past with drums beating and their fifes playing Yankee Doodle, the crowd gave them a huge cheer and the drunks, dogs and children skipped along behind them.

The Long Wharf was thick with people and more coming all the while, as the shops and taverns, the counting houses and salons, emptied their contents. Everyone was pointing eastward, out past Governor's Island and Deer Island, and the crossed yards of *Mercure, Calipheme* and *Declaration.* I got myself up on to a barrel and squinted under my hand, and I sighed with disappointment. Four or five miles off, the billowing topsails of a man-o-war were creeping in from the sea. I saw the flash of her colours and I think that even at that distance I knew what she was. But I borrowed a telescope from a man who'd got one, and had a good look. She was British all right, a big frigate. Damn, damn, damn!

The Bostonians weren't none too pleased, neither, and they wanted a fight even if I didn't. Here was a foreign warship of a hostile power seemingly trying to get her guns within range of their town. Plenty of those watching were old enough to remember British bombardments during the Revolution and they didn't cherish the memories.

"Declaration'll see her off!" says someone.

"Aye!" they cried.

"Powder and ball's the answer!"

"Aye!"

"Damn the British!"

"Give 'em hot shot from the forts!"

"No quarter!"

"No King!"

"No surrender!"

It was the only time I ever was in America when I feared to be recognised as an Englishman. I kept my mouth shut and wandered off as soon as I could. I went back to my lodgings and left the town buzzing furiously. When I left the Long Wharf there was a blue-jacket up on a box calling for volunteers to double-man the gun-crews aboard *Declaration* and to carry shot to the guns in the batteries, and men were running forward to do just that.

Back in Congress Street Mr Poole had found his courage. There was such a spirit in the town that even *he* now thought that the British would get a bloody nose and be driven off. He was busy hanging flags from the windows, like many other householders and he'd got out a little table with a bottle of some vile wine that his mother made from cranberries. This was on offer to all passers-by.

"Our brave boys'll save the town!" says he, "Don't you long to see our ship bear herself into action, Mr Fletcher?" says he, shoving a glass at me. "Don't you hope the battle'll be in daylight so we can see?"

No I did not. Not in the slightest. But I didn't tell him that. I drank his sickly over sugared wine and toasted *Our brave boys* and *God Speed to our arms* etc etc. But wasn't half so sure as he was, that *Declaration* could do the business. I'd trained her gunners myself, but that was nearly a year-and-a-half ago, and *Declaration* had been in harbour for months. I wouldn't like to wager money on her defeating a British frigate with a well-drilled crew. Not unless the Frog pitched in to help that is, and then what might the mutinied British ship do? It was all very uncertain.

I went into the house to sit down and consider what this might mean to me. But I hadn't been five minutes in my room when Poole laboured up the stairs again and tapped on my door. He didn't look none too pleased.

"Mr Fletcher," says he, "I made clear my requirements on your entering this house." He was high up on his dignity and something had upset him, because he was attempting to read me the rule-book. I don't like pompous little fat men taking that tone to me and he must have seen it in my face, and he backed off and took a different tack, "Now, now," says he, "No offence intended I'm sure, but in such an elevated part of the town as this, there are certain standards."

"Come to it, man!" says I, and I may have shouted a little, as I was preoccupied and had no time for this nonsense. He jumped and his chins wobbled and he gulped, "Well, sir," says he, "Fact is, there's a black woman wanting to be shown up here and offering this for you to see, and maintaining she has a respectable connection in…"

But I was up on my feet and snatching at what he was holding out to me. It was a piece of red ribbon tied into a bow. Last March I'd bought some yards of ribbon like that, for Daniel Cooper's housekeeper, Lucinda. And she'd turned out that very night, in my bedroom, wearing those self-same ribbons and nothing else whatsoever.

"Bring her up, man!" says I, full of delight and lust.

"But, but…" says he, and he'll never know how near he came to having his fat arse kicked down his own stairs. But I had a use for his lodgings now, and an urgent one, and I didn't want him coming back with a constable, to disturb me.

"Good heavens, Mr Poole," says I, "What possible impropriety could there be in this? Do you take me for one of those who would debauch a poor negress? Sir, you have not asked the nature of my business in Boston, but now I will tell you. I represent interests of the Presbyterian Congregation of Great Britain that is dedicated to evangelism among the blacks of the plantations. The poor child who waits below is one of our converts, who passed me the sign of the red ribbon, which is the symbol of Christ's blood. She is here on the work of our church."

(You see? I ain't just a big fellow with a pair of heavy fists, now am I? I defy any man to come up with a finer bucket of old cod's wallop than that, given equally short notice.)

He damn nearly believed me too. I could see the little piggy eyes flickering and blinking as I held forth. And in the end, I'd guess that he decided he was sufficiently persuaded for appearances sake and that he should not enquire too closely of a customer who paid up quite so readily in advance, and didn't mind being over-charged.

And so, down the stairs he went and up the stairs came the tall, lovely ebony-skinned creature that I remembered with such delight from last year.

"Lucinda!" says I, carefully shutting and locking the door behind her.

"Jacob!" says she, and leapt at me with shining eyes, folding me into her arms. By George that was a wonderful moment. She was so soft and splendid, and stood so straight and tall, and had such white teeth and long, slender limbs. She'd look down on most men from her six feet of height, but not me.

And I was damn pleased to see her again. One of life's joys is re-union with a friend, and Lucinda was that to me and more. I've had many women in my time and some of 'em (like those trollops Patience Jordan and Alice Powys) were no more than passing fancies, some of 'em passing pretty damn quick. In those cases, they got what they wanted and I got what I wanted and that was that. But the ones I remember are the ones that didn't make a habit of the thing. The ones to whom I was special because they liked me, even loved me, and who were special to me, because I liked them too, and loved them too. For I like women a powerful lot and it's hard for me not to fall in love with 'em. It comes of my being a sailor I suppose.

So I spun Lucinda off her feet and round and round the room and we said each others names over and over and I kissed her all up and down her neck and she caught my ear with her teeth and ran her tongue all over the side of my face. That was lively work which made me shudder with delight, and as I'd got her feet off the floor and it was only me holding the pair of us upright, we staggered backwards and came up against the wall with a thump and slip and slide till we jammed into a corner with her slipping her hand inside my shirt and running her nails up and down my back.

She let go my ear and fastened her lips on mine, all soft and moist and slippery. I hoisted her up by the rump with one hand and got the other under her skirt and hauled the material up like a furled sail. She gasped and hooked her long, naked legs behind my knees and as a matter of historical record, they didn't wear no drawers in those days.

"Now!" says she, throwing her head back with her eyes tight shut, "Now! Now! Now!" I did my best unbuttoning myself one-handed while holding Lucinda up by the soft round stern but it weren't easy. Just you try running out the guns when you're so excited that one touch on the barrel will fire the charge. As it was I missed first time, and missed fired half my charge, hauled back, tried again and hit the mark.

"Yes! Yes!" cries Lucinda, and we clung together panting and laughing and kissing, until I swept her into my arms and kicked off my breeches so I could take her properly to bed. I didn't get that right either, and trailed them across the floor still fast by one ankle. But one way or another, we ended up in my bed with our clothes scattered about the bedroom, and her curled up in my arms with me stroking her smooth back and telling her how much I'd missed her.

Later, I made love to her properly, taking my time and doing the thing right. A thundering gallop is all very well when you've just met, but a lady deserves pleasing properly when a gentleman has the time to do it, and to my mind the longer you can make it last, then the better it is for all concerned.

And then we fell to talking and everything changed. The joy and the pleasure departed and a heavy uncertainty fell upon me. Not that any of this was Lucinda's fault, and nor was it her intention. The trouble was that last time we met, she believed I was a British Naval Lieutenant acting as a spy on the Americans. It was approximately the truth and it kept her happy. But when we told each other what we'd been doing for the past year, I got a surprise. Lucinda was married.

"Yeah, married," says she "To Peter, him as was Butler fo' Cap'n Cooper. We got some money together and we bought a house and a parcel o' land. He's a good man."

"Oh," says I.

"Yeah," says she.

"He's a good, steady man," says she, "Don't drink, don't chase the skirt, and don't raise a hand to me."

"Oh," says I.

"Saved all his money too. So's we could buy our own place and not be beholdin' to them fine Coopers with their airs and graces. That's why me and Peter, we don't work there no mo'…" Then she laughed at me for she could see I was smitten with jealousy, "Why, yo' dumb man!" says she, "Was you gonna come back an marry a po' black girl?" I had no answer to that, so I changed the subject. This was an intelligent woman and I knew I could tell her no lies. You should have seen the way she had the tradesmen on the hop when she was Cooper's housekeeper, and they were trying to give short measure.

"So what're you here for, madame?" says I,

"Fo' you, you dumb man," says she, "'Cos I love you," and she wriggled herself closer in the most appealing fashion and smiled up at me with her great beautiful eyes and laid her head on my chest. By George it was cosy, I can tell you.

"An' I gotta tell you some things too," says she, "There's a man here in Boston, goes by the name o' Thomas Ratcliffe?" she paused and looked at me expecting some reaction, but got none. "Don't know him huh?"

"No," says I, "Why should I?" She blinked and grew nervous and held me close. She whispered very softly. "'Cos that Mister Ratcliffe, he knows you is a British Lootenant, and he knows why you was here last year."

"Does he?" says I, not realising what this meant. Then I grasped what she was getting at. She was telling me that this Mr Ratcliffe now believed that I was a spy in the British service. At first I sighed miserably and wondered what this might mean to the wonderful agreement I'd reached with Ezekiah. And then I sat bolt upright in bed as the full ghastly significance hit me. Oh Christ! Did the Yankees shoot spies or hang 'em? By the laws of war they were fully entitled to do either.

"Who told him that?" says I in a fright.

"Me," says Lucinda in a tiny little voice.

"What?" says I, "Why'd you do that?"

"Cos he asked," says she.

"What ?" says I and took her by the shoulders and shook her.

"Don't!" says she, "He came round askin' questions."

"Round where?" says I.

"Round the Cooper house."

"Asking questions?"

"Yes."

"What kind of questions?"

"Navy questions: about you."

"Me?"

"You."

"And did you tell him? What he wanted to know?"

"Yes."

"Why?"

"Cos he paid me, an' he promised no harm to you."

"Did he, by Jove!" says I, "And who is he? What is he?"

"He's the fishmonger. Came to the back door most every day, always smilin', always talkin' … an' askin'."

"And you told him about me?"

"Not at first. Not till I was sure you wasn't never comin' back. I thought you was long gone and safe in England. An' anyhow, he kept askin' and jokin' an' laughin' … an' offerin' money. There didn't seem no harm in it."

"When did this happen?" says I.

"Last year."

"Well what is this man? Does he write lines for the newspapers? Is he the town gossip? What is he?" She shrugged her shoulders and wouldn't meet my eye.

"Just a fishmonger," says she.

"Then why are you warning me about him?" says I.

At that, her lip quivered and the big eyes filled with tears and a second later she was in my arms sobbing her heart out. It put another fright up me, and no mistake. Presumably she thought this Mr Ratcliffe was some sort of officer of secret police. The Frogs, of course, have secret police like

236

a dog has fleas, for that's the sort of devious, cunning swabs that they are, but I wouldn't have thought the Yankees would've stooped to such a thing. Mind you, if they *were* secret then how was a man to know?

Meanwhile I soothed her down and told her it didn't matter, and thanked her for warning me, and said she was a brave girl, and that I loved her, and all the things a man says to a woman to send the tears away. Then when she calmed down I asked another question and got another nasty fright.

"Why are you telling me this now?" says I, "Why did you come here?"

"'Cos yo' was at the Cooper house last night, and after yo' left, there was a big fight between Mizzah Ezekiah and Mizzah Daniel."

"How'd you know that?" says I.

"We got friends in the below stairs, at the Cooper house," says she, "They tell me what goes on, specially when it's somethin' spicy."

"Well," says I, "Go on."

"Well," says she, "That's how I found out yo' was here, and I would have come to find yo' anyhow," she smiled.

"Would you?" says I.

"Course," says she, "But then them Coopers fell to a scritchin' and a hollerin' and a cussin' ' you, and then a-fightin' over some English Lady, name of Sarah Coignwood that bin' goin' round the town and that hates you, Jacob. She hates you bad."

"I know," says I with a feeling like a round shot in my stomach. That damned, bloody woman had got to the Coopers. What price my gold transactions with Uncle Ezekiah now? It all had to depend on trust for one thing. What chance his wanting to trust me now? If I'd had the least confidence that Ezekiah might still trust me, I'd have given it a try. I'd have gone to his office and brazened it out, for I don't give up gold without a struggle. But I'd seen Sarah Coignwood at work, bending men's minds to her will and I wasn't walking into any trap that she'd set for me. And then it got still worse.

"Jacob," says Lucinda, "If I heard that stuff from the servants at the Cooper house, then so did Mizzah Ratcliffe. He still go' there and he still asks his questions."

It was a very bad moment. Through blood, fire, shot, revolution and murder, I thought come through at last, and out on to the sunlit uplands of life. I'd even shaken off the Navy and was out of even their long reach. I'd lost two fortunes: first the Coignwood inheritance, my natural father's money, and then I'd lost the fortune I was building for myself in Jamaica. But by good luck I'd got my hands on a third, and the chance to build, and build upon it. And as you'll know if you've read this far in my journals, it's the building that really I was looking forward to.

But now, on the threshold of this wonderful opportunity, my business partners were poisoned against me and the Peelers thought I was a foreign agent. And the irony of it was that while, of course, I was *not* a British agent, I couldn't afford to be held in prison, or have my affairs looked into, or attract any sort of attentions of that kind, while beginning so ticklish and so sensitive an undertaking as I'd planned with Ezekiah Cooper. Not when the Yankee Government was itself after the gold. Cooper would run a mile and who'd blame him? I was balked and it was cruel hard fate and dastardly unfair.

Worse still, a feeling close on panic was arising from within me. I'd run from England. I'd run from Jamaica. And now was I to run from America? And if so where should I run? I didn't want to live my life among bloody foreigners that won't speak English. I wished Sammy Bone were with me and I wanted some safe place to hide while I thought things out. I looked at Lucinda, and I knew she could do nothing. She had her own life and her own man. As for the Coopers, they were poisoned by Madame, and that left Francis Stanley.

"I'll have to go, Lucinda," says I, getting out of bed.

"I know," says she and she followed me. We dressed in a hurry and without speaking. It was getting dark as we went down the stairs. We'd been up there for hours. Poole came out as we went past his door. I don't doubt he'd heard the bed creak above his head and he was trying to work up courage to say something, but I shoved past and stood aside to let Lucinda out. I'd paid in advance so there was no reason not to walk out with my belongings in a bag and never go back. So I did.

Lucinda had insisted we say goodbye upstairs. She said a white man couldn't kiss a black girl in the street. Not in Congress street. And he couldn't show no familiarity neither. So she walked off, tall and queenly with her nose in the air.

She weren't a woman that a man forgets in a hurry. If I'd had my way I'd have kept her in a nice little house with plenty of spending money and a piano and lady's maid, and an insurance policy on my life for her old age. That's how a gentleman manages these thing if he's got an ounce of decency in him. It's a pity she'd blabbed about me, of course, but who could blame her? She thought I was gone for good. So she went her way and I went mine, and I didn't see her ever again, more's the bloody pity of it. But what can you do?

My way was northwards towards Stanley Wharf. I was deep in thought as I went through the darkening streets and so it was some while before I got the feeling that I was being followed. Up in the north end of Boston there was still quite a bit of open land in those days, with big gardens and small fields and not much in the way of lighting. There were few people about, and most of them in carriages with flickering lamps, that rattled past and were gone. So I looked back and saw a small group of men coming after me. I quickened my pace. So did they. I broke into a run. So did they. But I'm no great runner. I'm too big and they gained on me. I threw aside my bag and cracked on all the speed I'd got.

"Fletcher!" cried a voice, "Jacob Fletcher!" And one of them sprinted up to me and clutched at my arm. He hung on and held me back for his mates to catch up, and then there was four or five of 'em hanging on to me and pulling me to a halt.

So much the worse for them. I raised my fists and put down two of them in as many seconds. Then I got my hands on the third and heaved him at the fourth by his coat collar and the seat of his breeches. With none other left standing I took to my heels again and ran all the way to Stanley Wharf where I hammered on the gate till Stanley's man Joe let me in.

Stanley himself was up working in his study and greeted me at the door of his wretched little cottage. At least he made me welcome and at least he was pleased to see me. He weren't much of a friend but he was a friend. And he weren't so pleased when I told him what had happened, neither. But he joined in with cursing Sarah Coignwood and put everything down to her baleful influence.

I told him about the misunderstanding with the police too. There was no point keeping it back. He groaned and sighed over that, for he was still hell bent on giving back his loot. And he glanced at me a bit sharpish and asked what truth there might be in this tale of my being a British agent. I was just telling him, pretty damn firmly what nonsense this was when there came a heavy knocking at his front door.

"That's odd," says he, cocking his head on one side, to listen, "Joe don't knock like that."

"Don't answer!" says I jumping to my feet.

"Why not?" says he and went to the door. I darted into the next room as soon as moved. It was dark but the moonlight shone through a window. I hauled up the sash and got my leg over the sill, and there stood a man with a brace of pistols levelled at my breast.

"Get back in there, or you're dead!" says he. I looked around. The house was surrounded. There were a dozen of 'em and they had Indian Joe trussed up and gagged.

"Where is Lieutenant Fletcher?" says a Yankee voice, coming from the parlour behind me, "Lieutenant Jacob Fletcher of the British Royal Navy?"

CHAPTER 29

"She is a dark-haired lady of middle height, though seeming taller, and of irresistible vivacity. She is not young but her beauty ravishes the senses and those who have once enjoyed her society must thereafter suffer the pains of the opium addict, who is compelled to seek another and yet another dose of his drug."

(From a letter of September 24th 1795 from Mr Harrison Otis of Boston, to his brother Edward in New York.)

To her surprise, Lady Sarah Coignwood found that she liked Boston. The urbane skyline of spires and rooftops was pleasing, there were theatres, libraries shops and churches, and after the success of the ball, the great and good of the town crowded to present themselves to her in the best drawing room of her lodgings. This room, which while far beneath own salon in London, none the less had a naïve elegance and was of a most appealing oval shape.

Many of the visitors were men, all were curious, all fell rapidly under My Lady's spell. She found the problem of being an enemy alien, to be non-existent. Three or four of the Selectmen fell over themselves agreeing that a passport could and should, and *would* be prepared without delay, since My Lady could be no conceivable threat to the town. Later still, various bankers assured her that Boston would accept payment for anything, in British silver or gold, and that Bank of England notes could be transformed by the larger commercial houses, into cash at a small discount. Beyond that, these Boston bankers – surprisingly sophisticated for colonials – were obviously capable of moving credit between continents, and were smilingly ready to grant her any amount of money, drawing on her vast reserves in London, given only her signature.

As for the ladies of Boston, having seen Lady Sarah's clothes (every stitch being in the latest Parisian mode, war or no war), caused the dressmakers, milliners and drapers of Boston to bless and worship Lady Sarah, as took their new orders.

In addition My Lady was entertained by Mr Charles Bullfinch, the celebrated architect, in his own grand house. This young gentleman proved to be as cultured as any European. He'd made the grand tour and had studied under the masters of French and English architecture. He and his wife were charming company except that they mentioned one Jacob Fletcher, an English Lieutenant whom Mr Bulfinch had met at the house of Mr Daniel Cooper last year. The same Daniel Cooper now in command of *Our fine new warship out in the bay*. Lady Sarah smiled at Cooper's name and turned the conversation to other matters.

After that My Lady threw the already stunned and admiring city of Boston, flat back upon its heels by achieving, all in one day, the incredible feat of moving into a new house, acquiring a staff of servants, and giving a dinner party for a select company of the bright and the beautiful. Those ladies who received invitations, fell to their knees and gave thanks to God in his infinite grace and mercy. Those who did not would have sold their children into slavery to get them, if only invitations were to be obtained by so cheap and easy a course of action.

The house was an imposing edifice in State Street, recently designed and furnished throughout by Mr Bullfinch for a client who ran out of money. Among her many guests on the day she moved in, there was a handsome young man by the name of Harrison Otis, a lawyer with a huge and lucrative practise and investments in land and property. He was a politician too and tended to draw the conversation down boring paths. But later on, when he was persuaded to get rid of his still more boring wife, Mr Otis returned to be admitted by the side entrance and to the intimate favours of Lady Sarah herself.

On the next day, Mr Otis, Mr Bullfinch and a party of ladies and gentlemen, hired a barge with boatmen and a hamper and wine, and an awning and comfortably cushioned seats, and took Lady Sarah to see the harbour and the approaches of the city. The trip included an impromptu boarding of the American warship *Declaration of Independence* anchored opposite a French ship and the mutinied British ship that Lady Sarah had seen (entirely without interest) on her arrival in Boston.

Being laden with Captain Daniel Cooper's close friends and social equals, the barge was readily taken alongside the great ship, and arrangements made to hoist the ladies aboard. Since there was an exceedingly great number of very fine young men on board of the ship, Lady Sarah enjoyed the visit, though Captain Cooper did not, being crushed in guilt and soon seeking excuses to be away from the party. This was amusing but regrettable, and threw Lady Sarah into reflection.

The fact was that Captain Cooper was proving ineffective in his given task of dealing with Fletcher, such that now (and having come so far, and having tried in so many ways) she was beginning to wonder about the wisdom of dealing with Fletcher. So troubled were her thoughts that her attention fell entirely within herself, she ignored the chatter of her friends, the wonderful animation of her expression faded, and all those about her noticed.

"My Lady?" said Otis.

"My Lady?" said Bullfinch, and the American ladies cooed and ahhhed.

But she was remembering that moment after the latest attempt, when she went clear over the edge into the abyss.

"It was a near escape," she thought "a near escape from *him* and not just him… but from *myself*." And she began to frame the question that her son had asked, "am I …" she thought, "could I be … am I …" But her sense of self was infinitely greater his and she laughed, sharp and sudden, and everyone breathed laughed with her. "Well and good," she thought, looking at them, "but things must settle. Things must be left for a while." Thus already, in depths of unconscious thought, the decision was made to go home: home to things safe and secure and where failures would fade, and new plans could be made.

Meanwhile the four hundred virile young men of *Declaration's* crew, while minding their manners and doffing their hats, were looking at Lady Sarah as a pack of wolves look at a plump young fawn. It was only the expectation of this delicious experience that had caused Lady Sarah to suggest going aboard in the first place, for what else was there of interest in a ship?

Later, the barge visited briefly the British Vessel *Calipheme* which the Americans somewhat gleefully pointed out had been beaten by the French. The crew of this vessel were observably not under proper discipline and

Lady Sarah thought the vessel seemed untidy. Mr Otis and Mr Bullfinch insisted that the barge did not approach too closely and hinted that political wheels were turning with regard to this ship.

The French ship, *Mercure* gave an altogether more satisfactory response. Again, Otis and Bulfinch would not permit the barge to stop, but it rowed around the Frenchman, to the admiring cries of the hundreds of matelots aboard, who instantly spotted the ladies and were up in the shrouds and astride the hammock nettings for a better view.

Sarah Coignwood had always loved the French. She spoke French as well as she did English. She owned a house in Paris, and before the French went mad and murdered their King, she'd been as well known to Paris as she was to London or Bath. Because of this, and because Boston's news had reached the lower deck of *Mercure*, she was agreeably and flatteringly recognised.

"Milady!"

"Madame la Belle!"

"La Coignwood!"

"La Belle Coignwood!"

Lady Sarah luxuriated like a flower in the sunshine. *La Belle Coignwood* was her favourite appellation in her favourite language. And these men were saluting her with it, of their own free will and at the tops of their voices. They were grinning and ogling and waving and it was intensely pleasing for this to happen before her new American friends in this far-away land. She glanced sideways at her companions to ensure that they were duly impressed. And indeed they were! Then a shouting and erupted from the French ship. The cheers died away, and a rough unshaven person dressed in a peasant's blouse and wearing a red cap of liberty, was seen to be furiously going among the men and cuffing their ears. The Americans did not follow his coarse and rapid French, but Lady Sarah did.

"You whore-sons!" said he, "Cheer a damned English Milady, will you? Take that you shit-eaters! Take that you pig-fuckers!" And then he himself leapt up into the mizzen shrouds and bawled down at the boat.

"Get off you slut! Get away you tart's tart of a cock-sucking aristocrat! We've got the way to deal with your sort in the new France! Get away from my ship!"

There was a brief silence. Three hundred and fifty Frenchmen peered down into the boat not ten yards from their ship. The puzzled Americans looked up, the boatmen rested on their oars. From the stern, among her cushions, La Belle Coignwood raised her voice, in the clear and perfect French of the Court of Versailles.

"Who is this person?" said she. The voice carried authority and drew an immediate reply.

"He's the Captain," cried a French voice, from the ship. And being French, and deeply loyal to his Captain, and being more emotional of speech than an Englishman or an American, he added, "He is our good Captain Barzan. He is our father!"

"How fortunate for *you* to know *your* father," said Lady Sarah, "For the gentleman appears to be one whose mother pleased so many men that he never could be sure of his own."

There was roar of laughter from the French ship and Barzan himself was seen to smile. Bulfinch understood Lady Sarah's French with ease, worked back to what must have been said, and explained to the others. And so the barge pulled away in triumph from the noisy, bawling, cheering French ship and took yet another chapter in the adventures of Lady Sarah Coignwood, to the eagerly awaiting salons, newspapers and magazines of Boston.

None the less, Lady Sarah had to take note of the fact that the quiescent war between the Americans and the British was about to leap thundering awake. This was a serious problem because it could mean herself being trapped in the Americas. Thus the already-made, homebound decision popped into her knowing, and she wondered how best to act upon it.

CHAPTER 30

As the voice in Stanley's parlour called out my name I knew I was trapped. I couldn't go forward or I'd be shot, and men were already running into the little bedroom to take me. I turned back into the room with the only weapons I had, my two hands.

"Here he is!" cries the first man into the room and rushed forward. The light was bad and I was balanced on one foot as I hopped off the window sill but I swung at him and I'd have brained him if the blow had connected properly. As it was I bowled him over and I went for the second man. They seemed not to be armed.

"No!" cried a loud voice, "Let up, sir! We ain't your enemies, we're all King George's men here!"

"Aye!" they cried and I stopped with a man's collar in my hand and a fist drawn back ready to strike. In fact what I had hold of wasn't a man. Not quite. It was a lad in a Midshipman's coat. His eyes were white with fright but I saw he'd a dirk at his side and a pistol in his belt. He'd not drawn either weapon, so I put him down and let him breathe and a busy, fussing man stepped into the room and took me by the hand.

"I'm Ratcliffe, sir!" says he, "Thomas Ratcliffe. I missed you last year and now I'm proud to make your acquaintance." He was man in his fifties, with a round face, prominent ears and a constant beaming smile and a constant flow of chatter, which only occasionally slipped to show the entirely different personality underneath. His voice put me on guard again: it was American.

"What's this?" says I, "You don't sound British to me."

"It's all right, sir!" says the Middy, "Mr Ratcliffe is a loyalist."

"Ratcliffe?" says I, recalling what Lucinda had said.

"Ratcliffe it is, sir!" says he, "I fought for my King in the rebellion and

246

saw the rebels drive out my kin and my neighbours after their victory. For all those that were loyal had to flee for Canada, with what they could take with them on their backs. Land and farms and stock were left behind, sir, for the damned rebels to steal!"

"Dreadful!" says I, for it seemed the thing to say, but I kept quiet about Lucinda, not knowing what to make of him, and it turned out that he was the same one right enough. The one who'd been asking questions, except now I knew he'd been asking in the British interest not the American.

"Dreadful indeed sir!" says Ratcliffe, "And now I've found you, Lieutenant, I'll beg a most urgent word with you for what me must do, must needs be done fast!"

"Ah!" says I, not liking the sound of that one little bit. It was all well and good that these weren't Yankees come to arrest me, but I didn't like being called Lieutenant, nor did I like the Middy's uniform nor the fact that the men crowding into the parlour were all of them seamen: British tars by the look of 'em. They had Indian Joe tied up and were starting on Stanley, with a length of line.

"Avast there!" says I, "None of that! Mr Stanley is a gentleman and a good friend to me. I'll not see a hand laid on him!" Instinctively I'd roared that out with a masthead bellow, which stopped the tars dead in their tracks, and they flinched and they looked sheepishly at Ratcliffe, while he positively *beamed* in delight and clapped me on the back.

"Tarnation!" says he, "You are the man we're looking for and no mistake!" He turned to the mid, "Mr Parry," says he, "I'd be obliged if you'd take your men outside and keep watch while I have a word with Lieutenant Fletcher. Take this gentleman," he pointed at Stanley, "And guard him well, but don't bind him!" then he looked at me all knowing, and winked, and said, "So, Mr Fletcher? Still claimin' you ain't a sea-service officer?"

They bundled him out while I was wondering about that one, and Ratcliffe took me to Stanley's table and we sat down. I didn't know what was happening anymore and was only too ready to listen. But what he came out with was half fairy-tale and half nightmare, because he'd worked it all out and got it all wrong.

"Mr Fletcher," says he, "We've little time so I'll come to the point. I know you act on secret orders and I'll not expect you to confirm or deny anything," he looked me in the eye all noble and sincere, "I'm King George's man sir!"

"Ah!" says I, "Splendid!"

"Now, sir," says he, "I know it, so don't deny it, that you are a British officer secretly in service with the Royal Navy."

"Oh?" says I.

"I know you are a gunnery expert. I know you are a fine seaman with special knowledge of submarine navigation. And I know how you fight!" He grinned again, "Unarmed and alone you beat five good men last night when they set on you!"

"Those were yours then, were they?" says I.

"King George's sir!" says he, "Loyal hands out of *Calipheme*. Loyal but stupid, or they'd have made themselves known to you."

"Well," says I, "Tell the buggers to say *please* next time!"

"Ah-ha!" says he, "I like you sir! Damn me if I don't!" Then he leaned across the table, smiling furiously, "Now here's the situation, Lieutenant: *Calipheme* lies in the hands of mutineers. *Mercure* waits to take her. The French Consul is in touch with *Calipheme* and is on the point of persuading those traitorous dogs to go over. And then there's the Americans! *Declaration* is ordered to stop *Calipheme* escaping. She is ordered not to interfere with *Mercure* and to seek by all means to persuade *Calipheme* to come over to the Americans. Captain Cooper is having little success in this regard and the Americans think the ship is as good as French."

"And what about our navy?" says I, "I saw a frigate come in this morning. After *Calipheme* I suppose?"

"Correct!" says he, "That ship is Sir Brian Howe's flagship, *Diomedes*, warned by myself of what was happening."

"You warned him?" says I.

"Yes," says he, "I send messages up and down the coast to the British squadron."

"Do you now?" says I.

"Yes," says he, "*Diomedes* will seek to cut out *Calipheme*. But if she does then *Declaration* will stop her and there will be a fight."

"And why not?" says I, losing the thread of the argument, "That's usually the case when ships of opposing navies meet during wartime. Or have they changed the rules?" He grinned like a big snake cuddling up around a little frog.

"I see you have a taste for humour, sir!" said he, "And in fact they have changed the rules. This war with the Americans is dead on its feet.

Neither side wants to prosecute it. Neither our navy nor the Americans wants a fight. But the Americans won't let the British take a ship out of an American harbour, and the British can't let *Calipheme* go over to the French," He thumped the table and swore. "Howe's between the devil and the deep blue sea! If he fights the Americans the war comes to life, if he lets *Calipheme* go over then President Washington and the Congress will most likely side with the French."

The swine was in actual anguish at this stage. He was your true fanatic and lived and breathed the cause he followed. In other words he was your typical secret agent. I've met a few of 'em in my time and they're all bloody lunatics, or why else could they do such work?

"The Americans are taking this as a test of the new France," says he, wringing his hands, "The new ideas that the French say they bring to history!"

"What?" says I, "Rubbish! No Government goes to war over new ideas. There's got to be a good reason like trade, or gold or land."

"Those reasons are equally poised on either hand, Sir," says he, "The Americans could go either way. We are at a crossroads of history. The fate of this single ship could swing the boundless resources of the American nation behind either France or our own dear King." Well, when he put it that way it made you uneasy. I suppose he had a point. It's true the Yankees had played both sides against the other. Maybe they were waiting to see which side to join?

"And as for yourself, sir," says he, "This is your moment of glory!"

"Is it, by Jove?" says I.

"Sir," says he, "The Americans have placed Captain Gryllis and fifty loyal hands under a generous parole. Provided they do nothing to interfere with the interests of the United States, they may pass freely."

"Huh!" says I, "They bloody-well interfered with Indian Joe and Francis Stanley!"

"That does not signify," says he (I said he was a fanatic), "And so we have the chance to prevent a disastrous engagement between *Diomedes* and *Declaration*."

"Do we?" says I.

"Yes, sir!" says he, "We have fifty men, I can supply arms and boats, and we shall go out this very night and re-take the ship while all their attentions are directed towards the sea and Sir Brian Howe!"

"And jolly good luck to you, Mr Ratcliffe!" says I, "I'll wave you off from Stanley's landing when you go out, and I hope you give the rogues what for!" The grin strained and strained and he laughed nastily,

"Now ain't you the one for a joke, eh Lieutenant? Modest and joking even in the face of danger!" he leaned closer, "Now see here, sir, for this is the heart of it. Captain Gryllis is a broken man and lies sodden with drink in his bed. The other sea officers are killed or wounded and we are left with the Purser, the Chaplain and Mr Parry, who is but sixteen. We have fifty British tars but no officer to lead them!"

"But what about yourself, Mr Ratcliffe," says I, "You could lead the attack."

"I ain't no sea officer," says he, "Do you think the tars'll follow the likes of me?"

He was right. Our sailors were cussed bone-headed particular as to whom they'd follow down the cannon's mouth. They'd want a *real* officer with a blue coat and shiny buttons and a gentleman's voice. And that was not Mr Thomas Ratcliffe. He was a sly, clever, active little cove, but that weren't nearly good enough for Jolly Jack Tar.

I sighed and bowed my head and closed my eyes. I had nowhere left to run and I was totally confused and I didn't know whether I had friends or enemies around me. Not here in Stanley's parlour, not in Uncle Ezekiah's offices, not anywhere in Boston. Not with that damned woman at work. Compared with the wheels within wheels that were spinning around me, a simple cutting-out expedition seemed the easiest way forward.

"How many men did you say we've got?" says I.

"Fifty one, counting you, Lieutenant," says he, "And a mighty great load off'n my mind it would be to see you come right, for it'd save me an onerous duty."

"Meaning what?" says I, sharpish.

"Meaning that if you don't come right, then you'd be failing your King."

He shrugged his shoulders as a sort of apology, and his right hand flicked a knife out of his left sleeve. It was no more than six inches long in the blade and the handle was wrapped with sticking plaster for a good grip. He spun it, caught it and slid it back, quick as thought. It send a shudder up my spine. If he'd drawn a firearm that would have been a different thing, but here was a fellow half my size but confidant that he could do me harm with a thing little better than a pen-knife. He took my eye and smiled steadily at me and I didn't have the least doubt that he was a very dangerous man indeed. But so am I, especially when folk annoy me.

"Don't you threaten me, you bugger!" says I, "I'll pull the limbs off you one by one!"

"Won't be necessary, Lieutenant!" says he all jolly again, "For we've just established that we're all King George's men here! And now come away, sir, the men must see you and you must see them"

He was a bright little toad and no mistake. He led me outside and bustled around and left a man to guard Stanley and Joe, and then out into the night we went. There was a boat moored nearby and some ten or twelve of us got in and Mr Midshipman Parry took command and we rowed swiftly round to Barton's point where Ratcliffe had the rest of the men waiting in a shed by an old rickety wharf. There was plenty of light inside and there was an old table and a map of Boston and its harbour. It was the one drawn up by Lieutenant Page of the Corps of Engineers during the siege of 1775.

The tars were sat on the floor looking miserable and a group of gentlemen were clustered round the table. One was sat on a barrel with a tar holding him up. He wore a Lieutenant's coat, and one leg was a mass of filthy, bloodied bandaging. His name was Mountjoy and he was badly sick. You could smell the rot in his leg as soon as you got within ten feet of him.

The others were *Calipheme's* Purser and the Chaplain both of whom were armed and clearly determined to come on the expedition. Ratcliffe introduced me, and Barrow showed me where *Calipheme*, *Mercure* and *Declaration* lay.

"You've a six mile pull out to the ship," says Mountjoy, gasping at every word, "then the faster you're on top of the swabs, the better. Oars are muffled with rags. Pistol and three rounds per man. Cutlasses freshly sharpened." If you ask me, Mountjoy had already done everything that could possibly be done to prepare the attack. I was given the thing already cooked and dressed. But of course, there was one more thing needed.

"A word in your ear, Mr Fletcher," says Mountjoy, and Ratcliffe nodded to him and got the others away while I was left holding him up. The stink of his wound was nauseating.

"I hear you're in the Service," says he, "But I've not had the pleasure of knowing you."

"No," says I.

"It's Gryllis's fault, you know," says he.

"Yes," says I.

"He's took to the bottle now," says he.

"I know," says I. He sighed and looked at the tars.

"Talk to 'em!" says he, "Put some fire into the swabs or you're lost!" He said the same thing in six different ways for emphasis and waved Ratcliffe to come back.

"Water…" says he.

Well, in for a penny in for a pound. Storming a thirty-eight gun frigate ain't a thing to be done half-hearted. So I took a breath and read 'em the rules and no mistake. I told them about duty and England and the King, and the just retribution that awaits all who perform the wicked, vile, loathsome, and despicable crime of mutiny, which crime is more than a crime for it is an affront against Father, Son and Holy Ghost and all conceivable standards of Christian decency.

Then I promised to cut the bollocks off any man who fired before I gave the word: a threat you youngsters should *always* make, should ever you lead tars in a night attack, because it is one of the cherished traditions of the service, and the men expect it, and sometimes they even pay heed to it.

When I'd done, I called for three cheers for the King and the men responded, though not half so well as I'd have liked. They looked glum and shifty and I could see they hadn't the heart for it. They'd have gone after the Frogs and loved the sport of it. You couldn't have held them back. But this was fighting their shipmates and that was another thing entirely.

But Ratcliffe cheered his heart out and so did the Chaplain and the Purser and Lieutenant Mountjoy too, so far as he was able.

As soon as the tide turned we set forth in two launches, each with twenty-five men aboard. Mr Parry the mid, young as he was, had the makings of a good officer and the men liked him. So I gave him one boat with the Bosun to back him up. I took the other with the Purser as my second in command. He was a considerable fire-brand for a *pusser* and no doubt he was anxious to get back all his stock that he'd been robbed of. Ratcliffe kept close by me and it crossed my mind he was keeping an eye on me.

It was a bad night for a sneak attack. The moon was popping in and out behind some thin, high cloud and the weather was calm. Any ship keeping decent lookout must see us coming from hundreds of yards away. But it had to be that night, since tomorrow Rear Admiral Sir Brian Howe and Captain Daniel Cooper might be exchanging broadsides.

In my experience there are many times in life when you've no better option than to go at the enemy like mad bull and hope to carry the thing off by pure dash. Look at the Light Brigade: most people forget that they did actually reach the guns and cut the gunners to pieces. So I told Parry to board *Calipheme* on the larboard and I would go for the starboard, to split their fire should there be any. Apart from that we couldn't do much more than conserve the men's strength by pulling steadily until it was time for the final dash.

With Page's excellent map, I steered north of the main channel to keep Governor's island between our boats and *Calipheme* and we sighted the masts of the three glowering warships as we passed south of Apple Island.

"Ship oars!" says I, and waved at Parry's boat. I wanted to be sure we went for the right ship. It wasn't too hard. *Calipheme* was the most northerly of the three and the closest to Deer Island. As I waited I clearly heard a ship's bell chime aboard Declaration followed almost at once by the bell of *Mercure*. It seemed American and Froggish time were in synchrony. But not British. No sound came from *Calipheme*.

"Give way!" says I and pointed at *the enemy*, for that's what *Calipheme* was.

Parry's boat pulled away beside us and steered so as to come round to take *Calipheme* on the larboard side, and in a couple of minutes we were close enough to see the long hull, with its white stripe and black chequer of gun ports. They were open and the guns run out. The complexity of the rigging came into focus and the dim shapes of men in the tops. She was keeping lookout all right and we were no more than a couple of hundred yards away. Now was the time.

"Pull!" says I and waved furiously at Mr Parry.

"Pull!" says he, clearly audible and the men heaved their hearts out and the two boats darted forward.

"Hurrah!" cries a voice from our boat, "King George for England! We'll show 'em lads!" it was the bloody Purser, up on his feet and waving a pistol in the air. Bang! The shot echoed round the harbour.

"Sit down, you lubber!" says I, "Sit down or I'll pistol you myself!" I turned to the oarsmen, "Pull you bastards! Pull!" In the other boat Midshipman Parry was yelling at the top of his boy's voice.

"*Heave* away! *Heave* away! *Heave* away!" He was calling the time steady as a veteran. The boats surged onward with a hundred yards to go and the men who weren't rowing bawling and yelling their hearts out. The thrill of the moment had put some fire into them at last. But I could see figures darting and running about on board of the big frigate. Figures were looming over the guns.

"Pull! Pull y'buggers!" says I and it was fifty yards to go. By George we were going to get alongside of her after all. Then:

Boom! Boom! Boom! The whole long side of *Calipheme* blazed into lightning flashes. Right in the line of fire, the full weight of sound and light beat down upon us from fifty yards range and the air shrieked and sizzled with hurtling metal. It was grape over round shot, and it wasn't aimed fire, for they'd simply hauled on their trigger lines when danger threatened, but so much iron was flying that we could not escape.

My boat staggered as the blows went home. Thummmmm! Some great projectile sang through the air within feet of me and blood and meat sprayed in all directions.

"She's going!" cried a man in his terror, and the bows of the boat went under with way still on.

"Crack-Bang-Pop!" came a volley of musketry from the frigate. It did no harm, but Booom! A carronade roared from her quarterdeck and the waters around us smashed into foam as a charge of canister hissed about our ears. Howls and groans of pain arose all round me and men were fighting for oars or thwarts or splinters or anything that would float as water rushed up to the stern of the boat, and rolled over the dead and the dying and rose cold up my legs. The boat was finished. I slid over the side and trod water.

"Parry!" I roared, "Mr Parry! To me!" Then a struggling drowning seaman in the last horrors of fear grabbed at me with maniac strength and tried to climb on top of me in the water. I hit him under the ribs and shoved him at the wallowing wreckage of the boat. He clasped hold and lived. Others went down around me, crying and bubbling as the water ran into their mouths. I saved another in the same way, but I had to fight him to do it, and if ever you are in that terrible plight well, then you just swim clear and leave 'em alone. Leave 'em alone or they'll drown you too. Even *I* pulled back after the second, for I'd not the strength to try a third.

Parry's boat came up just before the wreckage of my boat finally went under and they hauled out five men including myself. Three were wounded. That left twenty making their way slowly to the sandy bottom below. Parry himself was kicking and screaming in the bottom of the boat with a wound in him somewhere and five or six of his men similarly placed beside him. The Bosun was in command and those who were left unharmed manned the oars and pulled for Boston with all their might. Ratcliffe survived among them, the nasty little sod, when far better men were killed all round him, but that's the way of war.

The second broadside was even more ragged than the first. Probably they never even saw what they were shooting at. They nearly missed us entirely but three or four grapeshot came aboard the dense-packed boat and killed nine men outright. The attack was a total failure.

CHAPTER 31

"Acting in the interest of the great cause which we serve, I therefore assured the English mutineers that the attack upon their ship was by active connivance of the American Authorities."

(From a letter under diplomatic seal, dated Wednesday 30th September 1795, from Mr Abraham Bouchet, Hon. Consul of France in Boston, to Citoyen Henri Chapelle-Marie, Secretary to the Minister of Foreign Affairs, Paris.)

Early in the morning of Wednesday 30th September 1795 Boston harbour was buzzing with activity, following the deafening cannonade from the mutinied British frigate, that had split the previous night asunder and send round shot hopping across the water as far as Dorchester neck where the curious were busy digging them out of the beach as mementoes. The whole town spoke of nothing else, though less than a handful of the tens of thousands who'd heard and seen the gunfire, had the slightest idea who had been fired at or why.

One man who did know exactly what had gone on was Mr Abraham Bouchet, who for some years had looked after French interests in Boston. He was the son of a French music-teacher and a Boston lady of property who had travelled in France. He was an American by birth, a merchant by profession, a supporter of France by inclination and an implacable enemy of the British by sincere conviction.

Shortly after dawn on Wednesday morning, Mr Bouchet took a boat from Clarke's Wharf and had himself rowed out to *Mercure*. He was taken aboard and soon after, he and two others came back over the frigate's side and descended into the boat. A line of anxious faces watched the boat as it pulled for the English frigate a mile away. *Mercure's* people fretted and worried and shrugged their shoulders and peered at the little boat among the dozens of others out for curiosity and sight-seeing.

Unlike the dozens of other boats, Mr Bouchet's was allowed alongside of the Britisher. All others were warned off with ugly threats and handfuls of ballast stones hurled into any that came too close.

On the soiled and grubby quarterdeck a negotiation took place between Mr Westley (late of Westley and Pevensey) and Mr Bouchet. Mr Westley was backed by the two hundred and fifty gaunt and frightened men who'd thrown in with him, and Mr Bouchet was backed by Capitaine de Fregate Barzan and by a pinky-cheeked, little Enseigne de Vaisseau named Colbert.

These latter were objects of horrified fascination to the mutinied British tars. These were Frogs. These were the enemy made flesh. They should have been monsters. But they were not. Instead, Jean-Bernard Barzan, in his dirty clothes and red cap, managed to work on them, some of the magic that he worked on his own men. He boomed and laughed and stamped about and threw his arms around them. They grinned and shuffled in embarrassment and brushed his hands away and wondered at such behaviour from a ship's Captain.

Barzan spoke not a word of English but the warmth of his personality, and his straight honesty came across, and the boy in an officer's coat that had come with him, translated for him as best he could. He told them about the new France where no man felt the lash and all were brothers. He told them about the freedom that the French had won for all mankind, he told them that it was their own right and duty as free-born men, to throw over the oppression of those who held them down.

Westley and one or two others, who'd had some education, actually paid attention to the words. But for most of the poor desperate, seamen who'd been driven into this pass only by a mortally cruel and inept Captain, they simply saw the chance of escaping the Navy's revenge, and they felt that Captain Barzan was a man they could trust. And above all they respected the fact that Barzan had come aboard of his own free will, unarmed and placed himself in their power. Then the clinching argument was made by Mr Bouchet, the Yankee with the French name. He lifted up his voice and spoke to the nervous mutineers.

"Last night's attack was engineered by the American navy," he cried, "They hadn't the heart to face Lord Howe's guns and so they armed Gryllis and his men, and gave them boats and even hired the scum of the Boston docks to make up numbers, and then kept out of the way themselves while Gryllis tried to re-take the ship!" there was an angry murmur from the mutineers, "That's right!" yelled Bouchet, "So there's no use whatever your thinking to go over to the Americans, and all things considered, your best chance is to go with Captain Barzan to freedom in France!"

It was a cunning, clever speech and it was well received. But even so the deep-grained prejudice against the ancient enemy held back a large portion of the mutineers. They were not ready to take the last step; not quite, not yet.

"Leave them to me, Mr Bouchet," said Westley, taking him aside, "They've no choice any more. It is a matter of their coming to accept it." Westley turned to Captain Barzan.

"*Merci Monsieur Le Capitaine*," said be, pronouncing the words carefully and slowly "*Pour tout que vous avez fait.*" Barzan erupted with a flood of rapid French, smiled broadly and embraced Westley, swinging his feet clear of the deck. Enseigne de Vaisseau Colbert, translated.

"Monsieur Le Capitaine, says that he hopes to lead this ship back to France, with her people as our brothers and our friends. He says that we shall break past Admiral Howe together and *Mercure* will shield *Calipheme* so that there will be no need for you to fight your countrymen."

"*Merci Monsieur!*" said Westley, "*Merci beaucoup!*"

CHAPTER 32

"...and if His Majesty's ship 'Calipheme' is not given up to me by noon on Monday October 5th I shall enter the anchorage to restore His Majesty's authority within her. I shall scrupulously avoid all harm to the Citizens of the United States and to their property, but I must warn you that any attempt to intercept my actions will be met with force."

(From a letter of Saturday October 3rd 1795, from Rear Admiral Sir Brian Howe aboard *Diomedes* in Boston Roads, to Captain Daniel Cooper aboard *Declaration of Independence*.)

Late in the afternoon of Friday October 3rd 1795, Rear Admiral Sir Brian Howe, sat in conference with his officers in the great cabin of His Majesty's frigate *Diomedes*, was disturbed by a hail from the maintop lookout and the sound of cheering from the decks above. Howe frowned, and sighed miserably.

"I take it that friends are come to call," he said, and snapped at his Captain, "Stop that bloody noise at once!" The Captain glanced at the first Lieutenant. The first Lieutenant left, and soon the bellowing of the Bosun and his mates put a stop to the cheers. Then a deferential Midshipman arrived to confirm what Howe had already guessed.

"Officer of the watch's compliments, sir," said the boy, with his hat under his arm and stood stiffly to attention, "Sail in sight, sir: *La Syrene*."

"Very good!" said Howe, "You may go."

"Aye-aye, sir!"

Howe sighed again and went up on deck followed by his staff. Marines saluted with their muskets, Lieutenants raised their hats and all moved from

259

the weather side to leave that favoured position for Sir Brian, the Captain, Sir Brian's secretary and the first Lieutenant. Howe called for a telescope which was instantly put in his hand and he searched the approaches for the oncoming man-o-war. There it was. British without a doubt.

Then, and for the hundredth time he trained the glass on the anchored *Declaration*. He studied her gun ports, now closed and hiding the 24-pounders that so much out-classed the 18 pounders of his own ship. And he studied her massive hull, near three-foot of oak at the waterline, for *Declaration* was an old line-of-battle-ship re-built to make a substitute for a frigate, and a damned powerful one too. There was not a chance now of a cutting out expedition using boats because some bloody fool, Gryllis in all probability, had already tried that and failed miserably and warned *Calipheme* to beware.

So now if Sir Brian were to act at all, then he'd have to do the thing the hard way and take *Diomedes* into Boston harbour and risk a fight with the formidable *Declaration*; with the French joining in too, and very likely the mutineers aboard *Calipheme*! In the face of so dire a set of possibilities it was just conceivable that if the case were well argued, and if Sir Brian's mighty brother Lord Howe were to back him, then it was just possible, that Their Lordships of the Admiralty might agree with the wisdom of doing nothing. And *nothing* was what Howe was strongly inclined to do.

It wasn't that he was frightened, because the emotion of fear had been entirely bred out of his bloodline, and had it been two French ships guarding *Calipheme* he'd have taken *Diomedes* into action without a second's delay, and may God defend the right! On this occasion, however, he was happy for any excuse that might free him from the ghastly dilemma upon which he was so securely crucified.

But here (damn him) came Captain Nantwich, cracking on sail and doing his loyal best to bring his thirty-eight 18-pounders, plus six 24-pounder carronades, plus two hundred and fifty fighting men, to the aid of his Admiral. Very creditable action in a subordinate, but now, unfortunately, Their Lordships would never allow that two British frigates could not beat three of any other description that ever sailed the sea, and thus was Howe committed to action.

He put the telescope to his eye again and trained it on *Calipheme*. The last message from the agent Ratcliffe had warned him that the mutineers were in touch with the French and could be relied upon to surrender the ship within a few days. He ground his teeth at the thought of a British ship surrendered to the French by mutineers. The thought was an outrage, a monstrosity, an obscenity. He would die before he let that happen. His officers jumped as he cursed aloud and stamped his foot. The whole bloody thing was impossible! But if he *did* go into Boston harbour he'd have to fight the Americans and he'd be damned by all England for touching off the American war again. While if he *didn't* go into Boston harbour he'd be damned by a England for letting a British warship go over to the French.

"Signal!" he cried and a Midshipman ran up with the code book, "Make to *La Syrene*: Repair on board the flagship at once." Within seconds the necessary flags were chosen, snatched out of the lockers at the taffrail, bent to the halliard and shot up to the masthead. They broke and streamed out in their sharp, bright colours. There was the briefest of pauses before the signal Midshipman, observing the distant *La Syrene* through his telescope, cried,

"Acknowledged, sir!"

Later, Howe held another meeting in the great cabin, this time including Captain Nantwich and his first Lieutenant. He explained what must be done and showed them the letter he was about to send to the Captain of the United States ship *Declaration of Independence*: one Daniel Cooper.

"We shall enter harbour and take *Calipheme*," said Howe, "I can see no other way. I have done my best to avoid action if I can, and for that reason I do most strictly forbid that the British side should fire first. If firing there is, then history must record that it was the Americans who began it." There was a tense silence as this group of professional fighting men considered the implications of this order. Nantwich spoke for all.

"*Declaration's* broadside is eighteen 24-pounder long guns and five 32-pounder carronades, Sir Brian."

"D'ye think I don't know that, sir?" said Howe.

"But, Sir Brian, if we allow them the first fire, undisturbed, then…"

"Damn you sir!" said Howe, "If you've no stomach for the work then be comforted that *Diomedes* shall precede *La Syrene* so it shan't be *your* damn ship that's fired into, but mine!"

"I protest, sir!" said Nantwich, "That's not my meaning."

"I know that, damn you!" said Howe, "And I await any suggestions from any man here for any better way of coming through this business,"

He looked round the table and nobody spoke, "Failing that, I'll expect this squadron to be at general quarters and under fighting canvas, in three days time at 12 noon sharp, which is the hour of the expiry of my ultimatum to the Americans."

CHAPTER 33

*"The southern tip of Deer Island being low lying and unsure
ground, I shall place my guns on the northern part of Long Island
where firm and rising ground will enable me to sweep the channel
and pound the British as they come in."*

(From a letter of Sunday October 4th 1795 from Major James Abbot,
Massachusetts Militia Artillery, to Captain Daniel Cooper, United States
Navy, on board of *Declaration of Independence*, Boston Harbour.)

Captain Daniel Cooper was resting, alone in his day cabin. He'd sent
Howe's ultimatum ashore to the proper authorities. Boston was on fire
with excitement, every possible precaution had been taken, and for the
moment there was nothing for him to do, and in his idleness he fell prey
to sombre thoughts. He recalled the action he'd fought last year against
the British frigate *Phiandra*, and the fearsome speed and steadiness of
British gunnery. Broadside for broadside, *Phiandra* had fired twice as fast
as *Declaration* and he had been lucky to have the excuse to run when two
more Britishers hove in sight.

Cooper wondered if Howe's ships were as good as that? He wondered
how fast and steady his own gunners would fire, in action? He'd given
them plenty of drill, but not with live firing. And … and … he'd not got
Jacob Fletcher any more to train up the gunners. The man was a marvel at
gunnery. Could it really be true, as Uncle Ezekiah believed that Fletcher's
true gift was in commerce and that the man actually despised the sea service?

Cooper took out the two letters he'd received that day, one from his
Uncle making what passed for an apology for their quarrel, and the other
from *her*. The two letters were very different but had points in common.

Each referred obliquely to the fact that he, Daniel Cooper, stood an excellent chance of being killed on Monday morning, and each referred to that very same Jacob Fletcher; a subject upon which each writer held strong opinions. Uncle Ezekiah was firmly resolved to keep his bargain with Fletcher, concerning the gold, while she (adorable, sweet and gentle creature though was) could only see ill in the man.

Then came a rumbling of feet down the companionway outside, and a rapping at the cabin door. It was his first Lieutenant with a young artillery Major just come out from the shore, in his brown coat with the red facings, his leather helmet with its bright crest and his smart top-boots and his sword at his side.

"I have the pleasure to present Major Abbot, Cap'n," said he, "Whom we have been expecting."

"Come in Major," said Cooper standing up and offering his hand, "What support can you give me?"

"Four 18 pounders, sir," said the artilleryman. My men are surveying two possible sites. But either would do, and will enable us to play upon Howe's ships before they come into action with yourself."

"18 pounders?" said Cooper with a frown, "Nothing heavier?"

"No sir, not in the time available and with the paucity of trained men available to me, unless of course you could lend me men out of your ship?"

"No," said Cooper, "They are needed here in case Howe attempts a sudden attack. I am grateful for what you have achieved, Major. Four 18 pounders from shore batteries will render invaluable assistance to my ship," he forced a smile, "Do not think me ungracious!"

"It is an honour, sir," said the artilleryman. He paused and asked the question all Boston was asking, "Will it come to a fight, sir? Will Howe come in on Monday as he has promised?"

"Yes," said Cooper, "He'll come."

"And can we stop him? Can *Declaration* stop him if he passes my guns?"

"Yes," said Cooper. For this, taking everything into account, was his honest opinion, "And in any case, we are bound in duty to try," he sighed, "There can be no question of our suffering him to pass freely into an American port. If he comes in, he must receive the fire of every gun we can man."

"Will the French ship support us?" said the artilleryman.

"Oh yes!" said Cooper, "Mr Bouchet who acts for the French, was aboard yesterday. He says that Captain Barzan and his men will fight as our allies and brothers against the perfidious British. Those were his exact words."

"Hmm," said Artilleryman, "There's nothing the French would like better than us and them allied together against the British," and he frowned, for he was well aware of European politics, "You don't think, Sir … do you … that we're being manoeuvred? By the French?"

"Damned if I know, Major," said Cooper, "All I know is that if Admiral Howe brings his ships in here next Monday, then we must fight him, and I can see nothing in the world to prevent it."

CHAPTER 34

I spent the morning after our failed cutting out expedition, trying to sleep in a corner of Ratcliffe's grubby shed at Barton's point. There were twelve men laid out dead down at one end, and another row of poor devils moaning and twitching, bandaged up as best as their mates could contrive. Out of fifty-one men who'd set out the previous night, thirty-three were dead, including Mr Midshipman Parry, the Purser, the Chaplain and the Bosun. Five men were wounded; six counting Lieutenant Mountjoy who was now in a hot red fever and not likely to live much longer.

That left twelve men unharmed, including myself, but the tars were sickened and fearful, and I was thoroughly fed up with a fight that I'd never wanted to be part of in the first place.

But one man was never daunted one whit. That was Ratcliffe. He was the one who'd bustled about organising the care of the wounded when we staggered back into the shed. He was the one who brought us food and drink and he even brought round blankets to cover us so we could sleep. And then he went out to find a surgeon who could be relied upon to keep his trap shut.

It was past noon when he got back with a brace of the butchers, with their grey wigs and black coats and their bags of tools. I got up and walked out as soon as they rolled up their sleeves and sent for a tub for the *wings and limbs*. Most of the tars came out pretty quick too, except one who'd a messmate to take care of and one weren't really a tar at all, but a Landman who'd assisted the surgeon aboard ship. The tars sat down together trying not to listen to what was going on inside, and peered miserably out over the broad expanse of the Charles River. Then Ratcliffe came out, looking for me.

"Fletcher!" says he, "A check, sir! A serious check!" he looked tired but he'd still got his bounce.

"Go and be damned," says I.

"Now, now, Fletcher," says he, "That's no way to speak, for we ain't done yet, and we're all King's men here!"

"Bugger off!" says I, and I turned my back on him and stared northwards over the water, across the mudflats with their teeming waterfowl, towards Leachmore's Point and the distant forests of the Massachusetts mainland. It was the still morning of a beautiful day, but I was full of my own thoughts. I'd had quite enough thank you of daring-do and I was mourning over the loss of all that gold for me to work with. If only that damned bitch hadn't got to Uncle Ezekiah and turned him against me![12]

"Come now, Fletcher," said Ratcliffe, forcing cheerfulness, "Give hope a leg-up, and smile!" I looked at his round smiling face: smiling, always smiling.

"See here, Ratcliffe," says I, "Let me tell you something. I ain't no Navy Lieutenant, I ain't in anybody's service, and I ain't going out there again." I pointed east towards the waiting frigates. "Do I make myself clear?"

"So that's the way, is it?" says he, and shrugged his shoulders, "Can't say as I'm surprised. You *looked* like an officer and that's all I cared about," and then the smile came back, all fat and round and cunning. "I know more about you than you think, Mr Fletcher," says he, "For I've spoken to old shipmates of yours, out of *Declaration*, and *Amiability* and *Bednal Green*"

"*Bednal Green?*" says I, that was the merchantman I served in a year ago and that got took by Captain Daniel Cooper, then in command of the privateer *John Stark*, "Nosy little swab ain't you, Ratcliffe?"

"Aye," says he, "So I don't give a cuss for what you think you are, mister, for I can see with my own eyes you're a seafaring man and an Englishman and that you're a man used to command."

"Bah!" says I, "Leave me alone."

"Damned if I will!" says he, "You're all I have left, mister!" I sat down on the coarse scrubby grass and tried to ignore him but it was no good. He sat beside me and kept right on talking. "It's up to you and me, Mr Fletcher," says he and made a rough map out of stones and stalks of grass.

"Here's *Calipheme*," says he, "West of Deer Island. And here's *Declaration*

---

12   As Fletcher's secretary, it was my duty in later years to place into his hands certain letters informing him that Mr Ezekiah Cooper had not in fact been turned by Lady Sarah Coignwood, but had remained faithful to him. This was the only occasion upon which I ever saw him shed tears. S.P.

in the channel between the tip of Long Island and bottom of Deer Island. And here's *Mercure* just north of Spectacle Island. And here's Sir Brian Howe's *Diomedes* out in Broad Sound." He picked up the pebble that was *Diomedes* and moved it in towards Boston. "If Howe comes in, then he's either got to come between Deer Island and Long Island, and meet *Declaration*, or he's got to go all the way north, around Deer Island and come in through Shirley Gut."

"Never!" says I, interested in spite of myself. Shirley Gut was a narrow channel between Deer Island and Shirley Point on the mainland. To a landman, it *did* appear to be a possible way of avoiding contact with *Declaration*, but it wasn't. "It's all mudflats and sandbanks in Shirley Gut," says I and Howe won't have a pilot to bring him through. He'll either come past *Declaration*, or," I took Ratcliffe's pebble, "He'll come through the Western Channel, south of Long Island, then north between Thompson's Island and Spectacle Island. But if he does that," I put down *Diomedes* and picked up *Mercure* and *Declaration*, "He'd risk *Mercure* and *Declaration* getting between him and *Calipheme*, like this," and I blocked Howe's advance with two ships.

"How's a British Admiral going to know all this about Boston Harbour?" says Ratcliffe.

"Cos he *is* a bloody British Admiral!" says I, "Our navy surveyed all your harbours during your damned Revolution."

"Not mine damn you!" snarled Ratcliffe, "I serve my King, God bless him!"

"*Their* damned Revolution, then!" says I, "And the Royal Navy's been cruising off your – off *America's* – coast, ever since. And they're bloody obsessed with making bloody maps. They never let up!"

Ratcliffe looked at our map and thought a bit more.

"It's that Frenchman that's the real problem," says he, "We can't let them go home with a British crew gone over to them, and that's the cause of it all. That's what's going to set the British fighting the Americans again," he traced a line in the sand from the Boston direction out to the pebble that was *Mercure*.

"I know the answer," says he, "Why don't we find a barrel of gunpowder each, and swim out to the Frenchman and blow him up!" He laughed.

"Aye," says I, "And let's ask our fairy godmother to make us invisible so's the Frogs can't see us coming..." And I as I said that, the most staggering thought came to me. I'm not a man given to flights of fancy (except in commercial matters of course) and it's usually been my lot to do things the hard way where action is concerned. But not this time.

"God's Boots!" says I, and my heart began to slam against my ribs, "Ratcliffe, we could do it. We could do just that!"

"What?" says he.

"We could do it in Stanley's machine: the *Plunger*," Ratcliffe shuddered.

"That rat-trap?" says he, "It's a sea-coffin."

"No it ain't," says I, and brought myself up sharp as I remembered those ghastly moments on the bottom of Morgan's bay "Well, mostly it ain't. Most of the time…"

"Huh!" says Ratcliffe, "That's right nice to know I must say!"

"No," says I, "I've been down in her and she works. I've seen Stanley place explosive mines wherever he wishes, and by George, when they blow there's nothing to withstand 'em!" Ratcliffe looked at me intently.

"Could it be done?" says he, "There was attempts with such things in the Revolution. Bushnell tried it but his machines all failed."

"Never heard of no Bushnell," says I, "But I've seen Francis Stanley's machine, and I tell you it works!"

"Gracious God!" says Ratcliffe, "You're serious, ain't you?"

"Yes," says I, carried away with the fascination of the thing.

"Can you navigate this *Plunger*?" says Ratcliffe.

"I don't know," says I, "We'd need Stanley for that."

"Will he do it?" says Ratcliffe. I thought a bit and was inspired again.

"Yes," says I, "I think I could persuade him."

Within an hour, Ratcliffe and I and half-a-dozen men were pulling for Stanley's Wharf in the surviving launch, which was leaking badly and needed two men bailing all the way. But first the surgeons were paid off, the landman who fancied himself a surgeon was left in charge of the wounded, and a couple of tars were left to bury the dead, who now included Lieutenant Mountjoy, whom the medical gentlemen had killed in taking off his leg at the thigh.

He went into an un-marked grave with the others, without shroud or a flag or a coffin between 'em and with assorted bits and pieces thrown in for company. Ratcliffe insisted on this in case the Yankees found out what we'd been doing and threw us into gaol, and the tars didn't even whinge, which was a bad sign of broken spirit for such a flouting of their customs normally turns 'em nasty.

At Stanley's wharf the fellow left on guard had used his brain and kept out of sight with a cutlass ticking Indian Joe's ribs while that gentleman turned away Stanley's people as they came in for their day's work. Joe told 'em the master was ill and wanted no disturbing. So it was an empty yard that we found when we made fast the boat alongside of *Amiability* and walked along the wooden jetty. Fortunately no man gave us a second look from the other wharves and ships nearby, for tars all looked much the same whether British or American and there was plenty of comings and goings as the dockyards began a new day.

Ratcliffe and I spoke to Stanley in his parlour. which looked even more shabby and unkempt in daylight that it had at night. Stanley was sullen and hurt at first, as he'd a perfect right to be if you ask me, and told us bluntly he'd be no part of anything against his own country. What's more he called Ratcliffe a traitor to his face and the two of them fell into a furious, pointless quarrel as to who had done the worst things to whom during the Revolution: the loyalists or the patriots.

When I managed to stop this vicious exercise I pointed out that there was no question of our harming anything American, and that our entire plan was an attack upon the French using Stanley's submarine boat. At this, a most remarkable change came over Stanley. I'd been prepared to persuade him to help the British as payment for the money he'd stolen. But I didn't have to, because once Stanley properly understood what we wanted him to do, the idea touched on something within the depths of the man.

"You want me to take out the *Plunger* and place a charge beneath *Mercure*?" says he, with a faraway look in his eyes, "To attack a ship from underneath, where she is weakest."

"Precisely," says Ratcliffe, roused with an enthusiasm of his own, "Blow the damn Frenchman to pieces and then there can't be no alliance of France and America against the British."

"Of course," says Stanley, not even hearing and certainly not caring. He ignored Ratcliffe and looked at me, "And how might this be done, Mr Fletcher? How might the charge be laid?"

"Well," says I, "Where Mercure's anchored, there's only five fathoms of water, and less at low tide. If we was to place a charge on the bottom, I suppose it might do the trick." But I realised I hadn't thought this out properly, "Hmm … would it?" says I, "What do you think, Stanley?"

Stanley smirked as a schoolmaster does when he questions the scholars, all full of himself and superior.

"And how might the charge be placed, Mr Fletcher?"

"With your spar-pincers," says I, "Or you could just unscrew it, like you did in Montego Bay."

"No," says he, "The spar-pincers were destroyed," he pointed at me, "As you know! And I have no more sub-marine mines left."

"Yes," says I, "But can't the pincers be repaired? And can't you make another mine?" He said nothing. He sat in his chair in his miserable parlour with the dirty windows and the dirty ashes of the dead fire in the unblocked grate, and the remains of last night's food un-removed, and the un-washed pots and plates on his dirty table. He was thinking and thinking and thinking. I looked at him and at Ratcliffe, and Ratcliffe looked at me and shrugged and raised his eyebrows as if to say, "What's happening?"

And then Stanley stirred himself with the look of a man who'd come to a decision.

"I have something to show you," says he, "I shall need some keys from my study," he looked at Ratcliffe, "That is if I am free to move about my own house?"

"Now, Mr Stanley," says Ratcliffe with his jolly face on, "There's no need for that."

"Huh!" says Stanley and went and rummaged in his study. He came back with a big key on a ring and beckoned us to follow. He led us out into his yard past clutter and gear of all kinds and to one of a number of out-houses. This one was heavily padlocked. He turned the key, opened the door and turned to face us on the threshold. His eyes were gleaming with some strong emotion or other.

"I am going to show you something," says he "that no man has seen before. The practise of sub-marine warfare is older than is supposed, but has been much mocked and attacked, by the stupid!" he said that with bitter emphasis, "And so I have chosen to keep certain ideas to myself, in case ever my country should need them." He frowned, paused a bit and muttered, largely to himself, "But I cannot wait forever to be proven right," He stood aside, waved us in and announced, "Jacob, you talked of mere submarine mines. Now behold my *Gunpowder Porcupine*, which is the answer to all your problems."

271

Well, my jolly lads, I've seen some diabolical applications of engineering in my time: Gatling guns, steam hoses, explosive bullets and the like, but none to compare with Mr Francis Stanley's little wonder.

It lay on a bench in the long workshop, brightly lit by a row of windows set in the pitched roof above. All the ordinary windows were permanently boarded up. Tools and special tackles and kit of all kinds were scattered about in the untidy jumble that was the sign of Stanley's work. Heaven knows how he turned out the immaculate wonders that he did. The thing itself was the two halves of a large wooden cylinder, about five feet long and three broad. The two halves were hewn out of single pieces of heavy timber, shaped and smoothed to fit neatly together down the long axis.

One half of the egg was on chocks, round-side down, flat-side up, and you could see that it was scooped out to leave a large cavity in the middle, which was now empty. The other half was flat-side down, round-side up and lay on the bench like a great wooden tortoise.

But the smooth wooden hump (tarred all over like *Plunger*) bristled with long iron rods. There were ten of them, each about two feet long and an inch thick, rising out of iron sockets set flush with the surface of the egg. They splayed out aggressively in all directions and you could see why Stanley called it a porcupine. But what about the gunpowder? I must confess I was profoundly fascinated, as was Ratcliffe. Stanley preened himself and showed off the inner mechanisms of the device. He got his fingers under the half-egg with the rods and heaved it up, shoving a block of wood beneath it to keep it up.

"Look here," says he, and by crouching beside the bench we could see up into the interior of the thing. It was hollowed out with a cavity just like the other half, but running into the cavity was a set of iron tubes which corresponded to the rods on the outside. The tubes were closed by screwcaps at the ends which stuck into the egg, but each tube was drilled with a series of small neat holes just above the cap. They looked like touch-holes in the breech of a firearm.

"Now see here," said Stanley and we got up and followed him further along the bench to where some rods and tubes like those in the egg, were laid out. There were rows of evil-looking bottles too, and jars like those in an apothecary's shop. The place stank of chemical smells and the surface of the workbench was scarred with burns and scalds. Also there was a couple of wooden cases like those that new pistols come in. He flipped these open and each one revealed a row of odd little glass vials about the size and shape of a man's finger, nestling in the baize lining.

"This is the heart of my device," says Stanley and he carefully (very carefully) took up a vial from each case. One contained a thick liquid, the other a powder. He took the vials right to the end of the bench and laid them in a big iron mortar.

"Stand back, now!" says he and took up the pestle. He reached over and quickly smashed the two vials so their contents mixed, then darted back, as there came an angry hiss and splutter, and the mixture burst into flame! It burned furiously for a second or two and then consumed itself and so went out.

"What in the devil's name was that?" says Ratcliffe, "What's in those glass knick-knacks?"

"Sir," says Ratcliffe, "I would not tell you that, not under torture!"

"D'you think so?" says Ratcliffe with a sneer.

"I would not tell you under any circumstances!" cries says Stanley, and they started bickering again. They hated each other and were only cooperating out of a most rare and unlikely conjunction of their totally different interests.

"Ratcliffe!" says I, stepping between them, "What does it matter? Let Mr Stanley keep his secret, just so long as his machine works!" I glared at him till he shut up and turned to Stanley, "Please go on, Stanley," says I, "What's the purpose of what you've shown us?" So he told us, and I never did find out what his secret chemicals were[13], he picked up one of the long rods and showed us how it slid smoothly into its tube.

"The tube sits in the upper half of the porcupine," says he, "And the rod rests on two of my vials which are placed at the bottom of the tube. Certain mechanical devices which I shall also keep secret," he glowered at Ratcliffe, "Prevent the rod from crushing the vials until the desired moment."

He suddenly snapped the rod hard into its tube. It ran in about six inches and clicked sharply against the bottom. "But when that moment occurs, the rod breaks the vials and flame spurts out of these holes," says he, showing us the holes in the bottom of the tube.

---

13   Professor David Burkhill-Howarth, the celebrated natural philosopher and Master of Sidings College Cambridge, is of the opinion that the liquid in the vials would have been oil of vitriol, and the powder chlorate of potash. He reports that these ingredients, when mixed, will spontaneously inflame exactly as Fletcher describes. S.P.

"And that sets off the charge inside the machine? says I.

"Correct, Mr Fletcher," says he, "it ignites two hundred pounds of best black powder."

"But how do you force it against the enemy?" says I, for I could imagine the thing assembled, with the spines sticking out on top and the charge within, such that a tap on any of the rods would set it off. Then a nasty thought struck me, "Bloody hell fire," says I, "It's not your plan to drive this thing bodily into the target is it? With the sacrifice of the operator's life?"

"Certainly not!" says he with an insulted look on his face, "Do you take me for a fool? See here," says he and pointed to a ring-bolt screwed into one end of the upper half of the egg, "The mode of attack is for the sub-marine craft to dive beneath the enemy, towing the gunpowder-porcupine on a line. The porcupine trails behind the craft and floats upon the surface where It is drawn smartly into contact with the target."

"Ah!" says I.

"Ah!" says Ratcliffe.

"Yes!" says Stanley.

"And have you ever tested the device?" says I.

"No," says Stanley, "The opportunity never arose … until now!"

"Then how do we know it'll work?" says Ratcliffe.

"Because I'm telling you it will," says Stanley, "And if that ain't good enough for you, you can go elsewhere!"

This time I stepped in before they could maul one another and insisted that there were practical matters that needed urgent settlement. So Stanley locked up his great secret and we went back to his cottage, with the seven tars and Indian Joe looking at us and wondering, and we went inside and sat down and talked it over.

What we decided was this. We would venture an attack on *Mercure* so soon as everything could be prepared and the conditions were right: the attack would need to be at night and in still waters. The limiting factor would be getting *Plunger* seaworthy after the damage she'd taken Morgan's bay. As regards arming the porcupine, Ratcliffe said he could get enough powder to top up what was left aboard *Amiability* and at Stanley Wharf.

It was agreed that the ideal workmen for our business were Gryllis's remaining men and that Gryllis himself should be left in the lodgings where Ratcliffe had placed him in the confidant expectation that he'd drink himself to death. Of Stanley's own workpeople Stanley absolutely insisted that two men were indispensable for their special skills and that they could be trusted to hold their tongues. This set off another furious argument, with Ratcliffe declaring they'd tell all Boston, but Stanley wouldn't be budged and in the end we just had to trust him and his two men.

The rest of his people would be told that Stanley had no work for them at the moment and that they'd be told when they were wanted, while the rest of us it would be work night and day to get everything prepared because who knew how long Howe's patience would last? And the whole purpose of our effort was to prevent Howe coming into Boston Harbour, by removing the need for it.

Ratcliffe said he had much to do, out and about in Boston, and in any case he'd be little help at boat-building (normal or sub-marine) so it was agreed that he would come and go, and be our eyes and ears in the town. As for me I was in an odd sort of limbo. I was committed to this unholy enterprise for a mixture of reasons: I thought I'd lost my chance with Uncle Ezekiah and the gold. I didn't know how the Yankee authorities would treat me if they got hold of me. I certainly knew what the British would do, and so I didn't quite know who I was or what I was. And into that limbo came the one thing I was certain of, and that was Francis Stanley's sub-marine inventions.

My earlier fascination for Stanley's amazing craft, was returned and was grown bigger than before. And I'm not a man that can be happy when idle, so I put my heart into the job in hand and never had time to worry about nothing else. So first we got *Plunger* swung out from *Amiability* and lowered into the water. Then we got her into a little dry-dock, built just for her, inside of Stanley's Wharf, where we could set about her without half of Boston docks looking on.

There was much to do. The hull itself was sound but almost all her fittings were bent, crushed or damaged and the lead drop-keel, of course, was lying on the bottom of Morgan's Bay. Stanley looked glum at first and said there was six month's work to do. But I said he'd never seen British tars at work and that we'd do it in a week. As it turned out, we had to do a lot better than that.

CHAPTER 35

The work on *Plunger* went on night and day, and the usual resourcefulness of British seaman proved invaluable. Some of the gloom fell off of them too: the gloom of Gryllis's wretched, miserable ship and the gloom of the beating they'd taken from the men who'd once been their shipmates. Once they had a useful task to do and a difficult, ingenious one beside, they cheered up and worked with a will. Mind you, there was trouble at the outset, when I explained what we were going to do with *Plunger* and you could see by the sulky looks on some of 'em that they didn't approve of sub-marine mines nor blowing the bottoms out of ships and drowning poor seamen. Not even French seamen.

By Jove! There's cussedness for you. These same men would gleefully have fired treble-shotted into an enemy. But it was quite typical of tars. Fortunately, however, I was able to put their simple minds at rest by promising to punch the head of any man I caught slacking, and once I'd shown them that I meant it they were the busiest set of workmen that ever was. And just so long as they were busy, I didn't care what they were thinking.

Stanley I found an infuriating man to work alongside of. He lost tools. He dropped things. His mind wandered off. He was a superb craftsman but the most lackadaisical blighter that ever was. Finally I insisted that he should instruct me on what was to be done each morning, and then he'd go off to his secret workshop with his two trusted men, to perfect the porcupine and get it ship-shape and ready for action.

This increased the pace of our repairs to *Plunger* to a speed that Stanley found miraculous, and also it gave me the most detailed insight into the workings of the beast, which saved my life in due course.

And so the work pushed forward. On the Thursday we improvised a keel from round shot, nailed into a timber frame beneath the hull. It couldn't be dropped so we'd lost that safety margin but it would ballast her upright and stop her rolling. On the Friday we set about mending the bilge pump that had failed in Montego Bay. Drawing on my experience at Lee and Boswell's and with the help of one of Stanley's special craftsmen we fixed that too. It was devilish awkward and a crude job, but it worked. We cut away the remains of the spar pincers and their controls pulleys as well, since we weren't going to need them. But on Friday evening, Ratcliffe came running into the yard, shouting out my name and Stanley's.

"Fletcher!" says he, as I turned away from the dry-dock and walked towards him wiping the tar off my hands with a rag, "Hell and damnation!" says he, "Howe's been reinforced and he's sent in an ultimatum!"

"What's that?" cries Stanley running out of his workshop still holding the file he'd been using, and the three of us met in the middle of the yard with the tars looking on.

"Another British frigate's arrived and anchored beside Howe," says Ratcliffe, "And Howe's said if they don't give up the *Calipheme* he's coming in to get her on Monday at 12 noon!"

"Monday!" says I, "Christ we'll never do it in time!"

"What?" says Stanley, "Does this mean the war's already started?" The anger ran red into his face, "Then I'm done with these games," says he, and flung down the file, "I'm a true-born American patriot and I damn all Kings and taxations!"

"What? You damned rebel!" cries Ratcliffe, grabbing Stanley by the shirt-front, "Deny your King, would you? I tell you sir, it is still my hope to see King George restored to …"

"Shut up and be damned the pair of you!" says I, and pulled them apart, "This don't change a thing!" says I, "Not unless they've already fired into each other?" I looked at Ratcliffe.

"No," says he, "Howe's anchored out In Broad sound and *Declaration's* still off Long Island."

"There!" says I, "Then we might do it yet!"

"Stanley," says I, "Today's Friday, we've got tomorrow and Sunday to finish the work. The screws are working, she's ballasted and the bilge pumps work."

"But we've not repaired the compass, nor the depth-finders," says Stanley, "Nor the fresh air pipes, nor the bearings that failed in Montego Bay, nor…"

"Stanley," says I, "She'll swim, she'll sink and she'll rise. If need be we can run on the surface or just awash and you can con us by looking out of the upper scuttle."

"No! No!" says he, "We can't take the risk that…"

"Dammit, Stanley!" says I, "You said you were a patriot. Are you saying you won't stretch out your hand to save American lives? If Howe comes in he'll kill Americans by the hundred. And don't you want your work proved? Do you want to be remembered as a man who failed?" That touched a nerve in him. He jumped and looked at me with real venom in his eyes. And then he thought a bit and a shifty look came over him that was most unlike anything I'd seen of him before.

"It shall be me that cons the craft?" says he.

"Of course," says I, "You're the most skilful." That seemed to please him and he turned and went back to his workshop without another word.

"Can you do it, Fletcher?" says Ratcliffe, "The fate of England could depend on this. God help our cause if the Americans unite with the French."

"We shall have to do our best," says I and by George I meant it too. It ain't often in my life that I've gone into danger when there weren't no profit in it, and when I could have got out of it if I'd wanted. But as I'd worked away on *Plunger* and my thoughts fell into place I'd come to the conclusion that fighting between the British and the Americans represents an abomination, because it's obvious that The Lord God placed our two peoples upon the earth as an example of decent behaviour for the foreigners and heathen to follow, as best they might, in their own wretched fashion. Consequently, we didn't ought to let Him down in His great purpose by squabbling amongst ourselves.

With this pious thought in mind, I went round the yard, kicking backsides and otherwise inspiring the men, and I found Ratcliffe something to do to keep him out of the way (for he would take part, yet couldn't do anything useful) and I took it on myself to fix the air tubes that allowed fresh air to be drawn into the vessel when she was running just under water.

In the middle of my work it occurred to me that the brief conversation out in the yard had been the first time we'd discussed who was going aboard of *Plunger* for the attack. There was room for three men. One must be Stanley for his unrivalled knowledge of the craft and the gunpowder-porcupine. He would be Captain and would navigate her. The second had to be me because the task of cranking the propeller was a heavy one that called for a strong man. After all, we were planning a round trip of several miles. That left a place for a third man, to open valves and man the pumps as ordered. It was an unskilled rating but we found it the hardest to fill.

By working through Friday night, and Saturday night, with men sleeping in four-hour watches like they did at sea, we had *Plunger* and her mine ready enough at nightfall on Sunday for the attack to take place. In some ways Sunday was the best possible time, for the docks and the harbour were at their most empty and there should be little interference from the curious or the officious, when our launch towed *Plunger* out of Stanley's Wharf, around Hudson's point and under the eyes of any man or woman who might have been taking a stroll across the Charles River bridge.

With everything ready, including the demonic porcupine, secured by a long screw-bolt to *Plunger's* round back, and the dry-dock lit by torches, I assembled the men and called for volunteers to man the pumps. Dead silence followed.

"Come now, lads," says I, "Here's Mr Stanley going aboard, and myself besides, and going out to save Old England," (note well the manner in which an address to the tars should be constructed), "Will no man come along with us?" There was a shuffling amongst them and a man was propelled to the front with marked reluctance on his part. He stamped his foot, raised his hand to his brow in formal salute, and he spoke to me but never met my eye.

"Beggin-yer-pardon-sir," says he, "Deputation, sir. I speaks for one-an-all,"

"Speak up," says I just barely controlling the urge to knock the teeth from his head, "You have nothing to fear." He began slowly but what he said came from the heart and it came with the encouragement of his mates. By the time he was finished he was close to shouting and the rest of them growling along with him.

"T'ain't nacheral, sir, beggin-yer-pardon," says he, "We done our duties like hearts of oak, sir, under Cap'n *Gryllis*. An' then we stayed loyal an' went out agin' the old *Calipheme*, sir. An' now we's worked like slaves for you, sir, though you ain't no real officer beggin-yer-pardon-sir," By George he was on thin ice there, the lubber, but I clasped my hands behind my back and gritted my teeth, "We done all that, an' done it with a will," says he, and finally came to the point, "But we signed on as seamen, which is seamen aboard of ships upon the sea, not under the sea, which ain't nacheral, nor ain't it *right* sir. For it's goin' out to fight with no flag flyin'!

An' sneakin' up like no Englishman should … from below!" He sighed and straightened his back having come into port after a long and perilous journey. "An' that's it, sir!" says he, and saluted again.

"Aye!" roared his mates.

I could see there was no point arguing with them. You might as soon try to shift the rock of Gibraltar as move the minds of seamen. So I shifted tack instead.

"No man shall be compelled to follow me," says I, "But I shall do my duty to England even if you will not. And if no man will come aboard with me, will you at least pull an oar aboard the boat that tows me out to face the enemy alone?" They stepped forward at once, for that, the stupid bone-heads. Never accuse a British seaman of being consistent. So that was my boat's crew, but who should man the pumps aboard *Plunger*?

"Fletcher," says Ratcliffe, at my elbow, "I'll come."

"It's a seaman's work," says I.

"Is it?" says he, "There ain't no sails nor rigging in that!" he looked at the *Plunger*.

"But you," I searched for a tactful word, "you don't care for such things."

"If you mean I'm scared shit-less, then say so," says he, "But I serve my King."

And that's the crew that set forth. Just before eleven o'clock when the night was really dark the launch laboured out from Stanley's Wharf and towed the heavy bulk of *Plunger* out of the now-flooded dry-dock. She wallowed along behind, trimmed down so that little more than the uppermost copper dome and her cluster of mechanical metalwork, broke surface.

It was desperate hard to keep her under way and under control, and we had eight men at the oars. There was little other traffic upon the water and we passed slowly round the North Battery, and headed south-east out towards the mass of sand-banks and islands that lay between Boston and the open sea. We kept as far off from the lights of the town as we could, and after over an hour's heavy work we finally passed down-channel between Governor's Island on the larboard beam and the great glistening mass of Dorchester Flats on the starboard. That was as close as I was prepared to go with the launch. Already we could see the dim outline of *Mercure's* masts and crossed yards, some two miles off.

"Belay there!" says I, and the steady clunking of the oars ceased and the launch glided to a halt in a trickling gurgle of water from under her bow. Then bump! The black shape of *Plunger* caught up the launch and knocked slowly against her stern. It was perfect night for a sub-marine craft: still waters, soft weather and very quiet. At first all we could hear was the wind and some distant bird calls. Then, very faintly came the sound of busy voices and the thud and clink of tools from nearly three miles away on the northern tip of Long Island.

"It's the new battery," said Ratcliffe, whispering, "They're getting heavy guns in place to fire on Howe's ships tomorrow. They've been working for days … like us."

"Seems like they're not quite ready," says I.

And then it was time to unscrew *Plunger's* upper hatch and climb down within her. I went first, then Stanley, then Ratcliffe. It was black dark inside at first and the round hull rolled as it took our weight.

"God save us all!" muttered Ratcliffe and laughed nervously. I wondered If he had that infernal grin on his face now.

"We must have a light," says Stanley and called for a lantern to be handed down. There was a brief scuffling and bumping and the smell of hot tallow filled the vessel. "It reduces the air but we will achieve nothing without it," says Stanley and a shaft of yellow light lit up the narrow interior, like a scene from a mediaeval painter's view of Hell.

As the big copper hatch came down, and Stanley screwed it home and the launch cast off and left us, we three were shut into a tubular space some thirty feet long by five-and-a-half feet high. And that's five-and-a-half feet wide too, for the inside was entirely circular in cross-section.

The neat, shiny clutter of cranks and works and levers, I've already described, and the thrill of it too, that came upon me from the wonder of this unique machine that represented a new age of mankind. But what was different from my previous voyages in the *Plunger* was the fact that it was night-time and we were going out to war. The lantern-light threw more shadows than anything else and barely gave enough light for us to take our places without falling over the rods, lines, levers and stanchions that took up most of the space where you'd expect to plant your foot in moving from one end of the beast to the other. So we stepped carefully and moved like black demons in a nightmare.

What we'd agreed was that Stanley must take the helm and be in command, while I should crank the propulsive screw and Ratcliffe would control the pumps to send us up or down and would do such other duties as Stanley or I hadn't time for. In this odd craft, the helmsman's place was at either of the two copper domes, where cranks connected to long rods, running down the inside of the hull to act through water-tight shafts in the hull and so act upon the rudder.

Our plan was to do as much of the work as possible with the boat trimmed to run awash, so no more than her upper dome could be seen and yet we should be able to refresh the air inside through the copper breathing tubes. And so, Stanley took a few steps up the short ladder that was permanent fixture beneath the upper dome and swung a folding thwart across for himself to sit upon, in which position with his feet braced against the ladder, he could see out through the glass scuttles and could steer by turning the handles that controlled the rudder.

What's more, he had a sort of miniature binnacle fixed to the inside of the copper dome, with the hastily-repaired compass and also device to measure our depth beneath the surface. These instruments were painted with a phosphorescent compound which enabled Stanley to read them even in pitch dark.

My station was at the stern where I sat to one side, with both hands on the big, iron crank that turned the screw. This exercise was distinctly harder than rowing, and being unremitting, it slowly wore you down. It was a job for the strongest man you could find and I couldn't complain that it was mine. It was mortal dull, though, and the best effort that I could keep up for any length of time only sent us forward a slow walking pace.

Ratcliffe took his place amidships by the main pumps and had charge of the lantern for he was the only one of us who might need to move about and he was also the least familiar with the innards of the vessel. I never took to Ratcliffe one little bit, not as a man nor as a comrade. The fellow was too damn cunning by half and a fanatic besides, but you couldn't fault his courage, for he was terrified of what we were doing and all the bounce and affected jolliness was gone out of him. He cringed as the hatch came down and I actually heard him sob. And yet he did his duty and never complained.

And so we set forth, with the deadly mine fixed above our heads, to cover the mile-and-a-half to where the Frogs were anchored. I laboured and the sweat began to run down my back. From time to time, Stanley ordered Ratcliffe to pump out or let in water to adjust the trim, and about fifteen minutes passed. Then Stanley began to talk.

"Gentlemen," says he suddenly, "tonight we shall do a thing that no man has done before," he was excited, but I thought nothing of it for so were we all, "Others have tried and they have failed, but tonight there shall be no failure."

"I should say not, indeed!" says I, heaving away at my cranking handle and wishing he'd shut up. It was time for action now, not speeches. But he went on.

"Tonight," says he, "We shall deal such a blow against the mockers and the believers as shall ring around the world!"

"Aye," says I.

"Vindication, gentlemen!" says Stanley, "At last!"

"What's he talking about?" says Ratcliffe, his voice shaking with the fear that was upon him.

"Is it not propitious?" says Stanley, "Here tonight we have every condition fulfilled to demonstrate…"

"Stow it, Stanley!" says I, sharply, "Save your breath. The air's getting thick in here."

"Ah…" says Stanley, "Mr Ratcliffe, give a turn on the fresh-air pump. It's that one … no, not there… *that* one."

Ratcliffe did as he was bid and spun a handle that turned a sort of rotating fan within a casing that sucked air down a tube and into the interior. He worked busily for about five minutes but the air didn't get noticeably better.

We went on like that for nearly an hour with Stanley getting steadily more excited and the air getting steadily worse. It seemed that my hasty repair on the air pump had failed, for Ratcliffe was whizzing the thing around as hard as he could but to no effect. I grew worried. This was taking much longer than we'd planned, and Stanley showed no sign yet of unscrewing the mine to let it drift astern of us for the final stage of the attack. Crammed in my little corner I was deaf and blind to everything except Stanley's chatter and Ratcliffe's clumsy movements. Finally, with my chest heaving, and unable to catch my breath in the foetid air, I could stand it no more.

"Stanley," says I, "Throw the hatch open. Let some air in!"

"No," says he, "We dare not. If we ship water she'll go down and drown us."

"Oh, dear God!" says Ratcliffe.

"Open her up!" says I, gasping, "I can't breathe."

"No!" says Stanley.

"No!" says Ratcliffe.

It was all right for them. They hadn't been working like a coal-heaver. They weren't drenched in sweat with their muscles groaning. But I couldn't catch my breath and I was panting like an old dog on a hot day.

"Open one of the scuttles," says I gasping and wheezing, "I'll come and take a breath … we won't ship any water."

"No!" says Stanley, "Impossible!"

"Why?" says I.

"Because… Because they're stuck fast," says he.

"Let me," says I and struggled up out of my seat and pushed past Ratcliffe in the dark. My head was swimming and I knew that either I took a breath of clean air in the next few minutes or I'd keel over.

"No!" says Stanley, "Get back to your place. I'm in command here!" And he tried to push me back as I squeezed up the ladder beside him. But I was desperate by then and simply seized the wing-nuts that secured one of the glass scuttles and twisted them hard. They turned smoothly and soon I had the thick glass port hinged open and was gulping down breaths of clean, cold air fresh off the salt water. I soon felt better and even smiled when I saw Stanley's nervous face three inches away from mine in the moonlight that trickled in through the scuttles.

"Sorry Cap'n" says I, for I assumed I'd frightened him by disobeying his orders, "Shall I take my name for punishment?" But he didn't appreciate the weak joke. Instead he blinked at me, and I saw his eyes flicker and look away.

I followed his eyes and looked out. It was an odd point of view, about a foot above the water with the great expanse of Boston Harbour all around, dimly lit by the moon. There was the dull grey dark of the sky, the glittering, oily black of the sea and the intense black of the islands. But that wasn't what Stanley was looking at. He was furtively looking at an anchored ship not more than a cable's length ahead.

"By George!" says I, "Shouldn't we be diving? Shouldn't we rig the mine?" And the questions died on my lips for even in the dark I knew what ship it was. She was *Declaration of Independence*. "Stanley?" says I, "What the hell are we doing here? Where's *Mercure*?" He said nothing.

"What's going on?" says Ratcliffe from below.

"Stanley?" says I again, "What have you done?" Stanley blinked at me and sighed.

"I am sorry that it should come to this," says he, "but I must show you something of the very greatest importance."

"Fletcher?" says Ratcliffe, "What's he talking about? What's happening?"

"We're heading for *Declaration*," says I and twisted my head round to look astern. The masts and the black hull of *Mercure* were visible a mile astern of us, "Stanley's run us right past *Mercure* and we're heading for *Declaration*."

"Why?" says Ratcliffe, "We can't attack *her*. There's no sense in that!"

"Let me pass," says Stanley and lowered himself down the ladder, "There is a reason for this," says he, "Give me the lantern, Ratcliffe." He said it so calm and matter of fact, that Ratcliffe handed him the lantern and Stanley went to the bow and opened a little locker. After all we had no reason not to trust him.

There wasn't enough light to see properly what he did next but he played around with something or other and when he turned around he had an iron-bound wooden box in his hands. It was about the size and shape of a family Bible.

"Listen to me," he said, "Nineteen years ago I made an attack upon Lord Howe's ship *Eagle* in New York Harbour, using Mr David Bushnell's invention of a sub-marine boat. That attack failed and Bushnell who was my master and my friend, was broken by the failure. But I persisted and have greatly improved upon Bushnell's work. Tonight we shall make amends for that failure. We shall prove that a sub-marine boat may sink a man-o-war."

"*Declaration?*" says Ratcliffe, "But you're a Yankee! Would you sink your country's only warship?"

"Of course not!" says Stanley, "Do you take me for a poltroon? We'll pass safely by *Declaration* and go for Howe's ship *Diomedes*," He smiled, "Ain't it fitting that it should be a Howe that's in command?"

Ratcliffe and I started forward, but Stanley raised his box.

"Stop!" says he, "This is full of gunpowder! If I drop it, it blows. If I shake it, it blows," I stopped and grabbed Ratcliffe, "Now then," says Stanley, "I shall tell you what we are going to do."

CHAPTER 36

*"That which was said of me, it was all just the spite of them that
is dunning you for the money, Pa. There never was no meeting
of mine with the British, as I swear by dear mother's memory.
Instead pay heed to this. Viz: my latest business will take some
months, but on return I will place in hour hand enough ready
money and more, to pay off everything you owe, and keep the ship
and all besides."*

(From a letter of September 4th 1795, from Patrick Jordan, aboard 'Nancy
Ellen' in Boston Harbour, to his father Mr Absalom Gordon, Shipwright
of Pawtucket, Massachusetts.)

Lady Sarah received her visitor in the upstairs salon of her house in State
Street. It was late but the matter was urgent. He was admitted by her
butler, who tapped on her door, entered and announced,

"Mr Patrick Gordon, master of the schooner *Nancy Ellen*," the butler
bowed and left. He was black. All the servants here were black. Lady
Sarah was becoming used to it. Meanwhile here was the sharp-faced,
goggle-eyed young Mr Gordon, done out in his uttermost best, with
hair pulled behind his head in a sailor's queue, and his face washed and
his boots blacked, and himself looking every way at once as such luxury
of décor as he'd never seen in all his years, but mostly gazing at herself as
men had been doing since she was fourteen, such that she hardly even
noticed it any more. But still they did. And in any case, she'd put on a
muslin gown that left arms and shoulders bare, and much of her bosom
besides because she wanted this man's best cooperation.

"Do sit down, Captain Gordon," she said.

"My Lady," he said, blinking in the light of the dozens of candles that lit the big room and damn the expense. He smiled and sat in the upholstered, gilded, French chair that she indicated. There was a tiny, similarly gilded French table between them, bearing a silver tea service on a silver tray. But she made no move towards that. Nothing else stood between them, other than an iron-bound chest off to one side. She just smiled, and sat with the light gleaming from her naked arms and shoulders, and Gordon dared to dream (as all men do in such a case) that perhaps he was about to become the luckiest man alive.

"Thank you, My Lady," he said, careful to be polite, "I got your note," he shrugged, "and here I am!"

"My Lady?" she thought, "Not the usual ma'am, that these people began with. At least he'd taken some advice. Perhaps that indicates intelligence?" and it did. Mr Gordon understood what was needed. He understood fast.

"We ain't provisioned for so long a voyage," he said. "We'd have to put in somewhere to take on stores."

"But you have enough to get clear of Boston?"

"Aye, M'Lady."

"Good! So long as I am out of Boston tonight, we may then proceed to England thereafter."

"*Tonight*? This very night?" he thought about that. "Well, M'Lady, in that case the tide ebbs in less than an hour. Can you be ready for that?"

"Yes," she said, "Everything important is packed and everything else can be left."

"What about the British? They've got at least two cruisers off Boston. What if we're intercepted?" She smiled.

"I have taken careful advice about you and your ship, Captain Gordon. So is *Nancy Ellen* the fastest ship on the New England coast, or is she not?" Gordon smiled.

"She is that, M'Lady. But what if a spar got carried away? What if the sea got up so's she couldn't spread her wings? A big frigate might be faster than a schooner in a blow. And what if there was no wind at all?"

"Why should you fear the British? Is not this war a pretence?"

"Not if Howe comes in to take *Calipheme* M'Lady. If he does that – and I think he will 'cos that's what the British do – then if Howe comes in, it's war with all the trimmings and prizes taken."

"Mr Gordon, if we are taken by a British ship, then that ship's Captain will prostrate himself to offer me every luxury that he has aboard and will carry me home at best possible speed."

"Aye, M'Lady. *You* but not *me*, because Captain Howe don't like me one bit."

"Oh?" she raised eyebrows, "Are you acquainted with Captain Howe? I wonder how that might be since he has not yet come ashore." Gordon laughed.

"Never you worry about that, M'Lady, I'm just warning you that I'll not risk losing my ship. Not when a war's in the offing."

"Then look in there," she said, pointing to the chest, on the floor. "Open it. It is not locked." Gordon got up, knelt and opened the chest.

"God bless my soul!" he said, "It's full of silver."

"Yes," she said, "Spanish dollars from the Mexico mint, advanced to me on credit. Do not ask me how this was done, because I do not understand the process. But done it was, by one of your own banks here in Boston."

"Oh," he said. Just the one sound.

"That money is yours," she said, "I am assured it represents the full value of your ship. Another, exactly similar chest, awaits you in London," she smiled, "Though the chest may contain gold rather than silver." She stood, and looked into his eyes, noting that he was a small man, no taller than her. She stood so close that he could feel the heat of her body and smell her perfume.

"Tonight, on the next tide, Captain? Have we an agreement?"

"You most surely do, M'Lady." They shook hands.

"You may help my servants with the luggage," she said, "There will be a cart outside the door by now."

"Yes, M'Lady."

"I will need to change, but I will be quick about it."

"Yes, M'Lady."

Nancy Ellen went out on the ebb tide, passing the many other ships at anchor and in company with a few others making their way to sea. All these merchantmen passed the three big warships unmolested in the night, under the moon and stars. Once in the open sea, *Nancy Ellen* made all plain sail, raced like a stallion, and left behind every other thing on the face of the waters. But just before she entirely lost the lights of Boston, there came a bright glow, followed minutes later by the rumble of an enormous explosion. Men leapt into the shrouds to look. They yelled and pointed. Gordon, at the tiller, looked back over his shoulder.

"What the Hell and damnation was that?" he said.

"It does not matter," said Lady Sarah Coignwood, "It is behind us, and we are moving too fast for anything to catch us."

CHAPTER 37

As always in these pages, I offer you youngsters the benefits of my experience. Thus, should ever your duty oblige you to go into action on board of a sub-marine boat, then you should avoid any vessel with many of its fittings not working, and you should avoid any crew which is entirely composed of fanatics representing opposing interests. And finally (if at all possible) do try to keep the gunpowder out of the hands of the crew.

The device that Stanley pulled out of the locker was another of his little wonders. Exactly what mechanisms lurked within I never found out, but it seemed that he could it set off in a number of ways including a sharp tug on a line that ran out through a hole in its side, and which was now secured to Stanley's finger.

"So you'll see," says he, "That there ain't the least possibility of your overpowering me. Should you try it, then we all go up together," he looked down at the harmless-looking box, "I prepared this device in case of need. There's ten pounds of powder in here," says he, "And in this confined space that'll see us all mashed to splinters."

"Oh God!" groaned Ratcliffe. I could feel him tremble and I wasn't feeling all that jolly myself.

"So what do you want of us, Stanley?" says I.

"Only for you to go back to your stations and do my bidding," says he.

"What about our plan?" says I, "To stop the war with England,"

"No," says he, shaking his head, "That was your plan, Fletcher."

"Traitor!" says Ratcliffe.

"And what are you?" says Stanley. "An American who kneels before a foreign king?" Ratcliffe trembled and I grabbed his arm before he could do anything that might result in a lethal explosion. But Ratcliffe sank to his knees and covered his face with his hands. He groaned and wept and sank still further down so that his brow was touching the grating that covered the bilge below. It looked as if the terror that he'd mastered with such effort, had finally broken out and overcome him completely.

"Good heavens!" says Stanley, just as if we were in some drawing room together and Ratcliffe had broken wind, "Whatever is the matter with him?"

"Ratcliffe!" says I shaking his shoulder, "Buck up man, we ain't dead yet!" I looked at Stanley, "This is your fault!" says I, "It's more than the poor devil could bear. Now put that blasted thing down like a good fellow and let's get Ratcliffe back on his feet." It was wild stab, but such is the sheer damned perversity of human nature that it almost worked, and I could see Stanley dithering with his bloody box and his bloody piece of string round his bloody finger. But then he frowned and stepped back.

"Ohhhhh…" moaned Ratcliffe and beat his head on the grating.

"Dammit, Stanley," says I, "What sort of a man are you? Here's a fellow creature in agony and all you can think about is sinking ships!"

Ratcliffe crawled forward and grovelled at Stanley's feet, mumbling and slobbering to himself like a child. It was actually embarrassing. The fellow was clinging to Stanley's knees in his fright, with the snot and spit and tears sliding down his face.

Keeping a wary eye on me, Stanley tried to disentangle himself, while holding the box up out of the way. But he only succeeded in pulling Ratcliffe up on to his knees. Ratcliffe was far away in his own nightmare and didn't seem to notice.

"Enough!" says Stanley, "Be done, Ratcliffe! Be a man I say! He leaned forward to shout in Ratcliffe's ear … and *swish*! Ratcliffe had been faking. He picked his moment and moved like lightning. One hand grabbed the explosive box and the other whipped out the knife from his sleeve and cut Francis Stanley's throat from ear to ear, then severed the line that ran to the man's finger so there could be no pulling of whatever trigger lay inside the box.

It was done in an instant. Then there was Ratcliffe standing over his victim, clutching the box and the dangling trigger line, as the blood sprayed thick and strong out of the severed vessels of Stanley's neck. He didn't last long. Not more than a few twitches and a half-hearted drumming of heels as he lay sprawled over his own pipes and levers in the bottom of the boat that was his pride and joy. As soon as he was still (or a little before, in fact) Ratcliffe looked at me.

"We must get rid of this," says he, looking at the box, "Can we open the hatch, or is it too dangerous like he said?" but I just gaped at Stanley, who was still twitching, and I gaped at Ratcliffe who was still chattering, "Fletcher! Fletcher!" says he, "Do we dare throw the damn thing out, or is it too dangerous?" I forced myself to speak.

"It's no more dangerous than keeping the bloody thing on board," says I, and I shinned up the ladder and unscrewed the big bolts that held down the hatch. The harbour was very calm, and though *Plunger* was rolling a bit, there was little danger of taking water – which we could pump out in any case.

"Give it to me," says I to Ratcliffe's white face looking up at me from the dark interior of the boat.

"Careful!" says he, "Don't shake it!"

I reached down and took the box, slowly raising it up to where I could place it in front of me on the rounded bulk of *Plunger*, just inches above the water, in front of the big copper collar that the hatch hinged down on to. It was a strange feeling to be standing dry-footed on a ladder that sank into the depths below me, while my shoulders were level with the waters that lapped around the very uppermost parts of the boat. Also I was acutely conscious of the bulk of the gunpowder porcupine sitting on Plunger's back not six feet from me, astern of the hatch. If the box went off now, there'd be a monstrous wallop and no mistake.

I looked around, wondering what to do with the box. Ahead lay *Declaration* anchored between Deer Island and Long Island, and beyond her the British squadron in Broad Sound. Astern lay *Mercure* and away off on the larboard beam, and invisible against the bulk of Shirley's Point, was *Calipheme*.

I thought of throwing the box, but didn't for fear of setting it off. So I climbed further up the ladder, leaned out and put it carefully on the water and gave it as firm a shove as I dared before slamming shut the hatch and screwing up everything snug and tight. I clambered down the ladder and made for the wheel that let water into the ballast tank.

But Stanley's body was in the way.

"Ratcliffe," says I, "Haul him clear."

"Did you get rid of it?" says he.

"Yes," says I, "Here! Take him!" and I shoved Stanley into his arms. I found the wheel and spun it hard. Water gushed into the tanks and Ratcliffe dropped Stanley so his head hit the grating with a smack.

"What're you doing?" says he, as the fear rushed back: real fear and no mistake.

"Diving," says I, "This thing dives faster than it swims. The box is floating and we need to get well clear."

"Diving?" says he, "How deep?"

"She's safe in 30 fathoms," says I

And ... boom! The powder-box exploded and *Plunger* rolled heavily.

"Oh God!" says Ratcliffe and shuddered uncontrollably.

"By George," says I, "You're a precious funny 'un Ratcliffe! I thought you were play-acting when you said you were afraid."

"I was and I wasn't," says he, shaken by the discharge of a few pounds of powder safely over his head while the fresh body of the man he'd killed, lay in his lap with himself as unconcerned as if it was a spaniel.

"That'll wake the harbour," says I, "and it won't make our work any easier."

"D'you mean to go on?" says he.

"Yes," says I, for I was determined to see the thing done. I don't know to this day what was the complete mixture of my reasons but the sum total of them was for pressing on.

"Can you work this thing?" says Ratcliffe, looking at the mysteries of *Plungers* interior.

"I think so," says I.

"Then tell me what to do," says he.

"You'll have to turn the screw," says I, "While I take the helm. When we need to work the pumps, I'll have to do that too."

So that's what we did. But first we pumped out her bilge and brought her up again so we could run awash as we'd done before. We briefly considered heaving Stanley out but abandoned that as we didn't want him floating ashore and becoming the cause of embarrassing questions. We decided he could wait for a quiet burial later, like Lieutenant Mountjoy. So we shoved him up into the bow where he was out of the way. It's was a shame and a pity really. He wasn't a bad sort of cove for a fanatic.

Meanwhile I opened one of the scuttles when we surfaced and put an ear to it. As I'd thought, the harbour was awake. I could hear orders being shouted aboard *Declaration* and a boat was being lowered. But there was nothing for it than to press on, and with Ratcliffe heaving the crank around I gave *Plunger* full larboard rudder and brought her slowly round to head due west towards the masts and spars of *Mercure*, just under a mile away. Assuming we were making about two knots, that meant about half an hour's heavy work for Ratcliffe, before we could dive under the enemy, with our mine paid out astern.

While Ratcliffe sweated and grunted, I nipped between the conning hatch, the trimming pumps and the big screw bolt that held the porcupine in place. According to what Stanley had told me, once the thing was unscrewed, it would float clear and a spool of line would roll out until the mine floated a hundred yards astern. That distance he calculated to be sufficient to ensure the boat's survival when the mine exploded beneath the enemy. I could only hope that his calculations were soundly based.

About twenty minutes after we'd begun our approach towards *Mercure* Ratcliffe started to tire. He didn't complain nor say anything but the boat slowly lost steerage way. I guessed what was wrong and got down the ladder and went astern. He wasn't the man for such work, and he was no longer young. He was gasping and blowing and clenching his teeth.

"Ratcliffe," says I, "We shall have to change places. I'll show you how to steer," but then something ponderous and solid struck *Plunger* heavily and rolled her over. The new arrival ground over the upper hull and pressed down upon her. I staggered and Ratcliffe fell out of his seat. Then there came a clattering and battering upon the hull and the conning hatch and the unmistakable sound of gun-shots and bullets clanging into the metalwork and thumping into the oaken hull.

I leapt at the ladder and got my head up into the dome and peered out through the scuttles. It was a ship's boat full of men: matelots, marines and an officer. It had slid off of our hull and was close alongside with men taking hold of us with boat hooks. They were wide-eyed and staring and yelling and gabbling. They were Frogs. You could hear it even through the copper dome.

Then one of them saw my face pressed against a glass port and he levelled a pistol and let fly. Bang! The ball hammered into the dome not an inch away from the glass and left a heavy dent. The shouting redoubled and they fell to battering and slashing away at the dome with everything they could lay hands on: cutlasses, oars, pikes and musket butts. And then my heart stopped as I saw one of them take a swipe at the porcupine with a boat hook. He missed the spines but caught the woodwork a hefty blow.

Instantly I slid down the ladder and threw my weight on the, lever that flooded the ballast tank. Down we went and the battering and hammering stopped.

"God almighty!" says Ratcliffe, "What was that?"

"Ship's boat out of *Mercure*," says I, "They must have been rowing guard round the ship."

"That'll be Abe Bouchet's doing," says Ratcliffe.

"Who?" says I.

"He does for the French what I do for the British," says Ratcliffe.

"Does he now?" says I.

"Must have warned them to expect an attack," says Ratcliffe.

"How would he find that out," says I suspiciously.

"From Stanley's people, I'd guess," says Ratcliffe, "I knew they'd rat on us!"

"Why didn't you say this before?" says I.

"I tried to, if you remember," says he, "And neither you nor Stanley'd believe me! And any ways, I'm only guessing. But someone sure got them French all fired up and I don't see who else…"

But he was interrupted. Crash! SSSSSSSS … and a stream of water was pouring in through the copper dome and the shards of a glass scuttle were flying like canister through the air. Ratcliffe screamed in terror that this time was totally sincere. I threw myself on the bilge pump and worked it like a maniac to bring her up.

I heaved the lever, the water gushed in from above. I heaved and it gushed and foamed and sloshed about my ears. I heaved and heaved and heaved. Ratcliffe got himself on his feet and staggered down to join me, but there was room for only one on the lever and I doubt his strength was worth adding to mine.

"Block the hole!" says I, "Block the bloody hole. Shove anything in it or we're done for!" He cast about for something that would do and hauled off his coat. He fought his way up the ladder and thrust the bundle of material at the stream of white water and the leak became a trickle. We were very, very lucky that the scuttle had failed so near the surface. Nearly a third of the glass port had blown in, leaving a hole size of a man's fist. If that had happened a few fathoms deeper, the whole port would have gone and then nothing that we could have saved us. I soon cleared the ballast tank and broke surface again.

"Where's the boat!" says I.

"About twenty yards off, but they haven't seen us!"

"We've got to pull clear," says I and shoved Ratcliffe's hands on the steering handles. "Hold 'em steady," says I, "Like that!" and I got myself back at the screw-propeller crank and gave it every ounce of my strength as hard and as fast as I could go until I had to pause for breath.

"It's all right Fletcher," says Ratcliffe, "Can't see 'em any more. I can hear 'em though, calling to one another. Must be a couple of boats in the water." I got up and came to the foot of the ladder to have a look at the plugged leak. I was weak with the effort I'd just given, and had to hold on to the ladder. One look at the smashed scuttle was enough.

"Well that finishes it," says I, "We can't mend that and so we can't dive. And if the Frogs are rowing guard, we can't attack afloat. We'd best head back for Stanley's Wharf." The mention of Stanley's name sent a twinge of guilt through me and I looked at the grey figure bundled up in a heap on the grating. His blood was all over my clothes, and Ratcliffe's too.

"Wait," says Ratcliffe, "I ain't giving up so easy. Everything I've stood for the last thirty years is null and void if the Americans take the French side in this war. It could mean the end of England and the King that I serve."

"So it might," says I, "And if you can tell me how to get that porcupine alongside of *Mercure*, then I'm your man."

"Could we do the thing without diving?" says Ratcliffe.

"Possibly," says I, "We'd need to work ourselves into a position, with the porcupine was strung out on its line, so that when the tide turns the porcupine'll be swung like a pendulum against the side of the ship," I looked at him and shrugged my shoulders, "But it ain't no good, Ratcliffe, for we'd have to get within a hundred yards of her and then we'd be sure to be spotted by her boats."

"So it's the boats that are the problem?" says he.

"Yes," says I. There was a long silence, then Ratcliffe spoke.

"Calipheme has no boats," says he.

"What?" says I.

"She has no boats. They were smashed in the action with *Mercure*. It's my business to know such things."

"What are you saying, Ratcliffe?"

"It's obvious ain't it?"

"We can't do that…"

"Why not? The problem is *Calipheme*, and *Calipheme* is the problem!

Remove *Calipheme* and there's no need for Howe to come into Boston and fight the Americans."

"But she's British!"

"Yes, but her crew are mutineers and the penalty for mutiny is death!"

We argued like that for a while and all the time I knew that Ratcliffe was going to have his way. In fact I don't know why we hadn't gone after *Calipheme* in the first place. But still… to sink a British ship full of British tars, even mutinied tars? Hmmm … but what about mutinied tars that were on the point of giving up their ship to the enemy? And so, my jolly boys, you can amuse yourselves with philosophising over what *you* would have done in my shoes, and all hands'll give three hearty rousing cheers for the one of you that comes up with the best plan. But this is what your Uncle Jacob did.

First I showed Ratcliffe how to steer properly and how to hold a compass course. He was a sharp witted 'un and learned fast. Then I took my place at the crank once more and drove us due north towards *Calipheme*. I worked steadily until Ratcliffe called me up to have a look. It was *Calipheme*. I could see her clearly through a scuttle we'd opened for the fresh air.

"Guns run out and lanterns burning from end to end of her," says I, "And look! There's men in the tops and others moving about the quarterdeck."

"Not surprising," says Ratcliffe, "First there was Stanley's ten pounds of powder, and then those Frenchies shooting at us."

"At least there's no boats," says I.

"Like I said!" says Ratcliffe.

"See how she's lying," says I, "There's her bowsprit pointing due west and her rudder due east. We must pass ahead of her bow, and anchor a little less than a hundred yards off her starboard beam with the mine trailed astern. That way when the tide ebbs we'll stay put and the mine will swing under her bow."

"And up she goes!" says Ratcliffe.

"Aye," says I, and I went to unscrew the porcupine. The long bolt came free after a deal of turning and I hoped Stanley hadn't made a mistake and put in a time fuse. Then I went back to the crank and propelled us forward again. We both took a nasty fright as the porcupine bumped and scraped its way astern, but whatever were Stanley's secret devices to prevent premature detonation, they were effective. Ratcliffe watched the black-tarred hump vanish astern with its wicked spray of horns and the spool of line rolling out just as Stanley had intended. Finally the porcupine was towing astern of us with its hundred yards of line stretched taut and ourselves forging steadily onward, passing *Calipheme's* bow and myself not even tired.

Ratcliffe kept up a steady account of our progress for my benefit and for a while all went well. Then just as we passed Calipheme's bow, Ratcliffe sang out,

"Lot of activity on her fo'c'sle, Fletcher," says he, "Men in the rigging of her foremast and up on the bowsprit. They've seen us Fletcher! I think they've seen us!"

"How far off is she?" says I, labouring away at the stern.

"Thirty yards, maybe forty," says he, "Like you said. I can't steer any further off or the mine won't reach her."

"Just hold your course," says I. There's little enough to see of us. It'd be like shooting at a barrel. All that's above the water is the copper dome."

"Fletcher!" says Ratcliffe, "They're pointing a gun. One of the fo'c'sle carronades. Faster! Get us past!" But I was already giving it my all. I heaved like a maniac and the crank fairly whizzed around in its bearings. Then the gun fired and the brightness of the muzzle flash penetrated even down to my corner of *Plunger*. I distinctly remember seeing the scuffs on the toes of my boots and the dirt under my fingernails.

There was a huge roar from the gun, and a huge blow fell upon *Plunger* and Ratcliffe was thrown bodily down the short ladder, blown out of his thwart to lie blood-stained and unconscious on the grating beneath. *Plunger* rolled hideously and water slopped in from where the copper dome should have been. But the waft of cold air and the choking cannon-smoke that rolled down into the boat told me that the dome was gone.

CHAPTER 38

With the copper dome and its collar blown off and *Plunger* rolling, with the gaping hole flush with the water, she was shipping it in great gulps every time one side or the other of the hole dipped under. I thought she was gone and my first thought was to abandon ship. I was actually head and shoulders clear of the hatch hole with seawater slopping round my elbows when another gun fired and canister beat the water all around me, rattling into Plungers hull.

I dropped back into the depths of the boat, treading heavily on Ratcliffe, who lay as still as his friend Stanley and never even twitched. Boom! Another gun and *Plunger* twitched and shuddered as the shot struck home. I stumbled clear of Ratcliffe, gave up all thoughts of swimming and grabbed for the ballast pump lever. I worked it furiously to clear the water she'd shipped, and the heavy keel came to my aid by slowing the roll enough that she stopped taking water from the hatch-hole.

But *Plunger* was still in peril. *Calipheme* kept banging away with every gun she could bring to bear and every musket too. Sooner or later a round shot must hit her fair and square and open her up like a cask under a sledge-hammer. Deafened by gunfire and stumbling over the bodies of my late companions, I tried to lighten the boat by heaving out of the hatch-hole everything that wasn't bolted down. All the tools went from their racks, then the racks themselves, then gratings that covered the bilge tank, and finally Stanley's wretched dead body (and if you think that callous then I'll point out that I *didn't* throw Ratcliffe out 'cos I thought I heard him groan).

That did the trick and within a few minutes she stopped taking water, except what the splashing of *Calipheme's* shot threw into us.

Then I lashed down her steering levers with a length of line I'd saved for the purpose and went back to my crank to get *Plunger* out of sight of *Calipheme's* gunners and into position for the mine to be swung against her when the tide turned. And this I had to do bit by bit, darting between the hatch-hole, the pumps and the crank and with *Calipheme's* guns thundering and flashing furiously.

I was in a bugger's muddle of confusion and damn near sank myself with shifting my weight about and causing the hole to roll under. I kept driving her the wrong way and having to adjust the set of the steering levers. A round-shot caught her a clout at last and knocked a splinter off her hull and started a leak which I couldn't plug 'cos I'd thrown all the necessary tackles overboard and so I just had to pump all the harder.

But two things were on my side. First, it was still dark and second, *Calipheme* hadn't got a proper target to shoot at. The glinting dome was gone and with *Plunger* more under the water than on it, all there was to see was the thin black strip of the upper hull where it broke surface. Eventually as I clung to the hatch-hole gasping and panting from my efforts, I could see them swinging the frigate round by hauling on the springs to her cable: hauling her the wrong way thank the Lord, for her broadside went off with an appalling crash and sent its fire whistling away towards Governor's Island, well to the south of my position. They were firing blind or by guesswork.

And then things went quiet for a bit apart from a lot of shouting aboard *Calipheme* as they all talked at once and tried to spot the enemy. God knows what they thought was after them. Probably another boat attack from Gryllis's men, I suppose. But that gave me the chance to work myself into position for the attack, which brought me into even greater danger.

When I thought I was where I should be: about a hundred yards to the north of Calipheme's black bulk, and about twenty yards west of her bowsprit, I had to anchor *Plunger* so she'd stay put when the tide turned which couldn't be long now, so far as I could judge, so I decided to drop anchor and wait. But that meant clambering out on to the hull to cast off the anchor that was secured at her bow. So out I got on the slippery round hull, leaving my shoes below for a better grip, bare footed.

I slid my way for'ard on hands and knees, slipped clean off into the cold water, panicked for a while when I couldn't get back on, then swum to the anchor and hauled myself aboard by that. I cast it off and the cable unwound from another of Stanley's revolving spools till the iron flukes took ground in the sandy bottom below. Then I worked my way back to the hatch-hole, slipped back inside and took another spell on the pump to keep her from going under. Then I popped my head out of the hole again to see what *Calipheme* was doing and saw a sight that froze my blood.

Bobbing gently towards me out of the darkness, and riding smoothly on the flat, wave less waters was the familiar black hump of the gunpowder porcupine. With *Plunger* no longer under way, and the towline slack, the mine had drifted back to its parent. It was only twenty or thirty yards off and was spinning slowly in the water. Trickles of water ran off its tarred back and the spines turned and swayed and reached out for something solid. I thought of the fragile glass vessels within its belly and the heavy iron rods waiting to crush them, and the two hundred pounds of powder waiting for the flash of alchemist's fire.

For a second or two I hoped it would just go by, but no, the bloody thing was coming home to roost. And it was too close for me to swim off and hope to get clear. I'd have to push it away or say my prayers and hope the Lord would forgive me my trespasses when I met him in about thirty seconds time. I groaned with the unfairness of it all, kicked off my shoes that I'd only just put back on, slipped into the water and swam for the monster.

In actual fact, had the thing not contained live powder, then a child could have done it. I simply swam up, took hold of one of the spines by the root, so it couldn't slide inward and fumbled around till I found the ring-bolt and the tow line. Then I swam off towing the gunpowder porcupine behind me. At first all I had in mind was to pull the thing clear of *Plunger*, but then I thought I may as well do the job right and put the mine where the tide would carry it on to *Calipheme*. And that too was easy, really, apart from the yelling and shouting aboard *Calipheme* and the audible clanking of the capstan as they swivelled her broadside around looking for me.

When the line went taut I took a sight on *Calipheme's* outline, to check I'd placed the mine correctly. But I got a shock. I thought *Calipheme* was under way. The jutting outline of the long bowsprit was sliding forward against the stars. But she was still anchored, with not a sail set! Then it dawned on me that the tide had turned and the mine was being swung under *Calipheme's* bow, just as I'd planned, only I was swinging along with it.

Well, my lovely lads, I doubt any man in the entire history of aquatic exercise has ever swum quite so hard and quite so fiercely as I did for the next couple of minutes. I thrashed and splashed and gulped and put as many yards between me and the mine as ever I could. But this drew attention from the frigate, for I heard 'em shouting and pointing me out.

The trouble was I was going crabwise. As hard as I swam north, the tide was sending me eastward, out to sea with the waters of Boston Harbour, and as a result I was passing right under Calipheme's bowsprit.

Crack-Crack-Bang! Muskets went off above my head as men leaned over the fo'c'sle bulwarks and took aim. Splash-Splash! Cold shot plunged in beside me and if that wasn't enough, something was tangling my legs. It was the bloody towline for the bloody mine! It had caught me up somehow. I struggled to get free, swallowed half the harbour, came up gasping and choking, and saw the row of faces glaring down at me from the ship. I saw the flash and fire of small arms. I saw the fists raised to hurl round shot, and felt the tug of the tide as it drew me along.

Then down the length of the taut towline came a quiver and a jar. The line had come up against Calipheme's bow, which meant the mine would be alongside of her without delay. I struck out again, forging away from the ship's bow half mad with the fright of what might happen at any second. The trouble was that in doing so, what with the tide and my own efforts combined, I found myself sliding down the line of her open-mouthed guns while simultaneously working my way out and away from the ship, and so placing myself in an absolutely ideal position for receiving the full benefit of her broadside, should she chose to let me have it.

I was bearing fair on her beam and a nice fifty yards from her gunners as they hooted and yelled and pointed me out to one another and peered at me over their sights. I could see the dim black shapes busy at it as I glanced back over my shoulder. Any second now, they'd fire, and the whole long line of black gun-ports would light up in flame and blow me into food for the fishes. I could even hear the gun-captains calling out the drill to the crews.

"Train right!… Well!"

"Train left!… Left! … Well!"

And then night turned into day. A fierce dazzling, searing day accompanied by a colossal, thunderous explosion and a white water-spout of terrifying magnitude that leapt up high above Calipheme's mainmast, as the whole mass of the great ship lifted and broke and thundered into ruin and split in two at a point a third of the way down her length.[14]

I was deafened and blinded all at once and the force of the mighty discharge pummelled me through the very water as if I was being tossed by a bull. My ears and nose streamed with blood. Wreckage, spars and splinters began to rain down upon me in huge beams that could have killed me like a squashed bug. But they were the saving of me. I was too weak to swim but I got my arms round a piece of timber and so floated and did not sink.

I saw *Calipheme* go down in her two halves, with her mizzenmast yards still above water, for it was too shallow to swallow her completely. The other masts were blown to the points of the compass, the water was full of every loose floating thing, large and small, that's spilt out of a ship when she founders, and full of the remains of her people too. Some were smashed and torn and others seemed whole but all were dead that I saw.

It made no impression on me at the time, for I was sick and hurt and all my strength was needed just to hold on to the great timber that alone was holding me up. And so in an hour or two the tide took me out towards the sunrise, out past Deer Island and past *Declaration*, anchored in the straight that Howe had declared his determination to enter that very day.

In the dawn light I saw the boats working around *Declaration*, passing to and fro and fishing things out of the water. I tried to call out to them, but I passed too far away and I was low in the water and nobody saw me. So out I went into Broad Sound where there were more boats at work. Busy boats probing and watching and finding out. Boats with blue-coated officers peering past *Declaration* and observing with their telescopes: it was the ever-vigilant, ever-active, ever-diligent, omni-bloody-present Royal Navy.

I waved and shouted back towards *Declaration*. I didn't want the Navy to catch me. Oh no, please not that. Not after so much. But it was too late.

"'ere's a bugger wot ain't dead, sir!" says a voice and a boat came clanking up with bluejackets at the oars and Lieutenant in the stern.

"Out with him now!" says the voice of command, "Look lively!"

---

14   Fletcher later expressed the conviction that the tremendous destruction wrought upon Calipheme was more than could be effected by the 200 lbs of powder within the 'porcupine'. It was his opinion that some or all of Calipheme's magazine must have been exploded by the mine's detonation. S.P.

And so eager hands hauled me out and laid me in the bottom of the boat and a ring of weather-beaten faces stared down at me. I was entered back into the bosom of my own folk, my own kind, and my own nation. The officer leaned forward to welcome me.

Mutinous filth!" says he, "I'd as soon let you drown and spare the trouble of a hanging. So think yourself fortunate for British Justice you foul creature!"

Shortly after that I was taken on board of the frigate *Diomedes* where I was the subject of vast curiosity as I stood bare-chested and bare-foot in my breeches. The marines were paraded with bayonets fixed to keep a guard round me, I was next to naked, empty handed, back in the Navy's power and all the wealth and profit that had passed through my hands since I left England was gone.

Worse still, the Navy thought I was a mutineer out of *Calipheme*. Of course, all I had to do to correct them was to say that I was Jacob Fletcher who was wanted on a charge of murdering Bosun Dixon of the impress tender *Bullfrog*, then at least they'd hang me for the right crime. If I'd had the least confidence of being able to do it, then I'd have affected a Yankee accent and sworn I wasn't British. But I've no talent for that so I kept my mouth shut and said nothing when they took me below and secured me in irons on the gun-deck under the fo'c'sle.

And there I stayed for most of that day. They brought me food at dinner time and those whose duties took them within sight of me, took the opportunity to look me over, but there was a marine on guard to prevent my talking to anyone, even if such an idea had entered my head. I spent the time trying to think how best to present myself to the enquiries that would surely follow, but I was tired and aching and chafed by the leg-irons that bolted me to the deck, and in any case I didn't know who or what to say that I was, other than a mutineer or Jacob Fletcher, of course.

About half an hour after I was brought aboard there was a bellowing of orders and a shrilling of Bosun's calls and a flurry of orderly activity amidships. A steady chanting came from over my head as teams of men hauled on lines, intent on some heavy work. I was secured facing for'ard and all this was astern of me, but by twisting round and peering over my shoulder I could see what was going on.

The gun deck of a frigate of those days was beneath the fo'c'sle at the bow and the quarterdeck from just aft of the mainmast, but for most of the waist, the gun deck was open to the sky, apart from narrow gangways on either side and the spars and timbers secured across the gap for storage of spare spars and the ship's boats. But something else was being lowered into place where the boats should be. It was black and wet and I couldn't see it properly at first and damn near dislocated myself with trying, but then saw the jury-rigged keel that I'd helped build and knew that *Plunger* had followed me out on the tide. I wondered what the Navy would make of her. It was clear that they were mightily interested.

Then there was more shouting and stamping of marines' boots and a tarpaulin was lashed over the submarine boat and *Diomedes* fell back in to her routine and the hours passed, marked by the notes of her bell. Late in the day a Middy came to find me with the Bosun and a couple of his mates to look after him. They looked at me ever odder than anyone else had and the Mid handed me a shirt.

"Capn's orders," says he, "You're to put this on and come with me." With that the Bosun unlocked my irons and I stood up and made myself presentable.

To my great surprise I was taken aft to the Captain's great cabin and ushered in, past the sentries, to a meeting of Sir Brian Howe and his officers. I'd never met Sir Brian, but I recognised him at once as one of the Howe clan. He weren't so swarthy as his famous elder brother but he had the heavy brows and the damn-your-eyes expression. The others present were Captain Nantwich of *La Syrene*, three or four Lieutenants and an uncommon canny gent in civilian clothes who was called Dr Millicent and was Howe's Chaplain and trusted confidant.

They sat round Howe's table and considered me standing before them in my ruined breeches and a shirt too small by half and they simply peered at me, neither friendly nor unfriendly, but *oddly* like those examining some rare beast in a menagerie. There was a silence for a bit as if no man knew how to begin, and then Howe spoke.

"I learn that I am very deeply in your debt, Mr Fletcher," says he, and waved a disparaging hand at me as he saw my expression, "Don't bother denying your name. No less than three of my hands served with you in *Phiandra* under Sir Harry Bollington, and you have been made known to me."

He frowned, and drummed his fingers on the table in front of him. "Your friend Ratcliffe has a canister ball in his chest and is below in the hands of the surgeon," says he, "Ratcliffe sings your praises in such a manner as I never heard the like. He reports that you and he navigated a sub-marine boat to explode a powder-mine beneath *Calipheme* and Ratcliffe awards you the lion's share of such credit as appertains to this … remarkable …" he pursed his lips like Dowager sucking a lemon, "… this remarkable … *expedition* … and declares that without your energy and dedication, the attack could not have succeeded."

He paused and looked at his companions, as if for support. The clergyman, Millicent, spoke.

"You should know, Mr Fletcher, that Ratcliffe is a man in whom Sir Brian places great trust. Ratcliffe has been a loyal and valuable ally. Furthermore his testimony amounts to a dying declaration and bears the especial credence attaching thereunto." Then there was another long silence while my interrogators shuffled in their seats and sighed deeply and looked to Howe.

"Fletcher!" says Howe, finally, "This … *thing* … that you have done. This *thing*, I say, has undoubtedly averted a war with the Americans that must have proved disastrous in the extreme for our country." But he glared at me defying me to take any comfort from his words. "So I offer you my thanks, sir," says he, "For you've saved my reputation besides, and that of every man here." And then he drew breath and let rip, "But a more cowardly, loathsome, un-British and downright despicable means of making warfare, than that which you have practised, I am entirely incapable of imagining."

"Aye!" said all present, and with the utmost emphasis.

I licked my lips and said nothing, for there was more to come. I could see it in his face.

"I know of you, Fletcher," says he, "My brother, His Lordship, has told me of you. His Lordship says he owes you his victory of the Glorious First of June. But he says you are a self-confessed murderer whom the Navy owes a hanging, and a man whose given word can in no circumstances be trusted! In short, sir, I am at a loss as to how to deal with you and I'm sending you home to England with that … that *devil's engine* of yours … for wiser heads to pronounce upon. You will now accompany Dr Millicent to his cabin where he will examine you in detail upon these matters. Good day to you, sir. I shall not speak with you again."

And that was that. I never said a word. Millicent left the table and led me off and sat me down in the narrow corner of the lower deck where his cabin was squeezed in between the Surgeon's and the Purser's and got out pen and ink and a candle for light. Then the inquisition began.

"Mr Fletcher," says he, smiling like the man with the lever that stretches the rack, "I most heartily advise you to tell me your entire history." He paused and looked at me hard, "Because it may be that truth will save you from the hangman, but lies will not."

By Jove, but he was a spry 'un! He was a clergyman but he'd have made a damn fine lawyer, and you could see why Howe thought so much of him. I'm quick-brained and proud of it, but he was something beyond my powers to cozen or deceive. He cross-questioned me a dozen ways and drew every last detail from me, and next morning he and I went inside of *Plunger* where he took more notes, asked a great deal of penetrating questions, and took measurements and made sketches.

After that, Howe shifted his flag to *La Syrene*, and *Diomedes* was ordered to sail for England. He and Millicent clearly believed that *Plunger* was something so special and alarming that news of her must be carried home even at the expense of detaching one of the ships of his squadron. I went with *Diomedes*, and Millicent's notes went with me, together with a long despatch from Sir Brian.

The voyage home was tedious in the extreme. I had nothing to do and no place in the ship's little world. I wasn't a gentleman and I wasn't one of the hands. I was neither seaman, nor marine, nor prisoner nor a free man. I was an oddity, and slung my hammock on the lower deck, but messed by myself for the hands were ordered not to speak to me on pain of a flogging. I didn't know what Millicent had written about me, nor what Sir Brian Howe had written, except that the way that I was being kept isolated led me to suspect that I was going home to my death. On the other hand, and if so, then why didn't they keep me in irons?

Ratcliffe died of his wounds two weeks after the attack on *Calipheme* and without ever fully regaining his wits. They gave him full honours including the Union Flag over his sewn-up hammock as they slid him overboard. No doubt he would have approved.

Diomedes sighted the Lizard on November 20th and made Portsmouth two days later. There were storms like hurricanes in the Channel that November so I suppose we were lucky to make so easy a passage.

We anchored at Spithead which was relatively empty as the Channel

Fleet was out, and there we stayed for a fortnight until they came back in on an evil, freezing morning in the first week of December. Admiral of the Fleet Richard (Black Dick) Lord Howe was in command again, following another shuffle in Pitt's cabinet in August, which ended in Lord Bridport being thrown out on his ear and Howe reinstated, old and infirm though he was. I'd had plenty of time by then to read all the newspapers so I was well up on the politics that giveth command unto one and taketh it away from another.

Messages ran between *Diomedes* and *Queen Charlotte*, Lord Howe's massive three-decker, and on Thursday December 9th I was rowed across the icy grey waters of Spithead for my Court Martial.

CHAPTER 39

*"I have no news of your friend Stanley other than to confirm that
he has entirely disappeared. But I can confirm, on the testimony
of the sole survivor of the British frigate, that she succumbed to an
undersea explosion of the very kind which you sought to engineer .
against them while in General Washington's service."*

(From a letter of 12th November 1795, from Captain Daniel Cooper
aboard 'Declaration of Independence', Boston Harbour, to Mr David
Bushnell of Warrenton, Georgia.)

The miserable, sopping-wet urchin stood in his puddle on *Declaration's*
quarterdeck and cringed in the cold morning light before the gentlemen
and officers towering all around him. His thin arms and bare legs shuddered with cold and fright. It was October 5th, the day after *Calipheme*
had gone down following a massive explosion that had ripped her open
and split her in two.

"Speak up, there!" says a tall officer in a uniform coat and shiny boots,
who was Captain Cooper of the Yankee warship *Declaration*, "What
caused the explosion."

"Dunnosir." said the boy.

"Was it the magazines?" said the officer.

"Dunnosir." says the boy.

"Were you attacked?"

"Dunnosir."

"Was there an accident of *any* kind?"

"Dunnosir."

"What the tarnation *do* you know?" snapped Cooper, "How'd you like your britches warmed for you with the Bosun's cane? D'ye think that'd help your memory?"

Ship's boy Jimmy Randolph, lately of HMS *Calipheme*, wailed in fright and lapsed into self-pitying, terrified tears.

"Brace up there!" cried Cooper, "You've nothing to fear. Brace up or I'll flog the hide off you!"

"Aye-Aye, sir!" says the boy through his tears.

"What were you firing at?" said the officer, "Your main battery was in action for nearly fifteen minutes."

"We was shootin' at the *pahdah-moins*," said the boy.

"What?" said Cooper.

"Pahdah-moins, sir, pahdah-moins, floated at onner toid. Dem Yankees dunnit inner 'merican wore an' Cap'n Gryllis, 'e dunnit an' orl, juss like wot they dun."

"What?" said Cooper, mystified by the adenoidal, glottal-stopped, tones of the child's accent. He turned to his officers, "What's he saying?"

"Powder mines, sir!" said one who knew the British accent a little better than the rest, "He says that *Calipheme's* crew were afraid of mines floated out on the tide, just like Bushnell attempted in the Revolution."

"Ass-it, sir!" says Jimmy Randolph, nodding furiously, "Wottah-gemman-sed-sir!"

"There's some such rumour going round the town, sir," said the knowledgeable officer, "Seemingly spread by the employees of Mr Francis Stanley the sub-marine engineer."

"Well I'm damned," said Cooper, "Was Stanley helping Captain Gryllis?"

"It would seem so, sir," said the officer, "It's for sure that somebody exploded a charge of powder beneath *Calipheme*."

"Yessir!" said the boy.

"Good God in heaven!" cried Cooper, "Jacob Fletcher knows Stanley. He came into Boston in Stanley's ship!" He turned on Jimmy Randolph again, "What do you know of Jacob Fletcher?" he cried. But Jimmy Randolph knew nothing more about anything, no matter how they threatened him.

(In due course, having been pressed into service aboard Cooper's ship, Jimmy Randolph learned to speak properly and eventually came to think of himself as a New Englander. He became a citizen, made a decent living as a fisherman and married a girl from Yorktown Virginia.)

CHAPTER 40

Now pay attention, my lads, for your Uncle Jacob is going to open up the casing that encloses the Engine of State, so that you can take a peek at the works.

In 1724 Lord Emanuel Scrope-Howe married Mary Sophia, daughter of Baroness Kielmansegge who'd been mistress to King George I, making Mary Sophia the King's illegitimate daughter. Lord Emanuel and Mary Sophia had children, the second of them being Richard (Black Dick) Howe, who therefore was blood nephew to King George II, cousin to King George III, and it don't come better than that as relatives for a sailor to have.

Thus it's no wonder that having joined Uncle George's Navy as a boy and served a six-year apprenticeship, the young Richard Howe was promoted first to Lieutenant, then to Commander and then to Captain, all in the same single year of 1745, when he was only nineteen, and not even Nelson would rise that fast. Which is all very interesting and all very important to my story, because it was the same Black Dick, now sixty-nine years old and wielding all the powers that went with vast seniority and possession of the Blood Royal, who was President of my Court Martial, convened on board of *Queen Charlotte*, at Spithead, in December of 1795.

In plain words, what I'm telling you is that Black Dick was a man who, in Naval circles, could do just exactly whatever he wanted, and answer to absolutely nobody, and walk on bloody water if he chose to do so.

So, they brought me alongside *Queen Charlotte* after dinner, when the Court was comfortable and in all respects fit for action. I was dressed entirely out of *Diomedes's* slop-chest, and looked like a common seaman. But I'd nothing else and had to make do.

The Court was met in the magnificence of the Admiral's State Cabin at the stern and I was led in and stood before them. They had marines behind me to keep guard, a table and a clerk to one side of me to take notes, and finally, in front of me, the Court sat in its full dress. From right to left as they sat, the members of the court were: Captain Sir Andrew Snape Douglas of *Queen Charlotte*, Captain Sir Harry Bollington of *Sandromedes*, Black Dick himself, then Captain William Bedford of *Danossophos*, and finally Captain Charles Powell Hamilton of *Prince*.

Every one of these men was a well-known luminary of the Howe faction who could be relied upon to follow where Black Dick led, whether it be into the fire of the enemy or into putting their names to a prearranged, cut-and-dried verdict.

And so to business. The clerk asked me if I were Jacob Fletcher of Polmouth in Devon and I said that I was. The clerk explained the court to me and indicated that Captain Snape-Douglas was appointed my *friend* and would represent me. (That was a blow. I'd been hoping for Harry Bollington whom I'd served under in *Phiandra* and whose life I'd saved in a boarding action.)

Then the clerk read out the details of my killing of Bosun Dixon of the impress tender *Bullfrog* back in '93. They'd got witnesses and depositions and any fool could see that the case was proven beyond doubt. The fact that Dixon was a vicious brute who deserved what he got, didn't weigh one ounce in the scales. Then for good measure, the Court proved to its entire satisfaction that I'd broken my parole as a gentleman in order to escape from custody, and so on to Jamaica.

At this stage things looked grim for your Uncle Jacob. Every man of the Court was looking at me stone-faced. Even Harry Bollington, the ungrateful bastard. Then Black Dick slapped his hand on the table for silence and delivered a speech.

"Fletcher," says he, "We have heard the evidence against you, which evidence is clear and admits of no doubts." He looked at me steadily and I saw death in his eyes. What was one more poor devil's life to him, after half a century of blood and slaughter? "But," says Howe, "You have undoubtedly saved your country from the great threat of American hostile involvement in our war with the French." By George, but that sounded better, and it got better still. "Furthermore, Fletcher," says Howe, "I am conscious of the part played by you in bringing the French to battle in June of last year," he leaned back and looked at the rest of the Court,

"Either one of these actions, had they been performed by an officer of the Sea Service, could not but have resulted in his advancement and even ennoblement! Would you not agree, gentlemen?"

"Aye!" they said, and damned themselves if it weren't true. But *none* of the buggers smiled and none of 'em gave me a friendly look, especially Black Dick himself.

"However, Mr Jacob Fletcher," says Howe, "you are *not* in the Sea Service. You are very much in your own service, and the fact of the matter is sir, I don't like you, nor your methods, nor the underhand weapon that you have demonstrated to be a practicable means whereby a nation not in possession of a fleet, might attack the fleet of the greater power."

So that was it. Sammy Bone had been right all those months ago. It didn't matter how many times over I saved England, they weren't going to forgive me for doing it with sub-marine mines.

"Dr Millicent assures us," says Howe, tapping his finger on what I took to be a document written by Millicent, "That had not a struggle broken out among the people of your craft, then it must have performed as its designer had planned and so re-written the entire rules of war," He paused and dared to voice the nightmare that I had caused him to dream, "What if the French were to profit by your example?" says he, "What if even now there were a swarm of sub-marine craft working their way beneath this ship? This is just precisely the sort of un-manly, un-Christian, cowardly trick that the French would relish!"

Again the heads nodded wisely up and down the table.

"Fletcher," says Howe, "You have forced upon England's attention a device which she does not want nor need, and which only her enemies could profit by ... and yet ... you have single-handedly *saved* your King and your Country from disaster, and what is more, I hear on every hand that you are an exceptionally fine seaman, a master of gunnery, a leader of men and a very Hercules in a hand-to-hand fight!" He glared at me, "No sir!" says Howe, "Don't smirk! I state the facts and mean them as no compliment. The truth is, Mr Jacob Fletcher, that like my brother Sir Brian, I'm damned if I know what to do with you, and you may bless the day you were born that Sir Harry Bollington remembers a favour you once did him, and so has a certain proposal to put to you!" Howe glared at Harry Bollington, "Tell him!" says he.

Bollington looked at me and spoke.

"Fletcher," says he, "After the battle of Passage D'Aron where you saved me from a French bayonet, I offered to further your advancement in the Sea Service…"

"So did I, after the Glorious First of June!" growled Howe.

"Quite so, my Lord," says Bollington, "And now, Fletcher, it is come to this." I held my breath. The judgement was coming, "His Lordship and I, and the members of this Court are conscious of an obligation towards yourself that honour may not avoid. This obligation supersedes other considerations and we have struggled to find a way to discharge it."

"Get on with it Bollington!" says Howe, "Get to the point!"

"Aye-Aye, my Lord," says Bollington, "It amounts to this: all charges against you will be dismissed." Joy unbounded flooded through me. I'd escaped the rope and was a free man! Whatever they did to me after that it would only be a matter of time before I was safe on shore and free to follow my natural inclinations. It would be hard to build a new business, but it's the building that I enjoy, just as I've always said. "On condition," continued Bollington, "That you enter the Sea Service as a midshipman, in a ship of our choice, under a Captain of our choice, and you solemnly promise to abandon forever your unseemly connections in trade."

Damnation! That was a blow, but I'd promise whatever they asked to escape a hanging. And I could always get out of the Navy after a year or so. It was still a good way forward.

"You have my solemn word, Sir Harry!" says I, seriously.

"Not nearly good enough, you slippery villain!" says Howe, and jabbed his finger at me. "I know the value of your promises, sir!" he urged Bollington on with a wave of his hand, "Go to it, Sir Harry!" says he.

"Precisely, my Lord," says Bollington and fixed me with his eye.

"It is our decision, Fletcher," says he, "To kill two birds with one stone. We shall ensure that your undoubted gifts be put to your country's service, and shall discharge our debt to you by having you commissioned a Lieutenant after a decent interval of time: say six months after you join your ship."

"All matters of service time, certificates of proficiency, and the like, will be arranged for you," says Howe interrupting, "And you will sit an examination for Lieutenant, which you will pass."

"Quite, my Lord," says Bollington, "And then, Fletcher, you will devote your life to the Service, and to the exclusion of all other interests." He paused to let this sink in and added the clincher, "You are found innocent of the charge of murdering Bosun Dixon, but no charge has yet been laid regarding the mutinous assault which you made upon the person of Lieutenant Lloyd when you escaped from his custody in Portsmouth last year." A cold fright gripped me as I saw the trap they'd laid, these gentlemen who looked down upon me for my sub-marine activities. I'd knocked Lloyd senseless when he was escorting me to prison. I thought that little incident had been forgotten. "As you know, Fletcher," says Bollington, "The penalty for mutiny and assault upon an officer is death."

"So that's why we don't need your given word!" said Howe, smiling for the only time during the proceedings.

"Might I continue, my Lord?" says Bollington.

"Proceed!" says Howe.

"Your career will be followed, Fletcher," says Bollington, "And should you shirk, or twist, or most of all, should you go grubbing about in trade, then you'll find yourself before this court again..."

"And then, by God, we'll hang you!" says Howe, thumping the table, "We'll hang you for a damned ungrateful puppy who spurned the gift of the King's commission that thousands of better men than yourself, would give a precious limb to obtain!"

"We shall indeed!" says Bollington.

"And you should know, sir," says Howe, "That this shall be the end of my generosity. You leave my presence a free man and as good as Gazetted. But after that you shall look to me no more. You must make your own way. Neither I nor any other present will favour you nor advance you."

"Quite so," says Bollington.

"Well, sir," says Howe, "Speak up! Do you accept this offer or do you chose to hang?" I was so stunned I could barely think, let alone speak, so Howe spoke for me.

"We take silence for grateful acceptance, Mr Fletcher," says he, "I offer you my hand, sir, as a final act of thanks." He stuck out his hand and I took it. The rest of them did likewise but without the least warmth. "And now you may go," says Howe, "But my secretary will accompany you to arrange some final matters of detail."

And that was that. I staggered out numb and horrified. The clerk followed. We went into Howe's day cabin where more papers were laid out. Howe's final details were the provision of clothes, supplies, and a sum of money for my immediate needs, and a series of documents (ready sealed, stamped and awaiting only my signature) whereby I finally renounced all claim to the Coignwood inheritance, and to my monies, holdings or any other possessions in Jamaica and Boston.

"Must I?" I asked.

"Oh yes," says the clerk, "His Lordship wishes you to know that the entire settlement of your case depends upon it. You must abandon absolutely all pecuniary interests or commercial connections."

And that my boys, my very jolly boys indeed, is how the Navy turned your Uncle Jacob into a Sea Officer and how the buggers forever denied him his one true vocation.

CHAPTER 41

"Your offers of marriage, so oft repeated in your many letters, shall ever be held in my highest regard and shall go far towards obliterating any trace of recollection of the unfortunate event which passed between us. Rest assured that I strive to forgive you and that should you visit London, the doors of my house are open to you."

(From a letter of June 5th 1796 from Lady Sarah Coignwood, Dulwich Square London, to Captain Daniel Cooper, Boston.)

Lady Sarah signed the letter to the ridiculous Daniel Cooper and smiled happily at the barbed shaft she had let fly with her veiled reference to the events of the night of the ball. She folded over one third of the expensive, gold-edged writing paper towards the middle and then completed the manipulations whereby a sheet of writing paper was folded on itself to make a letter for the post.

She sealed it with wax, addressed it and put it with others just completed. As she did so, there came a discreet tap at the door and her new Steward, Blandish, entered her private dressing room. He carried a silver tray piled high with papers. He advanced and placed these reverently beside her on the ormolu-mounted, satinwood writing table at which she was sitting, in a gleaming fauteuil, with lions-head arms, decorated and finished en-suite with the writing desk.

"The submissions from the architects, my Lady," said Blandish, "For the new oval dining room."

"Ah!" she said and reached for the one on top of the pile. It was an impressive folio of watercolour illustrations, beautifully presented in an elaborately-decorated folder.

"Ahem," said Blandish, with the respectful tact of the well-flogged retainer.

"What?" said his mistress, and her eyes narrowed ever so slightly. It was not her practise to be prevented from the immediate gratification of her inclinations; not by a servant.

"The new footmen, my Lady," he said. "They are assembled in the garden, for your inspection."

"Ahhhhh!" the frown vanished. "Thank you, Blandish," said she, "I shall come at once. You may precede me."

She rose, he stepped aside. She glided forward in a rustle of scented muslin. He threw open the door. She descended the stairs. He backed and genuflected before her. She swept through the hall, to the library, to the great glass doors that led to the garden, with its gorgeous blooms, and its staff of outdoor domestics. Blandish contrived to cast open the doors and bow her through.

Outside the warm sunshine beautified the garden and beautified the four very beautiful young men, who were drawn up in line. According to the strict specifications that had been laid down, each was under twenty years old, each was smartly dressed in fashionable clothes, each was tall, slim and muscular, each was smoothly and glossily black. They swept off their hats and bowed gracefully as my Lady appeared.

Sarah Coignwood sighed happily. She had not forgotten anything. She had not forgotten her disappointment in never fully enjoying Rasselas. She had not forgotten the unspeakable torments of Jamaica. She had not forgotten the pleasant interlude of Boston (a pretty enough little town, but not to be compared with London or Paris).

Above all, she had not forgotten Mr Jacob Fletcher. But for today, Fletcher could wait and the memory of Rasselas could not.

POSTSCRIPT

On Sunday January 9th 1796, a poor bloody Midshipman clambered into a boat on Portsmouth hard, with his sea chest and his uniform coat and his cocked hat and his greatcoat and his muffler and his thick woollen gloves. He cursed the misery of cruel fate and the leaden grey skies and the evil wind, and the sleet that the evil wind drove across the vile, grey waters. He screwed up his eyes and peered out to Spithead and tried to spy out his ship, the brig-sloop *Serpant*.

This was myself: Mr Midshipman Jacob Fletcher, joining a King's ship as a *Young Gentleman*. I was in a foul mood, and I was greatly missing Sammy Bone, whom I never saw again to my sorrow, though I heard of him years later and took comfort that he survived the Maroon wars and lived happily with his musteefino girl. I was also missing Lucinda, and even Kate Booth strangely enough.

The boatman and his wife, red-faced, red-armed, and pipe-smoking the pair of them, took me aboard and shoved the boat into the water with the help of their brood of children. The boat swam, the boatman and his wife bent to their oars and I cursed the entirety of creation and by the time we came alongside of *Serpant* I was sunk in gloom. But I paid the boatman, and went up the side as men hauled my chest aboard, and I scowled at what I saw because there was slovenliness and slacking all around.

This was no great surprise because, by a little piece of humour on the part of Black Dick and his followers, the ship I was joining was under the command of one Cuthbert Percival-Clive, or *Poxy Percy* as he was better known. He was a dunderhead moron whom I'd served with in *Phiandra* but whose his father was the sugar millionaire Sir Reginald Percival Clive and his mother was sister to Billy Pitt the Prime Minister. So Percy had been promoted Lieutenant and then Commander, and given *Serpant* to rule over as lord and master. At the present moment, he was, and had been for weeks, comfortably installed in a hotel ashore and had left his ship under the command of the Bosun. The Bosun was an idle swab and the ship was gone to the dogs.

As I set foot on the greasy deck and looked about me, three petty officers approached. These were the Bosun himself and two of his mates. They fancied themselves hard men, and had wind-roughened faces and heavy hands. The Bosun had a rope's end swinging in his fist and the other two had cudgels in their belts. They were all swathed in winter clothes like myself.

"An' just 'oo might you be then, you lubber?" says the Bosun, insolently affecting not to notice the cocked hat that proclaimed my rank. His mates glared at me and stuck out their chins like bulldogs. And so the foul depression lifted. The one thing that I wanted was someone to punish for what had happened to me, and when you're my size, three'll do as well as one. So I said nothing but took off my hat, greatcoat, muffler and gloves, and stretched my limbs a bit, that had got cramped sitting in the boat, because it was going to be warm work for the next minute or two.